FULL
EXPOSURE

FULL EXPOSURE

TRACY WOLFF

HEAT

Published by New American Library, a division of
Penguin Group (USA) Inc., 375 Hudson Street,
New York, New York 10014, USA
Penguin Group (Canada), 90 Eglinton Avenue East, Suite 700, Toronto,
Ontario M4P 2Y3, Canada (a division of Pearson Penguin Canada Inc.)
Penguin Books Ltd., 80 Strand, London WC2R 0RL, England
Penguin Ireland, 25 St. Stephen's Green, Dublin 2,
Ireland (a division of Penguin Books Ltd.)
Penguin Group (Australia), 250 Camberwell Road, Camberwell, Victoria 3124,
Australia (a division of Pearson Australia Group Pty. Ltd.)
Penguin Books India Pvt. Ltd., 11 Community Centre, Panchsheel Park,
New Delhi – 110 017, India
Penguin Group (NZ), 67 Apollo Drive, Rosedale, North Shore 0632,
New Zealand (a division of Pearson New Zealand Ltd.)
Penguin Books (South Africa) (Pty.) Ltd., 24 Sturdee Avenue,
Rosebank, Johannesburg 2196, South Africa

Penguin Books Ltd., Registered Offices:
80 Strand, London WC2R 0RL, England

First published by Heat, an imprint of New American Library,
a division of Penguin Group (USA) Inc.

First Printing, January 2009
10 9 8 7 6 5 4 3 2 1

LIBRARY OF CONGRESS CATALOGING-IN-PUBLICATION DATA:
Wolff, Tracy.
Full exposure/Tracy Wolff.
p. cm.
ISBN 978-0-451-22596-2
1. Women photographers—Fiction. 2. Sculptors—Fiction.
3. Baton Rouge (La.)—Fiction. I. Title.
PS3623.O57F85 2009
813'.6—dc22   2008022730

Set in Sabon and Grotesque • Designed by Alissa Amell

Printed in the United States of America

For the Men in my Life:

My Father, who taught me how to Dream.

My Husband, whose Love and Support has helped make my Dreams a Reality.

My Sons, who are the reasons I get out of Bed in the morning.

Acknowledgments

Thank you Emily Sylvan Kim and Becky Vinter—for taking a chance on me and taking such very good care of me and this book.

Chapter One

Kevin Riley was the stuff fantasies were made of.

Her fantasies, to be exact.

Six foot five, heavily muscled, with the most beautifully intense blue eyes she'd ever seen, he captured her attention like no man ever had. And with his half-naked body in front of her and nature thrashing fiercely around her, it was all she could do to keep her clothes on, her mouth shut and her camera aimed somewhere besides his absolutely fabulous ass.

Not that he should mind—it was one of his best features, after all. And she was being paid—well paid—to take pictures that showed his *every* side.

Of course, she wasn't sure that fifty shots of his ass were quite what the publishers had had in mind when they'd hired her, no matter how glorious it was. Besides, her humming libido couldn't handle much more without going into severe overdrive anyway.

Serena snorted before she could stop herself. Who was she kidding? She'd passed overdrive a while ago, was now heading straight toward spontaneous combustion at an alarming rate. The thought disturbed her, and she moved restlessly, desperate to focus on something—anything—that could bring her traitorous body under control.

She glanced toward the large windows that covered an entire side of the old redbrick studio and tried to concentrate on the storm raging through Kevin's little slice of bayou. But the wildness of it—the utter lack of control—only made her more uncomfortable.

Rain pummeled the tin roof, flashes of lightning illuminated the darkness beyond the house and thunder shook the studio as it exploded across the sky. Mother Nature was in a frenzy, and much of southern Louisiana would pay the price on this steamy summer night.

She was just one more victim.

It was three a.m., and she should have been asleep, tucked safely into bed in her Baton Rouge condo. Nature whirled around her, and she should have been terrified as she witnessed the destruction caused by every gust of seventy-mile-an-hour winds. She was working, and she should have been focused, completely absorbed in taking photos for the book that could blow her career wide-open. But she wasn't.

She wasn't at home asleep, she wasn't terrified and she certainly wasn't focused.

What she was, was aroused.

Powerfully, frighteningly aroused.

Wetness pooled between her thighs, her nipples peaked and she had to work—hard—to stifle the moan threatening to part lips it was becoming harder and harder to keep closed.

She'd never been this out of control before, had never been so aroused that she couldn't focus on anything but the throbbing ache between her thighs. Serena pressed her legs together, desperate to stem the sensations bombarding her. But it was no use. Heat swept through her body. Her skin flushed a rosy pink, and her heart began to race as the fine tremor of arousal shook her, making hands that were normally rock-steady tremble with reaction.

It was all his fault, she thought resentfully, studying Kevin Riley through the camera lens. Because while Kevin was the living, breathing example of every fantasy she'd ever had, his unbelievable sexiness did nothing to put her at ease. Fantasies were just that—something she could escape to when her hard-earned control stifled her, when life got boring and she needed a little spice. But fantasies were supposed to *stay* fantasies—who expected to encounter them in real life?

This was her work, her livelihood, her big chance, yet all she could think about was that luscious mouth and how it would feel pressed against her own. She wanted to pull Kevin into the storm, to run her hands through his too long black hair and feel his muscles ripple beneath her fingers as water and wind lashed at them.

The musky sexiness of his skin called to her, and even with half the room between them, she couldn't escape his unique scent—a mixture of sandalwood and the crisp, clean outdoors. Passion, life, vitality rolled off him in waves, swamping her as her fingers fumbled another roll of film into her old Nikon. She'd used the digital camera earlier, but something about the time, the storm and Kevin himself had cried out for a more primitive approach.

She lifted the camera again, hands shaking as she snapped the first pictures on the roll. Kevin's jeans rode low on his hips as he bent, blowtorch in hand, to mold the lowest corner of the sculpture. Intensity and passion etched every angle of his fallen angel's face— his lush lips were molded into a grim line and his eyes burned with concentration. Despite the air-conditioning, sweat rolled slowly down his bare torso before disappearing inside the waistband of his much-abused Levi's. Lust roared through her, nearly bringing her to her knees, even as the artist in her recognized the power in his unconscious actions.

Click, whirr. This was it. *Click, whirr.* The picture she had been waiting for all night. *Click, whirr.* The shot that would make her famous. *Click, whirr.* Sculpting ecstasy. *Click, whirr.* Bending metal to his every command. *Click, whirr.* A work of art. *Click, whirr.* Of genius. *Click, whirr.* Was she speaking of Kevin or his work? *Click, whirr.* Perhaps both.

She slid to the ground, looked up through the lens. *Click, whirr.* His immense power overwhelming. *Click, whirr.* His talent huge, larger than life. *Click, whirr.* A giant in his field. *Click, whirr.* And she wanted him. *Click, whirr.* This man who was more a work of art than anything he'd ever created. *Click, whirr.* She burned for him. *Click.*

Serena snapped the last picture on the roll before lowering the camera to her lap with unsteady hands. Her chest rose and fell rapidly, and her breath came in short, jerky gasps. Lifting trembling fingers to her lips, she struggled for control. But she was shaky, wary, disturbed by the truth she saw through the camera's eye.

Kevin Riley, with his too long hair and too feminine features, with his Greek god body and devil-may-care attitude, was the most talented artist she'd ever seen. She'd known coming into this project that he was considered a genius, but knowing was a far cry from being hit in the face by the sensual power and talent he exuded without effort.

She shouldn't be here. The thought ran—unbidden—through her head. She couldn't take this. What thinking, breathing woman could? His work alone turned her inside out. She was afraid that any second she would careen over an edge she hadn't known she was close to. An edge she hadn't realized existed seventy-two hours before.

She cursed Steve, the agent she and Kevin shared, under her breath. This whole thing was his idea. If he hadn't called her, thrilled about the "absolutely fabulous" opportunity that came with photographing the many facets of Kevin, she wouldn't be here now. Of course, when Steve had called, she hadn't been able to say no. How could she? It was a huge career break for her, one that could send her rocketing to fame herself. Besides, she'd needed a distraction—desperately—something, anything to keep her mind off the upcoming hearing and her sense of impending doom. How could she have known that photographing Kevin would be nearly as disturbing?

The cell phone attached to her hip vibrated, but she didn't answer it. Refused to even look and see who was calling. If it was *him,* she didn't want to know about it, didn't want to think about it. And she really didn't want to spend the rest of the night tied up in knots over somebody's stupid idea of a joke.

Taking a couple of deep breaths, she pushed the unwelcome intrusion from her mind. Instead, she focused on Kevin again—a subject only a little less uncomfortable than her very persistent and obscene crank caller.

After all, the man was a walking, talking example of human perfection. His muscles strained as he bent the warm metal to his every whim. Faded denim molded every inch of his lower body, cupping his ass in a way that Serena would very much have liked to echo. She sighed unknowingly, absently pressing a hand against herself in an effort to stop the ache that was slowly turning her lower body liquid.

Not that he'd notice if she dissolved into a puddle of unrequited lust on his studio floor. Though he had been pleasant enough when she had shown up on his doorstep two and a half days ago, he'd paid her almost no attention since. Serena was used to a certain amount of attention from men, and his complete lack of interest both annoyed and intrigued her.

How could she be so attracted to a man who didn't even know she existed? She wasn't one of those women who always fell for the man who was just a little cold, just a small step out of reach. Or at least, she never had been before. She'd always liked her men hot, accessible and casual. Most important casual. For Serena, nothing was worse than having a lover who didn't understand her boundaries.

Yet she couldn't get Kevin out of her mind.

She snorted again. Talk about an understatement. For the last two hours, she'd fantasized about making love with him in nearly every position possible. Not to mention some positions she had her doubts about but was more than willing to try.

Despite the storm raging outside, cooling the nighttime air, it was stifling in the huge one-room studio. Kevin had the air-conditioning pumping full-blast, but it had little effect against the huge metal welding furnace throwing out heat in the corner of the room. Or the blowtorch Kevin wielded with amazing concentration.

Serena let her camera slide to the floor and fanned herself with a nearby magazine as she watched him. What was happening to her? Nothing ever distracted her or kept her from completing an assignment. But there was plenty of time, she reminded herself. And there was no way she could take any more pictures tonight, not if she had any hope of getting out of the studio without humiliating herself.

Absently, she slid her hand slowly down her bare arm, enjoying the silky smoothness of the skin. Imagined that it was his hand touching her, his fingers sliding slowly over her shoulder to find the hollow of her throat. She wanted to feel those rough, callused hands on her body, needed it with an intensity that shocked her. Her eyes trailed desperately over his naked torso, following the thin line of hair that disappeared beneath the button of his jeans. She wanted a man she shouldn't have. Couldn't have. Serena closed her eyes and silently willed away the need.

"Fuck!" Kevin cursed viciously as he burned himself for the third time in as many minutes. His concentration was shot, knocked to hell and back by the beautiful blonde staring at him through her camera lens. From the moment she'd shown up on his doorstep three days before—with her long legs and drop-dead attitude—he'd known he was in trouble.

How could he not be? Everything about her—from her pixie-cut blond hair to her serious brown eyes—screamed coolly professional. She even buttoned her oxford shirts to right under her chin, a habit that was driving him completely insane. All he'd been able to think about for the past two days was opening those shirts one button at a time, slowly peeling them away to reveal every inch of her smooth golden skin.

He'd worked hard to maintain his distance, to treat her with the same cool amusement with which she treated him. But while Serena gave every appearance of being oblivious to him and the hunger she ignited inside of him, he was anything but oblivious to her. Under her steady, detached gaze, he'd made a number of stupid mistakes in the last couple of days, and it was beginning to seriously piss him off.

Turning the blowtorch off and setting it aside, he stepped back to look at his latest sculpture, frowning. Something wasn't right, though he was hard put to figure out exactly what the problem was. While he planned every detail of his sculptures out before he ever began to build them, small variations normally occurred as he worked. A feeling he got that told him to bend this piece or twist that one. Intuition, really, that set his work apart from everyone else's.

He rolled his shoulders, working out the kinks that came from long hours crouching over steaming hot metal as he bent it to his will. Disgusted with himself, his work and his overactive libido, Kevin closed his eyes as he stretched, determined to block Serena, with her pixie eyes and curvy body, from his mind.

He'd been down this road before, he reminded himself, had learned his lesson well. After all, Deb had been one hell of a teacher. Yet here he was, lusting after another artist who wanted to use him to further her career. He shrugged restlessly, even as the old anger churned in his stomach. At least Serena was honest about what she wanted—something Deb had never been.

Deb had been drawn to his fame, had exploited it. And he'd let her. He'd been in love for the first time in his life, and he would have done anything to keep her happy. He had wanted to use his influence in the art world to help her make a name for herself. Why shouldn't he? He hadn't realized, then, that he was expendable; that the second she got what she wanted from him, she'd be out the door.

Kevin shook his head, loathing his inability to keep the past where it belonged. He'd buried this crap a long time ago, so why was he dwelling on it now? Why was it suddenly right there, front and center in his mind?

His lips curled sardonically. Who was he kidding? Serena was the reason it was all rushing back to him. She shook him up, invaded his mind, made him ache. Usually, when working, he could block out everything from hunger to nuclear holocaust, but not tonight and not with her. Tonight the hair on the back of his neck stood straight up—as did another notable part of his anatomy—and it took everything he had to even remember what the sculpture was supposed to look like, let alone why he shouldn't be thinking about her. Wanting her.

He ground his teeth together, conscious of the ever-present whirring of her camera. How she could concentrate on taking pictures right now, he didn't know. Between the storm, the heat and—he glanced at his watch—the time, his body was telling him that there were better ways to spend the remainder of the night. And every single one centered around the beautiful, sexy woman behind him.

Muttering a curse, he strolled to the refrigerator in the corner of the room and grabbed an ice-cold beer. If he couldn't work anymore, then he could at least try to quench with alcohol the desire she had ignited.

He chuckled grimly to himself. Of course, when you added alcohol to fire, all you ended up with was one hell of a flame.

"You want one?" he asked, keeping his back to Serena as he fought the strength of his arousal.

"Hmmm?" Her voice was soft and sexy. Shivers shot down his spine, and he felt his eyes narrow speculatively. What had put that sultry note in her normally crisp and businesslike tone?

He turned to her, a beer in his extended hand. "Here. I'm done tonight."

Her eyes were hazy, far away, as if she too were aroused. Kevin's eyebrows rose as he watched her blink several times, trying to bring him into focus. Maybe the attraction wasn't as one-sided as he'd thought.

"Thanks." Serena took the beer, twisted the top off and drank a long, slow swallow.

His eyes greedily followed her every move as she closed her full lips around the top of the bottle, tilted and drank. Her throat moved as she swallowed and her ripe, unpainted mouth slid in a subtle back-and-forth motion that had drool pooling in the corners of his mouth. Suddenly his cock was so hard he thought he'd explode.

When she lowered the bottle, a single drop glistened on her bottom lip, and he ached to lick it off. Before he could step closer, the tip of her pink tongue darted forward and swept across her lips, once, twice, a third time.

He cleared his throat in an attempt to disguise the groan he couldn't quite smother. He tried to turn away, but couldn't—he was literally frozen in place as his eyes wandered over her from head to toe.

The heat from the furnace was truly overwhelming tonight—he'd had to stoke it up to get the reaction he needed from the metal he was working with. Because of the heat, she had discarded the oxford shirt long ago, and now only a thin caramel-colored tank top covered her lush, high breasts. One of the spaghetti straps rode low on her shoulder, resting directly above a wicked-looking scar on her biceps and revealing the absence of a bra. An absence made even more obvious by the hard peaks of her nipples beneath the soft cotton fabric.

Though he knew it was rude to focus on those lush nipples, he couldn't force his gaze away. He wanted to touch them, taste them, draw them into his mouth and suck the sweetness from her until she writhed beneath him in ecstasy. What would she taste like?

He heard Serena's breath hitch, knew suddenly that she was as aware of him and his body as he was of her. He had never before lusted so obviously after a woman he was working with, had always tried to be considerate of a woman's feelings during working hours. But normal working hours had come and gone. It was the middle of the night and hot as hell. The storm raging outside was tying his gut into knots. He wanted Serena, had burned for her from the second he'd first laid eyes on her almost seventy-two hours before.

And though he had restrained himself, believing that she was not in the least interested, the answering arousal in her own eyes suddenly changed everything.

He took a step closer, his gaze still focused on her telltale nipples. They grew even tauter and he knew—he *knew*—that there was no way he could stop himself from touching her.

It was way too hot for her to be cold, way too steamy in the studio for him to question whether it was arousal making her nipples peak. As he drew closer to her, stalking her, he forced his eyes back to her face.

Eyes closed, head tilted back, lips soft and open, she rubbed the beer against the back of her neck and down the side of her face. A soft moan revealed the pleasure the contact with the cool bottle brought her. Opening her eyes, she noticed his predatory stance for the first time, saw his eyes blazing with a need he couldn't hide.

He watched her own widen in answer, watched them glaze over as the passion she too was fighting to hold off rose up and overwhelmed her. Her scent—a mixture of wildflowers and hot, spicy woman—teased him, drawing him closer and closer to the edge of his resistance.

Reaching forward, he plucked the beer from her hands and drank slowly, enjoying the taste of her as much as the beer. He watched as her eyes found a drop of sweat at the hollow of his neck, as they followed it helplessly down his bare chest and onto his stomach.

Serena wanted to reach her tongue out and sweep the drop from his body. Wanted to follow the lazy path made by the drop, testing, tasting every inch of his well-muscled torso before working her way slowly, oh so slowly, beneath the waistband of his jeans.

Serena's breath hitched in her throat, and her eyes met Kevin's for the first time in many hours. His breath, too, was coming in harsh pants, and she could tell that he was as aroused as she was. That he wanted her at least as badly as she wanted him.

She reached one still-trembling hand toward him, whether in invitation or denial she didn't know. But when he grasped her fingers with his own, she shivered at the strength in his work-hardened palm. And when he slowly, oh so slowly, lifted her hand to his lips, she shuddered with the power and the pain of her desire.

His tongue reached out and caressed her index finger, once, twice, before drawing her slowly into his mouth. His teeth nipped lightly at her fingertip, as he pulled her more and more deeply into him. He sucked her finger gently, his tongue sweeping in slow, lazy circles as his mouth slid back and forth.

Serena's breath came in short gasps, and her knees weakened until she feared their ability to support her. Her eyes drifted shut and her head rolled back on her neck. She knew this was wrong, knew she shouldn't be doing this. They had weeks of work in front of them before this book was completed and a one-night stand now would only make working together that much harder.

But she couldn't deny the need flowing between them. Didn't want to deny it. And his mouth on her finger felt so incredibly good. How would it feel on her lips? Her breasts? Between her thighs?

As Kevin slowly relinquished his hold on her finger, she bit back an instinctive protest. She was on fire, burning, her underwear soaked through. Glancing down at the front of his jeans, she felt her eyes widen at the erection the denim couldn't begin to disguise.

She reached to touch him, but he grabbed her hand before it could connect. "Not yet, *cher*," he whispered, holding her newly captured hand to his chest. His heart pounded heavily, riotously beneath her palm. Her fingers flexed, explored, slid lightly over one nipple, and his heartbeat grew faster, harder.

It echoed her own, she thought, as blood pumped hot and quick through her veins. The raging storm had moved inside, buffeting her from every angle, sweeping her into its powerful, chaotic embrace and leaving Kevin as her only anchor.

His stormy, heavy-lidded eyes burned into her own, midnight blue and fierce with desire. His musky scent overwhelmed her. Yet his touch was tender and his lips gentle as they moved slowly over her finger, down her palm, his tongue trailing a path of fire wherever it touched. Leisurely, as if he had all the time in the world, his mouth pressed long, lazy kisses across her hand—over her love line, her life line, slowly, slowly working his way down to the rounded pad at the base of her thumb. And there, right there, at the juncture where her palm met her wrist, he bit gently, firmly, his teeth sinking in even as his tongue laved away the hurt.

Serena's knees gave way, and with a cry of ecstasy, she slid, trembling, down the wall.

Kevin crouched beside her, his eyes on hers, searching for any sign of uneasiness. But she was too hot, too steamy, too far gone to think of the consequences. Reaching out, she tangled her fingers in his hair and pulled him forward until his lips met her own.

He tasted like the cinnamon gum he chewed obsessively, a combination of spicy and sweet that drove her to the brink of her control and then beyond. She knew he'd meant to take it easy, slow, but with the first powerful touch of his mouth, Serena was lost and her uninhibited response sparked his own. His tongue swept across her lips—ravenous, demanding, desperate—and she opened for him as lust burned through her.

They plundered each other, tongues testing, tasting, tangling together. She sucked his lower lip between her teeth and bit slowly; he groaned in response, his hands sliding down to cup her ass, to press her against him.

She was hot and wet and frantic to feel him within her. Kevin must have sensed her desperation, for he tightened his hold, pressed more firmly against her, began a gentle thrusting between her thighs that sent her pulse soaring. A high, keening sound escaped her— one that would have mortified her at any other time. But here, now, with the frantic grip of her hands on his body and the powerful thrust of his hips against hers, it seemed natural. More than natural. Perfect.

But she wanted more. Breaking free of his kiss, Serena slid her lips slowly over his cheeks, relishing the stubble on his unshaven jaw before her tongue darted out and explored the inner shell of his ear. Frenzied, frantic, she closed her teeth around his earlobe and bit gently, as her hands moved to caress the rippling muscles of his back.

Kevin growled deep in his throat and moved his hand slowly down her chest. As his fingers closed around her breast for the first time, a huge streak of lightning lit the sky beyond the studio, and the lights went out, plunging the room into still and eerie darkness.

Chapter Two

Serena stiffened, pulling away from Kevin as fear wrapped itself around her throat in a tightfisted choke hold. Bloody images flashed in front of her eyes before she could stop them. "What happened?" she demanded, hands pressing urgently against his shoulders.

"It's just the storm, *bébé*," he soothed, his black-magic voice calming the shock waves pulsing within her. "Anytime a big one hits, we lose power out here. I'm surprised we've had lights this long."

He lowered his head to her neck, let his tongue stroke lazily across the hollow of her throat. But she pushed at his shoulders again, shoving him away hard as she scrambled to her feet. "Do you have a flashlight?"

"A flashlight?" he responded dumbly.

"Yeah, a flashlight. Or a candle? Anything?" The urgency in her voice barely registered on him.

"Do we need one?" He ran a hand through his hair. "I thought what we were doing was pretty well suited to the dark. Not that I don't look forward to seeing you in the light." His voice was low and teasing as he reached for her again. A note of humor crept in. "So, where were we?"

"I don't want—" She pulled away, ran her hands down arms that were suddenly ice-cold.

"You don't want what?" he parroted, the warmth in his tone cooling several degrees as his eyes narrowed dangerously. "You don't want this? You sure picked a hell of a time to change your mind."

The flames in the iron-working stove had died down as he worked with his blowtorch, so it gave off just a small amount of light. Enough that he could see her outline, but her face and eyes were shadowed.

"Serena, answer me. What's going on here?" Impatience colored his words, making them cooler than before.

Serena pressed trembling hands to her eyes, desperate to block out the darkness and the hint of temper Kevin couldn't hide. Desperate to stop the memories bombarding her. Though her arousal was gone, killed by the sudden and imposing darkness, now she was shaky for entirely different reasons, and she couldn't stand this new and unexpected loss of control.

"I'm sorry," she said softly. "I know it looks bad, but I never meant to do this to you." And she hadn't—once she made up her mind, she rarely changed it, and she always, always followed through with what she started, whether it was an assignment for work or a project she did for pleasure. Making love with Kevin definitely fell into the pleasure category, but she couldn't do it. Not right now. Not while darkness closed in around her. Not while Sandra's screams echoed in her head and the stench of long-dried blood assaulted her nostrils.

"I never said you had." His tone was guarded, though warmer than it had been a few moments before.

"I don't . . ." Her voice was harsh, husky with a fear she couldn't banish as she forced the words passed the sudden lump in her throat. "I don't like the dark."

"What?" Kevin asked, confusion evident in his tone.

A hint of her own temper entered her voice—she hated being vulnerable. "I'm afraid of the dark, okay?" The words were evenly spaced, her voice defiant, as if daring him to make fun of her.

Feeling as if he'd missed a couple of steps, or an entire staircase for that matter, Kevin closed his eyes. Ran another hand through his hair. Clamped down on the desire still twisting his guts into knots. "You're a photographer," he finally said incredulously. "Half your life is spent in a darkroom!"

"It's different." Her voice shook, despite her best efforts to keep it steady.

"How?" But his voice was softer. He was too shocked at the difference in her—the complete transformation from cool and composed to trembling and terrified—to be annoyed. From the second he'd laid eyes on Serena, he'd wanted to see her with her control shattered. But he'd never envisioned it happening like this. He reached out a hand and found hers in the darkness, astounded at how quickly she had turned cold and clammy.

"My choice," she said in little more than a whisper. "I choose to go into that room, dark or no. And I have control of the light switch. Nobody else." Her trembling suddenly increased and he couldn't resist pulling her into his arms.

"Kevin," she said, hands once again pushing against him, "I don't want to do this right now. I can't—"

"I'm not asking you to do anything. But you're shaky, freezing. Let me hold you."

Her spine stiffened suddenly and her voice dripped ice as she answered. "I'm not a child to be comforted. I'll be fine if you just give me a minute."

Settling himself against the wall, Kevin pulled her into his lap before she could protest. "Sssh." One hand reached up to stroke her short hair; the other rubbed her slender back soothingly as he murmured nonsense in her ear.

Against her will, Serena relaxed into him. He felt safe, made *her* feel safe and secure. It had been so long since she'd felt this way that it took her a minute to recognize the feeling.

Seventeen. The thought echoed through her. She'd been seventeen the last time she'd felt this safe. At the time she'd thought she had everything she'd ever want—guaranteed entrance into one of the best photography programs in the country, a boyfriend she adored and the best twin sister in the world. But that was before Damien, with his good looks and insane jealousies. Before she'd known what it felt like to have a blade sink deep into her flesh. Before she'd heard her sister die.

Stifling the whimper that wanted to escape, Serena cursed herself. It wasn't like her to lose control like this, to curl up on a man's lap and let him soothe her like a baby. She didn't need comforting, had refused to need it for more than a decade. So why was she cowering on Kevin's lap just because the lights were out?

She started to move, to push him away again, but Kevin held her in place. And she let him without knowing why. She could have struggled, could have demanded her freedom. But it felt right sitting here, letting him hold her. When the lights came on, Serena knew she'd be embarrassed that he'd seen her this way. But for now, as fear stalked her and darkness fenced her in, she was content, if not happy, to stay exactly where she was.

Despite the heat of the past few minutes, there was nothing sexual in his touch, nothing passionate in hers. Yet, leaning against him in the dark, letting him support her, she recognized a small rekindling of the fire that had burned so brightly within her earlier. Who would have thought the fearsome, awe-inspiring Kevin Riley could be so ... kind?

Glancing around the still-dark studio, she shuddered before she could stop herself. She hated this terrible fear, hated that it had the power to control her. It had been ten years since Sandra had died. And while the first few years were a jumble of fear and hate, confusion and loneliness, she'd slowly pulled out of the tailspin her sister's murder had thrown her into.

Years passed and she began to go days, weeks, sometimes even months without feeling the crippling grief that literally brought her to her knees. But something always happened. A newspaper article, a movie preview, a blackout. And she would realize, once again, just how tenuous her grip on sanity really was.

Breathe in, breathe out. Breathe in, breathe out. The pattern was her mantra at times like these. If she did it long enough, the shaking would stop. It always did.

Silence reigned for a few minutes, though fierce bursts of thunder continued to shake the studio violently.

Sweat slowly slid down Serena's neck, pooled between her breasts. She should pull away from Kevin, give both of them some much-needed breathing room. The heat was becoming unbearable in the studio, even with the furnace in the corner dying down. Most months, the bayou was not a comfortable place to be without air-conditioning, but August was especially hot and sticky.

As she shifted away from him, Kevin's arms tightened around her. "Where you going, *bébé*?" he asked huskily.

"I figured you'd be sick of me by now. It's really hot in here."

"I'm used to the heat. But maybe you're sick of me?" He pulled back slightly, as if trying to see her face in the darkness.

"I'm not." She leaned forward, buried her face in the curve of his neck, inhaling his incredible masculine scent. "I should be, but I'm not."

"Then don't worry about it."

Desperate to shatter the tension that stretched between them and striving for a bit of normalcy in this very abnormal situation, she was determined to focus on something besides the fear that was slowly driving her out of her mind.

"So this book we're doing," she commented, "how do you see it?"

"As crap."

Serena stiffened immediately, pulled just far enough away to glare at him, even though she knew he couldn't see her. "Excuse me?" Her voice dripped ice.

Kevin smiled. It seemed that cool and collected hadn't totally deserted the field after all. "Not your part, Serena. The whole thing. Why do they need to do a book about me? My work's the interesting stuff, and I'm not even sure that *it* would make a good book."

"I don't know if it would make a good book or not, but my photo essay on you is going to make a fabulous one. I've already got some incredible shots."

"How do you know if you haven't developed any film yet?"

"Intuition."

He sighed, raked his hand through his hair in a gesture that was becoming incredibly familiar. "What do you expect the book to say about me?"

"What do you want it to say?" she countered.

"I don't know." His fingers tightened into fists, and she instinctively reached a hand out to soothe him. "I don't like people. I don't like them in my studio, and I sure as hell don't like them in my head."

Despite his vehemence, she felt his hands relax slightly beneath her own. "You let them into your head every day, Kevin. What do you think your art is doing if not letting people see inside you?"

"But only what I want them to see."

"Do you really believe that?" she asked, lifting an eyebrow. "You really believe that art critics, connoisseurs, other artists only see what you want them to see? Give me a break and the rest of them some credit. Watching you for the last few days, I know I've seen things you haven't thought you were revealing."

He stiffened and Serena immediately recognized her mistake. She waited for him to comment, to demand an explanation. He didn't say a word, but she could feel his withdrawal in his slackening grip, in the physical and emotional distance that suddenly swelled between them.

When he finally spoke, of the very mundane, his voice was hoarse and the easy camaraderie between them gone. "Do you want something to eat? I've got some Twinkies out here. Or we can head back to the house and see what I've got there. Everything's electric, so I can't cook, but I'm sure there's sandwich stuff. And I've got candles."

She missed his heat, the warm center of her brutally cold

emotional storm. And she regretted, deeply, the distance her careless choice of words had put between them. She'd known even before she met him that Kevin was a very private person. His deep-seated isolation was practically legendary in a field filled with the lonely and the odd.

"Twinkies? Do you know what's in those things?" She deliberately kept her voice light and unthreatening.

"I don't know and I don't care. All that matters is they taste good." Kevin's voice was a little warmer, though he was several degrees from relaxed.

"Are you kidding me? Do you know that they don't even bake them? The whole sponge cake thing is based on a chemical reaction."

"A chemical reaction that makes them taste *good*." He leapt to his feet, crossed the room in a few giant steps. "So do you want one or not?"

She shrugged. "I guess."

"Don't sound so enthusiastic." Opening the small refrigerator, he asked, "Do you want another beer or would you prefer something else?"

"Water, if you've got it. I can't imagine the gastronomical nightmare a combination of beer and Twinkies might bring on." Though she kept her voice light, Serena felt his absence keenly. Without him against her, it was much harder to forget the enveloping blackness.

Kevin heard the note of restrained fear in her voice, cursed himself for not realizing that leaving her would make her terror more pronounced. But he'd needed the space, needed a chance to regroup. He didn't put himself on display for anyone, had worked hard nearly his entire life to keep people at arm's length. It was both disconcerting and demeaning to think that some woman—some photographer—could see past his defenses.

But Serena wasn't just some woman or some photographer, he admitted to himself. That was the crux of the whole problem. She was the woman he wanted more than he'd wanted anything for more years than he could count. He felt vulnerable, exposed, and he detested every second of it. After Deb, he'd sworn no woman would make him feel this way again.

After handing Serena the bottle of water and a Twinkie, he sat and pulled her into his lap once more. They sat in silence for a few moments before he commented, "I love your voice." It was a peace offering, a weak apology meant to get them back on even footing.

"What did you say?" she asked, pulling away from him abruptly.

"Your voice. It's really low and husky. Very sexy."

"I hate it."

He tried in vain to see her expression. "Why? It's fabulous."

She didn't answer, simply turned her face away from him despite the darkness.

"Serena—"

"Leave it alone, Kevin."

He sighed in frustration but didn't say another word, just held her as the storm raged wildly around them.

How long they sat there clinging silently to each other, he didn't know. Long enough for the storm to slowly pass over them and for the wind to finally die down. Eventually the early-morning sounds of the bayou returned as the wildlife around them slowly relaxed.

Kevin was tired, knew that Serena was exhausted. But he couldn't sleep, couldn't relax enough to even consider sleeping. Sometime during their quiet talk, between the Twinkies and the beer, renewed desire began to pound through him.

His senses thrummed at the torture of being this close to Serena. He could feel her heartbeat—a slow, steady rhythm pounding in unison with his own. Her breath was as deep and relaxed as she was, and each inhalation pressed her soft curves more firmly against him.

Trying to control himself, determined not to fall on her like an animal, he brushed her hair softly back from his face. She made no objection as his hands smoothed her hair, as his lips softly grazed her forehead. He began to lower his mouth to hers, but as dawn's light illuminated her face, he realized that she was asleep.

Cursing himself and the overactive libido that had blinded him to her need for sleep, Kevin tamped down the lust that rode him hard. Instead, he climbed gingerly to his feet and—forgoing shoes for fear of waking her up—carried her out of the studio, across the yard and into the house, where he walked slowly to her bedroom.

Her scent teased him with every step, and as he laid her gently on the bed, he slid his fingers slowly down the curve of her cheek.

Her eyes blinked open, sleepy and confused. "Kevin?" she asked, her voice husky with sleep.

"I'm here," he reassured her, clasping the hand that reached for his. "Sleep, *bébé*. The storm's over and the lights should be on by the time you wake up."

"Are you certain?"

"Absolutely." His smile was cocky, reassuring. "I've been through this a lot."

She smiled back as her eyes drifted shut. "Stay with me." Her hand tightened around his.

His cock twitched eagerly, but he ignored it. "Are you sure?"

"Yes," she sighed, rolling onto her side. Then, clutching his hand against her chest, she wrapped herself around him and drifted back to sleep.

Kevin sat on the side of the bed, watching over her as daylight slowly crept into the bayou. Her gold hair gleamed against the dark sheets, making her look defenseless and nearly childlike. She would hate this in the morning, he knew. Would hate the vulnerability that had forced her to lean on him, would hate even more that he'd seen her asleep, without the mask she kept in place nearly all of her waking hours.

He couldn't say how long he sat with her warm body curled around his hand, how long he watched her face as she slept. But the sun was high in the morning sky and the bayou alive with noise when he finally pulled his hand from hers and walked slowly down the hall to his own room.

As he crawled into his bed, the air-conditioning suddenly kicked in, and his ceiling fan began its quiet turning. The electricity was back on. As he drifted to sleep, he wondered if the game between them was as well.

Chapter Three

He couldn't sleep. Not that that was anything unusual. It had been so long since he'd had a full night's sleep that he could barely remember what it felt like to live without this bone-weary exhaustion wearing him down. Why should today be any different?

Climbing out of bed with a sigh and a shrug, he padded into the bathroom to stare at his reflection in the dim light filtering through the edges of the blackout curtains. He could see himself, just barely, but he didn't bother turning on the overhead light. It hurt his eyes and often brought on the killer migraines he'd do almost anything to escape. Besides, he liked the shadows. Liked the vague outline of his face in the mirror, the many shades of gray he'd chosen to live his life amidst.

He ignored the vast array of yellow medicine bottles lined up against the mirror. They couldn't help him—it was already too late. He could feel a migraine starting, even without the added stimulation of light. Pain crushed through his head from all sides and his vision blurred. Nausea clenched his stomach in its slippery grip— once and then twice—and he barely made it to the toilet before becoming violently ill.

When it was over, he slid bonelessly to the floor; resting next to the toilet for a few minutes, he braced his head on the warm oak cabinet he himself had installed in better days. He wanted desperately to climb back into bed, but he was too weak to get that far. The pain, and sickness, had sapped him of all energy. Besides, this was only the beginning. The sickness would get worse—much worse—before it abated.

Goddamn her! Rage rushed through him, driving back some of the pain, some of the weakness. This was all her fault—disappearing for days on end. Didn't she know he needed her? Needed to see her. To hear her voice.

She made the pain bearable.

Images of her careened through his head, flashing in and out as the pain ebbed and flowed. Clutching his head, he struggled to ignore the agony and bring her face into focus. Long moments passed, filled with his harsh breathing and harsher groans as he tried to make sense of the rapid flashes of color bombarding his brain.

And then, suddenly, the flashes coalesced and there she was. Soaking wet after being caught in a summer rainstorm—her hair slicked back and her brown eyes alight with a rare and intoxicating laughter. The thin cotton of her shirt all but transparent while her nipples pebbled into tempting hardness.

His dick twitched, grew harder despite the pain still gripping his head. With a sigh, he wrapped a hand around himself. Began to squeeze and stroke as he imagined Serena on her knees in front of him—wet and willing—her warm, ripe mouth sucking him dry. The pain began to slide away.

He'd rip open her wet shirt, bare her creamy breasts to his starving eyes. Her nipples—hard, tight little peaks—would be so deeply pink they'd be almost red as her breasts thrust upward for his approval. He'd reach out and pinch them tightly enough to make her whimper—a little pain only increased the pleasure. She'd moan and cry out, and then he would take her nipples in his mouth, one at a time, rolling them over his tongue and between his teeth. He could taste them already—the strawberry tartness tickling his tongue, feeding his soul, before he pulled away and let her suck him like she'd be dying to do.

She'd play with him first, let her tongue lick delicately at his head before pulling him into her mouth and down her slender, elegant throat. He groaned—swiping his thumb across the head of his dick as he envisioned her soft, wet mouth doing the same—then increased his tempo as he imagined her tongue stroking up and down his dick while her lips and teeth and the soft suction of her mouth drove him to insanity and beyond.

His hips surged against his hand as he dreamed about her warm breath fluttering over him. She'd curl her tongue around him, moaning deep in her throat even as her teeth found the sensitive ridge at the base of his head. She'd bite down—softly, experimentally—and he'd tangle his hands in her hair, forcing his huge, powerful dick down her throat. Ramming it into her again and again as she struggled to take all of him. Her teeth would scrape against him, pain—once again—making the pleasure even sweeter.

Ecstasy shot through him, stealing his breath and his control. He stroked faster and faster, harder and harder, until he came with a scream. A giant flooding that stripped his soul bare and had fireworks shooting off behind his eyes as she swallowed all he had to give her and demanded more. Her body starving for all he could give it.

The soul-searing pleasure faded and he came back to himself with a groan. He was slumped—naked—on the bathroom floor, his come coating the cold, smoky tiles between his upraised knees.

Serena danced before his eyes—bare, aroused, dying for him—and he reached for her. The image disappeared and was replaced abruptly by one of the cool and composed Serena he'd seen in the last days of the trial—before the deal had been cut. Ravaged by pain but too brave, too stoic, to let it out. No one had seen how much she was hurting. No one had realized how distraught she was.

No one but him. He could see. Of course he could see—he knew her too well to be fooled by that mask she showed the world. He had stood in the shadows, watching her. Wanting so much to comfort her. Wanting to kill the animal who had tried to take her from him.

But she hadn't gone then, hadn't given up. Even then she'd known that she was his and she always would be.

The pain in his head was gone, swallowed by the earth-shaking pleasure Serena had given him. The absence of agony allowed him to take his first deep breath since awakening. He couldn't wait until he could repay the favor, giving her back equal measure of the ecstasy and agony she so often brought to him.

Climbing shakily to his feet, he reached for the largest bottle on the vanity table. She would be back in a few days and he had to be ready.

He shook out two pills, swallowed them dry. And tried to ignore the fine trembling that rocked him from the inside out.

Serena closed her laptop with a sigh. She'd spent the last few hours taking notes on each and every photo of Kevin she'd taken with the digital camera. But now it was time to come out of the bedroom—time to face the music, so to speak.

She glanced at the clock. It was two thirty and Kevin was finally awake. About twenty minutes before, she'd heard the shower turn on, and now the scent of coffee was drifting through her closed door.

She was already showered and dressed, had been for nearly four hours. Though she'd been exhausted when she'd fallen asleep on Kevin—her cheeks burned at the memory—she'd only managed to sleep about three and a half hours. The nightmare had woken her up, as it had every day for the last two weeks, and she hadn't been able to face lying in bed and staring at the ceiling.

She'd decided, instead, to make the most of her early start by examining the digital pictures she'd taken of Kevin over the last three days. There were not as many as she would have hoped, largely because she'd spent an awful lot of time taking photos with her Nikon. Now she had about thirty rolls of film to develop, something she planned on doing when she returned to Baton Rouge later in the day.

Kevin would think she was running away, and maybe she would have considered it if this thing in Baton Rouge hadn't loomed huge and irrevocable in her head. She dreaded the trip home. Dreaded facing what she'd buried for the last ten years. But the assistant DA was insistent—it was imperative that she testify at the parole hearing. She couldn't argue with him; she knew Jack wouldn't put her through it if he didn't think it absolutely necessary.

Her cell rang, interrupting her silent reverie, and she picked it up without thinking. "Serena Macafee."

"Hello, darling."

Her stomach clenched sickly at the now familiar, mechanically distorted voice, and she moved to hang up, but knew the gesture was useless. He would just call back and leave messages—twisted and explicit—until she finally listened to him. "What do you want?" She kept her voice steady, though her stomach churned.

"Just to talk. I've missed you—you've been away for days."

Chills skittered down her spine. "I don't know what you're talking about."

He laughed, the sound even more disturbing for its distortion. "Let's not play games, sweetheart. You're not at home and haven't been for nearly a week. Where are you?"

"That's none of your business."

The disembodied voice turned deadly serious. "Everything about you is my business. When are you going to figure that out?"

Hands clenched into fists, Serena fought for control—fought to keep the sick panic out of her voice. "Look, hasn't this gone on long enough? Aren't you bored yet?"

"You could never bore me. Talking to you is so often the highlight of my day."

"Well, it's not the highlight of mine. You need to stop or I'll call the police."

"No, you won't." The voice was confident, self-assured. "You hate the cops, hate the whole system. You wouldn't call them if you were dying in the street."

Serena froze, shocked at just how well this man knew her. She'd assumed, at first, that the calls were just a joke. A couple of kids crank calling for kicks. But the calls had gone on for weeks now, each one a little more personal, a little more disturbing than the last. He'd even managed to get her cell phone number after she'd changed it. Twice.

"Ahhh, that got your attention, didn't it? You think I don't know you? You think I don't know everything about you? Like right now you're in the middle of that godforsaken bayou taking pictures of some famous artist, aren't you?

"What's the matter?" he asked after a minute, as if her silence disturbed him. "Am I not supposed to know what you're up to?" His voice dropped to nearly a whisper. "Am I not supposed to know about the great Kevin Riley? They say women are crazy about him. Is that true? Are you crazy about him? Do you want him to fuck you?"

The mechanical voice dropped an octave, turned even uglier. "Or has he already?"

She didn't answer him, *couldn't* answer him as shock spun through her.

"Tell me the truth, damn it! Has he touched you? You've been way out there in the middle of the swamps with him for days. Has he kissed you? Sucked your gorgeous little nipples? Licked his way down that hot, little body of yours until—"

She hit the DISCONNECT button moments before the phone fell from her suddenly numb fingers. She couldn't listen to one more word—even if it meant the calls would escalate, get worse.

Serena sank slowly onto her bed, her shaking legs no longer able to support her. What had she gotten herself into? And, dear God, how was she going to get herself out of it?

Had she somehow managed to pick up a stalker, someone who watched her every move? She shuddered violently, fighting against the overwhelming need to close the blinds and curl into a ball. Fighting the urge to take a shower and scrub until she felt clean.

Sandra's death had taught her to be wary, had convinced her that the world could be a very sick place. She really should call the police, tell them about the phone calls. About the caller's sinister knowledge of her life and personality.

But he was right. She hated the Baton Rouge police, didn't trust them at all. Refused to trust them after the debacle surrounding her sister's death. Besides, she didn't have any proof. Unwilling, at first, to accept the seriousness of her situation, she'd erased all the messages.

Now, however, she wasn't nearly as certain. Now she was scared—for herself and for Kevin. What if this guy was violent? Jealous? Completely obsessed? She'd seen that kind of obsession firsthand, knew how vicious it could be.

Resting her head in her hands, Serena pressed the heels of her hands against her weary eyes. As if the next few days didn't already hold enough fun-filled activities to last her a lifetime, now she had someone following her every move—fixated on her and perhaps on Kevin as well.

With her eyes closed, she couldn't stop the events of the previous night from flipping through her brain. What had she been thinking? Her laugh was unamused as she realized the obvious answer—she hadn't been thinking at all. She'd been too caught up in the blazing desire generated from being in the same room with Kevin to even attempt to think rationally. There was no other answer for her behavior, no other reason for the heat flooding her still.

But she couldn't afford to use her suddenly raging hormones as a guide to living her life. Even without her obscene caller and his threats, her life was entirely too complicated at present to even consider starting a relationship.

She had to stop this thing with Kevin before it really got started. Had to stop thinking about him, lusting after him when she should be working. She wasn't afraid of the sex—that was the easy part. But she couldn't just fuck him and move on. Because no matter how casually she intended this thing with him to be, no matter how desperately she tried to keep her emotional distance, she had a feeling getting involved with Kevin would be the equivalent of emotional quicksand. He didn't have a casual, uncomplicated bone in his body, and even if he did, there was too much heat between them for things to be just sexual.

Already they were teetering on the edge of emotional involvement, and she didn't *do* emotional involvement. He'd held her last night when she'd fallen apart, had soothed her and rocked her to sleep like a child. That in itself put Kevin in a category far apart from mere sexual attraction. A small part of her—one that she had thought long dead and buried—warmed at the memory of his care and concern. The rest of her was a mixture of fear and humiliation. Fear because of the curious melting in the region of her heart. Humiliation because Kevin had seen her so completely defenseless.

She'd spent years cultivating her smooth outer shell—so many years that no one even remembered the girl she'd once been. Not even her. And now she'd let Kevin in—had let him see her with all her defenses down. She felt naked, exposed, and she couldn't stand the vulnerability. Forcing herself to take a deep breath, Serena inhaled and exhaled slowly. Battled the rising panic and slowly unfurled her clenched fists. She could handle this. Compared to what had happened ten years before, compared to what awaited her in front of that parole board, getting through the next hour was a walk in the park. She just had to get herself, and her emotions, under control before she did.

Pushing her chair back from the desk, she strode across the room and stared at herself in the mirror above the sturdy unfinished pine dresser. She looked pale, frazzled, on edge. She laughed, but it was a sound tinged more with cynicism than humor. She *was* frazzled and on edge. How could she not be? She was in the middle of the biggest project she'd ever been involved with, perched to blow her career wide-open, and she was falling apart.

Her shadowed brown eyes were made even darker by the purple circles underneath them. Her light summer tan looked sallow with her unnatural pallor, and her mouth was drawn into a tight line. Quite a difference from the sexually charged woman of the night before. But the blackout last night, followed by the nightmare, had been one stress too many on her already maxed-out system. It would be a miracle if she managed to get out of Kevin's house without making a complete and total fool of herself.

Serena laughed again, bitterly. Oh, yeah, she'd already done that. She picked up her brush, ran it through her hair one last time—more because it gave her something to do than because she cared what her hair looked like. When she was finished, she dropped the brush into her open luggage and slowly zipped the sensible gray case shut. Taking a bracing breath, she opened her bedroom door and headed down the hall to find Kevin.

He was making eggs. Bacon sizzled on the back burner and coffee dripped slowly into its glass carafe. Her stomach twisted violently, and for a moment Serena thought she'd have to make a mad dash for the bathroom. But a couple of deep breaths and a huge dose of willpower settled her down enough that she could walk sedately into the kitchen.

Her eyes fell on Kevin. Did the man ever wear a shirt? she wondered, shoving her hands into the back pockets of her jeans. She was determined to ignore the fine trembling that had started as soon as she laid eyes on him.

His faded jeans had a hole under his back left pocket, and if she looked hard enough she could see a tanned, lightly haired thigh. Not that she was looking, Serena reminded herself sternly, forcing her gaze away from his tempting flesh. His feet, big and bare, were tanned. She watched as they tapped in rhythm to a song only Kevin could hear.

She cleared her throat, prepared to speak, but Kevin whirled around before she could get a word out. "Oh, hey, there you are!" He grinned. "Did you sleep well?"

She nodded. "Umm, yeah, I did."

"Good." He gestured to the loaf of bread on the counter. "You want to make the toast? The coffee's just about ready."

Was he going to make it easy for her? she wondered, as she started the bread toasting mechanically. No mention of last night? Like he hadn't seduced her more thoroughly than any man ever, with a simple bite of her finger? Sudden anger burned in the pit of her stomach, though she wasn't sure why. Wasn't this what she'd wanted? Not to have to deal with her insane and impulsive loss of control? Not to have to make excuses for cutting things short?

She viciously buttered the toast, nearly ripping the first piece in half. Had he just been using her as a convenience, to scratch an itch? Her cheeks flared, the pallor of a few minutes before replaced by her sudden indignation. No man treated her like that, as if she were just a warm body in the middle of the night! She kept her affairs casual, true, but that was because *she* liked them that way. Who did Kevin Riley think he was?

"What did that toast do to you, *cher*?" he murmured, his voice warm with laughter as his arms circled her waist from behind.

Serena jumped, nearly sending the toast and butter knife careening across the kitchen. His breath was warm in her ear, sending shivers down her spine as his teeth nibbled leisurely at her earlobe.

"What are you doing?" She meant to sound outraged, but her voice betrayed her, coming out more than a little breathy.

"Saying good morning." His mouth coasted slowly down her jaw as he pulled her deeper into his embrace. "Good morning."

She melted before she could stop herself, her body turning hot and liquid. She wanted to stay there forever, letting his lips work their magic over her entire body. A moan rose in her throat, and she had to work extremely hard to stifle it. Forcing herself to stand straight up, refusing to lean into his body, was one of the hardest things she'd ever done. But she couldn't do this, not now, not with this man. No matter how badly she wanted to.

She cleared her throat, striving to sound professional. "Good morning."

He didn't get the hint, pulling her back flush against him. Her knees nearly buckled as she felt him rubbing, hot and hard, against her. Using every ounce of strength she could muster, she picked up the plate of toast and ducked out from beneath his arms. "Ready to eat?"

Kevin studied her with suddenly narrowed eyes. "I guess I am." He grabbed the two plates of food near the stove and strode to the table. "Here." He thumped hers down before sitting in his chair.

"Thank you." Her voice sounded strangled, but it was the best she could do. She felt bereft without his arms around her, but she had only herself to blame. It was better this way, she told herself as she settled down at the table. She had a feeling Kevin could make things extremely complicated when he wanted to.

Thank you. The words echoed in Kevin's head as he tried to tamp down on the fury slowly setting his body on fire. What kind of game was Serena playing? From cold to hot and back to cold? With no warning or explanation? He studied her closely, from the serenity of her expression to the rock steady hands slowly bringing the coffee cup to her lips.

Gone were the sexy siren of last night and the lost little girl of early this morning. In their place was the woman he had met three days ago. Calm, cold, collected, a small but superior smile tilting the corners of her lips.

"The eggs are very good." When she spoke, her voice was as steady as her hands, all traces of desire gone as if they had never been. But he'd felt her tremble in his arms, last night and again a few minutes ago. Had felt her body melt into his before she could stop it. So what was going on?

"Wine," he said, his voice sounding harsh to his own ears.

"Excuse me?" She looked at him inquisitively, that small and intensely irritating smile still on her lips. He itched to wipe it off, to bridge the distance that had sprung up between them.

"I put a little white wine in when I was mixing them. It's how my mother taught me." He caught her eye.

"Oh. It's good." She tried to look away, but he held her cool gaze with his hot stare, refusing to let her. He didn't know how long they sat like that, eyes locked, her fork poised halfway to her mouth, his hand wrapped around his coffee mug. But for a moment, just a moment, an answering heat blazed in her own eyes and her lips parted, as if she was having trouble breathing. The hand holding the fork trembled, and her other hand slowly closed into a fist.

So she wasn't as cool as she liked to pretend. The knowledge calmed him, temporarily subduing the beast that had begun to rise in him. He took a deep sip of coffee, ignoring the slight pain that came from the steaming brew.

"Are you hot?" he asked.

"Excuse me?" Her voice was strangled.

He raised one eyebrow inquiringly, and his lips curled in a smile that was more a threat than a sign of genuine amusement. "You're sweating." He gestured to the single drop of sweat slowly working its way down the side of her face. She definitely wasn't as cool as she wanted him to believe.

Her hand came up defensively, wiping away the condemning drop before she could stop herself. "I guess it is a little warm in here. With the stove, I mean."

He shrugged. "I'm pretty comfortable. But I can lower the AC if you want me to."

"No!" Serena stopped, took a deep breath. "I mean, I'm fine. And I'm not going to be here long enough for it to kick in."

Rage erupted inside of him, running up his spine to his brain at an alarming rate. Fighting to keep his head from exploding, Kevin clenched his fists and studied her through eyes that had turned nearly black with fury. He forgot to be detached. He forgot to act as if he didn't care. He forgot everything but the anger burning him from the inside out.

When he spoke, his voice was a low, furious throb. "I didn't take you for a coward."

"I am not a coward." Her voice was ice-cold. "I simply have things that I need to take care of, things that can't be done from here."

"Bullshit. You're running away." He raked a hand through his hair, even as his eyes bored viciously into her own. "What's the matter, Serena? Too scared to finish what you started?"

"I didn't start anything."

At his derisive snort, her spine stiffened even more. He hadn't thought it possible for anyone to actually sit that straight.

"I didn't," she insisted. "While I definitely ..." Her voice trailed off before she caught herself, cleared her throat. "While I definitely participated last night, I did so without any premeditation. You started it. I went along with it. But now I've changed my mind."

"Just like that? And I'm just supposed to go along with that?" He lifted one eyebrow sardonically, deliberately setting her teeth on edge.

"A woman's prerogative." She stared defiantly at him for a moment, before dropping her eyes to her plate. He felt, more than heard, her sigh. "Look, Kevin, it's a bad idea."

"What is?" He refused to make it easy for her. She set him on fire, made him burn hotter and harder than any woman ever had and then copped out at the last minute? Not in this lifetime.

He studied her breasts beneath the gray oxford shirt, saw her nipples pebble under his hot gaze before she crossed her arms defensively over her chest. No, he mused. Definitely not in this lifetime.

"Just because we—kissed—doesn't mean I have to sleep with you."

"You're right." He shrugged. "It doesn't."

She breathed a sigh of relief. "So, it's okay then. You understand what I'm saying."

He let his gaze linger on her breasts before slowly looking her in the eye. "No."

"Look, I'm sorry." Her tormented brown eyes met his blue ones. "But I've got to go." She stood up, carried her nearly untouched food to the sink.

Bluff called. She was walking out, without giving this thing between them a chance. "What about the book?" He despised himself for asking but couldn't hold the words back. "What about the gallery opening in San Diego?"

"What about them?" She shrugged. "I'll be back in four or five days, and we'll go from there." She froze, her eyes darting back to his face. "I mean, with the book only. We'll go from there with the book."

She was coming back. Relief swept through him at the thought. She wasn't running away permanently, just leaving to get some breathing space. He didn't like it, didn't want to see her go. But he could handle it. He could even understand it. For someone like Serena, who prided herself on being in control all the time, this thing between them must be pretty uncomfortable. For, much as he wished it wasn't so, things between them were hot, explosive, far, far out of control.

He watched her stride rapidly down the hall, her pert ass swinging with each click of her heels. She entered the room only to reemerge seconds later, her plain gray suitcase clutched in her hand.

"Let me take that for you." He strode down the hall, relieving her of her burden before she could protest.

"I can get it."

He smiled, his teeth gleaming warningly in the afternoon light. "I know you can, *chere*. But where I come from, a gentleman doesn't stand by and watch a woman struggle with a bag that weighs almost as much as she does." He headed outside before she could stop him.

"I didn't realize you were a gentleman," she shot at him, as she pushed the trunk release on her keychain.

His smile was predatory and sexy as hell. "I most definitely am. Look up the origin of the word sometime. It's a real eye-opener."

She dropped her keys. Grinning like a loon, he hid his face behind the open trunk lid as he loaded her bag. He closed the trunk to find her studying him, an uncharacteristically anxious expression on her face. Shoving his hands in his back pockets, he leaned into his heels and waited for her to speak.

"I'll be back in a few days," she said, her teeth worrying her lower lip.

He shrugged. "I'll be here."

She nodded, climbed into the car and shut the door. But he couldn't let her leave like that—she was biting her lip so hard, he was afraid she'd draw blood. He knocked on the driver's window and waited patiently as she rolled it down. "Drive carefully, *bébé*."

Her smile was reserved. "I will."

"Good." He stepped back and winked. "I haven't got the patience to break in two photographers in a week."

Serena gasped, outrage in every line of her face, before she slammed the car into gear and headed down the driveway as fast as safety allowed. Kevin stood watching her gray Volvo until it reached the end of the very long driveway. *Gray* clothes, *gray* suitcase, *gray* car. The woman definitely needed some color in her life. Wasn't it lucky he had more than enough to share? Whistling, he headed toward his studio to get to work.

Chapter Four

The metal gates of Angola Penitentiary clanged as Serena passed through them. She gazed straight ahead, afraid to speak, afraid to think, afraid to even blink. If she did—if she so much as moved the wrong way—she would shatter. So she concentrated on taking deep, even breaths. On swallowing the lump in her throat and keeping the tears at bay.

She had done all this for nothing. Left Kevin and the book. Dragged up a past she would much rather leave buried. Faced her sister's murderer. And for what? To see him paroled after ten lousy years? Louisiana sucked and the corruption that ran rampant in the state sucked even more.

As the prison doors shut behind her, the heat struck her like a fist. It was brutal, much like the parole hearing she had just left. And like the hearing, the hundred-degree humidity threatened to bring her to her knees.

Serena stopped, struggling for breath in the dense air. Her legs were shaky, threatening to revolt if she pushed them to continue. Her heart raced and pain exploded through her chest—was it possible to have a heart attack at twenty-eight? She pressed a hand between her breasts, fought the blackness that crept up on her with each passing second.

"Serena! Are you all right?"

She looked into the face of Jack Rawlins, assistant district attorney for Baton Rouge and the man who had been reassigned her sister's case as the parole date crept closer. It hadn't been required that he attend the parole hearing, but he had known how well connected Damien was. He'd been afraid things would go sour and he'd been right.

She put up a hand to ward him off, even as she struggled to suck air into her burning lungs. She'd lose it if he touched her. She knew it as well as she knew that Damien LaFleur, murderer and son of old Louisiana royalty, would be walking through these doors to freedom sometime very soon.

She wanted to scream, to claw Jack bloody. But it wasn't his fault that Damien was getting out, just as it wasn't his fault that first-degree rape and murder had been pled down to manslaughter ten years before. Money talked in Louisiana, more than almost any other place in the country, and Damien's family had a lot of money. Not enough to cover up the crime completely, but more than enough to keep Damien from spending the rest of his long life in prison. Like her, he was twenty-eight. He had years and years ahead of him to pretend that none of this had ever happened.

"Serena, answer me." Jack's face swam into focus again, his eyes frightened now, his mouth a grim slash as he reached for her.

"I'm fine." She forced the words past her too-tight throat, nearly choking on them. She closed her eyes and Sandra's beloved image hovered there, smiling, laughing, so full of energy that you felt she'd explode if she sat still for more than a couple of minutes at a time.

Again tears threatened and again Serena beat them back. Sandra's picture slowly faded, only to be replaced by the photos Jack had brought. He was wily and good at his job; instead of packing up the whole file for the parole board to see, he had packed the three most gruesome of the set. No reason to desensitize the board to the crime. Sandra's mutilated body swam before her eyes and Serena's stomach revolted. She barely made it to the trash can in time.

"It's okay. *Ssshh*, it's all right." Jack's hand stroked her back soothingly as Serena fought for control. When the dry heaves finally stopped, she stood slowly, wiped her mouth with the back of her hand.

"Here, take this." Jack handed her a bottle of water and Serena rinsed her mouth gratefully.

"Thank you." When she spoke, her voice wasn't back to normal, but it was audible and nearly steady. She took a few more breaths, relieved that the crushing chest pain had eased slightly.

Jack nodded, placed a hand at the small of her back and guided her toward his car. "Let's get out of here." He too seemed aware of Damien's imminent release. Damien's younger brother, Michael, was already there—though he hadn't said a word throughout the proceedings, he had sat in the back of the room watching everything. Serena remembered him and his unnatural stillness from school, from a time when they could be—if not friends, then at least not enemies.

He'd smiled at her when she'd first arrived, but she hadn't been able to smile back—not when his very presence at the parole hearing reinforced everything she already knew. The LaFleurs had bought Damien's sentence and now they were buying his freedom. Michael hadn't shown any reaction at all when his brother's parole had been granted. Not even a flicker of his eyelashes or a quirk of his lips betrayed any surprise he might be feeling. But then again, why should he have been surprised? The outcome was a guaranteed certainty before any of them had set so much as one foot in the room.

Serena followed Jack to his car and settled into the passenger seat, grateful for the blast of cooling air that hit her face within seconds. They drove in silence for a while before she finally worked up the energy to speak. "I'm sorry."

He snorted. "For what?" Stopped at a red light he turned to her, clasped her hand in his and looked straight into her eyes. "*I'm* sorry.

I never should have brought you here. But I thought, if they could see you, then maybe ..." His voice trailed off.

"Then maybe the money wouldn't matter?" Serena asked bitterly. "I didn't realize you were an idealist."

His mouth tightened, but he said nothing. What could he say? Serena wondered. No matter how pale and unsteady Jack looked, or how sorry for her he felt, nothing would make it okay that her sister's rapist and murderer would soon be wandering free—years before his full joke of a sentence had been served.

The rest of the two-hour ride was accomplished in near silence. Jack tried, more than once, to start a conversation, but Serena could think of nothing to say. She stared out the window, regrets beating at her as she eyed the threatening sky. It looked like another thunderstorm was due—she couldn't think of a better day for it.

After Jack had dropped her off at her Baton Rouge condo, Serena wandered aimlessly around for a few minutes, unable to sit. If she kept moving she wouldn't have to dwell, wouldn't have time to think about Damien getting on with his life in a way Sandra never could.

The phone rang, but she couldn't handle talking to anyone right now. What was there to say? Her mother had refused to go to the parole hearing, saying that it would only stir up bad memories. Was that all her twin sister was? A bad memory? And Mom wondered why Serena had so little to say to her these days. If she was calling to see how things had gone, she could wait and hear about it on TV. At the moment, Serena didn't feel up to breaking the bad news.

Her answering machine clicked on and she half listened, expecting to hear her mother's voice. Shocked that she'd managed to break away from husband number six—or was it seven?—long enough to make a phone call. A high-pitched giggle came over the line—one that definitely didn't belong to her mother—and chilled Serena's blood. Not now, she wanted to scream. She couldn't deal with him, too, not on top of everything else. She had to give the guy credit, though. If he wanted to shake her up, now was the time to do it. The creep had an impeccable sense of timing as well as a twisted sense of humor.

"Are you there?" His voice was muffled, but no less frightening because of it. "Are you listening to me right now, wondering if you should pick up the phone?" He laughed again, the sound grating on her already taut nerves. "I'm glad you're back home again. Back where I can see you and smell you and touch you. Back where you can remember. You remember, don't you? You remember even now?"

She crossed to the phone, her hand hesitating over the handset. *Remember what?*

"I do. I remember everything," the disembodied voice hissed. "And I bet you do, too. Remember, my darling. Remember and dream of me."

The machine clicked off and she moved to erase the message, as she had the previous ones. But something stopped her, some sense of self-preservation long forgotten. She wasn't ready to go to the police, wasn't ready to even contemplate it—but she should keep the evidence, in case she ever changed her mind. Not that the police could do much, except tell her it was some random crazy guy. After all, Louisiana was full of crazies. Look at Damien LaFleur.

With that incredibly depressing thought in the front of her mind, Serena wandered into her darkroom. Maybe she could work through the devastation, get the hearing out of her head. But after a few minutes of puttering with her chemicals, she gave up. For the first time in a number of years, the darkroom felt oppressive, disturbing. A sense of doom—of being watched, though she knew that was ridiculous—permeated the silence of the empty apartment, closing in on her and making work impossible.

Another shiver of fear shot through her, and she gave up. It was stupid to think she could stay here, stupider to make herself when she was jumping at shadows.

Back in her bedroom, Serena grabbed the suitcase she had unpacked just two days before. She yanked clothes out of her closet and threw them in without so much as a second glance. Moving quickly, she added her toiletries case, blow-dryer and a couple pairs of shoes. What had she been thinking, coming back here today? She should have known better. While she'd planned to return to Kevin's bayou tomorrow, after the storm had passed and she'd gained some perspective, she couldn't sit there fighting old and new demons for one second longer.

She needed to see him. Serena refused to question herself, refused to deal with why she so desperately wanted to be with Kevin. She only knew that if she stayed in her lonely apartment any longer she'd go insane. And the only other place she wanted to be right now was at Kevin's, basking in the warmth and safety he offered without reservation.

Dragging her suitcase down to her car, she dropped it in the trunk and climbed behind the wheel seconds before the sky opened up. Ignoring the danger and the streets that were already beginning to fill with water, Serena negotiated her way onto the highway and headed toward the swamps.

Lightning slashed the sky and rain buffeted her car. The windshield wipers barely made a dent in the water pouring from the sky, and it took all of Serena's concentration just to keep the car on the road.

Despite the risk, she was absurdly grateful to the storm. She had dreaded the three-hour drive out to Kevin's and the time it would give her to think. But the raging storm held all of her attention; it took all her strength and skill just to keep the car moving forward. There was nothing left over for thinking, even as the three-hour drive stretched to four and beyond.

The storm abated just as Serena pulled off the highway and onto the private bayou road that would take her to Kevin. She spotted his driveway amidst the lush vegetation of the swamps and gratefully turned left, taking the winding gravel-covered road up to his house.

"I don't know where she went, Steve, and I don't know why she's not answering her cell phone." Kevin thrust a hand through his hair, frustration and worry drumming through him. "She told me she was heading back to Baton Rouge for a few days to develop film. Maybe she's too busy to answer the phone."

"If it was you, I could understand that. But Serena doesn't have a temperamental bone in her body, Kevin. Clients like her make up for having clients like you."

Kevin snorted. "You knew what you were getting when you chased me down, so don't give me your poor-little-agent routine. I was doing fine on my own."

"You were getting scalped, selling your work for peanuts! That's hardly fine."

"Sure, it is. I might not have been rich, but I was free to do whatever I wanted, unencumbered, with no monkey on my back demanding more and more from me. Seriously, Steve, I don't know why I keep you around."

"You keep me around because when I first met you, you could barely afford to pay for your materials, let alone have anything left over to feed yourself. If nothing else, I've given you the means to buy more Twinkies than any man will ever need."

Kevin inclined his head. "There is that."

"Yes, there is. And it should make up for any aggravation my small interference causes you."

"Small?" Kevin snorted. "World wars have caused less aggravation than you. But you've grown on me, so I guess I can't fire you."

"Be still my heart," Steve replied, drily.

Kevin glanced up in time to see a car turn onto the long road leading to the house. Frowning, he watched it creep up his muddy driveway, swerving numerous times to avoid potholes. Every time his mother came, she complained about the driveway, asking when he was going to get it fixed. But he liked it—it kept all but the most determined people away from his door, doing more to guard his privacy than a two-hundred-pound rottweiler ever could.

Whoever it was wasn't noticeably discouraged by the unwelcoming road—something he would be more than happy to remedy. He was in a foul mood and definitely had no use for company. Taking his angst out on an unsuspecting tourist had a lot of appeal.

He'd been miserable since Serena left, anger and desire gnawing at his stomach, making it impossible to work, to sleep, to eat. He'd focused on the anger, ignored the desire and spent his rage on physical activities. Which is why he now had enough firewood cut to last him through the next three winters, his kitchen and family room were freshly painted and, in about three months, he'd have one hell of a garden. What he didn't have, however, was one piece of work he was even close to happy with.

Steve continued to prattle on on the other end of the phone, but Kevin was beyond listening as he stared with narrow eyes at the car, preparing to toss the driver out on his ear. But as it came closer and closer to the house, he realized that the car creeping up the lane was a Volvo. A *gray* Volvo.

Serena.

"I'll talk to you later, Steve," he interrupted, hanging up without waiting for a response.

Tension he hadn't known he was carrying eased slowly from his shoulders, and the lead weight that had settled on his chest three days before suddenly disappeared, making it much easier to breathe. She'd come back. Wiping his suddenly sweaty palms on his ratty jeans, he headed down the porch steps to greet her.

The car had stopped a few yards away from his front door, and Kevin crossed the distance easily, oblivious to the mud. He wrenched the car door open, desperate to see her, to touch her, whether she wanted him to or not. She'd had no business driving through the storm, and he would give her hell about it, but first he wanted to look at her. Just look.

He reached a hand in to help Serena out of the car—proper manners had been beaten into him by his mother, and years later he was hard put to forget them—even with this stubborn, distant woman, who had turned him inside out from the moment he'd first laid eyes on her.

Serena grasped his hands, allowed him to ease her from the car, and his first good look at her had his hands tightening on hers in alarm.

"*Mon Dieu, bébé! Êtes-vous blessé?* Are you hurt? Did you have an accident?" His heart raced as he skimmed his hands over her lightly, looking for injuries. She looked like hell. Her face was drawn, her eyes sunken pools of misery, her body shaking like a leaf.

"I'm fine." Her chin lifted at his snort of disbelief. "It was a long ride and the storm was bad."

Momentarily distracted, Kevin answered, "You had no business driving up in a storm like this. You could have been killed. As it is, you look like death warmed over."

If possible her pallor grew even more pronounced, and he cursed himself. She was obviously scared to death—he didn't need to rub it in.

He took a deep breath, shocked to realize he was trembling. Because they both needed a moment to regroup, he went around to the trunk to get her bag—determined to rein in his rampaging emotions.

"I had to see you." Her glorious voice was quiet but steady.

His eyes flew to hers. "What did you say?"

She shrugged, an uncomfortable motion. "I wanted to be here. I couldn't wait any longer."

He studied her, eyes narrowed dangerously. "Exactly what game are you playing, Serena?"

"I'm not playing anything." This time her voice trembled, despite herself.

"Then why the sudden change of tune?" His voice rose and he was helpless to stop it. "Three days ago you made it completely clear that you wanted nothing more to do with me outside of the book. Yet here you are, back early, claiming you couldn't stay away?"

He shook his head. "I just don't get you."

"I—" Her voice broke and she closed her eyes, as if the simple act of speaking to him was too much to handle. "I don't mean to be ..." Her head dropped and he saw, for the first time, the glimmer of tears rolling down her cheeks.

"Serena, what's wrong?" He dropped the bag in the mud, was at her side instantly. "What happened to you in Baton Rouge?"

She shook her head, defeat in every line of her body. "I can't ..."

"Look at me." Putting a hand under her chin, he tilted her head up until he could look her in the eye. He fought to keep his tone gentle, even as rage pounded viciously through his system. Someone had hurt her, badly. Gone was the cool, collected woman who had everything together. In her place was the lost child he'd glimpsed only once, the little girl searching for comfort in the middle of a storm. "What happened?"

Tears poured silently down her face as she shook her head. With a muttered curse Kevin pulled her against him, shocked anew at how cold she was. He kept her body pressed to his as he grabbed the suitcase in his free hand and propelled her toward the house.

He helped her climb the stairs, fought the urge to simply sweep her up in his arms and carry her the rest of the way to the couch.

He didn't release her until they reached the comfort of the family room. Directing her toward the sofa, he commented, "I'll put this in your room and then make some tea. Get comfortable and I'll be back in a minute."

Kevin pulled his arm away and watched, shocked, as Serena's knees gave way and she crumpled to the ground.

"What the hell?" Scooping her up, he plopped down in a leather recliner, Serena cradled on his lap. Strangled sounds, horrifying in their intensity, worked their way out of her throat. Devastated, he rocked her, not knowing what else to do.

"*C'est tout le juste, bébé. C'est tout le juste. Je vous ai, mon amour.* It's okay now. I've got you. I've got you now. Just relax.

He leaned forward, brushed a kiss against her temple, and just like that, she shattered. Sobs, deep and brutal, broke the silence of the bayou, shocking him once again with their intensity. Her hands fisted in his torn T-shirt, clawing his chest even as her hot tears burned against his neck.

Minutes ticked by, one after the other, as Serena's heart broke. He didn't know how long they sat like that, with his hands gently soothing her painful, bitter tears. Didn't care. But the storm finally passed, and while her sobs grew quieter and quieter, her body still shivered with each breath she took. He reached behind him, snagged the blanket he always kept on the back of the couch and covered her. They continued to rock as the tears dried on her face, and her shudders became more and more infrequent.

"I'm not usually a basket case." Her voice was more hoarse than usual, scratchy from the long crying jag.

"Who says you're one now?" he asked gently.

She laughed, sadly, and pressed her face more firmly against his chest. She didn't speak for a long time, and he couldn't bring himself to press her. If she told him, it would be because she wanted to.

Finally, when he was just about to give up hope, she spoke again. "My twin sister was murdered almost eleven years ago. Today was the parole hearing for the man who killed her."

She was gone. Rage threatened to strangle him before he could get a handle on it. With a bellow of fury he crushed the stupid fast food cup in his hand and got a strange sort of satisfaction from watching Serena's favorite diet soda explode in his fist and drip slowly down his arm. It looked almost red in the slowly coming twilight, and the image of blood—Serena's blood—turned him on hard and fast. He tamped down on the reaction, deeming it unacceptable in the present circumstances, and concentrated on the problem.

If she wasn't here, where was she?

Her mother's? He discounted the idea immediately. From the moment Sandra had died, Serena's relationship with her mother had been strained at best, outright hostile at worst. It was the same with her older brother. Tragedy and crisis had a tendency to pull families together, but something about this one had ripped Serena and her family apart. He remembered watching them at the trial, wondering why it was so hard for them to connect.

So who would she run to? he wondered. She didn't have any friends, really—her sister's murder and her subsequent breakdown had driven them away. As for the rest—a few comments here, a car accident there, and Serena would be his. All his.

As it was meant to be.

So where was she? The condo was dark, a surefire way to tell that she wasn't at home. The two lights his investigator said she kept burning all the time—the one in the family room and the one in her bedroom—had been extinguished. He'd already gone around the back to check.

An ugly suspicion darkened his mind—had she gone to him? To that bayou rat with his long hair and power tools? Or was she with the agent? He'd seen how the man had touched her in the pictures the investigator took, watched the care and concern he poured into her. Maybe she had gone to him—it made more sense than the manual laborer, after all.

But still, the indignation was almost more than he could bear. She wouldn't. She couldn't. She didn't dare turn to another man. Not after everything he'd gone through to ensure that she'd turn to him. Not after the long, long years he'd waited so that they could be together.

The ten long years since Sandra's death.

The time spent studying everything about her.

The loneliness.

The headaches.

One was coming now. He could feel the prickling behind his eyes, the tension seeping slowly into his scalp. He had to get home before it got too bad. But he couldn't leave here yet, not without being sure. Maybe the tension had been too much, and she'd simply fallen asleep.

Or maybe she really was playing the role of whore, like her sister had before her.

Reaching a casual hand into his pocket, he pulled out a lock-picking set from his younger, wilder days. He was inside in under a minute and turned to deactivate the alarm. But the green light blinked harmlessly, another surefire sign that Serena wasn't home. She'd never leave her alarm system off if she was inside. Not after Sandra.

Fury lived inside of him, grew with each breath he took. He wanted—needed—to throw something else. To smash everything in the house into irreparable pieces. He reached for the lamp on the entryway table. It was strong and sturdy and beautiful like Serena herself. He longed to destroy it—punishment for her duplicity. For the error in her ways.

But he'd already lost control once tonight—he couldn't afford to do it again. Besides, it wasn't time for that yet. Serena could still be redeemed.

He set the lamp down with a clatter and wandered from room to room. He avoided her bedroom and the clichéd search though the underwear drawer that came with it, though he longed to touch something so intimately connected to her.

Because he wanted it so badly his hands shook, he deliberately turned away. A loss of control—now—was totally unacceptable. It wouldn't get the job done. He walked, deliberately, into her dark-room and an almost orgasmic pleasure overwhelmed him.

This was where she spent her time. This was where her most intimate connections existed. He caressed a bottle of developing fluid, ran a hand over one of the trays she used to develop. The thrill was sexual—like being inside of her. He hardened in response.

He took a deep breath and smiled. He could still smell her in here—the lingering sent of jasmine touched him with every breath he took. It calmed him, relaxed him, reminded him of the connection they would always share.

Another breath told him she'd been in here today—the jasmine lingered despite the harsh smell of the chemicals. But no pictures hung drying, none stood developing—but why?

Maybe she'd been too upset to work. Too upset to think. And who could blame her, really? It had been a truly terrible day for her.

The realization calmed him as nothing else could have. Serena was too upset to know what she was doing. That was why she hadn't waited for him. That was why she'd torn out of there without bothering to set the alarm. She couldn't stand the silence.

He could understand that. Respect that, at least for now. So often he had the same problem.

Flipping off the red light, he closed the darkroom door and headed back toward the entryway. He could afford to be patient for a little while longer.

A very little while.

Kevin's eyes flew to Serena's, horror rocketing through him. As he'd sat there listening to her weep, he'd struggled to find an answer for her behavior. But even in his worst imaginings, he'd never pictured this. He searched for something to say, anything, but there was no soothing platitude for the occasion. Or if there was, he'd certainly never heard it.

Finally, he settled for truth. "He got off."

Her eyes, a deep melted chocolate, caught his and held. "Obviously. Five years before his pathetic excuse for a sentence was up."

"What happened?"

Her mouth trembled. They both knew he was asking about more than the parole hearing. But when she spoke her voice was rock-steady, as if she were reciting a story she'd told many times. "When we were sixteen, Sandra—my sister—fell in love for the first time. He was rich, good-looking. Everyone thought he walked on water."

He was watching her closely, saw the grimace she couldn't hide. "But not you."

"No, not me. There was always something that seemed just a little bit off about him, you know? Even though he did and said all the right things. Sometimes, he'd get this look in his eyes—like he owned the whole world and dared someone to try to take it away."

She shrugged. "I don't know. Maybe he did own almost everything—after Sandra's death it sure felt that way. Either way, I didn't like him. I tried to, especially since Sandra was so crazy about him. But Damien and I rubbed each other the wrong way from the first day she introduced us."

Her voice broke and he nodded encouragingly, needing to know the whole ugly story but wanting her to get it out at one time so she wouldn't have to revisit it again later.

Serena seemed to understand, because after a minute she continued. "Anyway, I tried telling Sandra how I felt, but she didn't want to hear it. She loved him, more, I think, than she loved me. At least at the beginning.

"So I backed off." She shook her head and tears welled in her eyes. "Even though I knew something wasn't right with him, even though I didn't trust him, I backed off. My distrust was driving a wedge between us, and I couldn't stand it. She was my twin, my best friend. I couldn't let a guy come between us. So I shut up, went on double dates with them, tried to ignore the fact that my skin crawled whenever he looked at me."

He stroked her hair back from her face. "You're not actually blaming yourself for trying to hold on to your relationship with your sister, are you?"

She laughed, a bitter sound that hurt his ears. "Hell, yes, I blame myself. That night, when he came over, I knew—I knew that he was up to something. But I let him in, let him get near her. If I had slammed the door in his face like I'd wanted to, Sandra would still be alive."

"No, she wouldn't." He tilted her chin up until he could look straight into her eyes. "If it hadn't been that night, it would have been the next. You know it, Serena. Much as you'd like it to be otherwise, you know it."

She looked away, shrugged her shoulders, absently rubbed her hands up and down her arms. "When they first started going out, she was so happy. She laughed all the time, zoomed from school to the library, from his house to home and back again. She'd never been one to sit still—she was always the outgoing one, but when she was with him, her energy was supersonic. She practically glowed.

"But things started getting ugly after about six months." She bit her lip, jiggled her legs up and down as she searched for words.

"He started getting jealous, really jealous. Didn't want her hanging around with anyone but him, wanted to know where she was at all times. The same old warning signals, same old story. I recognized them, tried to tell her once, but she was too far gone to listen.

"We had a huge fight and she didn't talk to me for days. It felt like my heart had been ripped out. So I shut up, kept out of his way. I tried to tell Mom and my stepdad, but they were blinded by his pedigree." This time the laugh was bitter. "Even after he'd killed her, after he'd raped and mutilated her, all Mom could say was that there must be some mistake. He was a *LaFleur*."

"Jonathon LaFleur?" Shocked, Kevin couldn't stop himself from butting in. He'd designed a sculpture for the LaFleur Building in downtown New Orleans years ago, had spent quite a bit of time with Jonathon and his wife. He'd liked them and their younger son, Michael, as well.

She snorted, nodded. "Jonathon is Damien's father. He's at least as charming, and as amoral, as his sons. He's the one who bought off the police and got them to destroy evidence. He also put pressure on the DA and got Damien an incredible plea bargain that never should have been offered."

"Are you sure?" He could have bit his tongue the second the question slipped out, but the story she told was so at odds with the man he knew.

"Of course I'm sure!" She looked at him scathingly, pushed herself off his lap before he could stop her. "Damien LaFleur murdered my sister in cold blood. When he was arrested he was charged with first-degree murder, felony rape and first-degree attempted murder. They had him dead to rights—a witness, the fingerprints at the scene and on the murder weapon—a weapon he'd brought with him to the house. They even found her blood on his shoes. And then suddenly the knife is gone, his shoes are lost and he's being offered a manslaughter plea. You think it was out of the goodness of the DA's heart?"

Kevin shook his head, stared at her. "I'm sorry."

"You should be."

He couldn't stand the way she was looking at him, as if he was a bug deserving to be squashed. But, he admitted bitterly as he replayed their conversation in his head, he deserved it. Wasn't he the one always talking about how appearances could be deceiving?

Wasn't he the one who rarely trusted people? As he cursed himself, his mind seized on something that she'd said. "Attempted murder? There was someone else involved?"

Her gaze slid away from his and she shrugged her shoulders, obviously uncomfortable. "Yeah."

A sick feeling started in the pit of his stomach. An image of the scar on her arm flashed into his head. "What happened, Serena?"

"He killed my sister."

"I know that. But you said you opened the door, let him in. What happened?" he demanded, grasping her arms in his, looking her straight in the eye so there could be no evasions, no half-truths.

She tried to turn her head, tried to lie. But something in his eyes stopped her. She shrugged, cleared her throat. "I let him in, called for Sandra. Then I turned to close the door and he stabbed me—in the back. I started to scream, to warn her before she came downstairs, but he punched me, hard. I don't remember what happened next, but I came to in the coat closet. He'd locked me in, shoved something up against the door so I couldn't get out. It was dark, pitch-black. I couldn't see anything, but I could smell the blood underneath me, around me. I could feel the cold slowly seeping into my skin.

"And I could hear. I could hear everything he said, everything he did to Sandra. I heard her scream as he raped her, heard him curse as she kicked and scratched. I even heard the knife go in again and again." He wiped away the tears slowly slipping down her cheeks, but she was too caught up in the past to notice.

"Everyone thinks that guns are the noisy way to kill, that if you stab someone it's silent. It's not—at least it wasn't with Sandra. It makes noise, a lot of noise, when something cuts through flesh to the organs beneath. When the knife hits bone and is deflected. When the person being stabbed screams her killer's name, begging him to stop."

She was miles away, years away. Kevin wanted to grab her, shake her, bring her back to him, but he couldn't. He couldn't do anything, so he sat. And he listened, bile churning sickly in his gut.

"I screamed, too, over and over again. I kicked the door, pounded,

desperate to reach Sandra. And then it was over. I felt her die. I actually felt it—a blankness in my soul where she had been. An absence.
We were twins. We shared everything. Half the time I could read her
mind, and I know there were times when she read mine. Then suddenly that connection vanished. I was alone."

His stomach twisted as he watched Serena relive the pain. He'd
wanted to take it away from her, but instead, with a few careless
words, he'd managed to hurt her all over again.

Disgust swamped him. He'd built a sculpture for LaFleur, had
taken his money. Hell, he'd even eaten at the man's house, never
knowing the kind of monster he'd been associating with.

"I couldn't stop screaming. The other day you said you liked my
voice, that it was sexy." She shrugged, avoided his eyes. "While he
was killing Sandra, I screamed so much that it broke. Changed pitch,
went lower."

She pulled the blanket more tightly around herself, took a couple
of deep breaths before continuing. "Anyway, once Sandra was dead,
Damien remembered me. He came back to the closet, started stabbing me. If my brother hadn't come home when he had ..." Her
voice trailed off.

Chapter Five

If her brother hadn't come home. Rage, hot and unadulterated, exploded through him, turned his spine rigid and his stomach to molten steel as the words reverberated in his head with every shallow breath he took. Fists clenched tightly, he closed his eyes as everything that could have happened flashed through his brain at hundreds of miles per second.

As he fought for control, it was his turn to breathe deeply, his turn to desperately fight the shaking that was ripping him apart. He had to move, had to put some distance between them before he lost it completely. Springing to his feet, he crossed the room in two long steps.

She'd almost died. Some madman had almost killed her and he'd never have had a clue.

He began to pace—anger and fear formed a ticking time bomb in his chest.

He'd sat at LaFleur's table. Shaken his hand. Made him a fucking sculpture. *And he'd never had a clue.*

He wanted to tear the world apart—to rip Jonathon and Damien and Michael LaFleur into such small pieces that all the money in the world wouldn't be able to put them back together.

"How bad?" he ground out before he could stop himself, his voice low and dangerous.

"I already told you—"

Kevin shook his head, eyes blazing. "I mean, how badly were you injured?"

She shrugged again, a gesture that was rapidly becoming a habit. "It was no big deal. A few cuts—"

"Bullshit!" He crossed to her, fury crackling with every move he made. "Don't lie to me! How badly were you hurt?"

He grabbed her arms, pulled her up on her tiptoes so that she was a little closer to his eye level. Despite the soul-deep weariness that had plagued her from the moment she'd heard the parole board's decision, Serena could feel her body responding to Kevin's nearness. Her breath quickened and a startling heat sparked deep inside of her.

"Serena!" Kevin shook her gently to get her attention.

"Oh, for God's sake!" she exclaimed. "If you have to know, I was in the hospital for almost two weeks. But my recovery was so slow because I couldn't handle Sandra's death. It pushed me right to an edge I don't ever want to get close to again."

He nodded and pulled her into his chest. She didn't know if the embrace was meant to comfort him or her, but she could feel her body relax inch by tightly wound inch as his warmth once again seeped into her.

Before she realized what she was doing, Serena had wrapped her arms around his waist and pressed herself, full body, against him. She rested her cheek on his chest, inhaled his musky, male scent and felt a small bit of peace creep into her heart. Not enough to make her forget the look on Damien LaFleur's face when his parole was announced. Not enough to make her forget her sister's mutilated body. But enough to make the next hour seem worth living. Just enough to make her believe that tomorrow would be a little better than today.

Refusing to give herself time to think, Serena pressed an open-mouthed kiss to Kevin's chest. She reveled in his muscles, in the careless strength that he took for granted. Her hands stroked softly over his strong back, delighting in the shiver of response she felt move through him.

She pressed closer, pushing her breasts even more firmly against him. He drew in a breath audibly and she grinned for the first time in a long time. Maybe this wasn't the wisest move on her part, or the best-timed one, but she wanted Kevin. She wanted to lose herself in his arms for a few blissful hours, wanted to forget the pain that waited for her with nearly every breath she took.

Her mouth skimmed, again, across his chest. She longed to touch his naked skin, to sink her teeth into the resilient flesh that beckoned to her with each rise and fall of his chest. The steady rhythm of his heart increased, and she placed a hand over it, relishing the power and life that flowed through him with every heartbeat. Her thumb lightly skimmed his nipple and she felt his indrawn breath.

Kevin pulled away from her, his beautiful blue eyes wary. She could still see traces of rage in them and his response warmed her. He cared. He really cared about what had happened to Sandra, about what had nearly happened to her. That, more than anything else, made what was about to happen seem right.

Even though she told herself it was simply recreational sex, something to take her mind off the trials of the day, she knew better. Sex with Kevin would be a lot of things—hot, mind-blowing, explosive. But it would never be something as bland as recreational, as mild as simple feel-good sex often was. Sex with Kevin would be intense, messy and everything she'd always dreamed making love could be. Not to mention everything that had ever frightened her about the act as well.

"What are you doing?" His voice was rusty when he spoke, dark and sensual despite his desire to keep things on an even keel.

"I thought that would be obvious." Serena's voice held a teasing note that she almost didn't recognize. She trailed her fingers lightly down his arms to his hands. Grasping his left hand, she brought it to her mouth and bit him in the exact place he had bitten her four days before.

His eyes darkened and his mouth twisted with desire. "Not now, Serena. We can't do this now."

"Why not? I can't think of a better time." Her tongue licked one finger and then another, slowly, like she was savoring a particularly wonderful treat.

"You're not thinking straight." His voice was desperate, his eyes nearly black.

"I am thinking straight. Maybe for the first time in a long time." She pressed a hot openmouthed kiss to his wrist, even as her lower body bumped sensuously against him.

Kevin picked her up, set her a few feet away from him, backed up even more. She was killing him, with her cat-and-the-cream grin and her mind-blowingly hot body. He could still feel every inch of her pressed against him, though almost half the room now separated them. "I don't take advantage of women in pain," he said aloud, though he didn't know if he was talking to her or himself.

Her eyes narrowed and her mouth twisted into something that looked remarkably like a pout. "I'm not asking you to take advantage of me. Just to take me."

His breath left him in a whoosh of desire and his cock hardened painfully. So much blood had left his head, he was shocked that he could remain upright. But thinking was becoming a struggle and he was determined to bring her to her senses. Before it was too late. Before he did something stupid, like take her in his arms and devour every sweet, tempting inch of her.

"Serena." He pitched his voice low, trying to be reasonable. Someone had to be the voice of reason here.

She walked toward him slowly, stalking him with every sensuous movement of her body. "Yes."

"Four days ago we stood here, and you told me that you didn't want to make love with me, that you wouldn't make love with me." He was desperate, a drowning man searching for a life preserver in a tsunami.

"I was stupid." Her brown eyes blazed. Her tongue darted out to caress her plump pink lips. She continued to glide slowly, steadily toward him.

"No! You were right." Was he actually backing up, running from a woman half his size? He felt the wall at his back. Nowhere left to go.

She shook her head. "I was very, very wrong." She was next to him now, her eyes holding his, enthralled.

"Serena, you can't decide something like this now. It's been a traumatic day. You aren't thinking straight. Get some sleep and then we'll talk." No, no! his hungry body screamed at him, called him every name in the book. Take what she's offering!

But he couldn't. She was hurt, in pain. And he wanted more from her than one night between the sheets. Though it'd be a hell of a night.

His cock strained with every breath he took, desperate to be inside her. But he was a man, not an animal, and he was determined to think this through rather than acting on pure instinct. He studied her, this gorgeous femme fatale who was seducing him with just her voice, just the look in her eyes. And if he hadn't been watching her as closely as he was, he would have missed the flash of uncertainty cross her face, the momentary shyness that she tried to hide.

"Don't you want me?" For a moment, she sounded forlorn, lost.

Kevin's breath came out in a rush of air and he reached for her. "Of course I want you. More than I want to take my next breath."

"Then why—?"

"I want you to be sure. You can't be sure right now."

"I am sure. Kevin, chase away the ghosts. Make me remember why life is worth living."

A better man would have walked away, would have settled her in her room with a cup of tea and a good book. But Kevin had never claimed to be a particularly good man, nor a particularly wise one. And as Serena stared up at him, her gorgeous brown eyes shining, her cheeks flushed a rosy pink, her mouth a moue of discontent and need, he felt his resolve slip. He was going to make love to her. He couldn't stop himself, though he knew it was a mistake.

He dreaded seeing her eyes in the morning, when she was once again herself. But as she reached out a hand to touch him, as her fingers blazed a path of fire down his chest and over his stomach, Kevin told himself that tomorrow was hours away.

He grabbed her hand, lifted it to his heart as he looked deep in her eyes. "Are you sure?"

"Very sure." Her smile was sassy, victorious.

Without another word he reached down, swept her up into his arms and carried her down the hall to his bedroom.

Serena knew she was taking a risk, but she couldn't bring herself to care. She wanted Kevin, craved him with every breath she took, every unsteady beat of her heart. If it was a mistake, it was her mistake and she would live with it. It would be just one more in a long line of screwups that continued to haunt her.

But as he lowered her feet gently to the floor, his blue eyes burned with every wicked, wonderful thing he wanted to do to her, and she couldn't believe that making love with Kevin was wrong. It might be unwise, was certainly premature, but it wasn't a mistake. From the moment she'd first laid eyes on him, she'd known that they would end up here. Whether she had wanted to acknowledge it or not.

"Last chance?" he murmured softly, stroking her hair from her forehead in a gesture she had come to love.

"Damn straight," she answered, wrapping her arms around his neck and pulling his gorgeous mouth down to meet her own.

The moment Kevin's warm lips touched hers, Serena's tenuous grip on control vanished. Her hands tangled in the cool silk of his hair, holding his head to her as his tongue gently parted her lips. But she didn't want gentleness now, didn't want him to hold back anything out of concern for her. She wanted Kevin, with his black moods and steamy passion, and she would have him. Tonight. Now. This instant.

Her tongue met his, tangled, explored his mouth as he had explored hers. She sucked his lower lip between her own, nipped softly and laughed at his groan of arousal. Her hands slipped between them, teased his nipples for a moment before she pushed him, hard.

He landed on the bed and she followed him, straddling his thighs as her mouth skimmed hotly over his lips, across his cheek, up to his ear. "I want you," she whispered softly, urgently. "I need you. Now."

Her fingers pushed at his shirt, lifting it out of the way so she could caress, lick, bite her away across his heavily muscled chest. Her tongue darted out, licked his nipple, darted back in. Again and again, even as her fingers fumbled desperately with his belt buckle.

"*Bébé*, slow down." He reached between them, took hold of her hands and lifted first one, then the other, to his lips. "We've got all night."

"I don't want to wait that long." Her voice was low, teasing, but with an underlying urgency that was hard to ignore.

Kevin felt his cock grow harder—who knew that was possible?—as lust, hot and demanding, consumed him. He pulled her face to his, ravaging her lips with his as he explored every centimeter of that sexy, sultry mouth. He reached for her breasts, frustrated to find them still covered by the light cotton of her shirt. He wanted to touch her, to feel every inch of her lush body pressed against his. He *had* to feel her. He grabbed both sides of Serena's shirt, his body raging, desperate for relief. With one strong downward motion of his hands, he ripped the material apart. Buttons flew, but neither paid any attention as his lips fastened over her nipple and he pushed the tattered shirt down her arms.

The scars on her chest and abdomen stood out in stark relief against her bronze skin, and he paused, once again fighting the murderous rage that threatened to overwhelm him. That son of a bitch had stabbed her. Had tried to kill her. And now he was going to be free. It was too much—

"Kevin, Kevin." Serena drew him back to the moment with her breathless pleas. She was out of control, her hands yanking his jeans halfway down his legs, her breathing ragged as she finally succeeded in freeing his cock to her questing fingers.

He deliberately put LaFleur out of his mind, refusing to let his memories of this night be ruined by that *fils de pute*. He would deal with LaFleur later. Much later, he acknowledged as Serena moved against him, her long legs jockeying with his for position.

He wanted to slow down, to savor every inch of her, but Serena's passion was as infectious as it was out of control. Suddenly, he was desperate to feel her—to taste her with nothing between them. He worked feverishly on her bra as he sucked her nipple through the fragile lace.

When finally, finally, the clasp gave way beneath his unusually clumsy fingers, Serena sobbed in relief. She clasped Kevin's head to her breast, her body arching up. She had to touch him, to feel every inch of him pressed against her. Pressed inside her.

Kevin lifted his head and she nearly whimpered in disappointment. Don't stop, she wanted to shout. Don't give me time to think. She reached a hand between their bodies, circled his cock and slowly, slowly began to stroke. He was as hard as the metal he sculpted, and as immense. As her hand stroked up and down, finding his tip and teasing the small drop of fluid she found there, she had a moment's concern about whether or not they would fit.

She wasn't a small woman, but he was huge. She should have guessed. Tall, large hands and feet. Only an idiot would have been caught by surprise. But she wanted him, was desperate for him if the truth were told, and his pulsing erection aroused her unbearably.

Again she stroked her thumb over his head, again it came away just a little wet. Staring into his bottomless sapphire eyes, she brought her thumb to her lips and licked it slowly. "Mmmm," she purred, as she tasted the incredible earthiness that was Kevin.

Eyes blazing, heart pounding, Kevin kissed his way down her body, praying that he wouldn't embarrass himself. He hadn't been this unsure of his own control since high school, and he wanted—needed—this to be as good for Serena as it was for him. Better.

She might be cool and collected most of the time, but in bed she was hotter, wilder than he could ever have imagined. He licked his way, slowly, down her rib cage to her belly button. His tongue darted

out, teased the slight indentation of her navel—played with the sm
gold hoop there—before continuing down her abdomen to her dark
blond pubic hair.

She moaned, fisting her hands in his hair. "Now," she breathed,
her entire body taught with desire. "Kevin, it's got to be now."

"Soon, *cher*," he murmured, as he slowly—oh so slowly—
slipped a finger inside her. She was incredibly hot, deliciously wet,
and his entire body clenched with need. But two could play her
game.

He slowly pulled his finger out and she whimpered, hips lifting,
before she could control herself. "Kevin," she gasped. "Please."

He smiled, darkly, as he raised his finger to his mouth. He
breathed deeply, loving the spicy-sweet scent of her. "Delicious," he
murmured before sliding his finger into his mouth and taking her
essence inside him.

She moaned, her fists twisting in the sheets as she bucked frantically. "Kevin!" Her voice was high, sharp, and he knew that he had
pushed her as far as she could take. But he wanted to do so much
more.

He wanted to bury his face between her thighs and feast until she
screamed in ecstasy. He wanted to kiss every inch of her body, make
her crazy with desire until she could think of nothing, of no one, but
him.

But she was whimpering, frantic, and he couldn't take any more
of her cries without exploding. He grabbed a condom and quickly
rolled it over himself before reaching between them and flicking a
finger once, twice, over her clit.

Ecstasy claimed her and Serena screamed, her fingers grabbing at
his shoulders, her body wildly arching against his. He plunged into
her as she came, moving hard and fast against her. Intensifying her
orgasm, building toward his own.

Her legs twined around his, her feet digging into the back of his
thighs as he pounded into her. "Again," she murmured. "Again."

"And again and again and again." He grinned, watching her
beautiful eyes dilate with passion. She was hot, disheveled, sweaty.

And he loved it. Loved knowing she could let go like this, loved knowing that she wanted him as much as he wanted her.

Kevin reached down, drew her nipple into his mouth. He sucked hard as he continued moving inside of her. He was close, so close he thought he'd explode any second. His balls were boiling, his cock throbbing, but he wanted to make her come again. Needed to see her face as it ripped through her. Had to be inside of her when it happened this time.

She was sobbing, her hands tangled in his as her body shuddered over and over again. "Please, please."

"That's it, baby. Come for me again. I have to feel you." His words were strangled as he moved faster and faster, loving the warm, wet feel of her muscles clenching around his cock. He lowered his mouth to her breast, sucked hard as he reached between them and stroked her clit.

Serena screamed, her body bucking wildly against him as a second orgasm—more intense and out of control than the first—ripped through her. He rode her through it, took her higher and higher until nothing existed but the intense, rolling pleasure that went on and on. Grabbing her hips, he tilted them until she was open fully to him.

He was going to explode. He couldn't hold back any longer. He had to— With a groan of ecstasy he came, harder, longer and more intensely than he ever had before. The world went black and he was lost, totally, to the insane pleasure overloading his senses. He was dimly conscious of Serena's own cries, of her body convulsing again and again, milking him as he emptied himself inside of her.

Serena's head was swimming. Pleasure, satiation, confusion, fear— they chased one another around in her brain even as her limp body relaxed into the warmth of Kevin's. Her breathing was still harsh, her head muddled, and a part of her wanted nothing more than to roll over and start the whole wonderful, confusing ride again.

But she'd been wild, out of control, totally unlike herself. She wanted to say something, anything, to keep the most beautiful experience in her life from becoming awkward. But she could already feel the tension returning; her skin felt too tight and her muscles were slowly turning rock-hard. She'd poured her heart and soul out to Kevin, and now she felt raw.

They'd planned a simple sexual encounter and she'd gone and complicated it. She could feel his eyes on her, studying her, his fingers tangled in her hair. She knew she should look at him, deal with the whole situation, but she was afraid. Afraid of her lack of control, afraid of her emotions, and perhaps most important, afraid of the pity she thought she'd see in his eyes. If he turned the most amazing sex of her life into a pity fuck, she'd completely lose it. And once she did, would she ever get it back?

With a deep breath she pulled away, forcing a smile that she didn't feel. "I'm going to go clean up."

His eyes narrowed and a fierce frown turned his lips downward. "Already?" he asked.

She shrugged and turned away. "I'm hot. I'll take a quick shower and be out in a few minutes." She gathered her clothes as she spoke, darting into the bathroom and closing the door before Kevin could say another word. Holding her breath, waiting to see what Kevin would do, she finally released it in a shaky puff when she realized he wasn't following her. Serena's trembling legs refused to support her any longer, and she sank slowly to the bathroom floor, wrapping her arms around herself as tears flowed, slow and silent, down her cheeks.

Chapter Six

Fuck, fuck, FUCK! Kevin rolled out of bed and began to pace the length of his bedroom, naked, as anger turned his stomach inside out. He'd damn well known better. He'd known it was too soon, known she'd regret it. But he hadn't been able to keep his hands to himself or his cock in his pants. Instead, he'd made love with a woman who was using him to forget the pain of her past. He'd taken Serena when she was lost and vulnerable, and now they were both going to pay the price.

Fuck! He thrust both hands into his hair, sinking heavily onto the bed. What the hell was he supposed to do now? Pretend he hadn't just had the most mind-blowing sex of his whole life? Act like he didn't want her so much it was painful to breathe when he wasn't inside of her? Ignore everything but the work?

No way. His teeth ground together. No fucking way. There was no way he was that good of an actor. And even if he was, there was no way he'd do it.

Serena couldn't stumble into his life, turn him inside out and then stumble out again, pretending nothing had happened. She might be able to compartmentalize her life into neat little boxes, but he didn't work that way. He *couldn't* work that way. Besides, the thought of never being inside of her again, of never again hearing the soft, sexy sounds she made as she came, was too awful to contemplate.

He heard the water start, and images of Serena, naked and wet and in his shower, tormented him until his cock stood straight up and the mere act of existing hurt. He studied the door through narrowed eyes, weighing his options as he listened to the water pound against the glass shower door.

He could play things Serena's way for a while, give her some time and space. His mouth twisted in displeasure. He could wait for her to come out of the bathroom and have a civilized conversation about where they would go from here. His frown deepened and his eyes narrowed to little more than slits. Or he could go in there and demand to know what the hell was going on.

Before he could talk himself out of it, Kevin crossed to the bathroom and rested his hand on the doorknob. He would simply go in and talk to her about why she was upset—before she could get her defenses back in place. He knew, instinctively, that she'd fled because she couldn't stand for him to see her vulnerability, because she couldn't stand for him to see the rawness that was still in her. But he couldn't fight her if he didn't know what she was thinking— confronting her before she had herself completely under control again was the way to go. With a decisive nod, he turned the handle and pushed the door open.

And froze. His hands clenched unconsciously into fists and a hand squeezed his gut with every heavy beat of his heart. Steam had slightly misted the glass shower door, but he could see Serena's silhouette through the fog. Her back was to the tap, her head thrown back and her hands lifted to her head as she slowly rinsed his shampoo from her hair. Her back was arched, her perfect breasts thrust forward and her nipples peaked as water cascaded slowly down her breasts to her stomach and lower still to the dark, sexy nest of her pubic hair. Her eyes were closed, her lips parted.

Kevin's cock hardened to the point of pain, and he fought to hold back a groan of absolute lust. She was the sexiest thing he'd ever seen, and he would die if he couldn't be inside her again. Soon.

Without giving himself time to think, without worrying about the consequences, Kevin slid the door to the oversized shower open and slipped silently inside. Serena's eyes flew open, startled, worried, and his instincts took over. He pulled her gently into his arms, cradling her head against his neck as his hands slid slowly up and down her back. She stood stiffly against him for a minute before the soothing rhythm of his caress slowly penetrated the fear that gripped her with an iron fist.

Kevin felt Serena relax against him, and the tightness in his chest slowly eased. They could still fix this. If he took things slow and easy, if he didn't startle her or make her nervous, it would be okay. He took a deep breath, ignored his throbbing cock and slid his hands gently into her wet hair.

Serena gasped as Kevin softly guided her head back under the spray, his fingers gently massaging the remaining shampoo from her hair. He stroked her scalp soothingly, fingers sliding softly through each strand. He reached for another bottle, his big body still sheltering hers as he squeezed a small amount of conditioner onto his palm.

She sighed and allowed her eyes to drift shut as she savored the feel of Kevin's strong, talented hands slowly rubbing conditioner into her hair. His long, beautiful fingers gently rubbed her scalp in a circular motion, setting every nerve ending in her body on fire. He nudged her and she obligingly tilted her head back so that the warm water could slowly stream over her head and down her body again. His fingers continued their talented massage and her nipples tightened, despite the warm water cascading slowly over her shoulders and down her breasts.

When her hair had finally been rinsed clean, Kevin rubbed a bar of soap between his hands and slowly began to lather up her body. His talented fingers slid down her neck, over the slope of her shoulders to the small of her back, before slipping around to tickle her belly button, setting the charms of her belly ring jangling. He gently skimmed her rib cage before stopping and slowly, oh so slowly, cupping her breasts.

"When did you get that?" he asked.

"Get what?"

"The belly ring. I love it."

Serena sighed, leaned into him for support. "Sandra and I got them done on our sixteenth birthday. I've kept mine because—because it helps me remember how things used to be. It's a connection between us—the only one that's left."

"Oh, *bébé*," he sighed. "You've had such a rough time of it."

She stiffened against him. "I don't want your pity."

He pulled away, looked down at her. "Pity? I don't pity you. I couldn't. I admire you."

She snorted. "Yeah, right."

"I do. You're the strongest person I've ever met."

Serena shook her head, tried to turn away despite his hands clutching her shoulders. "I've been a basket case since you've met me."

"You've been in pain." Lowering his forehead to hers, Kevin pulled her back into his arms. "There's a huge difference."

"But—"

"*Sssh, bébé.* Later. We'll talk later."

He reached between them, used his thumbs to gently flick her nipples. Serena moaned before she could stop herself. It felt so good, so incredibly good, to have Kevin's sensitive artist's hands on her body. To have him touch her in the most mundane and the most secret places.

He continued to stroke her breasts and Serena arched into him, her lower body pressing suddenly against his erection. She felt him stiffen, heard the sudden increase in his breathing and smiled. It was good to know that she affected him as crazily as he affected her.

"Serena." Kevin's voice was husky, low and warning. Her scent was wrapping itself around him—a combination of his shampoo and her own spicy sweetness that was driving him out of his mind. He'd never been the possessive type, but something about Serena covered in his scent aroused him beyond bearing.

"Hmmm?" she asked, allowing her own hands to slide sensuously up his back. She hooked her hands behind his neck and pressed tightly against him. She loved the feel of his chest against her nipples, his long, hard cock against her thighs. She tried to remember why she'd escaped to the shower, why this incredible pleasure had seemed like a bad idea. But as Kevin's hands cupped her ass and lifted her flush against him, her ability to reason deserted her.

"Inside," she murmured, her hands slipping from his neck to cup his face as she fastened her lips to his. "I want you inside me. Now."

Kevin pulled away gently, his blue eyes gleaming devilishly as he eased her to the ground. "No."

"No?" Serena tried to focus on what he was saying, but his hands felt so good as they toyed with her nipples. He pinched them slightly between his thumb and index finger and leaned down to blow a stream of hot air across the tight ruby buds. "What—what do you mean?" she asked, breathlessly, her knees threatening to collapse beneath her.

He chuckled. "I mean no." He rinsed the last of the soap from her aching body, turned her slightly. "We did it your way a little while ago. Now we do it my way." He eased her down onto the shower bench directly across from the spray.

Serena jerked as her overheated body sank onto the cool marble seat. She started to protest, but Kevin had sunk to his knees, spreading her legs and situating himself between her thighs. "What are you doing?" she asked, watching as he slowly lifted her foot and pressed his mouth to the inside of her ankle.

"Whatever I want, *cher*." His tongue slid tenderly up the side of her foot until he reached her toes. He looked up, his intense blue eyes holding her own as he slowly slipped her toe into his mouth and began to suck.

Serena's eyes widened and she instinctively tried to pull her foot away. But he wrapped a hand around her ankle and held her heel firmly against his chest as he continued his tender ministrations. His tongue slowly stroked the bottom of her toe even as his mouth continued the intensely erotic sucking. She could feel each pull deep in her womb, could feel hot liquid pool between her thighs as longing so intense it bordered on pain took control of her body.

She was helpless, caught by the intensity of his eyes, lost to the black magic of his mouth. Serena tried desperately to hold on to the shattering remnants of her control but everything was fading beneath Kevin's touch. Not again, she told herself, even as her head rolled back on her neck. She wouldn't lose control again, she promised, even as her eyes closed and her body arched on the hard bench.

Though it was slight, Kevin felt her sudden withdrawal and grinned. She could try to hold out as long as she wanted, but he already knew her. He knew the passion that bubbled just under the surface, and he was going to find it again, stoke it and shatter her control once and for all.

With the rest of the world she could be as controlled as she wanted. She could be cool, collected, always on top of things. But not with him. He wanted the real Serena, both in and out of his bed. He wanted the Serena she kept hidden away, the one no one else got to see. And he would have her. No matter how many walls he had to break down, no matter how many barriers he had to shatter, he would have her. He grinned again as his tongue traced a leisurely path along the bottom of her foot, enjoying the contrasting tastes of the cool, clean water and the spicy honey of her skin.

He found her arch, swirled his tongue around it before gently sinking his teeth into the smooth indentation. Serena let out a strangled scream, her body arching convulsively against the marble. He grinned and put a hand on her abdomen to keep her in place. Control, his ass. Nobody needed that much control and certainly not when they were making love.

Kevin skimmed his mouth up the inside of her leg, his lips blazing a hot trail over the cool porcelain skin. He wanted to rush wildly to the prize, to take her clit in his mouth and sink his tongue deep inside her. He wanted to taste her, lick her, bring her to orgasm again and again with his mouth.

She was his and he wanted to claim her, to brand her as his in the most primitive and obvious ways. He'd never felt this way about a woman, had never known this bone-deep connection. He refused to look too deeply at the feelings and focused, instead, on the sizzling-hot woman in his arms.

As he felt his own control slipping, he fought the overwhelming need to bury his head in the hot pink flesh between her thighs. Within seconds he could be tasting her, making her scream. Taking a deep breath, he exhaled slowly in an attempt to get a grip on himself. He took another deep breath and bent his head back to her insanely beautiful legs. He forced himself to go slow, to savor every inch of her body as his lips caressed her ankle, her calf, the exquisitely sensitive spot at the back of her knee.

He trailed hot kisses along the inside of her thighs, higher and higher until he finally reached her. He inhaled, savoring the sweet jasmine smell of her before placing his mouth as close to Serena's clit as he could without actually touching her. He spread her thighs, pulled her lips apart to expose her gorgeous clit. Then he blew out a long, slow, steady stream of air directly on her.

Serena moaned, high-pitched and desperate, her hips bucking wildly against his restraining hand. Her hands reached down, tangled in his hair and tried to bring his lips down to her as she pressed desperately against the hand holding her in place.

"Kevin—"

"What?" he whispered, keeping his lips over her so that the vibration would reach her as he spoke.

She arched again. "Please."

"Please what?"

She leaned against the glass of the shower, her head thrashing back and forth, unable to say what she wanted. "You know."

He did, but he refused to get any closer. Her hands were still fisted, and though she was powerfully aroused, he could feel the tension of control in each move she made. Her control was strained, her arousal making it harder and harder for her to hold on, but she wasn't ready to let go. At least not yet.

Smiling grimly, praying his own control was as strong as he thought it was, he licked her clit. Once. Twice. Three times. She began to relax. He felt the tension slowly leave her muscles as she calmed down. She was still aroused, true, but she was calm, convinced her control would not be breached. He licked her one more time, loving the honeyed cinnamon of her, before forcing himself to lift his head.

She whimpered, her brown eyes flying open and finding his. Her eyes were dazed, aroused, and he fought against the powerful reaction just a look from her created inside of him. Clenching his fists, he fought to regulate his suddenly ragged breathing.

He turned, flipped the shower off, grabbed a towel off the door. He wrapped her once-again trembling body in the towel, drying her tenderly.

"What's wrong?" she asked, reaching a shaky hand to his mouth. "Why are we stopping?"

His smile was dark, sensuous against her hand. "We're not. But the shower was getting cold. I thought you'd be more comfortable in the bedroom."

He watched her eyes narrow, could see her mind working beneath the suddenly sharp brown eyes. He even knew the second she reached a conclusion satisfactory to her.

"No condom," she said.

He raised his eyebrows, stopped in the motion of toweling himself dry. "Excuse me?"

"You stopped because we didn't have a condom, right?" she asked.

He inclined his head, a gesture that was neither affirmation or denial. She could believe what she wanted. He hadn't needed a condom to bring her release, had known she was teetering on the edge of satisfaction. A couple more strokes of his tongue and she would have come, magnificently. He knew it and so did she. But then he would have lost the chance to push her past a different edge, to see her finally lose that damned control once and for all.

He scooped her up in his arms. "Let's go to bed, *cher*." He carried her into the bedroom, dropped her on his lake-sized bed. His eyes blazed at the picture she made—her short hair carelessly tousled around her face, her pale skin a warm rosy pink, his towel half open around her, leaving one breast bare.

She smiled—a sexy, self-assured grin—and twisted onto her knees to reach for the nightstand. He groaned, nearly foaming at the mouth at the sight of her round, curvy ass wiggling in front of him. He wanted nothing more than to grab her hips, pull her ass firmly against him and thrust into her, over and over, until they both came harder and better than they ever had before. But she wasn't ready for that, and he wasn't ready to take a woman, again, who was not as fully involved in his lovemaking as he.

"What are you doing?" he asked, desperate to distract himself from the need burning away his own control.

"Getting a condom. Aha!" she crowed triumphantly, rolling over, a small, plastic packet in her hand.

"We don't need that yet."

Her brows furrowed and her lips turned down in the most adorable pout he'd ever seen. "We don't?" she asked, disappointment obvious in her tone.

"No." He shook his head and continued to watch her.

"Then why—?" Confusion gleamed in her sexy brown eyes, but she stopped herself from completing the question.

He sank down next to her on the bed, his hands gently cupping her face as he brought her mouth to his. Her lips moved softly against his, parted, her tongue slowly exploring the corner of his mouth. Serena slid her tongue, teasingly, temptingly over his lower lip, across his bottom lip, before finally, finally slipping inside his mouth to taste him.

His tongue met hers, dueled gently as she explored the recesses of his mouth. His cock tightened, and he nearly whimpered with the need to be inside of her. But this wasn't for him—it was for her. And he got more pleasure from simply touching her than he'd ever gotten making love fully to any other woman, even Deb.

His mouth skimmed over her cheek, nibbled her ear, before

working its way down her long, slender neck. "I love your neck," he whispered between kisses, his tongue caressing the pulse that beat at the base of her neck again and again.

"I love your ass."

He leaned back, eyebrows raised as he grinned at her. "Really?"

She bit her lip, a little embarrassed, but then she nodded. "Oh, yeah. The first couple nights I would watch you sculpt and struggle not to take pictures of your ass over and over again."

He went back to what he'd been doing, but grinned as he nibbled her neck, loving the shivers that swept through her. He licked the hollow of her throat, reveled in the pulse that beat more and more rapidly beneath his questing tongue. "Did it work?"

"Did what work?" Her voice was breathless, strained.

"Did you take pictures of something other than my ass?" His tongue dipped into the valley between her breasts, lapped at a stray drop of water.

She moaned and arched against him, her hands gripping his shoulders as her legs wrapped around his hips.

He moved to her left breast, nuzzled the nipple teasingly. "Well, did you?" he asked again, his hand caressing the underside of her breast as he pressed wet openmouthed kisses in a ring around her nipple.

"Did I—did I what?" she asked breathlessly, pressing her breast more firmly against him.

He grinned, pulled her nipple into his mouth and firmly sucked for a minute before releasing her. She groaned in frustration, her hands fisting in his hair. "The pictures?" he prompted.

She tightened her legs around him, lifted her hips so he was pressed tightly against her. She shimmied, circled her hips and took the tip of his cock inside of her. He groaned, beads of sweat appearing on his forehead as he fought the driving need to take her as fast and as hard as possible.

"What pictures?" she asked, clenching her muscles and pulling him a little more deeply inside of her.

"Forget the damn pictures," he growled, thrusting into her

s. She laughed, lifted her hips to meet him, relishing
seated deep inside of her.

d his head, stared down at Serena's beautiful, aroused
face. She was grinning, her eyes fierce with triumph and arousal. He
pulled back and thrust into her again, watched her lips part as pleasure swept through her. But her eyes, fierce and aroused though they
were, still held a watchfulness—a wariness—that set his teeth on
edge.

Clenching his teeth against the lust roaring through him, Kevin
used superhuman strength to pull out of her. "No!" she gasped, her
body bucking against his.

"Yes," he answered grimly. "You're not ready yet."

"If I get any more ready, I'll—" She stopped herself.

"You'll what?" he asked. "Lose control? Fall apart? Come?" His
voice dropped a little more with each word and his Cajun accent
grew more and more pronounced.

"Die," she answered, eyes blazing with fury and arousal.

"*La petite mort*. The little death. Not such a bad thing, hmm,
chere?" He smiled wolfishly, as his eyes searched the area around the
bed, desperately looking for something he could use. When he found
it, he kissed Serena fiercely, grabbing her arms and lifting them above
her head as his mouth devoured hers. At the same time, he reached
down, shook his belt free of his pants and looped it around the headboard and then her wrists again and again. He gave a final tug, satisfied that it would hold, and then sat back and studied her.

Kevin moved away from her and Serena became gradually aware
that her hands were anchored above her head. She tugged gently,
then harder as they refused to move. "What did you do?" she asked,
twisting to look at her wrists. "You tied me up?" Her voice rose.
"You tied me to the bed? Let me go!"

"No."

"No?" Outrage raced through her, followed by overwhelming
uneasiness and more than a little curiosity. "I don't know what
you're into, but I don't play this game."

His eyebrows rose, and his beautiful blue eyes were more serious than she'd ever seen them. "I'm not into anything and I'm not playing." He lowered his mouth to her nipple, bit gently and then laved the tiny hurt with his tongue.

She arched at the first touch of his mouth on her breast, damning herself for the unrelenting passion she felt for this man. "Kevin, don't ruin it. Let me go and make love to me."

"I'm going to make love to you, Serena." His hand circled her other nipple, flicked back and forth across it. "But I'm going to do it like this."

Heat overwhelmed her, painful in its intensity, and Serena was deathly afraid that she was going to let Kevin have his way. She wanted him, desperately, would do almost anything to have him.

She twisted against her bonds. Anything but this. She never gave up control. Never. "Don't ruin it, Kevin. Please." She felt tears burn the back of her throat, felt them well in her eyes. She turned her head so he wouldn't see, but she knew it was useless. Kevin saw everything.

His hand slipped down her stomach, his fingers tangled in her pubic hair as he thrust first one, then a second finger inside of her. "Do you want me to stop?" he asked as his finger found her G-spot and began to stroke.

She gasped and her insanely aroused body responded by arching into his wicked, wonderful hands. His fingers thrust back and forth inside of her, rubbing against her G-spot again and again. His thumb flicked gently across her clit and Serena nearly sobbed with sexual frustration.

"Serena?" he asked, his mouth teasing her breast as his hands continued to work their magic. "Do you want me to let you go?"

Her pride demanded that she say yes, that she make him free her and then storm from the room. But there was something intensely exciting about being chained for his pleasure. For her own pleasure, because she was certainly getting more pleasure from Kevin than she had from all the other men she'd been with put together.

She glanced up at the ceiling and noticed—for the first time—the huge mirror positioned directly over the bed. She stared at herself, shocked at the picture she made. Her legs spread, her body rosy pink with arousal, her arms anchored to the headboard so that Kevin could do whatever he wanted with her.

Her nipples were peaked, her breasts heaving as she strained against her restraints. Was *this* what he saw when he looked at her, she wondered, as her eyes coasted over her flat stomach to the glistening pubic hair at the apex of her thighs. Not the scared little girl she so often felt, not the basket case she tried so hard to bury, but this—this siren? Her eyes heavy-lidded with arousal. Her lips full and plump from his kisses. Her body moving restlessly as arousal coursed through her veins. Curiosity filled her, a need to explore the boundaries of this woman she barely recognized.

"Serena?" He lifted his head, his concerned blue eyes staring into hers as he lifted a hand to the headboard. "Do I need to untie you?" He began to fumble with the belt, obviously reluctant to have his other hand leave her to join the first.

She closed her eyes, took a deep breath. Did she want him to let her go? The question echoed in her head, taking on dimensions of its own. No. She didn't want him to, not now and not later. She didn't want to lose the woman she was just beginning to acknowledge.

"It's okay," she murmured, her legs moving restlessly against him. With a shuddering sigh, she forced her body to relax. "You don't have to untie me. But you'd better make it worth my while." Her brown eyes blazed with meaning.

A huge grin split his face and Kevin dipped his mouth to her breast again. "Oh, I will, *cher*. I will."

His mouth found her nipple, and his tongue flicked back and forth across it while his hand continued to work its magic deep inside of her. He began to increase his tempo, his fingers thrusting deeper and faster. Each thrust rubbed against her G-spot, bringing her closer and closer to the edge.

She was nervous, scared. Never in her adult life had she yielded control so thoroughly, and she was frightened of how she'd feel tomorrow. But, as her hips bucked desperately against Kevin's hand,

needing more, she gave herself up to him and v
ing together.

Kevin felt her surrender, felt the stress le
her body push more and more tightly against
been waiting for.

Joy swept through him and he pressed his fingers more in....,
against her, allowing his thumb to begin the circular motion she'd
been so desperate for. He pulled her nipple deep into his mouth at
the same time he circled her clit. His fingers stroked faster and faster,
and with one final pull on her breast, he sent Serena careening over
the edge.

Her body exploded and she cried out, her hands clutching at
Kevin. "I can't—oh my—Kevin!" she wailed as her world spun out
of control.

"I'm here, *bébé*. Trust me. I won't let you fall," he murmured,
kissing his way tenderly across her rib cage, down her stomach. He
traced the thin scars crisscrossing her torso with his tongue, gentling
her as her body continued to buck wildly against his.

The contractions became fewer and further apart, and he could
feel Serena begin to float back to earth. As her body relaxed, he positioned himself between her thighs, her legs draped over his shoulders. She sighed, braced for his penetration, and he leaned down and
captured her with his mouth.

She screamed, her eyes flying open as he thrust his tongue deeply
inside of her. Her hips twisted against his mouth, and he licked his
way up to her clit, his tongue swirling around and around.

"Stop! Kevin, I can't. Not again."

He ignored her, pulled her clit into his mouth and sucked as his
hands cupped her beautiful ass and held firmly in place. She whimpered, then moaned, again and again, as he began to stroke her gently between her cheeks. His tongue speared inside of her at the exact
moment his finger slipped into her anus, and she came again, sobbing, clutching his hair and struggling for breath.

Kevin rode her through it, his mouth merciless in its possession

Moments later she came a third time, her body twisting, her breathing harsh, tears and sweat mingling as they ran down her face.

He reached for the condom she had picked up earlier, rolling it on and freeing her hands in a series of quick, coordinated movements. Within seconds he had spun her around, pulled her to her knees and thrust inside of her.

He groaned, seeing stars as her body clutched at his, the remnants of her orgasm milking his cock again and again. He didn't want it to end yet, didn't want to give up this connection he had to Serena. So he ignored the clawing, urgent need to come, concentrating instead on Serena's incredible, unbelievable, unselfish response.

She gripped the rungs of the headboard, her body thrusting back against his as he pounded into her. Harsh sounds tore from his throat, high-pitched screams from hers as he thrust as deeply as possible. He reached his hand around her, found her clit and tapped. She shattered, her body going rigid as screams of surrender ripped from her throat. Her body clutched his tightly, her muscles contracting on his cock again and again. He couldn't hold back any longer, and with a bellow of intense satisfaction, he came, his body rhythmically emptying itself into her as he struggled desperately for breath.

Chapter Seven

Serena woke gradually, keenly aware of the empty spot beside her in bed. She rolled over and buried her face in Kevin's pillow, loving the fresh, clean smell of him that rose from the sheets.

Her body ached, but the feeling wasn't an unpleasant one. Memories of the previous night clicked through her head—an erotic slide show that set her body humming all over again. She had made intense, glorious, wonderful love with Kevin and the joy of all that had passed between them lingered inside her.

Despite her satisfaction, she couldn't help wondering if it was all a huge mistake. Had she really given everything to Kevin last night? She was always in control, always took the dominant role in every aspect of her life—from her career to her relationships. In one night, Kevin had stripped that identity from her. He had turned her inside out with the most intense, insidious pleasure she had ever experienced. And it had felt amazing.

As the morning light of the bayou leaked through the closed blinds, she still felt wonderful. But she was no longer so sure that she had done the right thing. Her control, and the distance that it provided her, was the only thing that had kept her sane after Sandra's death. Even her profession had helped her keep that distance. The world looked different through a camera lens—sharper, clearer, but also farther away. She'd needed that distance when she was seventeen, the ability to control her environment after it had been so violently disturbed. But she was older now. And wiser? She grimaced, not knowing the answer to that particular question.

How wise had it been to sleep with the subject of her latest project? How wise was it to let him strip her of every defense she had, leaving her standing, raw and naked, before him? But try as she might, Serena couldn't bring herself to regret it. Kevin had opened her up to an entire world of feeling and sensation that she had forgotten about. He had, in one night, shattered the wall she had hidden behind for almost eleven years. Now she had to figure out if she could function without it.

Rolling over, she glanced at the clock. It was barely six, but Kevin was already gone. Though the tempting aroma of coffee drifted down the hall from the kitchen, she knew he wasn't in the house. When he was around, the whole world seemed to pulse with the sensual energy that poured from him. And while her body was pleasantly humming from the most incredible sex of her life, she wasn't melting into a boneless puddle of lust—something she seemed to do whenever Kevin was in the immediate vicinity.

Serena stretched her overworked muscles and climbed gingerly out of bed. She'd bet that he was in his studio, blasting away, and she would give anything to be able to catch some candid photos of him. Admittedly, he always worked like he had no idea she was around, but what would he be like if he really didn't know she was there?

She rushed through her shower, ran a comb and some gel through her wet hair before slipping into a pair of jeans and a tank top. She started to put on the long-sleeve shirt that had been part of her "uniform" her entire adult life, but then discarded it. Kevin had already seen everything she had to offer. What good would her armor do her now?

A quick stop in the kitchen yielded a cup of coffee and, of course, a Twinkie. With an even quicker stop at her car for her camera bag, she was ready to go. Pausing for a moment, she looked around the bayou that surrounded Kevin's house—everything seemed greener, more vibrant than it had during her first trip. A few pictures wouldn't hurt, she thought. After all, this was Kevin's domain, and it said a lot about the man that he would choose to live in the middle of an alligator- and snake-infested swamp.

She brought her camera up, snapped a quick picture of a raccoon half hiding behind a tree. A hummingbird sipping nectar from a flower. Kevin's well-kept house. The great iron sculpture that sat a little to the right of the driveway. There was so much to see here, so many clues to who Kevin was and what he wanted.

She snapped another picture of the sculpture, then another. It was immense. Ten feet tall and at least four or five feet wide, it was an abstract piece full of sharp angles and long, thin spears. She zoomed in, taking shot after shot. The whole piece, sections, a particularly intriguing angle. The closer she got to it, the more she studied it, the more she grew to believe that she was studying Kevin's soul. Why was this piece, in particular, standing in front of his house? What did all the angles mean, all the confusing twists?

Serena lowered her camera slowly. She looked at the sculpture without the distance provided by her camera lens and felt a deep, erotic pull in her stomach. All sharp angles and wavy lines, myriad pieces and disconnected shapes—with one look, she knew that *this* was Kevin. She was sure of it. And while she didn't know what all the different pieces meant yet, she knew that if she could figure out this sculpture, she could figure out the enigma that was Kevin Riley. That was what she needed—for the book and for herself.

Her pocket began vibrating—and for a few seconds she stood, actually frozen in fear. Let it go, she told herself. You don't have to deal with this now. Not on top of everything else going on. She hesitated—hand over her pocket—until with a sigh of derision she flipped the phone open.

She'd spent too much of her life in fear—afraid of the dark, of commitment, of dying and of surviving. She'd be damned if she'd be afraid of her stupid cell phone, too. Or the sick and twisted psychopath on the other end.

"Hello." Her voice was clipped, abrupt, but she couldn't help it. Any more than she could make herself look at the caller ID. If it was him she didn't want to know one second before she had to.

"Serena."

All the tension inside of her poured out in a big sigh of relief. "Jack, how are you?"

"Actually, I was just about to ask you that question. I'm so sorry I couldn't stop what happened yesterday."

She sank onto the top step of Kevin's porch with a small sigh. "It's not your fault—I guess it was stupid to even get our hopes up."

"Not stupid, Serena. Human. I really thought, maybe—"

"I know." She interrupted him before he could finish. She couldn't bear to hear the words out loud. Not while the wound was still so raw. "Nothing we said would have made any difference. The LaFleurs—" She broke off, a bitter taste in her mouth.

Jack hesitated, and she could tell he wanted to say more. But he must have known how she felt, because at the last second, he changed the subject. "Well, then, if you're feeling up to it, I'd love to take you to lunch. It's a great day for it."

She couldn't hold back the grin—that was good old Jack for you. Always a gentleman, even when you didn't deserve it. She pictured the young, senior ADA perfectly—dressed in a suit, seated behind his desk, his hands steepled in front of him while he spoke on speaker phone. Just the kind of man she usually dated—cool, professional, casual. Not that she'd ever consider dating him—way too much history there. Besides, in the years after Sandra's death, he'd become a friend. But he was definitely her usual type—too polite to dig too deep, too nice to make her face things she'd rather ignore.

Not like Kevin, who pushed and prodded until she gave him everything. Who paid no attention to the boundaries she set—for her mind and her body. Kevin, who was a lot of things—incredibly hot, unbelievably sexy and terribly brooding—but who could never be called casual. Or nice.

"Serena." Jack's voice interrupted her reverie. "Are you still there?"

"I'm here, Jack." She cursed herself. She'd never drifted off in the middle of a conversation *before* she met Kevin Riley. He—obviously—was having a horrible influence on her. "But I'll have to take a rain check on lunch. I'm not in Baton Rouge right now."

"Really? Where are you then?"

"In the bayou, about three hours out."

"That's right—you told me. The book on Kevin Riley."

"Exactly."

"So, how's that going? Is he as difficult as everyone makes him out to be?"

She shrugged before she remembered he couldn't see her. "I don't know. He's certainly not easy."

"The best things in life never are."

She snorted before she could stop herself. "What are you—a Hallmark card?"

He answered with such a careful show of affronted dignity that she knew it was fake. "I was simply explaining that sometimes one has to work for happiness."

The laughter bubbling in her throat died abruptly. "You're kind of preaching to the choir, don't you think, Jack? If you want to use old euphemisms, I mean."

"Oh, Serena, I didn't mean it that way." There was a long silence in which she could tell he was trying to decide how to get around the elephant that had suddenly entered the room. The silence stretched—along with her nerves—until she couldn't take it any longer.

"Jack—"

"Serena—"

They both laughed as they tripped over each other's words, and the awkward moment ended. "Well, how long are you going to be out there? We'll have lunch when you're back in town."

"I've still got a couple of weeks, at least. But that would be wonderful. It's been a while since we've talked about anything but the parole hearing."

"That's true." His voice was suddenly much more subdued. "I am sorry, Serena—"

"Don't be. It's not your fault. It's no one's fault but the people in that room and the LaFleur family. You've been wonderful—through everything."

"Not wonderful enough, obviously, or Damien—"

"Stop."

"But—"

"I mean it. End of discussion. Besides, we've spent so many weeks talking about this that I have no idea what you're doing. We haven't talked about *you* in forever."

"I'm fine. Nothing unusual here—just working another big case."

"Aren't you always?"

"Only when I'm awake." There was a pause and then, "Good luck with Riley. From what I hear, you'll need it."

"He's really not that bad. At least he's resigned to the project."

"Well, that's half the battle then."

"With Kevin, it's two-thirds at least."

"And call me when you get back to town."

"You'll be first on my list."

Serena hung up with a grin, which quickly turned to a grimace. Something suddenly felt off—as if someone was watching her. She glanced around the bayou uneasily, but everything was as it had been before the call. It was just her imagination—the fear she just couldn't shake—acting up again. That one moment when the phone rang and she'd thought it was *him* had made her paranoid.

She turned back to the sculpture and took a few more pictures, refusing to let her fear ruin another day. Maybe she should have told Jack about the phone calls. Not that there was a lot he could have done, but still . . . she could have gotten his take on the situation. She opened her phone, began to dial his number, then stopped. If the guy didn't stop, if he took it to the next level—then she'd tell Jack. For now— She sighed. For now, she'd just wait and see.

When the camera clicked, signaling that she'd run out of film, she lowered it with a sigh of regret. She could stand here all day, taking pictures of this most personal piece of art. But while it might give her a better understanding of her lover, it wouldn't get the rest of her work done. Reloading her camera, she stepped silently into Kevin's studio, hoping to get a few shots before he noticed her.

She needn't have worried. He was in a frenzy, heating, bending, twisting metal, an almost crazed look on his face. Stunned, she watched him work with none of his ordinary stealth and precision. He flew through the studio, picking up one anvil, discarding another. Metal forceps, wrenches and even his favorite blowtorch rotated through his hands so quickly Serena had trouble distinguishing one tool from another.

Raising her camera to her eye, she took shot after shot of this delicious, haunted Kevin. He wasn't working from a sketch as he nearly always did. This vision burned inside of him, so desperate to get out that it had completely taken Kevin over. Obsession was upon him, the muse firmly on his shoulder, and it was the most fascinating thing she had ever seen. Sweat poured down his sculpted chest. His muscles strained to bend the iron to his will. His glorious hair was swept into a short, haphazard ponytail at the base of his neck, and his eyes glowed with a vision only he could see.

Her fingers flew over the camera, adding another roll of film, determined not to miss more than a second of the artistic frenzy that gripped him. He bent, his well-worn jeans cupping his ass as he strained to lift the base of the sculpture. A long, thick line, it was as fluid as waves rolling in off the ocean. She hadn't realized it was possible to do that to metal—to make it as soft and flowing as water. A lesser sculptor could never have accomplished it.

Kevin lifted an arm, absently wiped sweat off his face as he studied his work. And caught sight of her silhouetted against the doorway, her camera a natural extension of her body.

He grinned, full of excitement and exuberance. Serena found herself smiling back even as she captured the look on film. His eyes widened as he heard the click of the camera, and he prowled toward her. A sleek jungle cat stalking his prey, he advanced slowly, deliberately. Her breath caught and alarm coursed through her. But she wanted these photos, needed these photos. The real Kevin Riley—genius, predator, madman.

Her heart beat wildly and her breathing grew ragged. She'd had him more times than she could count last night, but she wanted him again. Here, now. Her body craved him, craved what only he could give. And he knew it. She could see his knowledge in the seductive curve of his mouth, in his sapphire eyes blazing nearly black with need.

His bare, wet chest reflected the sun, and its light surrounded him with fiery red tongues of flame. He was temptation personified—conquering general, obsessed artist, ardent lover—and Serena could feel him pulling her farther and farther into his dominion.

She clicked the last picture before lowering her camera. He came to a stop directly in front of her and his hand reached out to brush a stray lock of hair off her forehead. He was, once again, just a man, and when he opened his arms, she sank into them, resting her head directly above his heart. She breathed in the dark, musky scent of him, listened as his heart beat harder and faster. And laughed at herself, at the flight of fancy that had, for a few brief moments, had him looking something more than a man. But as she let her eyes drift shut, savoring the closeness of him, that last frame stayed with her. Fear, contentment, and desire churned in her stomach, dampening her thighs and making her nipples harden painfully.

"Did you sleep well?" he asked, pulling away to study her. His smile was warm, but his eyes were watchful as they skimmed over her face.

"I slept wonderfully," she purred. "You tired me out."

"I tried hard enough." His hands slid up and down her back and she felt his arousal press against her stomach. "Are you still tired?"

Her eyes gleamed wickedly. "Not too tired, if that's what you're asking."

His grin was wolfish. "That's exactly what I'm asking."

She pulled away from him, walked toward his work. "What are you working on? It's new, right?"

"Yeah." He shrugged, followed her. "I woke up at about three with this idea burning in my head. I had to see if I could capture it."

"Did you?"

"I don't know." His eyes were shadowed as he studied what he'd done. "I don't know if I'm good enough to capture what I'm seeing in my head."

She gasped, whirled to face him. "Don't say that. I've never seen anything like this." She gestured to the piece in front of her. "I didn't even know it was possible."

"I'm not sure it is. But I have to try."

"What's it going to be?" she asked. "It's hard to tell at this stage."

Kevin studied her for a moment, eyes grim, before his mouth curved enigmatically. "You'll see."

She raised her eyebrows, answered drily, "Or I won't."

"Exactly." He shrugged again.

Serena wandered through his work area, taking a few pictures as she went. He watched her work, silently, for several minutes before asking, "How do you know what picture you want to take? Why this workbench and not that one over there?"

"How do you know which way to bend a piece of metal?" she answered.

"It tells me. I feel it in my gut."

She nodded. "Exactly."

He brushed a kiss along her brow. "Are you ready for the trip to San Diego?" he asked.

"Sure." She shrugged, though it was far from the truth. It was one thing to be with Kevin here, in the bayou. Taking a trip with him—even one that was work-related—took their relationship to a whole new level. One she was far from certain she was ready for.

But as she didn't have a choice in the matter—the publishers had demanded the San Diego pictures be part of the book. Dwelling on her concerns would do nothing but make her crazy. "It's not like I have much more to do than what I'm doing here. You're the one with all the responsibility."

"It's no big deal."

"No big deal?" she asked incredulously. "The opening of an exhibit of your work at the San Diego Museum of Art? The unveiling of a sculpture in the new Matthias Building? Your first showing at the Price Gallery? It doesn't get much huger than that. Aren't you excited?"

It was his turn to shrug. "Yeah, I guess. I love seeing my work where it's meant to be—the Matthias sculpture took such a long time and is designed so precisely for its environment. I really like that part."

"But not the rest?" she asked. "A museum full of people admiring your work one night, a gallery of people buying it the next?"

"I don't like the show, all the airs people put on at those things." His eyes darkened. "I can't stand the fake crap."

"Why are you so sure it's fake?" she asked.

"How can it not be, *cher*? A bunch of people standing around in designer wear talking about what they *see* in my art, how it makes them *feel*!" He snorted. "Spare me the wannabes and their need to discuss the 'esoteric' details of my work with me. Particularly when ninety-five percent of them don't have a clue what they're talking about."

She leaned back and studied him for a minute. His eyes were contemptuous, his mouth twisted in disgust. "I never would have guessed it," she commented. "You're a snob."

"Excuse me?" His voice fairly crackled with indignation and his eyes turned glacier blue. "They're the snobs, with their hundred-dollar caviar and their thousand-dollar dresses. I don't care about any of that shit."

"And you think anyone who does is weak and stupid."

"A lot of them are weak and stupid." He raised an eyebrow, daring her to disagree.

"And you think because you wear faded jeans and live like a hippie in the middle of nowhere that you're better than they are? You're just as narrow-minded in your own way."

"Wait a minute! I never said I was better than them. I said I couldn't stand them. There's a difference." His eyes narrowed dangerously.

"Oh, really? What's the difference?" She smirked, challenging him.

He stared at her, nonplussed, trying to find an argument that would help him win their debate. When he could think of nothing, he simply shrugged and said, "I don't know. But there is one."

She laughed, wrapped an arm around his waist and snuggled into the curve of his arm. "Great answer."

"Why are you defending them? Someone just like that killed your sister and bought his way free."

Serena stiffened against him and he cursed himself, wanting to take the words back as soon as they had left his mouth.

"You think I don't know that?" She pulled away to glare at him. "You think I don't live with that every day of my life? But you can't condemn everyone because of what a few people do."

He watched the light go out of her eyes and cursed himself again. "I'm sorry. That was totally uncalled for."

She shrugged, the ice maiden back in place. "Don't apologize. It's true."

"True or not, you don't need me to throw it in your face." He put a finger under her chin, tilted her face up so that she couldn't avoid his eyes. "It was a crappy thing to say, and I'm sorry for it."

She studied him with expressionless eyes for a minute, then two. Just as he began to fear that he had really blown it, she shook her head. "Don't worry about it. Truth is truth, whether it hurts or not."

His fingers tangled in the hair at her nape. "Oh, *bébé*, I never meant to hurt you."

"Forget it." Her eyes warmed, and with a quick grin, she reached up and pulled the rubber band from his hair.

"My turn," she murmured, pressing her soft body against his burning one as her hands danced through the cool silkiness of his hair.

"For what?" His voice was hoarse, his eyes aware.

"For this." She pulled Kevin's mouth down to hers, wanting, needing, to taste him. Her tongue teased the corners of his mouth, traced his upper lip. When his mouth opened on a groan, she slid his lower lip between her teeth and nipped just hard enough to have his eyes flying open and his hands reaching down to cup her ass. He lifted her slightly, pressed his throbbing cock between her legs.

But Serena pulled away, shaking her head as she wiped a smudge of charcoal off his cheek. "No way," she murmured, lowering her head to lick a bead of sweat slowly making its way down his chest. "You got to do what you wanted last night."

He raised his eyebrows, even as he brought his hands back to rest on his thighs. "You have a complaint?"

Her eyes slowly ran over his body from head to toe, and she smiled sensuously. "No," she shook her head. "No complaints. But turnabout's fair play."

She reached a hand up to his face and delicately traced the hard angles she found there. Her fingers swept gently across his forehead, down his nose, over those seductive cheekbones and down to his chin. His breathing grew harsher, and Serena smiled, thrilled that she could so easily pull a reaction from him.

She turned, moving her body away from his so that her index finger was the only point of contact between them. Slowly, sensuously, she slid it back and forth over his lips. First the upper one, with its perfect cupid bow then the full, voluptuous curve of his lower lip.

Kevin's eyes, nearly black with arousal, scorched her as he turned his head and bit the tip of her finger before drawing it into his mouth, his tongue swirling around it.

Serena closed her eyes, enjoying the smooth, wet pressure for a moment before she slowly pulled her finger away. His hand reached up to grab her, to pull her against him, but she laughed as she evaded his grasp.

Swirling her tongue over her own lips, she trailed her still-wet finger into the deep vee between her breasts. His eyes followed her every move, his breath growing harsher with each moment that passed.

With a teasing grin, she dragged the tank top over her head, relishing his sharp intake of breath as she stood before him in only her black lace bra and threadbare jeans. She cupped her breasts, rubbed her thumbs over her nipples, enjoying both the contact and his response to it.

"Serena." Kevin's voice was low, warning.

"Something wrong?" she asked, flicking the front clasp of her bra open so that her breasts tumbled free. She licked her fingers, swirled them around her already hard nipples, moaning softly as energy shot from her breasts to between her legs.

He reached for her. "If you keep doing that, I'm going to come before I even get to touch you."

"Really?" Her eyes taunted him as her lips formed a perfect, inviting O. His arousal was huge, and it made her heart beat faster, just looking at him. Stepping forward, she hooked a finger in the waistband of his jeans and tugged him closer. "That looks uncomfortable," she said teasingly.

He smiled wickedly, his cock jumping beneath her gaze. "It could be better."

"Oh, really?" Her eyebrows lifted inquiringly, as she slowly slid the button free. "I don't think I could take it if it got much better."

Kevin's indrawn breath was audible as Serena eased the zipper down and slipped her hand inside his jeans. He wasn't wearing underwear, and her fingers made immediate contact with his aching erection, curling around him as she began stroking over and over.

Kevin's head fell back and he groaned, thrusting himself against her questing hands. "*Chere*, please. Let me—" His voice broke as she ran a hand over the thick head of his cock.

"Let you what?" She slid his jeans over his hips, kneeling as she slipped them down his legs and over his bare feet. She looked up, her face level with his truly magnificent erection.

Leaning forward, she rubbed her cheek along his hard, silky length before turning her head and softly kissing just the tip. She swirled her tongue around the head and reached between his legs to cup and massage his testicles.

Kevin groaned, his hot eyes following every move she made. His hands tangled in her hair as she leaned forward and slowly flicked her tongue up the length of him.

"Serena!" he gasped. "*Mon Dieu, bébé*, you're killing me!"

"Kevin, *bébé*," she mocked, "I haven't even started."

She turned her head and took his throbbing cock into her mouth, pulling him deep as her tongue continued to swirl around him. Her hands reached up, grabbed his ass to anchor herself as she slowly pulled back until only his deep purple head was between her lips. She sucked him gently, her tongue flicking back and forth across the small bundle of nerves centered on the bottom of the tip.

He clutched her hair, groaned, but she was relentless. Slowly, incredibly slowly, she took all of him in her mouth. Around and around she swirled her tongue, savoring his musky, masculine taste as her throat milked him.

Kevin watched her through heavy-lidded eyes, loving the sight and feel of her gorgeous mouth on his cock. He thrust against her, watched himself slide in and out of her raspberry-colored lips. He wanted her to continue, wanted to come in her mouth with a desire so intense that it make him shake. But he wanted to hold her, too, to pleasure her as she was pleasuring him.

"*Cher,*" he said huskily, forcing the words through his too dry throat, "stop. I don't want to come yet."

Serena released him almost instantly, and he didn't know whether to be relieved or disappointed. Looking at him through her lashes, she ran her tongue up and down his length as he murmured in approval. "I want you to come."

She was breathless, her body nearly as hot as his. Her nipples were painfully tight, her jeans soaked through, and she wanted nothing more than to make this man come, to taste the sweet saltiness of his release as she brought him pleasure. "I need you to come for me."

Her lips closed over him again, and her tongue continued to move back and forth as she reached behind his balls and touched a spot he hadn't known existed. It was too much stimulus, too much sensation, too much everything. He tried to pull away from her, tried to stop the orgasm flowing through him.

But Serena was having none of it. Cupping his ass, she pulled him tightly against her as once again she slid his entire length into her mouth and down her throat. Her tongue stroked the tender underside of his cock, her fingers rubbed the spot next to his balls and her mouth continued to suck until he was nearly out of his mind.

She hummed sexily, and the ensuing vibrations sent him into sensory overload. With a deep, lusty groan he emptied himself into her mouth in the most blindingly intense orgasm of his life. His knees grew weak, his entire body shook and he sank gratefully to the floor, pulling her on top of him as he did.

Serena's lips glistened as she reached a hand forward to stroke his cheek. Her hair was tousled, her cheeks flushed, her eyes pools of molten chocolate. She'd never been more beautiful to him. This gorgeous, generous woman who had turned him inside out and now held him more tenderly than anyone ever had.

He breathed deeply, inhaled her spicy scent. She was such a mass of contradictions—with her sexy perfume and tailored clothes, her burning eyes and cool, cultured voice. Which was the real Serena? Did he even care, as long as she continued to let him love her?

Make love to her, he corrected himself, suddenly uncomfortable with the fierce beating of his heart—a pounding that didn't come completely from his recent exertions. But her lush ass was rubbing against him and his cock came to life once again, sending all other thoughts fleeing from his head.

Turning her so that her high breasts brushed against his cheek, Kevin captured a taut, pouting nipple in his mouth as he peeled her jeans down her thighs. He rolled her nipple between his lips, pinching softly, loving how it tightened for him even more.

Resting one hand on her back to anchor her to him, he slipped his other hand between Serena's legs. She was wet, hot, burning, and he groaned as he slid one finger inside of her, followed closely by a second. He worked them back and forth, his thumb rubbing against her clit as she rode his hand.

Serena's head lolled back on her neck, her entire focus on Kevin and the wicked, wonderful things he was doing to her body. She straddled him, heat shooting through her as his cock nestled between the cheeks of her ass. His fingers moved harder and faster inside of her, thrusting against her. Orgasm flooded her, tightening every muscle in her body as she came, screaming his name.

He reached for his jeans and drew a condom from the back pocket, slipping it over his pulsing erection and sliding home as contractions continued to rock her. Serena rose onto her knees, riding him in ecstasy. Their eyes met, held, as need arced between them. She wanted to look away—the pull between them was too intense to bear. But Kevin reached up, held her chin between his strong artist's fingers, kept her eyes focused on his as he pounded into her. His eyes blazed, burned, promised things she didn't want to think about, things she wasn't ready to accept. But another release was close, beckoning, growing stronger as his eyes seared into hers.

His hand slipped between them, firmly stroking her clit as another orgasm loomed closer and closer. She closed her eyes, but his fingers tightened on her chin. "Look at me," he demanded hoarsely. "I want to watch you while you come."

Serena's eyes flew open and her body convulsed, his words sending satisfaction streaming through her. His dark, dangerous eyes trapped hers, intensifying her climax as his own roared through him. She felt naked, vulnerable, more revealed than she'd ever been before. Even so, she continued to stare into his eyes as her orgasm went on and on.

When the last ripple of sensation finally faded, she collapsed against Kevin's chest, burying her face in the crook of his neck. She was raw, emotionally drained and strangely shy after the intense emotional connection they had just shared. She'd known it was more than sex between them, but she had been woefully unprepared for the emotions surging through her at such an alarming rate.

What would she do if she fell in love with him? What could she do?

Chapter Eight

She wasn't answering. Again. He clicked the DISCONNECT button gently, stared at the phone for a few long seconds. Then slammed the phone against the table so hard it shattered.

Why was she doing this? Why now, when he was so close to making all of his plans a reality, was she shutting him out? He strode to the bar and grabbed a bottle of seventy-year-old Scotch. Without bothering with a glass, he unscrewed the top and took a long swig from the bottle. Then another and another.

Fire raced down his esophagus to his stomach, briefly burning away the cold that had lately taken up permanent residence there. But he couldn't take too much, couldn't afford to be drunk when he met his parents. With his past, a little drunkenness would totally freak them out, and he didn't want to do anything to rock the boat. To call attention to himself when he'd made blending in an art form.

He climbed the stairs and walked down the hall to the back bedroom, the one with the window that looked straight into Serena's kitchen. He'd been watching since last night and she hadn't returned.

No lights had gone on in her condo. No signs of life to say she was back, tucked into bed like a good girl.

So where was she? What was she doing right now that was so important she couldn't answer his calls? She knew how angry it made him when she wasn't available to him.

Had she seriously gone running out to that bayou, out to that gutter rat with his callused hands and dirty clothes? He couldn't imagine Serena actually letting him touch her—she wasn't the type to let some filthy laborer get his hands on her. But the man would have to die anyway. For his thoughts alone. No man, no one, could be alone with Serena and not want her. Not think about taking off her clothes and licking her delicious body from top to bottom. He should know—he'd done nothing but think about that body for ten long years and plan every single thing he would do to it.

Serena was his. His! And any man who thought otherwise was asking for a death sentence. He reached into the drawer of the desk that sat beneath the window. Pulled out his father's gun. Ran loving fingers over it. Cupped its cool smoothness against his cheek. A death sentence he would be only too happy to provide.

He hardened to the point of pain. Unzipping his pants with his free hand, he stroked his dick while he imagined what it would be like to stick it in her. To slam into her—over and over again—while he used his teeth on her nipples. Would they be the same bright red as her sister's? he wondered as he moved his hand harder and faster. Or would they be unique—like Serena herself? A pale pink, a dusky rose, a muted brown?

"Oh, God!" He squeezed harder and nearly came—the pleasure-pain almost more than he could bear. Would she like the combination as much as he did—the pricks of pain that made the pleasure only more intense? She would like it, he determined, because who could be better for her—to her—than he could? He would be in her, on her, in every way imaginable. And she would scream for more.

"Fuuuuuuuck ..." He came on a tidal wave of pleasure so intense he nearly passed out, so incredibly, unbelievably, fucking good that it overwhelmed and buried—just for a few seconds—the pain slowly winding its way through his head.

That was when it came to him, in that funny afterglow of pleasure after a particularly intense orgasm. If he had Serena he could fuck her all the time, over and over and over until the pain went away for good.

They lay together a long time, her head pillowed on his chest, his right leg wrapped around her—anchoring her in place. One of Kevin's hands gently stroked her hair as the other wound itself around her waist. She breathed deeply, savoring the smell and feel that was uniquely Kevin. But soon touching wasn't enough and Serena's tongue darted out, caressing his nipple with a soft, wet touch.

Kevin groaned, shifted so that his hands cupped her ass as she rested completely on top of him. "*Mon Dieu*, Serena. You are insatiable." He heaved a long, put-upon sigh. "But I suppose, if you insist—"

She giggled, a sound he had despaired of ever hearing from her, as she slapped a palm firmly against his chest. "Oh, no. I don't think so!"

Disappointment flashed briefly in his eyes before he muttered, "No? Are you sure?" He leaned forward, took one of her gorgeous raspberry nipples in his mouth.

She arched her back, sighing as he continued his tender onslaught. "I'm sore, Kevin. Any more and I won't be able to walk."

He pulled away instantly. "*Je suis desolé*. I'm so sorry, love. I didn't think." He leaned down, pressed a kiss on her slender patrician nose before slowly easing to his feet.

Serena watched him pad, naked and totally unself-conscious, across the studio to the refrigerator. He grabbed a bottle of water, twisted the top off and drank deeply. Wide-eyed, she watched his throat work as he drank. A dark arousal started low in her belly; her nipples peaked and her breathing became harsh. She shifted. Maybe, if they were careful—

Her tender muscles screamed in protest, and she ruefully admitted that no matter how willing the spirit was, the body definitely needed a break. Maybe just a short one, but still definitely a break.

"You want one?" he asked, gesturing to the water bottle.

"Sure." He bent down, his magnificent ass displayed in full glory. Serena couldn't help herself. She grabbed her camera and snapped two pictures in quick succession.

The whirr of the camera alerted him and Kevin turned around, eyes narrowed. "You did not just take a picture of my naked ass!"

She smiled impishly and clicked another picture. God knew, his front view was even better than the back. He stalked toward her, his erection growing with each click of the camera. Drool pooled in her mouth but she ignored the overwhelming urge to put the camera aside and touch him.

"Serena!" His voice was sharp.

He was standing over her, ruining the angle of the photo. She scooted back, leaned down to get the shot. "Hmm?" she answered absently, totally focused on the image in her camera lens.

He frowned. "None of these are going in the book!"

"Why not? Your body is unbelievable—these would totally boost your popularity. Not that you need it," she added hastily, as his face clouded over.

"I am not a *Playgirl* model!"

"And isn't that a shame?" she answered, licking her lips. "You'd sell an awful lot of magazines."

Or photo essays? he wondered before he could stop himself. He hated the suspicious twist his mind had taken, the sudden distance he felt from her. Serena wasn't Deb. She wouldn't make him fall for her, use him and then toss him away once she'd reached her objective.

But what exactly *was* Serena going to do? he asked himself again. When she was done shooting for the book, would she walk out of his life before he could convince her to stay?

"Kevin?" Serena's voice broke into his reverie. "Are you okay?"

"Of course. Why?"

"You've been standing there, lost in thought, for almost five minutes." She patted the rug next to her. "Come sit here."

He gratefully sank down next to her, reached to pull her in his arms. But she evaded him, scooting as far back as the wall allowed as she shrugged into his shirt.

"Lie down," she murmured. "I'm not done."

His eyebrows rose. "Not done with what, *cher*? 'Cuz I don't think we can get much done with you over there."

"The pictures, silly." When he didn't move, she sighed and moved toward him again. She leaned forward and kissed him, easing him down as her glorious tongue tangled with his. Just as he was getting into it, she pulled away and reached for her camera again.

She took a couple pictures of him openmouthed with shock. A few more with a pouty little-boy look she hadn't even known he was capable of.

But when his eyes began to gleam wickedly, she asked warily, "What are you up to?"

"I was just remembering what you taste like." His Cajun accent had thickened dangerously. "Thinking about how much I want to slip my tongue inside you again."

She nearly dropped the camera as a blush spread from her breasts to her face. "Stop it!" she hissed. "I need to concentrate."

"Me, too, *cher*," he commented, grinning. " 'Cuz the only way I'm gonna sit here and let you take naked pictures of me is if I get to fantasize while you do it."

"Fantasize all you want," she said with a stern look. "But keep your thoughts to yourself." She raised the camera again, loving the mischievous look on his face.

"That's not nearly entertaining enough for me. Now I *would* be highly entertained if I could pull your gorgeous little nipple into my mouth. I would roll it around on my tongue, savoring every sweet centimeter as my hand crept down and stroked your clit."

"Stop." She was breathless.

"Stop what, *mon amour*? Stop thinking about you? Stop touching you? I can't." His eyes gleamed and he licked his lips. "You want me to stop swirling my tongue around your nipple? To stop stroking your clit with my thumb? Stop thrusting my fingers inside that hot little ass of yours? Inside your beautiful cunt? But you're so hot, so wet and tight around my fingers. You feel so good. I can't stop and you wouldn't want me to if I could."

Serena tried to block out his voice as she snapped picture after picture. But it was no use. He was seducing her—with the looks he gave the camera and the words that wrapped themselves intimately around her. "Kevin—" Her voice was a husky plea.

"Spread your legs for me, Serena. Let me see what you won't let me touch."

She whimpered, tried to fight the black magic of his voice, but her need for him was too strong. With a sigh, she spread her legs, incredibly conscious of the air-conditioning hitting her bare ass.

His eyes blazed as he stared at her. "That's it, *bébé*. That's a good girl. You're so beautiful there, like a flower unfolding just for me. So many shades of pink. Have you ever seen yourself spread open like this? Have you ever really looked?"

She shook her head, bit her lip as desire crashed through her. "Sit up," she said, desperate to regain control of the situation.

His eyes laughed at her, as if he knew what she was trying to do. But he sat, bringing his knees up to hide his incredible erection from the camera.

"No," she said. "Bring your knee down. Let me see it."

Kevin's eyes turned heavy-lidded with his own need, as he moved to follow her instructions. His cock grew longer and harder under her gaze, and for a minute she could think of nothing but kneeling in front of him. She wanted to pull him into her mouth again, needed to taste the salty sweetness of him as she slowly licked him up and down.

"Should I tell you what I see?" he asked, his voice lower, huskier than before.

Their eyes met through the camera lens, held for a moment. Then he looked away, his eyes burning a trail between her legs. "You're swollen and slick. I can see the wetness glistening on you, like morning dew on flower petals." He reached for his water bottle as her numb fingers reloaded the camera.

"You grow darker, pinker with each layer of petals. Your inner-most folds are deep rose, nearly red. Especially when you're aroused." His breathing was harsh, his chest shuddering with each inhalation. "You are aroused, aren't you, Serena?"

She couldn't answer. She tried to concentrate on his face, on the look of intense concentration he wore. But he was huge, magnificent, and she couldn't stop herself from lowering the camera, from looking at his erection as it stood straight and proud.

She clicked the picture, wound the film, clicked again. He was right. These pictures weren't going in the book; they were for her eyes only, each one more delectable than the one that came before.

"Serena?" He called her name, his eyes still focused on the bounty between her legs. "You *are* aroused. I can see you getting wetter and darker. You're swelling, your hips moving back and forth to ease the ache. Put the camera down and let me touch you." He weaved a spell around her with his voice. "Let me taste you."

She shook her head, pressed back against the wall. "Not yet." Her voice was strained, her nipples tight and aching.

"No?" He shrugged. He leaned back on his elbow, let his hand stroke his cock under her hungry gaze. "Then touch yourself." Her eyes widened and he laughed. "You do touch yourself, don't you, *chere*? Late at night, when you're all alone? You rub your nipples, stroke yourself between your legs, circle your finger around your hot, little clit. I know you do." He continued to stroke himself, his thumb catching the drop of moisture that escaped from his tip and slowly rubbing it into the dark purple head of his cock.

Her mouth watered and the camera clattered noisily to the ground. She wanted him, needed his hardness inside her. But Kevin had no mercy as she reached for him. "Oh, no, *bébé*. You had your fun. Now it's time for me to have mine."

She glared at him, whimpering, as her hips moved helplessly against the floor.

"Put your finger in your mouth. Get it nice and wet," he murmured, his eyes watching her intently as she followed his directions. "Now swirl it around your nipple. That's it, nice and slow. Squeeze your nipple between your thumb and finger. Harder, *bébé*. Rub your thumb over it. Does that feel good?"

"Yes," she whispered as her head fell back and she rubbed both her nipples. Fire shot down her body and she could feel herself growing hotter, wetter just as he said she would. With a moan, she slowly lowered a hand to her thighs. Under Kevin's watchful gaze, she began to stroke herself.

"Slide a finger inside. Oh, yeah, that's fantastic. Now another one. Find your sweet spot and stroke, slowly—in and out." His eyes gleamed wickedly as her hips rocked against the floor, desperate for relief from the intensity of his words.

"I love touching you there, feeling how wet and hot you are for me. You are wet, aren't you, *chere*? Wet and hot and dying for me?"

"Kevin—" she moaned, her voice sounding as desperate as she felt.

"Serena," he mimicked, his eyes searing hers. "Now put your thumb on your clit. No, keep your fingers inside while you do it. That's right, *cher*. That's right. Now tap softly. No stroking yet. Just that soft up and down with your finger. How's that feel?"

She struggled for breath, shocked at how incredibly good it felt to do as he said. "Fabulous," she gasped, intensifying the motion as she felt her climax growing closer and closer. She wasn't sure what was more erotic—touching herself in front of Kevin or watching him stroke himself into even fuller arousal.

"Good." He grinned. "Does it feel as fabulous as my cock inside of you? As my tongue on you, licking you, slipping inside you?"

His words intensified her feelings, and with one more stroke, Serena shattered. Her mouth dropped open in a surprised *O* as she rode out the waves of her orgasm, her legs spread, fingers thrusting desperately inside of herself.

Kevin watched her pleasure herself, heat spiraling through him at an unbelievable rate. His cock was full, ready to explode. His balls ached with the pleasure-pain of restraint. But he refused to move, refused to do anything that might prematurely end the exquisite

sight of Serena coming. Cheeks flushed, eyes blazing, lips swollen—
she was the most beautiful thing he'd ever seen. A melting tenderness
spread through him, even as his need grew urgent.

Serena gasped a little as her orgasm waned and he grinned, imagining the pleasure in making her shatter again and again. If he wasn't
careful, making her come could become an incredibly addictive pas-
time. Her head lolled back against the wall while her hand lay intimately draped between her still-spread thighs. Other women might
have been embarrassed, but not his beautiful little photographer.
Still caught up in the power of her release, she lay quiet, savoring the
sweet aftershocks he could see rocking her body.

He scooted forward and wrapped a hand around her delicate
wrist. Her eyes opened drowsily and she smiled. He stopped for a
moment, stunned by the power and beauty of that smile. He had to
re-create it, had to find a way to make it a part of the art that was as
necessary to him as breathing. A part to hold on to when she was
gone.

He shrugged away the unwelcome thought, bringing her into the
shelter of his arms. "You are magnificent," he whispered against her
lips.

"You're pretty terrific yourself." Her hand slid down between
their bodies, capturing him and pumping back and forth. He saw
stars.

"You're playing with fire," he warned, thrusting back and forth
against her warm palm.

"Then aren't you glad I'm not afraid of getting burned?"

"Damn straight." Though it cost him, he put his hand over hers,
stopping the incredible motion. "I can wait, Serena."

She rubbed her thumb over the drop on the head of his cock,
then brought it to her mouth and sucked. "It doesn't look like it,"
she murmured with a grin.

His cock jerked in reaction to her sexy smile and honesty. "If
you're sore ..." His voice trailed off as she pressed her body against
his.

Her smile was wicked. "Not that sore," she murmured as she crawled over him.

Kevin's cock settled between her legs and Serena gasped at the first touch of it against her delicate inner folds. She was so sensitive that just the touch of him sent waves of pleasure skating up her spine. Desire—hot and hard—hit her, and suddenly all she could think about was getting him inside of her.

She rocked against him, whimpering softly as need overwhelmed her. But Kevin misunderstood her desperation. "Too sore?" he rasped as his hands, trembling softly, locked onto her hips and tried to lift her away.

"No!" She struggled against his restraining fingers as swells of need rushed through her. She was going to die, to spontaneously combust at any second.

"I don't care. I—" Her voice broke and desire swamped her—shook her—until Kevin was all that was solid and steady around her.

"*Bébé*—" His hands moved soothingly along her back, but she was too far gone to be calmed by a soft touch.

"Kevin—" she whimpered, her hips moving frantically against him. "I need—" Her voice broke again.

"I know, *cher*—" And then he was lifting her, ignoring her cries of protest, until she was poised above him. Her knees on either side of his head. Her pussy directly above his mouth.

He whispered something low and guttural and obscene, his breath hot and welcome against her. And then he thrust his tongue deep inside of her.

She came with a scream, her body spiraling completely out of her control until she shattered—completely and irrevocably. She felt herself break into a million myriad pieces, her mind fragmenting until she couldn't speak, couldn't think.

Serena spun outside of herself to a place where only feeling existed, sensation after sensation flooding her, frightening her with its intensity. She struggled against the tidal wave for long moments, terrified of losing herself in the never-ending pleasure. She bucked against his mouth but he held her still, his incredible strength allowing her no surcease from the emotions all but ripping her apart.

"Kevin, stop. I can't—"

"You can." His voice was lower, harsher than she'd ever heard it, and when she glanced into his eyes, she was trapped by the flames flickering there, building to a towering inferno that threatened to consume every part of her.

His tongue—his wicked, wonderful tongue—went from deep thrusts to long, luxurious licks that had ecstasy trembling along nerve endings that hadn't yet recovered from his first embrace. His teeth found her clit and closed gently over it even as his eyes stared deeply into hers—claiming her, branding her, demanding a response she wasn't sure she could give.

She made a high keening sound, her hips moving against him as he thrust first one finger and then another inside of her. He stroked her G-spot—once, twice—then pulled out to spread the hot liquid of her response over and around her anus. He circled the tight bud again and again, and she nearly screamed, pleasure rocketing through her.

Finally—finally—he thrust his finger inside at the same time his tongue swept over and around her clit. Another orgasm slammed through her—fast and hard and never-ending—and this time she screamed in total abandon.

Kevin grinned against, then pulled her clit into his mouth and began to suck. His hands held her hips still, poised above him for perfect access. He continued to torment her—sucking, licking, spearing his tongue deep inside of her—until one orgasm blended into another. And another. The more sensitive she grew, the further he went. She couldn't talk, couldn't think, couldn't breathe, and still he persisted. She bucked wildly against him, twisting and pulling in an effort to get away from his ravenous mouth. But he refused to relent.

"Kevin, no," she finally gasped. He had to stop. He *had* to. She couldn't survive another—

His tongue speared deep and hurled her into another climax. She'd lost count of how many times she'd come, lost track of everything but the ecstasy ravaging her body with each movement of Kevin's mouth. He was *devouring* her, pushing her beyond any and all limits until she couldn't recognize the tormented, pleading woman she was fast becoming.

"Yes," he growled as his tongue fluttered from her clit to her anus and back again. "You'll come for me over and over and over again. I'll never get enough of you, Serena. I'll never get enough of *this*."

Once again he pulled her clit between his teeth and began to suck and once again she came, stars exploding in front of her dazed eyes as she trembled and sobbed and pleaded with him to take her.

Finally—finally—when she was on the brink of insanity and control was a word she could no longer comprehend, he pulled her away and rolled so that she was suddenly beneath him, her body shaking as yet another orgasm ripped through her.

She grabbed on to his shoulder, her nails digging deep without her knowledge or consent as she pleaded, "I'm dying, Kevin. I'm *dying*. You have to fuck me. You have to—"

Serena's breathy pleas ran through him like a live electric current and he felt his control snap. With one powerful thrust, he buried himself balls deep within her. She was slick and wet and so fucking hot that for a moment he was afraid he'd come before he could bring her to orgasm again.

Then she whimpered—her hands pulling at his hair, her legs wrapping themselves around his waist, her cunt pulling at his cock— and he knew he wasn't ready for it to end yet.

He rode her hard, his hands braced beneath her hips to lift her higher, open her wider, for his penetration. Over and over he thrust into her velvet heat until he was on fire, flames of ecstasy burning through his brain, down his spine, over his cock. And still he slammed into her, determined to make the pleasure last. Determined to bury himself so deeply inside of her that she could never get him out.

Sweat beaded on his chest, rolled down his back, and still he continued thrusting, over and over again—as hard and as deep as he could go. His arms trembled, his cock screamed for relief, and still he pushed himself inside of Serena.

She was sobbing, screaming, her muscles clutching more tightly at him with every thrust. Her nails were digging into his back, drawing blood with every push of his body. Her back was arching, her legs shaking as he drove into her—over and over—with all the power and strength that he had.

He was buried deep when he felt the climax rip through her—a deep, dark tsunami so powerful that it swamped him, buried him, dragged him under. He felt his own orgasm tear through him, the never-ending pulses of her body sending him so far over the edge that he feared he'd never recover.

It started at the base of his spine and spread outward—through his cock, his stomach, up his back, around to his chest. Pleasure, pain, passion roaring through him, flowing from him to her and back again as he emptied himself inside of her in a series of powerful, all-encompassing waves.

When it was over, when he'd given her everything that he had, he rolled so that she rested above him. And wondered, grimly, if it was enough.

Chapter Nine

That bitch! He'd trusted her, loved her, taken care of her from afar for years, and she would dare throw it in his face like this? Bad enough that she stayed out in that bayou with him taking pictures for that absurd book. Worse still, that she'd come to San Diego with him. But to cancel her room—to decide to stay in his suite with him. Had she no shame?

He imagined that filthy laborer's hands all over her and he wanted to scream in denial. Serena was his. His. How dared this man think to touch her? How dared she let him?

The fury was back—so hot and uncontrolled that it spewed out of him in fiery sparks.

"Bitch! Whore!" He wasn't aware of throwing his Scotch until the glass shattered against the mirror lining one wall of the luxurious hotel suite he'd checked into only hours before. The mirror cracked and he walked toward it, fascinated. Amber liquid dripped from it, catching in the cracks and sliding slowly unto the plush carpet. The closer he got, the more of himself he could see in the mirror. But he was distorted, in pieces, his features randomly placed on his face.

"No!" He screamed in agonized denial. Not here, not now—

when he was so close to having her as his own. "It's just the mirror," he muttered to himself. "Just the broken mirror." He was whole, normal, perfect. It was just the mirror that—

His hand—a tightly curled fist—lashed out and struck the broken glass. He roared in agony as the skin over his knuckles shredded. But a few pieces of the cursed mirror had fallen, and the pain was worth it. With a hoarse cry he hit the mirror again, this time slicing a deep gash into the side of his hand as more pieces of the mirror crumbled away.

He watched, fascinated, as blood slowly dripped from his hand onto the carpet—decorating the long shards of glass lying facedown on the plush thickness. He grinned—he couldn't help himself. It was such a beautiful sight.

His hand hurt and the bleeding continued, but he made no move toward the bathroom. Blood dripped, pooled in front of him, around him, and still he didn't go for a towel. Instead he watched the crimson stain spread, watched a little bit of himself slowly leak into oblivion.

The headache was back, creeping up from his shoulders and neck to the top of his head—until the pain from his hand was but a small annoyance compared to the searing heat behind his eyes.

They were getting worse, coming more often, until he'd almost been unable to work last week. But control was everything, and he refused to let the pain take over his life. He'd have her soon and then everything would be okay.

When the bleeding slowed to a trickle, he walked to the bathroom and absently wrapped a towel around his wounds. Such a shame to cover up all that beautiful blood, but he had an appointment tonight he didn't want to miss. It wouldn't do for him to show up a bloody mess. It wouldn't do at all.

He crossed to the bar, poured himself another Scotch. Wondered what Serena was doing right now. Pondered whether or not she'd found his surprise—or better yet, if that bayou rat had found it.

It hadn't been easy, getting that close to her things without being seen, but he was more than pleased with the result of the extra effort. Hurting her wasn't his intention—at least not yet—but still, there were rules. She had to pay for her duplicity. Pay for letting that animal, that laborer lay his filthy hands on her.

Tonight was just a warning, but if things continued this way—the punishments would be much worse. For both of them.

Serena was his and he would have her. And once he did, no one would ever take her from him again. He'd kill anyone who tried.

Serena studied herself critically in the hotel mirror. She looked good. Really good, if she did say so herself. She had been a little leery when the boutique manager had proclaimed it perfect for her, but with her makeup and hair done, she could see that the woman had been right, though the raspberry silk was a little low-cut for her taste. She tugged at the halter bodice for the third time in as many minutes.

What had possessed her to buy a new dress? *Two* new dresses. Especially since she had two perfectly good ones still packed in her suitcase. When she'd packed for the trip to San Diego, she'd had every intention of wearing her old cocktail standbys. But when she'd gone to unpack last night, suddenly they hadn't seemed right.

She snorted as she shook her head. Meaning they weren't beautiful enough—sexy enough—for Kevin. She wanted to wow him, to make his mouth drop open and his cock get hard at his first glimpse of her.

She couldn't help herself from contemplating her reflection for a few, long seconds. Who was this woman who had invaded her body, and when was the real Serena Macafee planning on making an appearance? This was so unlike the real her—dressing up for a man, planning to seduce him. The real Serena didn't have incredible sex with the subject of her assignment. She didn't wear red lipstick *or* red dresses. And she certainly didn't leave her hotel room without a stitch of underwear on. Unless a red garter belt counted?

With a sigh, she spritzed cologne at the hollow of her neck, at her wrists and, after a moment of debate, between her thighs. Who was she trying to fool anyway? The best part of wearing this dress was imagining Kevin peeling it off her in a few hours.

A knock sounded at her bedroom door. "Serena, are you ready?" Kevin asked.

"One more minute," she called, reaching for her jewelry bag. She heard Kevin prowling the sitting room of the suite, and she couldn't blame him. She was the one who had insisted they leave early. Really early. He thought she was crazy, but she had plans for the extra ninety minutes. Big plans.

She slipped the pearl necklace her mother had given her for her twenty-first birthday around her neck, grateful that it suited the dress. Her earrings hadn't, and the saleswoman had talked her into spending a lot more than she had planned to on a pair of ruby-and-pearl chandelier earrings that were totally wrong for her.

But they didn't look wrong, she admitted, taking one final glance in the mirror. They made her look sexy and just a little bit wild. Of course, that could also be attributed to the raspberry Jimmy Choos she hadn't needed to be conned into buying. The second she'd laid eyes on the five-inch sequined stilettos, it had been love at first sight. Her feet would be dying by the end of the night, but it would be worth it. No pain was too great for these shoes.

She reached for her purse, started to slip her cell into the small evening clutch. She hesitated, her hand frozen in midair over the small phone. He'd called again, twice while she was shopping and then once more as she was doing her makeup. He'd left messages the first two times, spewing obscenities, demanding to know where she was. By the time she'd accidentally answered his third call, he had calmed down, had tried to keep his voice low and his words sweet. She'd found the attempt at seduction more disturbing than the threats—especially as it had been delivered by a voice so digitally distorted it barely sounded human.

Taking a deep breath, Serena turned toward the door without picking up the phone. She didn't want anything to ruin her night with Kevin, particularly explanations about an obsessed and un-known caller.

With a sigh, she grabbed her wrap and stepped into the sitting area of the suite the Matthias Corporation had booked for Kevin. He was on the balcony, leaning negligently against the iron rails as he watched the boats cruising the bay.

Her nipples peaked at her first sight of him. He'd been gorgeous in dirty jeans and bare feet and even more beautiful naked. But nothing could have prepared her for her first glimpse of his public persona. She'd seen pictures, of course, but they didn't do justice to him. She wasn't sure anything could.

His suit was perfectly fitted—black with a barely visible silver pinstripe. Beneath it he wore a silver silk shirt open at the collar. His glorious hair was pulled back into a short ponytail, and he'd traded his signature gold hoop for a small diamond stud. Her mouth watered.

Telling herself to get a grip on her out-of-control libido, Serena crossed to the open door and murmured, "I'm ready."

"Good." He turned and the look on his face was worth all the damage, and more, that she'd inflicted on her poor, unsuspecting American Express.

Kevin clenched his fists and shoved his hands in his pockets. Tried to turn away, to focus on the ocean view. Anything to keep from grabbing Serena, throwing her on the nearest bed and saying to hell with the museum opening. And to hell with the dedication and gallery opening tomorrow. As good as she looked, there was no way he'd let her out of his bed for the next twenty-four hours. Maybe forty-eight.

Her dress, what there was of it, was red—the same red as her nipples, he thought and then regretted it as he felt himself harden uncontrollably. The top tied behind her neck, halter-style, and bared an amazing amount of her beautiful breasts. He couldn't stop himself from staring and was rewarded when he saw her nipples harden beneath the silk. He wanted to kiss her, to put his mouth over the thin fabric and suck those luscious nipples into his mouth. He wanted to— Kevin cleared his throat, forced his eyes to follow the rest of the dress, though it cost him to look away from her breasts. Of course, the rest of the dress wasn't any better. While it fell straight to just above her knees, it was tight enough to mold every delicious curve. Definitely tight enough to give him a heart attack.

Her hair was tousled, wild, like it was after he'd made love to her. Her eyes were dark and mysterious, her lips a slick red that begged to be kissed. Delicate earrings dangled from her lobes, shivering gently with each breath she took. Layers of pearls circled her throat, enhancing its delicate lines. And the thin ice-pick heels inspired more fantasies than he could give voice to.

"You look—" Amazing, fabulous, sexy as hell. None of the words came out—he was tongue-tied for the first time in his adult life. "Good."

Her eyes narrowed. "I look ... good?"

He licked his dry lips, reached for her with a hand that was far from steady. "Good enough to eat."

Serena's eyes traveled over him, lingering at his broad chest and then at his obvious arousal. "I'm looking forward to it." A quick grin flitted across her lips before she turned to get her camera bag.

His hands itched to touch her and he waged a hard-fought battle to keep them to himself, but he managed to control himself. Barely. Her excuse for a dress was cut all the way down to the top of her ass, leaving her delectable back completely bare. Her golden skin glistened and his mouth actually watered.

To hell with control. He would spontaneously combust if he didn't get his hands on her soon. Placing a hand at the small of her back, he was rewarded by her slight shiver, by the humming awareness that swept between them.

She leaned into him, briefly pressed her body against his as she placed her lips next to his ear. "I want you so bad," she whispered, before turning back to check her equipment.

His whole body tightened, his instincts on red alert as he watched her bend over her camera bag, her glorious ass swinging in rhythm to music only she could hear. He reached for her, determined to feel her body pressed against his, even if only for a minute. Her sudden scream distracted him, and he watched in shock as she shoved her camera bag away and stumbled backward into his arms.

He caught her, and swept her behind him as he looked for the unseen threat. "What's the matter?"

She pointed a shaky finger at the bag. "Sc-scorpion." She took a shuddery breath. "Really big scorpion."

"What?" he demanded incredulously, his eyes sweeping across the carpet surrounding them.

"There's a scorpion in my camera bag!"

He settled her on the couch behind him and reached for the bag. "How'd it get there?" he wondered aloud as he stooped to pick up the bag.

"I don't know, but it's there."

He turned the bag over, shaking its contents gently onto the floor. Then watched, in shock, as two cameras and numerous rolls of film fell to the carpet, followed quickly by the hugest, ugliest scorpion he'd ever seen.

"Kevin!"

"I've got it." He brought his shoe down firmly on the poisonous arachnid, not at all concerned that he was squishing it into the expensive carpet.

When he was sure the thing was dead, he picked up her camera case and shook it vigorously before searching every pocket and compartment thoroughly. Serena remained quiet as he searched, her face pale as she studied the squashed scorpion.

"Where was it?" he asked grimly as he crossed back to her.

"In the side compartment." She shook her head. "I can't imagine how it got in there."

"When's the last time you opened that part of the bag?"

She shrugged. "Yesterday? The day before? I keep extra rolls of film in there, so I'm constantly digging through it."

"Well, I'd love to know where you picked it up," he commented. "There aren't any scorpions in the bayou, so it had to be somewhere here or in one of the airports."

"I don't know." She shook her head again as she began to put her equipment back in the case. "It's barely been out of my sight."

He retrieved a few Kleenexes and picked up the arachnid's remnants as Serena secured her cameras. When she was finished, she picked up her purse and wrap again before asking, "Shall we go?"

"Absolutely." He opened the door with a frown, his gaze still focused on where he'd killed the scorpion. "It could have stung you."

"It was just a random thing, Kevin," she murmured, her hand soft and trembly on his arm. "Right?"

"Yeah, sure." But he couldn't get the image of Serena—poisoned and dying—out of his head.

She seemed to sense his preoccupation and pulled him around until they were standing stomach to stomach, her arms resting lightly around his waist. "Don't let it ruin the night."

He pulled his gaze back to hers with effort. "I wasn't planning to."

"Good." She licked her lips and winked before gliding through the door. " 'Cuz I've got big plans."

His eyes narrowed. He didn't know what her game was, but two could play it, even if he didn't know all the rules. "I can't wait." He followed her, closing the door behind them and double-checking to make sure the latch had caught. He couldn't help grinning as he watched her hips sway as she strolled down the hall.

"Have I mentioned how much I love those shoes on you?"

She glanced over her shoulder, her eyes wide and wicked and more than a little bit aroused. "What's not to love?"

He inclined his head with a grin. That was a sentiment he could definitely get behind.

One of the hotel's limos stood waiting at the curb when they got downstairs, and he helped Serena into it, before settling next to her. "Balboa Park—Museum of Art," he told the driver.

"Actually, the Museum of Photographic Arts," Serena corrected him. "I have a friend who's on exhibit right now. That's why I wanted to leave early—to see Glenn's work."

Kevin felt a brief stab of jealousy, but beat it down mercilessly. What the hell was wrong with him that the mere mention of another guy's name had his stomach tying itself in knots? "You didn't tell me."

She shook her head. "No. I wanted it to be a surprise."

"What kind of surprise?"

"You'll see." Her smile was mysterious, enchanting. And when she slid her small hand into his much larger one, his gut relaxed. It didn't matter how many people Serena had in her past. She was with him now.

"Are you nervous?" she asked.

"About your surprise?" His eyebrows rose inquiringly.

"No." Her mouth twisted impatiently. "About the opening tonight! I'd be a nervous wreck. My own permanent place in a major, world-famous art museum. I can't imagine."

He laughed, though the words were eerily reminiscent of ones Deb had spoken to him years before. "It's not such a big deal."

"It's a very big deal. Maybe not to you, Mr. Big Shot Sculptor, but to the rest of us mere mortals, it's really exciting."

He shrugged, shifting uneasily in his seat. "I guess. It's just always been about the work, you know?"

"Your vision." She smiled into his eyes.

"I know it sounds corny."

"No. You're right. It is all about what you see. But, Kevin, what you see and how you see it is so extraordinary."

"Serena—"

"No. I know you don't want to hear it, but I need to say it. I was impressed, hugely impressed, with your work long before I met you. It's a big part of the reason I took this assignment. But now, having seen you work, I'm awed. Your talent, what you can create, awes me." She squeezed his hand as her eyes gazed steadily into his. "Really."

He swallowed past the sudden lump in his throat, nodded because he didn't know what to say. "Thanks."

She nodded back. "Not that you aren't an incredible pain in the ass when you're working."

He grinned. "That goes without saying."

"Oh, no. No, it doesn't. It is, however, a sentiment that bears repeating."

He gave a fake smile. "Ha-ha, aren't you funny?"

"It's a gift." She winked at him before leaning over and resting her cheek on his chest.

Wrapping his arms around her, he pressed her as close as possible. He loved this new, relaxed Serena, with her easy smiles and loving gestures. She still had moments of darkness, times when she was so far away he despaired of ever reaching her again. Not that he blamed her—if he'd had her life, he doubted that he would have half her courage or grace.

He snorted. Who was he kidding? Even with his relatively normal life, he was no match for her kindness and composure. A curious tightness started in his chest as he held her against him, a tightness that told him more than he wanted to know about his feelings for her.

He was oddly disappointed when the limo glided to a stop a few minutes later, as close as the driver could get them to the Museum of Photographic Arts.

The driver came around to help them out, and Serena listened as Kevin and he debated where and when to meet. As she waited, she studied the Spanish architecture that was so much a part of Balboa Park. Most of the museums were two- or three-story stucco buildings with tile roofs. Flowers and trees abounded, as did sunshine, and Serena drew a deep breath of the cool, clean air into her lungs. The bayou might be Kevin's all-time favorite place, but she loved San Diego, had always promised herself that when her photos really caught on, she would buy a place here to spend half the year. Not that she didn't like Louisiana, but the peace and tranquillity that permeated most of San Diego really appealed to her. Maybe because she'd had so little peace in her own life.

She continued contemplating the building as she took a few deep breaths. Excitement thrummed through her as she thought of what the next hour would bring. Not just a look at her good friend's truly wonderful photos, which was exciting enough on its own. But also something more … stimulating. She looked at Kevin through her lashes as he escorted her past the little coffee stand doing brisk business and into the building.

The contrast between the bright, warm outdoors and the cool darkness of the photography museum took a few moments to get used to. As Serena paused to get her bearings, Kevin reached for his wallet to pay the admission price, but Serena stopped him.

"My surprise, my treat," she said, pulling out a twenty-dollar bill.

Kevin eyed her in surprise. "I don't mind—"

"I do." She squeezed his hand before turning to the elderly woman behind the desk. "Two please."

"I only charged you half price, since we're closing in about forty-five minutes," she was told as the woman gave her more change than she'd expected. "That's why we're just about empty."

Perfect. Tingling with anticipation, Serena tugged Kevin into the main collection room. "Thanks. That's great," she called over her shoulder. "We just want to look around a little."

They strolled through the main gallery, looking at the photos by numerous photographers. Kevin stopped before two photos with artificially bright colors that ran together. "I like these," he murmured, studying the pictures of a street fair. In the first, all the people and booths blurred together in a surreal riot of color with only the perfect sand castles in the distance in focus. The second had the same blurred colorscape, but it focused on the once perfect sand castles being destroyed as children in brightly colored suits ran through them.

He glanced down to see the photographer's name, felt a jolt when he realized they were Serena's. His eyes flew to hers and she shrugged. "My one and only museum pieces."

"They're fabulous. I didn't realize—"

"Didn't realize what?" she teased, dragging him away. "That I actually know what I'm doing?"

"No!" he protested. "Just that—"

She leaned forward and kissed him, effectively shutting down his argument. "Come on. I want to see Glenn's work." She pulled him into one of the smaller rooms off the main one.

It took him a moment to adjust to the near-total blackness in the room, the darkness illuminated only by the small spotlights focused individually on each of the photos on the wall. As his eyes gradually adjusted, he took in the images closest to him. His body stiffened a little more with each frame that he looked at.

He reached out, snagged Serena's hand as she moved away from him. "Exactly what kind of exhibit is this?" he asked.

She grinned slyly, tugging her hand from his. "Glenn specializes in erotic photography."

Kevin sucked air through his teeth as he hardened instantly. He stared at a particularly provocative black-and-white photo of a man on his knees in front of a woman. They were both dressed, but her skirt was hiked up to her waist. And though the camera was angled in such a way that it was impossible to see the details, the look on the woman's face spoke volumes about what was going on.

His overactive libido substituted Serena's gorgeous face and body for the woman's in the photograph, and he felt himself growing harder still. He shifted, trying to make his erection a little less noticeable.

Until he saw the next picture in the series. The same woman was lying on a bed, her dress gone and her thighs spread open as she rested on her elbows. Though her underwear covered as much as a bathing suit, once again it was the look in her eyes that told the story. Last night, Serena had been in just that position. Her beautiful back arched, her gorgeous breasts lifted for his mouth, her silken thighs laid open for him.

A surge of lust hit him so powerfully that he was afraid to move in case he totally lost it. What the hell was wrong with him? He was an artist, had studied erotic art and photography in school and had never reacted to it like this. So why now, when he wanted to be cool and suave, was he reacting like a sex-crazed teenager?

Serena's spicy perfume tempted him almost beyond bearing as she came back to him, reaching out a hand to grasp his. "Do you like?" Her voice was low and teasing.

He cleared his throat, tried not to embarrass himself. "What's not to like?"

"That's what I say," she said with a grin. "Come here, I want to show you my favorites."

She dragged him over to a corner display of three black-and-white photos. The second he was close enough to see, his entire body tightened to the point of agony. The first photo showed a man and a woman in evening clothes. They were running in the rain, and though they had an umbrella, the woman's white dress was plastered to her body, revealing shadows of both her nipples and her pubic hair. In the second photo, the man had her backed up against a brick wall. His body pressed intimately against hers while his hands tangled in her wet hair and his mouth brushed kisses on her neck.

The final photo showed him cupping her ass while she wrapped her legs around his waist. Her skirt was bunched between them, and her head rested against the wall as he sucked her nipple into his mouth. As Kevin stared, wordlessly, at the picture, flashes of Serena in just such a position whirled through his mind. Her beautiful breasts spilling over the top of her dress. Her long, elegant legs wrapped around his waist. Her head thrown back in ecstasy as he pumped into her again and again.

The image was so real he nearly came right there in the middle of the museum. Clearing his throat, Kevin blinked and shook his head, trying desperately to chase the image of Serena in the middle of an orgasm from his mind.

"So, what do you think?" she asked.

"About what?" He didn't turn and look at her, knowing that he'd grab her if he did. Not that looking at the photographs was doing much to calm him down, but he'd take what he could get in a crisis.

She laid her hand on his arm, waited patiently until his eyes met hers. "About the pictures."

He cleared his throat again—a gesture that was getting to be a habit around her. "I like them. Especially the last one. It's very ..." His voice trailed off.

"Sensual?" she asked, her voice dropping to a husky whisper. "Realistic? Arousing?" She stepped closer, glancing down at his very obvious erection as she did.

"Uh, definitely. All of those." He took a step back, his pride smarting over having to retreat from her. But Serena was so into the photos he didn't want to ruin it for her by acting like a total pervert who couldn't handle some really beautiful adult art.

"I think so, too." She moved another step closer to him, her breasts nearly brushing his chest before she turned back to the photos. "I saw them before, right after Glenn finished them. The last one's my favorite too. You can see the passion between them, not just in the obvious sexual position. But in the details.

"See how her hands are on his shoulders? They're not just resting there. They're clinging, the fingers digging in as she arches her lower body against him." Her hands rested on his shoulders, lightly caressing him through his jacket.

"And his hands aren't just grabbing her ass so he can fuck her. Look at him. He's pulling her into him possessively—claiming her as his, branding her with more than just his cock." One hand skimmed down his back to rest firmly on his ass while the other continued to massage his shoulders.

"Look how she's offering herself to him. He isn't just taking— she's giving. See how she's thrusting her breast into his mouth? You can tell that she's begging for more. That she wants his mouth every- where at once." She stepped behind him, thrust her breasts against his back as her hands crept around to his chest, her fingers lightly flicking against his rapidly hardening nipples.

"Her head's thrown back, exposing the slender column of her throat. A totally defenseless position. Her legs are wrapped around him, once again giving him the position of power. She's so vulnerable that he could hurt her, easily. A hand around her throat, a too violent thrust. But he doesn't. He's as vulnerable to her as she is to him." She rested her head against his shoulders and began to stroke his erection through his pants, hand over hand.

Kevin reached down, trapping her hands against him as he thrust helplessly into her cupped palms. He couldn't remember ever being this turned on in his entire life. Each breath burned violently through his lungs. Each beat of his heart thudded painfully in his chest. Each caress of her fingers pulsed through him, until his cock was so hard he felt like it could hammer nails through concrete. Literally.

He thrust one more time against her hands and then stilled. He turned, pulling her into his arms as he lowered his mouth to her ear. "Let's go find the limo," he murmured.

"The limo?" Her eyes were almost as glazed as his.

"I'll die if I'm not inside you. Soon."

She licked her lips, wrapped her arms around his neck and pressed against him. "Here. Now."

"Right now?" He wanted to protest, to tell her all the reasons it was a bad idea. But her words whirled through him, rendering him incapable of rational thought.

She nodded, pulling him into the dark and shadowed corner. "Right now." She opened his belt and unbuttoned his pants. He nearly shouted in ecstasy when his cock sprang free of the confining clothes as her talented fingers slowly lowered his zipper.

But he had to be sure she knew what she was doing, had to be sure she really wanted this. "Serena, we should stop. Go somewhere more private." Though it cost him dearly, he stopped her gentle stroking with his own hands.

"I don't want to." She licked her lips again, pulled him with her as she backed up against the wall.

He pulled back, studied her face. "Are you sure?"

"You worry too much," she murmured, leaning forward and blowing a stream of warm air against his ear. "Touch me." Serena guided his hand under her skirt and up to her hot, wet folds.

His fingers found her, began to stroke her hard, pulsing clit. "You're not wearing any—"

"Nope. Just a garter belt and stockings. Nothing else."

"Damn," he breathed, slipping a finger inside her. "You feel so good."

She moaned low in her throat, arched her hips and pulled him deeper inside of her. "So do you. Now fuck me before I explode."

The vulgar words speared through him, increasing his excitement to a fever pitch. With a groan, he slipped his hands under her ass and lifted her against the wall. His cock pressed urgently against her, wetness already leaking from its head.

"Wait," she cried breathlessly, reaching into the very top of her stocking and pulling out a condom. "You need this."

How could he have forgotten? He moved to take it from her, but she tore the package open with her teeth and slowly, slowly rolled the thin barrier over him. By the time the thing was on, he was desperate for her. With one hard thrust he buried himself to the hilt, loving the feel of her tight, wet muscles around him.

"*Mon Dieu*, Serena. You're wicked." Again and again he pounded into her willing body.

"I know." She pushed against him. "Harder, Kevin. Please. Harder."

Her long legs were locked around him. Her head was thrown back. Her nipple was in his mouth. One hand was wrapped around his shoulders and the other slipped between them to stroke her clit as she pleaded with him. He gave her what she wanted, thrusting harder and deeper than he ever had before.

As he filled her completely, as he pounded into her as hard and as fast as possible, it came to him. He loved this woman. Loved everything about her, from the calm and cool woman she showed the public to the hot-blooded, passionate woman who made love to him better and hotter than anyone ever had. He loved holding her in his arms, loved watching her sleep, loved her strengths and her vulnerabilities.

As the realization of his feelings for her swept through him, so did the urgent need to come. "Serena, *mon amour*," he gasped, "I can't last much—"

With a low, keening cry, she shattered, her muscles milking him until he too let go of his control and came apart in her arms.

When the last shudders passed, Serena rested her forehead against Kevin's. Mission accomplished. She'd set out to seduce him, and she'd done one hell of a job, if she did say so herself. Not that it was exactly difficult. He was the most passionate, responsive man she'd ever known. And while she had never considered doing something like this with any other man, with Kevin it felt right.

She sighed, allowed herself to drift as Kevin stroked her hair and pressed soft kisses against her forehead, her cheeks, her neck. "I could stay like this forever," she murmured.

"Me, too, *cher*. Me, too." But as Kevin was speaking, the lights blinked, warning visitors of the museum's impending closure. With a sigh of regret, he lifted Serena's dress back into place before settling her on the ground.

She reached up and stroked a finger over his mouth. "I love the way you make me feel."

He closed his eyes, breathed in her intoxicating scent. He wanted to pour his heart out, to tell her of the riot of feelings bouncing around inside of him. But it wasn't the time, and some vulnerable part of him he had thought long dead shied away from telling her too much, too soon. He settled for a flip "I love the way you feel, too," and leaned down to kiss her again.

"Sssh." She put a hand to his mouth. "Do you hear something?"

He listened for a moment and a huge grin split his face. The staccato tap of heels echoed in the room, as heels clicked in the hallway leading to the erotic photo exhibit. "Someone's coming."

"Shit!" Serena tried frantically to make herself presentable, shoving her breasts back into her dress as fast as possible. Kevin laughed, but moved to shield her with his body even as he buttoned and zipped his own pants.

"Not so collected now, are you?" he teased as she shoved her fingers through her well-tousled hair.

"Shut up," she answered with narrowed eyes. "Or this will be the last time I surprise you."

That wiped the grin off his face, she noted with satisfaction. Taking a deep breath—something she seemed to be doing a lot of lately—she turned to face the docent headed their way, a serene smile firmly in place.

"We were just leaving," she called out, grabbing Kevin's Armani-clad arm and pulling him toward the front of the exhibit.

"Wonderful," said the woman as she ushered them out. "Did you enjoy it?"

Kevin glanced at Serena, a mischievous smile lighting his face. "Did we, *cher*?"

"Oh, absolutely," she answered, stepping on Kevin's foot as she moved in front of him. "It was fabulous."

"I'm so glad. I just wish you had had more time. Normally, we're not sticklers on the closing time, but I've got tickets to a fabulous exhibit opening over at the Museum of Art tonight. I'm very excited."

"The Kevin Riley exhibit?" Serena asked, ignoring Kevin's sudden grip on her arm.

"That's the one. He's simply brilliant, isn't he? Though I hear he's a bit of a recluse."

"Brilliant," Serena echoed, tongue-in-cheek. "But a recluse? Not at all. In fact—"

"In fact, we're going to the same place ourselves," Kevin quickly interrupted. "Maybe we'll see you there?"

The woman looked startled. "That would be splendid." She leaned in closer. "But do you mind if I ask how you got the tickets?

I had to pull in every favor I've ever given anyone just to get one."

"Oh, that's easy," said Serena, jerking her head toward Kevin. "He knows the artist." And with a wink for Kevin, she headed jauntily down the stairs.

Chapter Ten

Groaning with frustration, Serena studied the long, hard surface of the building. She wanted a background shot for the book cover—maybe—of where Kevin's newest private sculpture was being installed. But she couldn't get the shot right.

She lowered her camera and studied the imposing steel-and-glass structure in front of her. The Matthias Building was one of the most beautifully designed modern buildings in the U.S.—nearly as recognizable as the Empire State Building or the Sears Tower. She wanted to capture that legacy, along with the admiration and awe the powerful lines of the building inspired.

She'd deliberately waited until this time of day, when the sun was at its highest, because she wanted the dramatic contrast of the building with its shadow. No ordinary picture for this extraordinary structure—she hoped to use the darkness of the shadows to highlight the shocking architecture of this icelike palace.

But she'd been through three rolls of film, and she hadn't gotten what she wanted. No matter what angle she tried or what position she contorted her body into, she couldn't get it exactly right. There was no tingle of awareness, no shiver along her spine telling her that she'd taken the *perfect* picture. Like Kevin with his sculptures, she instinctively knew when a picture was right—even before she'd developed it.

With a weary sigh, Serena sank cross-legged onto a street-side bench, pushing her sweat-soaked hair out of her eyes. San Diego was known for its mild weather, and ten months a year the reputation was well-deserved. But the end of August and the beginning of September were brutal. Not Louisiana brutal, but not particularly comfortable for anyone lugging camera equipment around under the hot sun for two hours either. She was tempted to forget the image in her head and go back into the air-conditioned building. Kevin would be in the middle of installing his truly magnificent sculpture, his truly magnificent body twisted into any number of attractive contortions as he built, nailed and hammered it into place.

A pleasant ache started between her thighs as she imagined Kevin bent over with his incredible ass in the air. What would he do if she walked up and squeezed it before moving on to even more interesting body parts?

Probably bite her hand off. While he was usually more than willing to let her touch him anyway and anytime she wanted, Kevin had a tendency to be downright prickly where his work was involved. Unless you counted museum openings as part of his work.

Her eyes drifted shut as she remembered just how many times she had come the night before. While the photography museum had been truly inspired—and she was taking full credit for that—Kevin had more than matched her in creativity and enthusiasm.

He'd fingered her in the Impressionist room, so long and so well that she'd come three times and hadn't been able to walk for a good ten minutes afterward. He'd lured her into the second-floor conference room and taken her from behind, despite her fear of discovery. She'd had to bite her lip hard enough to draw blood to keep from screaming his name as he'd pounded into her again and again. And when they gotten to the limo, he'd instructed the driver to give her a tour of the city, but she didn't see much at all during the journey. The second the doors closed, Kevin dropped to his knees and went down on her for the entire ride—she'd lost count of how many times she'd climaxed by the time the car finally pulled into the hotel's driveway.

Serena's nipples peaked and she grew wet. Not for the first time, she wondered what Kevin had done to her. She never acted like this, never had sex in public—let alone twice in one day. And while she had a very healthy fantasy life, her sex life had been somewhat lacking before she'd met him. Though she'd dated, she had trouble lowering her guard enough to really enjoy sex, always worried about maintaining control of herself and her environment. Always frightened of trusting a man enough to be vulnerable in his presence. That was a fear Kevin blasted out of the water, at least when they were in bed together. Or anywhere else, for that matter—as long as some part of him was inside some part of her.

A cloud moved across the sky, momentarily obscuring the sun, and Serena shivered despite herself as her thoughts turned bleakly away from Kevin. She'd done a good job of ignoring everything but work and her new lover, but Damien was always there in the back of her mind. Especially when she could have sworn she'd caught a glimpse of his brother at the gallery opening last night. But when she'd turned to look, Michael was gone and it was easier to put it down to paranoia than to try to deal with it.

Except the uneasiness was back. The hair at the back of her neck was standing straight up as a chill that had nothing to do with the weather crept down her spine.

Someone was watching her.

But when she looked around, turning in a circle to cover all the angles, none of the people on the street or the benches were paying her the slightest bit of attention. She shook her head ruefully as her nervousness turned to embarassment. She was a grown woman of almost thirty—when the hell was she going to stop jumping at shadows?

Better to focus on Kevin and the fact that he made her happier than she'd been in the last eleven years. It was a happiness tempered by guilt—she couldn't do anything about that. After all, how was she supposed to feel about finding contentment when her sister's murderer was free? How could she enjoy her life when Sandra was dead?

She'd spent more than ten years living in a kind of penitential limbo—trying to gain some kind of forgiveness for living while her twin had died—and though she knew it wasn't healthy, she wasn't sure she was willing to let those feelings go. Who was she kidding? She wasn't sure she was *able* to let the guilt go. How could she just forget Sandra and move on with her life like nothing had ever happened?

Deep in thought, Serena glanced up at the Matthias Building, and everything inside of her froze for a moment. This was it. This was the picture she wanted. Not the shadows cast by a brilliant sun, but those cast by one dwarfed with clouds. Here was the mystery and the awe. She groped for her camera, brought it to her face and shot. Again and again. But the angle wasn't quite right so she stood and backed up, step by step, frame by frame, until she had what she wanted.

She took the picture, wound the film, took another one, oblivious to everything but her art and the satisfaction rushing through her. This was it. She knew it. She snapped another picture.

"Serena, look out!" She was so focused that Kevin's voice invaded her consciousness slowly, despite its urgency. A scream sounded behind her, and suddenly she was flying through space, Kevin's arms hard around her. He twisted in midair so that he took the brunt of the fall, and then she was on the pavement, struggling to take a breath into lungs that had totally shut down on impact.

He was shaking so badly he could barely hold the steering wheel. That had been stupid. Irresponsible. Weak, when he knew better than to show the slightest hint of weakness.

He didn't know what had come over him. This was supposed to be a simple recon mission. Gather information. Observe Serena and the bayou rat. Make plans to get close to her. But his first sight of her had driven all those plans out of his head. Rage—burning hotter than any he'd ever felt before—had coursed through him as he re-membered how she'd looked last night.

She'd been gorgeous—the most beautiful woman in the room. Sparkling so brightly that she'd overshadowed every other woman there. And it had all been for him. The insult, the disgust, was almost more than he could bear. She'd been so wrapped up in that laborer that she'd hardly known anyone else was in the room. And worse, she'd let him touch her—right there, in the open, where anyone could see.

They'd thought they were alone, had thought they'd succeeded in sneaking away from the crowd. But he'd seen them ... and fol-lowed.

Sweat beaded on his brow, then rolled down his cheek as he re-membered how she'd looked straddling that bench. Her legs spread and her fucking beautiful cunt wide open to his starving eyes. How he'd wanted to grab her, to thrust his huge, pulsing dick inside of her and fuck her until she begged him to stop.

But he hadn't done it, couldn't bear to think of fucking her when she stank of another man. Because she'd been spread for his benefit. The filthy rat had had his disgusting fingers inside of her, right there under the priceless Monets that hung in the Impressionist room. It had been Riley who had whispered obscenities in her ear, Riley who had held her while she came again and again. Her skin flushing pink, her cunt clenching around him and glistening with the power of her release.

The pain hit him hard and fast, so fast that he nearly blacked out before he could temper it. Only the loud honking of the cars next to him as he swerved into the right lane kept him conscious. With effort—great effort—he blocked out the pain and focused, once again, on righting the car and getting back to the hotel safely.

He concentrated on his breathing. Slow, deep breaths. Even breaths. One after the other. Again and again and again until he got the anger—and the pain—under control. Control was the secret. Control kept him sane.

He pulled into valet parking, stumbled into the hotel without waiting for one of the valets to hand him a ticket. Just a little farther. A few more steps to get to the elevator. A few floors to get to his suite. He could make it. Losing control in front of all these people wasn't an option.

He lumbered into the elevator, counting the seconds as it sped toward the fifteenth floor. He lurched out, shuffling down the hall until he all but fell against the door. He fumbled for his card, slid it in the lock and then he was inside. Safe. Free.

Whimpering, he careened toward the bar, where he grabbed his pill bottle. He wrenched it open and the pills spilled everywhere, but he didn't care. He grabbed a handful and tossed them back with a few large swallows of the Glenlivit Scotch sitting on the bar.

Then he threw back his head and howled, the pain in his head— the agony of Serena's betrayal—searing through him until oblivion, blessed oblivion, came and he slumped, unconscious, on the gray carpet.

She could see Kevin's concerned face, could hear the sound of tires squealing in the background and excited chatter coming from the rapidly gathering crowd, but she couldn't respond. Eyes wide, hands clenched into fists, she focused entirely on trying to take a breath. Seconds that felt like minutes passed before she finally could. She gasped, hand to her chest, as she greedily sucked in air, relishing the feel of her lungs inflating.

When she was finally able to speak, Serena asked, "What happened? Why did you hit me like that?"

"Hit you?" Kevin stared at her, incredulous. "That car nearly killed you. It was tackle you or watch the coroner's office peel you off the sidewalk!"

He pulled her into his arms, his heart beating frantically against hers. He'd never been as scared in his entire life as when he'd seen the green SUV careen onto the curb and head straight for Serena. What if it had hit her? he asked himself again and again. What if she had died before he'd gotten the chance to tell her that he loved her?

He knew that he should get up, check her for injuries, see if anyone had gotten the license plate of the car before it had sped off. Damn drunk driver. But he couldn't move. Serena felt so good, so right, in his arms. So safe when only moments before he'd been sure he would lose her.

What if he hadn't stepped outside to check on her? What if he'd been so absorbed with his work that he'd forgotten all about her? What if he'd lost her before he ever really had the chance to have her?

Kevin ran shaking hands over her body, searching for injury. "Are you all right?" he asked, again and again, as he kissed her hair, her face, her neck. "*Mon Dieu, bébé*, I almost lost you. I almost lost you."

The frantic beating of his heart finally got through to her and she pulled away. "What happened?" she asked again as people began to crowd around them.

"I saw the whole thing." A man in a navy suit stepped forward and helped the two of them to their feet. "It was like that guy was aiming for her."

"Aiming for her?" Kevin stared at him blindly as scenarios played out in his head.

"Yeah," agreed a blond woman who had retrieved Serena's camera cases and her now-smashed Nikon. "It didn't look like he'd lost control. It looked like he spotted her and hit the gas. I think he jumped the curb on purpose."

"I couldn't get the license plate," commented the first man. "I tried to write it down, but both were almost completely covered in mud. I can describe the car, however."

"Thanks," commented Kevin, watching Serena take her camera from the other woman. She didn't say a word, but her sorrow was palpable as she cradled the Nikon in her hands.

"Come on, *chere*. Let me get you settled inside and then I'll call the police."

Her eyes were little-girl lost as she looked at him. "Police?" she asked, as if things weren't adding up.

"Yes, police," he answered firmly, ushering her through the dispersing crowd. "Look at this." He gestured to the mess around them.

Serena looked beyond Kevin for the first time, turning white as she did. The bench she had been sitting on minutes before was crushed, as was one of the huge wooden planters filled with flowers that the Matthias Corporation took care of. Her notebook was torn and muddy, and one of her shoes, which had flown off when Kevin tackled her, had black tire marks across its smashed sole.

She stared at the once-white mule in morbid fascination. "That could have been me," she said, taking a step closer to Kevin as things began to sink in.

"Why do you think I'm so shaken up, *bébé*?" he demanded, pulling at his hair as frustration welled up inside of him. "You scared the hell out of me."

Before he could say another word, two police cars pulled up, sirens blaring. "It looks like someone already called the police," Serena commented, absently running a hand through her hair. She felt naked, exposed.

"I did," commented the man who had helped her to her feet. "As soon as it happened."

"Thank you." She studied the policemen as they made their way past the destruction, obviously looking for the people involved. Panic crawled through her and she desperately wanted to run and hide. She didn't want to talk to them, didn't want to remember the last time she'd had to deal with the police.

Kevin must have sensed her trepidition, for he placed a soothing hand at the small of her back. She closed her eyes briefly and squared her shoulders as he called the cops over to them. She could do this. Really, she could. If her knees would just stop shaking.

Taking a deep breath, she slipped her mask into place. This wasn't about Sandra, she reminded herself. This was about a stupid accident. And the sooner she got this done, the sooner she could move on with her day. Kevin's day.

Serena made it through the questioning in a kind of daze, her mind jumping from the present to the past, despite all her attempts to stay focused. Kevin never left her side, answered most of the questions for her, and generally lent her as much support as he was able to.

She'd never felt more cosseted—or more undeserving. This was Kevin's big day and she should be the one supporting him. Instead, he was the one lending his strength to her. It was an occurrence that was becoming depressingly regular and she couldn't help hating how one-sided their relationship seemed to be. She was the needy one; he was the strong one. For a woman who'd always prided herself on her ability to take care of herself, it was a bitter pill to swallow.

After the cops finally left, Kevin ushered her into a side office that Richard Matthias had given him the use of for the day. The security people were still milling around, but he firmly shut the door in their faces. Serena needed a little quiet time and so did he. He still couldn't get the image of the green SUV bearing down on her out of his mind.

With very little fuss he managed to get her settled into a large wing-back chair. She barely seemed to notice, so lost was she in a world of her own. He found himself frightened all over again, as he took her ice-cold hands in his. It was as if she wasn't there. He could feel her hands in his, see her body in front of him, but her mind was far away and he didn't know if he would be able to reach her.

"Serena, *mon coeur*, look at me." Her eyes remained hazy and unfocused. "*Mon Dieu, bébé*, you're scaring me. Look at me. Please look at me." He pressed his lips to hers, shocked by their iciness.

She pulled away, lifted a hand to his cheek. "I'm fine, Kevin. The police, the questions. It just makes me remember—"

"I know, *cher*." He settled into the chair across from hers, then pulled her into his lap and cradled her as he would a child. "I wish it hadn't needed to be like that."

She shrugged. "I don't know why it bothered me so much. I'm not usually such a ..." Such a what? she asked herself. Idiot? Basket case? Psycho? "Honestly, Kevin, you're seeing me at my worst."

His strong artist's fingers brushed her cheek and his lips skimmed lightly over her hair. "And here I've thought it was your best. You're doing fine, Serena. Better than fine."

"I'm never like this, Kevin. Why now?"

"Because you almost died today? Because your sister's murderer's on the streets? Because you can't carry the world on your shoulders all the time?"

She stiffened against him. "I don't want to talk about Sandra."

"I hadn't intended to. But why not? Why won't you talk about your sister? You'll never get past the pain if you don't."

"You don't know what you're talking about."

"I know that you've tortured yourself for ten years over something you had no control over. I know you're so caught up in the past that you can't see the present. Or the future."

Serena went ramrod stiff against him, pulling away to stare at him with injured eyes. "How can you say that to me?"

He looked her in the eyes. "Because I care about you. A lot more, apparently, then you do about yourself."

"That's not true. I've moved on with my life! I don't talk about Sandra to anyone—except you. I don't wallow in self-pity. I don't—" Her voice broke and silent tears streamed down her face.

Compassion moved through him as he continued to stroke her hair, refusing to let Serena leave him despite her struggles. "There's nothing wrong with discussing what happened to Sandra."

"I know that! I think about it all the time."

"You dwell on it," he corrected. "You blame yourself for not stopping it. You hold your feelings inside until you're ready to shatter. I'm afraid one day you will."

She pushed against him, eyes blazing as a sense of betrayal choked her. "And I should do what? Wear my feelings on my sleeve? Throw them around for everyone to see? Hide out in the bayou instead of living my life?"

"I'm not hiding out there," Kevin answered smoothly. "I love it. It's home. But you—you hide wherever you go, *bébé*. With your perfect manners and your buttoned-up shirts, you hide the real Serena behind a mask. That's not healthy."

"We've known each other two weeks, and you presume to tell me what's healthy?" Her eyes turned cold and she withdrew into her protective shell. He was seriously beginning to hate that shell.

He grabbed her and pulled her back against him, ignoring her resistance. "I know you." His fingers dug into her shoulders as he forced her to look at him. "I know you're scared of losing control. I know you ache every day because of what happened to Sandra. I know this parole hearing has ripped you apart."

He stroked her cheek, ran a hand down her back to anchor her body against his. "But I also know that you are so much stronger than you think you are. If you let the emotions go, you aren't going to shatter." He pulled back, looked into her eyes. "You've got to give yourself a break, *cher*. You're so incredibly strong. You've got to be strong enough to bend, before you end up destroying yourself with guilt."

Serena stared straight ahead, hoping to block out Kevin's words. But they made sense and they worked their way, insidiously, into her consciousness. "I can't."

"Yes, you can." His voice was firm, implacable.

"I'm not like you, Kevin. I'm not brave. I do care what others think of me. I do care about my career and the future and what I'll do if nobody likes my work."

"I'm not asking you to be like me. I like you the way you are." He tilted her chin up, made her look at him again. "And you are very brave."

She moved to protest, but he stopped her. "I can't believe how brave you are. I couldn't do what you do. I couldn't wake up every morning and function despite the pain. I couldn't go to that parole hearing and dredge up a past I despised. I couldn't control myself when anger threatened to rip me apart."

He pressed a soothing kiss to her forehead. "You are so incredibly courageous, Serena. How can you not see that? How can you not take the next step and allow yourself to begin to heal? How much penance do you think you need to do? Eleven years is long enough to torture yourself."

Her voice was rusty when she spoke. "I was there. I let him in."

"And if you hadn't, she would have gone running after him. You know that." She tried to look away, but he refused to let her. "You have to stop blaming yourself. You're letting the actions of one sadistic bastard rule your life. Hasn't he taken enough from you? It's time to stop letting him take your self-respect."

She shuddered, leaned into him. "I can't stand knowing that he's free while my sister's stuck in some cold, rotting tomb. I can't stand the idea of running into him somewhere—at a party, a wedding, the supermarket. If I don't have control of myself, I'll lose it completely."

"No, you won't. You'd never give him the satisfaction." Kevin leaned down, kissed her gently. "I know your sister's death will always be a part of you. I know you'll never let it go. But you can't let it destroy you anymore. You have to care for yourself, take some time to heal."

"I don't know if I can."

"Then let me help."

Her eyes flew to his, startled. "You?"

His stomach clenched, but he ignored it. "Yes, me. I'm not going anywhere, Serena. This isn't just until you've got enough shots of me for the stupid book."

"I thought ..."

"You thought what?" His eyebrows rose imperiously.

"I thought you wouldn't want ..." She struggled to find an answer he wouldn't think offensive.

"Wouldn't want what? Wouldn't want you? I want you so much I couldn't sleep the days you were gone. I want you so much my hands ache when they can't touch you."

She moved to interrupt, but he silenced her with a finger against her lips. She looked so shocked that doubts began to assail him. Had he read her completely wrong? Was she just killing time with him? Using him like Deb had?

But Serena wasn't like that. He closed his eyes for a minute, saw again the joy on her face last night as she stood surrounded by various pieces of his work. He remembered the light in her eyes when she photographed him, the passion between them as they made love. No, she wasn't using him.

Serena was as serious about him as he was about her, whether she knew it or not. Now it was just a matter of treading carefully until she reached the same conclusions he'd already drawn. He reached up, stroked a hand through her hair. "I know it's only been a couple of weeks. I know it's too soon to talk about the future. But you need to understand that this isn't casual. I won't let you walk away from me when this book is done."

Serena stared at him for a minute, the room totally silent except for the ticking of the clock hanging on the wall near the door. Kevin was asking for a lot, for more than she'd ever been willing to give. When she was with a guy—which wasn't that often, she admitted ruefully—she was always careful of the ground rules. Keep things hot in bed and cool everywhere else. Remember that the relationship won't last. Keep it casual.

From the very beginning, Kevin had blown that credo out of the water. Cooking her breakfast after she'd freaked out, holding her when she'd cried, making love to her until she screamed. None of those actions were casual.

Panic rushed through her, making her stomach clench and her head hurt. What was she supposed to do about him? He was a good man, surprisingly good. But there wasn't room in her life for a serious relationship.

Why not? an insidious voice inside her head cried out. Why can't you be with him? He's right. You can't wallow in guilt forever.

Sandra's dead, she answered the voice.

But you're not.

Taking a deep, shuddering breath, she concentrated on counting to ten as she exhaled slowly. This was getting her nowhere, getting *them* nowhere. Kevin's thing started in—she glanced at the clock—fifteen minutes and she didn't even know if he'd finished installing the sculpture. She'd been so numb when he ushered her through the lobby that she wouldn't have seen a nuclear warhead sitting there.

"We need to go," she told him.

"Go where?" he demanded.

She gestured toward the lobby. "Your presentation."

"Screw my presentation. I want to finish this."

She sighed heavily. "Kevin—"

A knock sounded on the door and she grabbed onto it like a lifeline. Serena rushed across the room and threw the door open, and was surprised to see her agent standing on the other side.

"Steve! What are you doing here?" She stretched to kiss his cheek, leaning into his wiry, compact body for a quick hug.

"I wouldn't miss Kevin's big day, luv." His clipped British accent always made her smile. It seemed so incongruous coming from such a flamboyant man. Today he was wearing bright orange, a color that should have clashed horribly with his red hair but somehow looked just right. Of course, the orange shirt *was* tucked into a pair of khakis, making the combination downright conservative for Steve.

"Kevin, the sculpture looks magnificent!" Steve commented, reaching out to shake his hand. "After ten years, I still can't understand how you can design something so exquisitely perfect."

"You're just glad I can, right?" Kevin answered, a wolfish smile on his face.

"Damn straight. You Yanks always know how to hit the nail on the head." He glanced at his watch. "But what are you two doing, cowering in here? I expected Rena and her favorite camera to be all over that incredible structure out there."

"We're running a little behind."

He rolled his eyes. "You're always running a little behind, Kevin. Out of choice, not necessity. But I expected better of my best girl. Serena, darling, what's happened to you? You look quite a mess and you aren't brandishing the whip very well over Kevin, now, are you, my girl?"

"Serena was nearly killed today," Kevin interrupted before she could say anything. "A car jumped the curb and almost hit her."

"Serena!" Concern replaced humor in Steve's eyes as he crossed to her. "Are you all right?" he demanded, running his hands over her arms as he checked her visually for any damage.

"I'm fine, really." She glared at Kevin over their agent's shoulder. All she needed was Steve in full mother-hen mode. "All the bumps and bruises I have are from Kevin tackling me."

He shrugged. "I did save your life."

She snorted. "You busted my favorite camera. Not to mention ruined the absolutely fabulous pictures inside of it."

"Such is life, *bébé*. At least you still have one."

"Children, children," Steve interjected, a fascinated smirk on his face. "However enjoyable I find this, Kevin needs to be changed and ready to go in"—he checked his watch—"five minutes. Which means the two of you need to hustle."

"I am ready." Kevin shrugged as they both turned incredulous looks on him. "You know I'm not big on these things, Steve."

"I know. But you still need to look presentable. At the moment you look like a cross between happy construction worker and crazed serial killer." His eyes narrowed as Kevin snorted. "But not to worry. I brought you a change of clothes." He tossed Kevin his briefcase.

Kevin eyed Steve's colorful ensemble with a sneer. "I don't think so."

"But I do. And I'm always right." Steve turned to Serena, winked at her fascinated expression. "I figured you would look fabulous in a nice hot pink—"

"No way!" Kevin's roar was outraged.

Steve sighed hugely. "But, alas, I know you. So everything in the bag is black. Now be a good boy and put the clothes on. You have exactly three minutes, and if you're ready in time, I'll even throw in a couple of Twinkies." Steve reached in his pocket and pulled out three of the snack cakes.

Kevin glared furiously for a moment, his eyes alternating between the Twinkies and Steve's face. Serena was sure that he'd tell Steve exactly what he could do with the clothes in the most impolite manner possible. She found out how wrong she was when Kevin simply heaved a sigh of disgust and began undressing.

Steve flashed a satisfied grin at Serena, whose mouth had fallen open in shock. Kevin never let anyone tell him what to do, yet he'd barely put up a fight with Steve.

"How did you do that?" she whispered, as Steve crossed to her and began straightening her collar.

"Magic, luv. Pure magic."

"I guess."

"And I keep him on a very short leash."

"I heard that!" Kevin pulled the fine silk T-shirt over his head and tucked it into the linen trousers Steve had picked out for him. "Can we go now?" he asked in an aggrieved tone.

"As soon as you put on your new shoes, we can," Steve answered.

Kevin eyed the black loafers in disgust. "I don't do preppy shoes."

Steve opened a Twinkie. Took a bite. "You do today."

Serena watched, fascinated, as Kevin snarled at their agent. Right before he put on the shoes.

Chapter Eleven

Kevin pulled off his tie, sinking gratefully into the relative comfort of the hotel room sofa as he did. He put his feet up, closed his eyes and spent a few minutes just soaking in the quiet. Silence was his favorite sound, he decided, as he studied the paint swirls on the ceiling above his head. Or at least his second favorite. His absolute favorite was the incredible noises Serena made as she came—high, breathless sounds that made him hard just thinking about them.

Serena. His heart beat faster at the thought of her. He'd only known her a couple of weeks, yet the thought of returning to his life without her held no appeal. The privacy and solitude that he craved—that inspired him—seemed empty without her. Self-indulgent. Lonely.

What the hell was he going to do when she left?

And she *was* going to leave. He had seen it in her face when they'd talked this afternoon. He could feel it in the distance that was suddenly between them. He knew that he'd scared her with his talk of permanence, but he hadn't been able to hold it inside any longer. He didn't know where they were going, didn't know where they'd end up. But he knew he wanted to try to build something with Serena. For the first time since Deborah left him, he felt something for a woman. And what he felt for Serena made his feelings for Deb seem like child's play.

Tonight hadn't been nearly as bad as he'd expected. It hadn't been good—particularly with Steve prodding him every ten seconds, expecting him to jump through hoops for the art patrons who'd shown up. More than once he'd been ready to tell Steve to go to hell, but then Serena would touch him. A hand on his shoulder, an arm around his waist, a kiss on his cheek. She calmed him without even trying, relaxed him in an environment that usually set his teeth on edge.

Not that he was dying to go to another opening anytime soon, but at least he'd made it through this one without incident. Something, Steve had joked, that would go into the record books. He smiled briefly, remembering his last gallery show. A group of patrons had been standing around discussing the meaning behind two of his sculptures and doing a piss-poor job of it. He'd finally had enough and told them in no uncertain terms how stupid and unimaginative he thought their interpretations were before knocking a full champagne tray to the floor and storming out of the gallery.

His smile widened. Steve had had to do a lot of cleanup on that one, which, in his mind, made the whole thing even sweeter. The fact that more than fifty pieces had sold that night just proved what he'd been saying all along—it really was all about the art. Nobody cared if he was suave and sophisticated or brash and backward. The art was the important thing.

But there had been no such outbursts tonight—no flaring tempers, no need to escape. Serena had calmed him, centered him, and he'd found himself, if not enjoying his time at the gallery, then at least tolerating the forced interaction with others.

The water in the adjoining bathroom stopped running, and his entire body tightened with anticipation. He might have Serena for only a little while longer, but he was going to put every minute of that time to good use. She'd seduced him last night—now it was his turn to return the favor.

He got up and dimmed the lights. Lit the candles he'd asked room service to deliver. Answered the knock at the door indicating that their late-night snack had arrived. He tipped the waiter and ushered him out of the room just as Serena opened the bathroom door, wrapped in a brown silk robe he'd never seen before.

Her dark chocolate eyes found his across the shadowy room and clung, watching him as she tightened the robe's sash around her waist. She looked ... nervous, he decided. Good. He liked knowing that he unsettled her, that he could break through her cool reserve without even trying.

"Champagne?" he asked, reaching for the open bottle behind him.

Her eyes widened as she saw the table that room service had set up. "Where did that come from?" she asked.

"Steve's not the only one who can work a little magic." He filled a champagne flute before holding it out to her. "Are you hungry?"

"Starved." She accepted the glass, her body brushing against his as she reached for a strawberry. "It's been a long day."

"Tell me about it." He grabbed the lapels of her robe, pulled her close for a kiss. Their lips met, clung. What he'd intended to be sweet turned wild in an instant.

Serena moaned and pressed tightly against Kevin as her body ignited. No one ever made her feel the way he did. No one even came close. He'd shaken her up with his earlier talk of the future, but she was sure she could get around him. Convince him that the present was the only place that mattered. Talk him into enjoying what they had as long as they had it.

His lips sipped tenderly from hers. His tongue lightly stroked her bottom lip. His hands slid gently over her back, afraid of pressing too hard on the bruises that had formed on her delicate skin.

"Thank you," she murmured against his mouth.

"For what?" His lips skimmed across her forehead, over her cheek, down her neck.

"For saving my life. For holding me when I fell apart. For taking such good care of me."

"I'll always take care of you, *bébé*. *Je t'aime*. I love you."

Serena shook her head, shut out the incredible sweetness of his words. Unable to answer Kevin, she returned his sentiments in the only way she could. Pulling his mouth back to hers, she nibbled his upper lip before sliding her tongue against his. And in an instant, what she had intended to be fast and frenzied turned soft and sweet.

Moaning low in her throat, she closed her eyes against the sudden, insistent sting of tears. She took a deep breath and inhaled his familiar musky scent. She licked her lips and tasted him there. Reached out her hands and felt his smooth skin, his hard muscles. How could she walk away when the book was done? How could she give him up when all she wanted to do was hold on forever?

But happiness was fleeting and there was no guarantee on human life. She'd learned that lesson early and well. Determined to enjoy the time they had left, she slowly unbuttoned Kevin's shirt before pushing it off his shoulders.

Her head dipped and she traced the strong lines of his chest with her tongue. Kevin groaned, fisted a hand in her hair and tugged her face up to meet his.

"Tonight we do it my way." He traced the soft outer shell of her ear. Ran his tongue over the hollows of her throat. Skimmed his lips over her chest until he found one ripe raspberry nipple and pulled it into his mouth.

Serena's knees went weak. Her hands fisted in his hair and she arched her back, offering him everything that she had, everything that she was. To hell with the future and to hell with the consequences. She wanted him, needed him, and for this brief moment of time, he was hers.

Kevin eased her onto the bed, untying her robe as she went so that she was bared to him. He stretched out beside her but didn't touch her. Serena moved restlessly, frustrated and aroused nearly beyond reason. He was close enough that she could feel his breath against her cheek, but whenever she turned toward him, he moved just a little farther away.

"Kevin!" She sounded petulant, demanding, but couldn't stop herself. Her breasts throbbed and her inner thighs ached. She wanted him to take away the pain.

"Serena!" The word was low, mocking and his voice was filled with laughter. "Do you want something?"

"Yes." She reached a hand toward him, but once again he moved beyond her grasp.

"What do you want?"

"You know." She kept her voice low and her eyes averted.

"I don't." He waited until her eyes lifted to meet his. "Why don't you tell me?"

"Kevin!"

He skimmed his lips over her shoulder, then pulled away abruptly. "What do you want, Serena?" His voice was hoarser than it had been, but she was too aroused to notice.

Rising on her elbows, she glared at him with hot eyes. "You! I want you." Her eyes narrowed as she rubbed her leg against him. "But that could change at any second."

He merely laughed at her threat, and for a moment she was afraid her concession hadn't been enough. But then he leaned over her and licked a slow, hot path from her collarbone to her navel. She gasped, arched up, clutched at him desperately. He laughed again, and her stomach tightened as the sound vibrated over her abdomen. "Somehow I doubt that," he murmured, continuing his trail from her belly button to the top of her well-trimmed pubic hair.

Serena wailed his name before she could stop herself. "Fuck me. Please fuck me." The words poured out unbidden.

"How?" he asked. His mouth was hot against her, his tongue poised over her clit.

Her hips arched involuntarily, and she gasped with relief as his tongue swept over her. Once, twice. He pulled away and she nearly sobbed with disappointment.

"You didn't answer me, Serena. *How* do you want me to fuck you?" His voice was an aroused growl, and she took solace in knowing that she was driving him nearly as crazy as he was driving her.

"You know." She wanted to beg, but some vestige of pride prevented it.

"Tell me anyway." He leaned over her, his blue eyes burning bright. "Where do you want my cock?" He ran his tongue over her suddenly dry lips. "In your mouth?" he asked, before licking his way to her breasts. "Between your tits?"

She whimpered, bucked against him as her need shot out of control. "Yes," she gasped. "Yes!"

He straddled her, his eyes gleaming. "But I haven't finished listing your choices." He kissed her breasts, drew first one nipple and then the other into his mouth as his talented fingers rubbed teasingly over her breasts.

He rolled her over, worked his way down her spine, one delicious lick at a time. Without warning, his teeth sank into her ass, nipping her before his tongue soothed away the sting. Straddling her, he grabbed a wrist in each hand, spread-eagling her body before she knew what was happening, holding her in place while he explored every inch of her back.

"Is this what you want?" His black-magic voice was darker, more seductive than usual, as he traced the line of her ass teasingly. "Do you want it here?"

He followed the line around until he found her, hotter and wetter than she'd ever been. He pulled her onto her knees, slid his hand under her to get better access to the slick, hidden folds, his fingers running back and forth against her slit over and over again. Dipping inside just enough to make her crazy, rubbing her inner lips just hard enough to have her gasping for breath and pressing back against him.

"This is what you want, isn't it, *bébé*? You want me right here, between your thighs." He thrust one finger inside of her hard, followed it with another and another. Her inner muscles clutched at the fingers greedily, and Serena screamed in pleasure.

"You feel so good," she gasped, moving her hips in rhythm with his questing fingers. "So good."

She glanced behind her at Kevin, saw a dark intensity that she'd never seen before shining in his eyes. For a minute he looked wicked, wild, and she knew that she should be afraid. Afraid of the passion and the darkness inside of him. Afraid of those same qualities he brought alive within her. But she was too far gone to worry about it, too aroused to do anything but ride out the unbelievable pleasure he gave her without any effort at all.

"It's about to feel better," he murmured, shifting so she was straddling him, her legs on either side of his head.

His tongue—talented, terrible—darted out, caressed her inner folds again and again. Serena spread her legs wider, desperate for something more, something deeper. With a groan of ecstasy, he clutched her ass, spread her legs as wide as possible and thrust his tongue deep inside her.

She came instantly, screaming and bucking wildly against his mouth. He held her in place, his strong hands immovable as he continued to lick and suck her through the first climax and into a second and a third before finally relenting.

When he let her go, Serena settled herself against Kevin with a low, satisfied moan. She kept her eyes closed as aftershocks of incredible ecstasy continued to rack her body. She savored them, one after the other, even as her hips moved restlessly against the quilt, searching for Kevin.

And he was there, of course. Right next to her, smiling, as he stroked her hair and ran his fingers lightly over the pearl necklace she still wore. "I couldn't get it off when I undressed," she answered his unasked question as she stretched against him. Her smile was lazy, her voice content even as she reached for him. "Your turn."

"Not yet." He shook his head, his eyes as deep and mysterious as the secluded waters of the bayou.

Her hand closed around his erection, and she pumped gently as she ran her thumb back and forth over the tip. "Now." She leaned forward and took him in her mouth, loving his low growl as much as the feel of him against her lips, in her mouth.

His fingers tangled in Serena's hair, anchoring her in place as she did the most amazing things with her mouth. He watched her lips sliding up and down his cock, watched her tongue swirl around him, pausing to flick at the drop of moisture on the tip. He hadn't thought it possible, but he grew longer, thicker, harder.

He ran a finger lightly down her cheek, marveling at the delicate skin. She was so beautiful, so fragile, that he feared breaking her every time he put his hands on her. Even so, he couldn't let her go. She was his and she would remain his.

Groaning as she took his entire length in her mouth, Kevin couldn't stop the involuntary thrusting of his hips against her. But she didn't mind—instead, she reached beneath him, cupped his ass and held him to her as she curved her tongue around his cock and savored every movement of his body against her mouth.

He endured the mind-blowing torture as long as he possibly could. But when he was as close to coming as he dared get, he sat up abruptly and flipped her onto her back.

She looked up at him with passion-glazed eyes, licked her lips as if savoring his taste. Sweat trickled down his forehead and over his chest as he fought for control of his raging body. This night was for Serena, he reminded himself. There was plenty of time, later, to take care of his own needs. Besides, watching her come again and again was almost more pleasure than he could bear.

"What's wrong?" she asked, eyeing the rampant proof of his desire for her.

"When I come, it'll be inside you." His voice was harsh, rusty with a need he didn't even try to hide.

"Sounds good to me," she purred, turning behind her to the nightstand and the brand-new box of condoms that rested there.

He took advantage of her turned back, reaching up and unhooking her necklace in one quick move. She turned back, eyebrows raised questioningly. "What are you doing?" she asked.

His grin was wicked. "I can think of a better use for these."

"Better use?" She frowned as she mulled over his words. He knew the exact second they sank in because her eyes widened in surprise. And interest. "Really? That's not just an urban legend?"

"Definitely not. Now lie down."

She followed his directions, her eyes both wary and interested as he began arousing her yet again. His lips were everywhere at once—her neck, her face, the back of her knees, her shoulders, her breasts. Everywhere he touched flamed for him, and soon she was thrashing against him, her body begging for his possession.

He reached a finger between her thighs, gratified when it came away soaked. He didn't know how much longer he could last. "Are you ready?" he asked, rolling the pearls slowly over her collarbone to her breasts and stomach.

Her eyes met his, clung, and he saw her trust for him. A trust that at once awed and humbled him because he knew how much it cost her. "Yes."

He stopped for a moment, lightly kissed her cheek, the corner of her mouth. "I love you, Serena."

And then he began slipping the necklace, pearl by pearl, inside of her, murmuring encouragement until only a few remained outside. "Does that feel okay?" he asked, brushing soft kisses over her breasts and abdomen.

Serena wiggled her hips experimentally, more nervous and aroused than she'd ever been in her life. The pearls shifted inside of her as she shifted, and she moaned, astounded by the sparks of pleasure the simple movement sent shooting through her. "It feels good," she answered, looking into Kevin's bold, beautiful eyes. She shifted again and nearly came. "Amazingly good."

His grin flashed, dark and dangerous. "I'm glad." And then he shoved a finger inside of her without warning, rubbing the pearls against the walls of her vagina as he did so.

She whimpered, arching off the bed as a wave of pleasure more intense than anything she'd ever felt slammed through her. The pearls were everywhere at once, touching every single spot inside of her. Kevin found her G-spot with his finger and rolled pearl after pearl against it until she screamed with frustration.

"I can't take it, Kevin. I swear I can't."

His grin was the sexiest thing she'd ever seen. "Should I stop?" His voice was low and teasing, his accent dark and pronounced.

"Yes." Her hips arched against his hand. "No. Oh, God, I don't know. Do something. Do something!" Her hips spasmed with each word, her pleas getting louder and louder as he continued to play with her.

"How about this?" He leaned down, blew warm air against her beautiful clit, and she screamed, her hips coming completely off the bed.

"Finish it," she begged. "Please. Don't leave me like this. I can't take it. I can't—" Her hips jerked against him, again and again, while her head thrashed back and forth on the pillows. "Kevin!"

He grinned, watched sweat pour down her body as she undulated against the sheets, desperate for release. Then he closed his mouth over her clit and sucked until she was at fever pitch. Her hands grasped the sheet greedily, her legs moved restlessly against him and tears poured, unnoticed, down her cheeks.

This was what he wanted. Serena lost in ecstasy, on the brink of an orgasm so fantastic she couldn't think, couldn't worry, couldn't control herself at all. He reached between her legs and slowly, slowly began to pull the string of pearls out. One bead at a time, letting each slip against her clit as he did so.

She began coming with the third pearl, clutching his hair and screaming his name loud enough to wake half the hotel. But he didn't stop—he continued to draw the necklace out slowly, steadily, making sure each bead rubbed both her G-spot and her clit as it came out.

When the last pearl was removed, she was still orgasming, still screaming. He flipped her onto her stomach and pushed into her from behind. He slammed into her again and again, harder and harder, riding her through the contractions rhythmically milking him. He felt her tension build, felt his own orgasm approaching, and when she spasmed again, he finally let himself go, pouring everything he was inside of her. Hoping, praying, that she could find it inside of her to give him just a little of herself back.

Chapter Twelve

Serena took a few deep breaths as she plunged the room into darkness. Her heart raced and shivers danced up and down her spine, but she ignored them as she always did. Today was no different from any other day. The fact that this was her first trip home since the day Damien had been released a few weeks ago would have no effect on her. She wouldn't allow it to affect her. This was her darkroom, and she would damn well do the work that she was trained to do.

She crossed blindly to the high counter where her equipment lay, the path as old and familiar as her own face. Today, she wanted to develop the black-and-white photos she'd taken of Kevin in his studio—the day after they'd made love the first time. Yesterday she'd spent nearly sixteen hours in her darkroom—fighting this ridiculous uneasiness as she developed roll after roll of film in a marathon session that she would prefer not to repeat.

But she'd already been away from Kevin for three days, and she wanted to get back to him as soon as possible. He'd tried to stop her from coming home, citing progressively more outlandish reasons for why she needed to stay in the bayou. But her work was at a standstill—how could she take any more pictures until she really had a chance to look at what she had?

So she'd ignored his craziness, his pouting, and even his wild, glorious lovemaking, and she'd come home to work—something she'd never had trouble doing before. Work had always been her solace. From the time Sandra had bought her first real camera, if she had a problem, she went to the darkroom with it—either to hide from it or to let her mind work on it as she followed the well-rehearsed steps to developing film. In the last twelve years, she'd developed enough film to do the basics in her sleep. Which was why her darkroom was such a great place to think up solutions.

She reached for the first roll of film, removing it from the 35mm canister with a can opener—a method her first photography instructor swore by. She unwound the film and peeled off the tape that connected it to the spool. Behind her, an old Aerosmith CD played—Stephen Tyler crooning about not wanting to miss a thing.

Her heart beat faster as she ran her fingers lightly over the negatives. This was the roll she'd been dying to see—the one of Kevin working alone the morning after they'd first made love. She'd reveled at the drive and passion pouring from him as she'd taken the pictures. He'd been in his own world, lost in the power and beauty created by his own mind and the challenge of bringing that beauty to everyone else.

Her hands shook at the memory, and she fumbled a little as she loaded the film onto the metal reel necessary for developing. He was magnificent—so fiercely private and isolated, yet so willing to open up once his walls were bridged. Where did he get the courage? she wondered. And where could she find some to match?

She placed the film in the tank and covered it out of sheer habit as her mind continued to work on her relationship with Kevin. What was she going to do with him? How was she going to leave him when the book was finished? Could she even if she wanted to?

With the film safely covered, she flipped on the light. Stared at her unsteady hands in disbelief. What was happening to her? How had she let one man turn her so inside out in so short a time? She never stayed in a relationship very long, never let it get serious enough to shake her up. Never, never let a man tell her that he loved her.

Je t'aime. I love you. Kevin's voice haunted her as she checked the temperature of the soup. She'd let the developing fluid warm a little—wanting it warmer than usual so that she could get a coarser, grainier effect for the roll. More primitive—like Kevin himself.

She checked the thermometer. Seventy-nine degrees. Seventy-nine. The number echoed in her head, again and again. The number of stab wounds in Sandra's body when Damien was done with her. The number of times he'd plunged his knife into her while she'd screamed.

She poured the soup into the spout and covered it, ignoring the shivers chasing themselves up and down her spine. Seventy-nine. Just a number, she repeated to herself again and again. Just a stupid number. One day she'd be able to see it and not think about Sandra. Someday. Just not today.

Je t'aime, Serena. *Je t'aime.* Kevin's words flowed through her as she waited for the photos to develop. He'd said them every time they'd made love since San Diego. He'd said them again as he helped her into her car as she headed back to Baton Rouge.

She'd wanted to return them. Had wanted to throw her arms around his neck and kiss him senseless, then tell him how much she loved him, too. But she wasn't ready. Didn't know if she'd ever be ready.

I love you. I love you. I love you. The last time she'd said those words it had been to her sister. The last time she'd heard them Sandra had been screaming them at Damien as he killed her.

I love you! Why are you doing this? I love you, Damien. I love you! Why won't you stop? I love you! Why? Why? Why?

Sandra had died before she'd gotten the answer.

When Kevin had said those words, Serena had been nearly overwhelmed with the need to run, to hide. She didn't want to know, didn't want the pain or the responsibility that came with holding someone's heart. Didn't he know this was supposed to be casual? Had to be casual—her relationships always were. Couldn't he see what a bad risk she was, how she was too screwed-up to love anyone?

She poured water into the spout for sixty seconds to stop the film from overdeveloping, then added a fixer so she could view the images in normal light. The second time he'd told her, she'd been nearly as frightened. Scared for him. She was going to hurt him. She didn't want to, but she would just the same. She was always the one causing the pain when a relationship got too serious and she had to end it. She didn't want it to be like that for Kevin. Didn't want to see pain in those beautiful eyes.

She pulled the lid off the tank and ran cold water into it for a few minutes before adding a clearing agent and stirring the mixture around. Then she washed the film one more time, wishing that she could cleanse herself as easily. Wishing she could stand under a shower and just rinse away all the parts of her life she didn't like— the parts she didn't want to remember. The parts she couldn't live with anymore.

She pulled the film out, careful not to touch the surface of the negatives as she hung them up to dry. As she fastened the last clip, she was caught by the final image on the roll. Kevin walking toward her, his muscles rippling with fluidity and grace. His hands were outstretched and the look on his face nearly took her breath away. He was completely focused on her, love and concern already laid bare for the world to see. She stared at the tiny negative for a long time, until it blurred and she was forced to blink unexpected tears from her eyes.

What was she going to do about him? A headache began to creep up the back of her neck, and she took yet another deep breath to try to calm herself down. The sharp chemicals of the darkroom assaulted her nose and the resultant coughing nearly brought her to her knees.

Did she love Kevin? Did she love him the way he deserved to be loved, the way he said that he loved her? The questions chased themselves around her mind throughout the day as she worked at a frenetic pace. Developing film. Looking for strong pictures in the finished project. Even blowing up a couple of pictures of Kevin she couldn't live without.

When morning bled slowly into afternoon, she still didn't have the answers.

She was in there—just a few steps away. He could feel her through the walls, through the closed door. All that passion and life just waiting for him to take it. To take her.

Not yet, he cautioned himself. Things weren't in order yet. It wasn't time.

Oh, but how he wished it was.

He ran a hand over the supple leather of her couch, tangled his fingers in the silver throw she had resting across the back of the couch. With a groan he buried his face in the soft velvet—it smelled of her. Honey and heat and ripe, warm woman.

Lust slammed through him, made his hands clench against the soft fabric until it was balled tightly within his fists. He took a deep breath and forced his trembling hands to relax before smoothing his careless marks away. The fabric was delicate, easily damaged—much like Serena herself.

He would have to remember that, have to keep his temper under control, lest he mar her too severely. Yet it galled him—bitterly— the knowledge that some other man had so recently been where he would soon be. He didn't take other men's leftovers, didn't like the idea of taking a woman who had so recently had some other man's dick in her mouth, in her cunt. His scent and filth all over her.

But Serena was special—he would make an exception for her. Eleven long years he'd waited to be with her. And once he got her, he would cleanse her until she was pure again. It took all of his willpower to tamp down on the excited laughter that wanted to bubble out of him at the thought of her purification. Of the fire—the burning—of her rebaptism. His dick stirred to life and he palmed himself absently through his pants.

But first she must atone for her sins. Suffer for letting that bayou rat touch her, lick her, come inside her, where no man but he belonged. Excitement bubbled through him at the image of her begging forgiveness. His forgiveness.

Of course, he would grant it to her. But not for a while. Not before she'd paid.

And she would pay.

Soon she would pay and pay and pay.

Today was only the beginning.

Her stomach grumbled and Serena glanced at her watch as she surfaced from her frenzy. It was four thirty and she'd worked straight through lunch. No wonder she was hungry. With a heavy sigh, she washed her hands in the darkroom sink and gave the photos she'd been developing one last look as she reached for her purse.

Glancing at the last few photos—the ones on the last roll of film she'd taken outside the Matthias Building before the accident—she froze. Then, springing into action, she ripped down the last picture on the drying hanger with one hand while she grabbed her photographer's loupe with the other.

Surely she was mistaken. Surely that wasn't— She leaned closer, her stomach churning sickly. But it was.

Michael LaFleur was in the crowd outside the building. Dressed in a suit, hands in his pockets, he blended in beautifully with the other businessmen strolling the streets of downtown San Diego. Only his erect posture and wary eyes set him apart.

What had he been doing there? And how could she have missed him? After everything that had happened, she'd assumed that she had some built-in radar where the LaFleurs were concerned. It was humbling—and frightening—to realize she didn't.

Serena's knees trembled, but she forced back the panic threatening to overwhelm her. It was just a coincidence—a horrible, horrible coincidence. She pushed away the memories of how uncomfortable she'd felt outside the Matthias Building, of how she'd feared she was being watched.

It was a free country after all—she couldn't live her life worrying about running into one of *them*. They were rich and well liked, and she was bound to end up in the same place as them sometimes. Louisiana—and the rest of the world, it seemed—just wasn't big enough to keep them apart.

She hung the picture back up with a shudder. Though her appetite was gone, she was determined not to let Michael's unexpected appearance ruin her day. After all, how on earth could she hope to build a normal life with Kevin if she was so easily derailed?

She couldn't.

So she'd just have to forget about this. She'd take a break like she planned—grab something to eat and maybe take a walk. Then she'd come back here and work late. If she was lucky, she could head back to Kevin's in the morning. Or late tonight, if she really pushed it.

Her heart jumped at the prospect of being in his arms again, despite all the warnings and worries she'd sorted through while she worked. Serena closed her eyes on a sigh—it seemed like she was going to be totally impractical when it came to Kevin. She could only hope they would both survive her folly.

She locked her doors and turned toward her driveway. It wasn't until she was nearly at her car that she realized that something was wrong.

He was bored. He, who never tired of his own company. He, who found women attractive, interesting, and utterly forgettable. He, who could spend days in his studio with no human contact whatsoever.

He was bored. And—for the first time in his life—lonely.

Kevin groaned, swiped a hand over his face as he contemplated another night spent alone. He missed Serena. A lot. He missed everything about her, from her cool smile to her hot eyes. From her buttoned-up shirts to her silky lingerie. And he most definitely missed the incredible sounds she made just as she was about to climax.

He put down his blowtorch and studied the sculpture in front of him. He'd been working night and day on it since they'd come back from San Diego. Though he had started it before they left, the true image for the piece had come to him in the Museum of Photography as he'd been buried deep inside Serena. In that moment after he'd come, when he'd gotten his first inkling about his true feelings for her, he'd gotten a clear picture in his mind of what he wanted for this piece. And as he studied the nearly completed sculpture, he saw that the vision was as close to perfection as he could ever hope to achieve.

The heat of the furnace was getting to him, so he grabbed a cold beer and headed outside. Not that it was much cooler there, but at least a breeze fluttered by occasionally, cooling the sweat from his skin.

He opened the beer and took a long swig before settling himself on the porch steps. It had been four days since he'd seen Serena—what he was rapidly coming to think of as the four longest days of his life. He'd worked sixteen-hour days in the studio, surfed the Net endlessly, even cleaned his house in the middle of the second night, though he had a housekeeper who came twice a week. He'd even chopped more wood, adding to the gargantuan pile he'd created when she'd left the first time. And he still couldn't walk into his room without smelling her. Couldn't sleep without dreaming about her. Couldn't close his eyes without seeing her face on the backs of his eyelids.

He was totally and completely screwed. There was no other word for it. He was in love with a woman who didn't believe in love, who couldn't believe in it. And he didn't know if he was optimistic enough to believe for both of them.

He glanced back inside the studio, awed yet again when he saw the sculpture of Serena. Long, fluid lines predominated, some the thickness of a human thigh, some the wispiness of a human hair.

Though it was an abstract, anyone looking could see the delicate arms and smooth thighs of a woman. When he was finished he would polish it until he could see his reflection in it—something he saw every time he looked in Serena's eyes.

He took a long, deep swallow. The critics were gonna love it. Steve would wet his pants when he saw it. *If* Kevin let him have it. Part of him wanted to shout loud enough for the whole world to hear: *Look at my beautiful, amazing woman. See what she's inspired me to do.* But the bigger, selfish part of him—a part he had learned to listen to almost unconditionally—told him to hold the sculpture as close as possible. Not to let anyone see it. Serena was his and his alone. No one else needed to know what beauty and light he had found with her.

The cordless phone inside his studio rang, but he kept his butt planted firmly on the porch. He didn't want to talk to anyone except Serena. And she wouldn't call. She never did—if he wanted to talk to her, he'd have to be the one to pick up the phone. It irritated him to no end that he mattered so little to her that she never gave him a thought when she was away from him. Especially since he could do nothing but think about her.

On the fifth ring the answering machine picked up and Kevin waited for the message with idle curiosity. Probably Steve. His mom was on a cruise and his best friend was currently searching for himself on a pilgrimage to the Far East. Kevin grimaced—artists could be so fucking pretentious.

He was struck, again, by the difference between his life and Serena's. Sure, he was a recluse, but he had a mother who called and visited regularly and a best friend who would go to the wall for him. His brother was a bit of a flake, but even Shawn checked in once a week—just to see how things were going. Who did Serena depend on when things went bad? Who did she talk to after a bad day?

"Kevin? I know you're there. Pick up the phone." Steve's voice interrupted his reverie, and Kevin raised his beer in a toast, congratulating himself on guessing correctly. Probably calling to harangue him about doing some article or showing up at some party. There was no way he was answering that phone. He wanted to wallow in his loneliness, not perform for a crowd of art patrons like a trained ape.

"Damn it, man!" Steve's voice crackled with impatience and an underlying note of concern. "It's about Serena." He paused, let his words sink in. Then, with a weary sigh, "When you get this—"

Kevin was at the phone in three strides. "Steve? What's wrong?"

"I knew you were there. Look, Kevin, someone destroyed her car. I mean, totally destroyed it."

"She was in an accident?" Fear coursed through him, making his heart race and his throat constrict so much that he nearly strangled on the words. "Is she all right?"

"No, man, not an accident. She's fine. Physically, I mean. But someone really did a number on it. Broke the windows, slashed the tires. Graffiti, urine. The works."

"You're kidding me. What was it, a bunch of kids getting their kicks?" Alarm bells rang in the back of his mind even as he spoke, though he wasn't sure why. The vandalism was disgusting, disturbing even. But it happened everywhere, and it was just a car after all. But still, something felt off.

Steve snorted. "Hell, no. The cops said this much damage means personal. Like crazed-ex-boyfriend personal. The guy jacked off in her front seat and scrawled *whore* across her hood in huge red letters."

For the first time in his life, Kevin understood what it meant when people said their blood ran cold. His literally froze in his veins, even as his stomach churned with fury and disgust. No one fucked with his woman. No one.

"Where is she?" he demanded, heading toward his house at a dead run, the cordless phone still pressed to his ear.

"At the police station on Magnolia. Giving a statement and looking at some mug shots of sick and twisteds who do this kind of thing on a regular basis. What a world!" Steve's voice was thick with his own disgust.

Kevin grabbed his wallet, slipping his feet into a pair of Birkenstocks as he searched frantically for his keys. "She called you?" he asked, not sure if he was more pissed about that or about the car. He pulled a clean T-shirt from his closet, shrugged into it without moving the phone from his ear.

"No, man. I called her to discuss this showing I just got her, but she was in the middle of this." He paused for a minute, cleared his throat. "Look, Kevin, she never calls. If you want to be with her, you have to know that going in. She never calls, never asks for help, never expects anything from anyone. She'll give you the shirt off her back, but she'll never let you far enough in to hurt her. Or love her."

Too late, Kevin wanted to shout. But he was wasting time. He needed to see Serena, to run his hands over every inch of her and convince himself that she was really all right. This time he wouldn't call—she was too good at lying about her feelings, with her words and her voice. But if he saw her, if he looked in those bittersweet chocolate eyes and held those trembling, emotional hands in his own, he would know exactly how much this had messed her up. Messed *them* up.

"Thanks for the warning. Look, I'm heading to Baton Rouge now."

"I figured you were. Call me later and let me know what's going on. How she is, you know."

"Yeah. Absolutely." He pressed the OFF button and tossed the phone on the couch as he spotted his keys next to the stove. Within five minutes he'd cleared the long, winding road to his house and his low-slung Ferrari was on the highway, cruising to Baton Rouge at nearly one hundred miles an hour. Usually he drove his old, beat-up truck, but today he wanted to get to Serena fast and his 599 GTB Fiorano would definitely do the trick.

He cruised for a while, passed a cop at one hundred ten without even batting an eye. The cop wouldn't be able to catch him, and if he was smart, he wouldn't even try. A quick look in the rearview mirror assured him that the cop was indeed smart.

With an angry growl, he thought over his conversation with Steve. Fury was a living, breathing entity inside of him, crawling around his stomach and sending razor blades through his heart. She hadn't called him. She hadn't fucking called him.

Didn't she get this whole relationship thing? Didn't she realize that if something happened to her, he'd want to know about it? He was far from an expert on having a girlfriend, but even he knew to call when there was trouble. His fingers drummed restlessly against the steering wheel as his foot pressed down on the accelerator. He barely caught a glimpse of the sign stating that Baton Rouge was fifty miles away.

Good. He glanced at the clock. He'd already gone sixty miles in a little over half an hour. Forty minutes more and he'd be at the police station—thank God, he'd grown up in Baton Rouge and knew exactly where Steve was talking about.

Who would do this? Who the hell would mess with Serena like this? She never hurt anyone, never bothered a soul. He thought over various comments she'd made—about how casual she'd always kept relationships, both romantic and platonic. How there hadn't been anyone serious in a long, long time.

But this destruction didn't sound casual—it sounded wanton, brutal and very, very personal. He'd never set much store by Louisiana cops, and if even they knew this wasn't random, he figured Serena damn near had a huge bull's-eye painted on her back.

But why? She kept to herself. Lived her life with little true human contact. She teased him about hiding in the swamp, but they both knew the truth. She was the one hiding—she just did it in plain sight.

So why? What had changed recently? For the second time in an hour, his blood ran cold. Two things had changed. Serena was involved in a serious, or at least semiserious, relationship—with him. And Damien Lafleur was out of jail for the first time in ten years. He thought back over the accident in San Diego that had nearly killed her, suddenly remembered the man's statement claiming the SUV was aiming straight for Serena. Things clicked into place, and the alarm bells that had been sounding in the back of his mind finally took center stage.

Had someone actually been trying to kill her in San Diego? And if he had, was it somehow connected to this vandalism? Could they afford to think that it wasn't?

As the city came into view, he glanced at the time. Six fifteen. Rather than going straight to the police station and taking the chance of missing her, he slowed the car to a reasonable eighty miles an hour and dialed her cell phone.

She answered on the second ring. "Hello."

"It's me." His reply was terser than he might've liked, but his anger had ballooned all over again upon hearing the controlled stress in her voice. "Where are you?"

"I just got home. I've been out ... running errands and things."

His blood boiled at the lie. "Yeah, like to the police station to deal with your vandalized car?"

Her sigh was weary. "Steve called you."

"*You* should have called me." His fingers drummed out a staccato rhythm on the steering wheel. "Where do you live?"

"Why?" she asked, and he could almost see the wariness stiffening her spine.

His words came from between clenched teeth. "Because I'm five minutes from the city, and I want to know where to meet you."

"You're on your way to Baton Rouge?"

"*Bébé*, I'm *in* Baton Rouge. Now give me some basic directions."

He listened as she rattled off directions to one of the nicest areas in the city before listing her address. *Mon Dieu*, how the hell had someone vandalized a car in that neighborhood in broad daylight?

"You didn't have to come, you know," she said softly.

"You're going to want to stop while you're ahead, *cher*."

"But—"

"Seriously. Stop. I'll be there in about fifteen minutes."

"Call me right before you get here. I'll open the garage so you can get in. I don't think you should park on the street anymore. Not with this going on."

His fingers tightened on the steering wheel at the strain and hurt evident in her voice. Someone was going to pay, and pay big, for messing with her. He struggled to keep his voice even. "Fine. See you soon, *bébé*."

He disconnected and made the next turn so that he was headed her way.

Chapter Thirteen

Twenty-five minutes later Kevin pulled his car to a stop in her garage. He would have been fifteen minutes earlier except he'd stopped for food, figuring Serena hadn't eaten all day. "A Ferrari?" He climbed out of the car, clutching a couple fast food bags and two Cokes, to find Serena staring incredulously at his car. "You actually own a Ferrari?"

She looked like hell. Her face was composed, her clothes neat and buttoned to the neck as always. Even her hair was in perfect order. But she was pale, her face lined with strain. He glanced at her hands—they were steady, but the nails were bitten to the quick.

He started to comment on it, but one glance at her eyes changed his mind. They were dark and dazed and pleaded for a little normalcy. So he simply shrugged. "If you've got it, flaunt it, *cher*." There was time enough later to talk about what had happened. Now he just wanted to hold her.

Her laugh was a little strained, but basically real. "Way out there in the bayou, hmm?" She turned and headed into the house, leaving him to follow.

"There is no place on earth, *bébé*, that a Ferrari doesn't fit in." He dumped the paper sacks on her kitchen counter and then pulled her into his arms. "It's like a magnificent piece of art—everyone can relate to it."

She held herself stiffly against him for a minute, while his hands gently rubbed her back. "Just let me hold you, *'tite belle*. I was so worried."

Serena relaxed gradually, sinking into Kevin's warmth despite herself. All afternoon she had told herself that she didn't need him. Not when she'd seen obscenities scrawled all over her car. Not when she'd found the come and urine drenching her front seats. Not even when the insurance company had told her she'd have to call the police and file a report. As she'd sat in that police station and listened to the police talk about the psychos in the neighborhood, she'd been thrown back to those long, difficult weeks after Sandra had been killed. But she'd gotten through it, had kept her composure when all she'd really wanted to do was run screaming for the nearest door, Kevin's name on her lips.

But as he held her against him, the steady beat of his heart soothed her spirit in a way nothing else ever had. Warning bells went off in the back of her head, but she was too tired to heed them. With a sigh, she laid her head on his chest and wrapped her arms around his powerful waist. "I'm glad you're here." The words escaped before she could censor them.

"I would have been here a lot sooner if I hadn't had to hear about this thing from Steve." He pulled back and leveled the full power of a Kevin Riley glare at her—the same glare that froze paparazzi from fifty feet away and made art critics weep at his lack of accessibility.

Strangely it neither intimidated nor frightened her as it did so many. Instead, it warmed her—made her feel safe and secure.

"You were working. I didn't want to bother you."

If possible, the glare grew fiercer. "You couldn't be a bother if you tried, and you know it. You wanted to handle this all by yourself, just like always. Big, bad Serena. She can handle anything the world throws at her."

"That's not—" The instinctive protest died in her throat as his eyes caught fire beneath the lowered eyebrows. "All right. Maybe that was part of it."

"All of it."

It was her turn to glare as she pulled away. "Part of it. I'm not used to having someone there to lean on."

He pulled her back. "Well get used to it, Serena, 'cuz I'm not going anywhere." He rested his chin on the top of her head. "Okay. Enough said. Now do you want to tell me about it?"

"Not really. It was nauseating. Disgusting. Absolutely horrifying." She shuddered. "Can we eat first? I'm starving and I don't want to lose the first appetite I've had in hours."

"Sure." He settled her at the table and snagged the two bags, making quick work of distributing the burgers and fries. They ate in near silence for a while, Kevin keeping an eye on Serena to ensure that she actually ate the food, rather than play with it as she usually did when upset.

After he'd eaten his food and she'd done fairly good justice to hers, he cleared the sacks away and she let him pull her toward the living room couch.

"I've waited long enough. Now tell me exactly what happened."

Serena bit her lip and clasped her hands together, but her gaze was steady as she looked him in the eye. "I've been working like crazy, taking very few breaks, not eating much. I—" Her voice faltered for a moment. "I missed you and wanted to get back as soon as possible, so I was working as hard and as fast as I could."

There. She'd said it and he wasn't running for the hills, wasn't trying to put as much emotional and physical distance between them as possible. In fact, his grip on her hands had tightened, and those beautiful, blue eyes seemed to warm gradually. She cleared her throat, fought against the panic rising in her chest.

It was just typical that she'd managed to face her desecrated car and a legion of police without a whimper, but one look from Kevin and she was nearly panic-stricken. She cleared her throat again, took another sip of her Coke as she bought herself some time. But when she looked back at Kevin, his gaze was just as steady, just as encompassing as before she'd admitted her feelings.

She reached for the silver throw she always kept on the back of the couch and dropped it over her legs. She'd been freezing for hours, despite the overwhelming heat and humidity.

"Anyway, it was about four o'clock and I was hungry. I'd been working since six thirty, when I got back from the gym."

His eyebrows rose. "You were at the gym before six a.m.?"

"I couldn't sleep." She shrugged. "And I haven't been getting much exercise at your place, since you take up every free minute of my time." Her look was pointed.

"Point taken." He grinned, reaching a hand up to stroke her hair away from her face. "So it's four o'clock and ..."

"And I don't have any food, since I've been staying with you. So I thought I'd run out for a sandwich. When I got to the street ..." Her voice wavered, but she steadied it with sheer will. "When I got to the street, the damage had already been done. My car was totaled."

"You didn't hear anything while it was going on?"

"I was in the darkroom at the back of the house. I had music playing." She shrugged again. "And when I'm working ..."

"A bomb could go off and you wouldn't notice."

"Pretty much."

"Your neighbors? It's hard to imagine that no one saw anything."

"Harder to imagine that they sat back and let it happen without calling the police."

"Speaking of which, I'm proud of you for calling the police."

She avoided his eyes. "Don't be too proud. I called my insurance company first, and they insisted I file a report with the police before they'd take a claim from me. If they hadn't ..." Her voice trailed off.

"What'd the cops say?"

His voice was even, but she could tell he was annoyed with her idiocy. But that was too bad—she didn't trust cops and had a pretty damn good reason for her distrust. He'd just have to learn to deal with it. "They wanted to know who I was seeing now, wanted to know about previous boyfriends and any sour relationships. The usual. Especially with the crank calls—" She broke off midsentence, but it was too late.

"Crank calls?" he demanded, eyes suddenly blazing. "You've been getting crank calls and you haven't told me? For how long?"

Serena cursed the tiredness that made her say things without thinking. She tried to shrug it off, to think of something else, anything else, to say, but her exhausted brain wasn't working well enough for that. So she tried to underplay it. "Look, it's no big deal. He—"

"How long, damn it?" Kevin grabbed her arms, turned her so that they were face-to-face.

"A few weeks." She shrugged out of his grip. "They started before I met you, and at first I thought it was just some kids. But now—"

"Now that's not looking real likely, is it?"

She shook her head miserably.

"He calls you at home?" He looked around her condo suspiciously. "But you haven't been here."

"He calls on my cell, too."

"He's got your cell number?" He stared at her incredulously. "Has he called you while you were with me?"

"Kevin ..."

"He has. And you didn't tell me. What's wrong with you?"

Her spine stiffened and her eyes turned cold. "Nothing is *wrong* with me, Kevin. Despite appearances to the contrary, I am not in the habit of spilling my problems to anyone who walks by."

"That's the biggest bullshit you've ever handed me." His hands clenched on her upper arms, and he shook her gently, fury rolling off him in waves. "You don't sleep with everybody who walks by either, but you're sleeping with me. That entitles me to some privileges when it comes to you."

She'd never seen him so angry, and a long-forgotten part of her wanted to soothe him. To let him pull her in and take care of her. That feeling—that utter neediness—had her straightening her spine before she could think twice about it. She wasn't Sandra, desperate to make some guy love her. "You only have the privileges I give you."

"Fuck that." His hands clamped more tightly on her arms, and though he was careful not to hurt her, she definitely felt the dominance in the gesture. "You're mine, Serena."

She narrowed her eyes at him. "You're going to want to back off."

"You're going to want to fall in line." His eyebrows lowered, and he stared straight at her with eyes even narrower than hers. "Because I've got no give in me about this, *cher*. Not when it comes to your safety."

They stayed that way for long moments before she pulled away, unable to maintain eye contact with him for another second. Desperate for a little space, she sprang to her feet and crossed the room. Seconds passed slowly as she stared at the painting above her dining room table, concentrating on the colors as she took one breath and then another and another. In, out. In, out. She fell back on the familiar mantra.

When she finally had herself back under control, she turned to walk back to the sofa and ran directly into Kevin's broad chest. He'd been right behind her the whole time and she hadn't even known he was there. The knowledge pissed her off like nothing else could have.

When had she let down her guard enough that he could sneak up on her like that? When had she started feeling so safe with Kevin that she stopped noticing every move he made?

"Back off." She ground the words out from between clenched teeth. She was suffocating under the weight of everything that had happened these last few weeks, and he wasn't making things any better. "Can't you see I need a little space?"

His eyes were pained as he stared back at her. "Can't you see that the more you run, the more I want to chase you?"

She sighed disgustedly. "Look, I don't have time for your poor-abused-boyfriend act. You came to me, remember? I didn't call you and ask you to come. If you don't like how things play out, that's not my problem."

Kevin gritted his teeth, her words making him even angrier because he knew she was right. She hadn't called him, hadn't asked him to be here with her. He walked to the window, thrust his hands through his hair as he tried to get his rampaging emotions under control.

"You're right," he said.

"What?" she asked incredulously.

"You're right. You didn't ask for help and I don't have any right to expect you to. It's not like we're in a real relationship, right?"

"That's not what I meant." She sighed, her fingers playing with the hair at her nape. It was a gesture she only made when she was nervous and confused, and it melted his anger despite his best efforts to hold on to it.

"I'm frightened for you, Serena." He kept his voice soft, compelling. "It frightens me to think of some psycho gunning for you."

"You're not playing fair." Her eyes were sad, her mouth trembly as she studied him. She was waiting for the other shoe to fall, and he was suddenly, overwhelmingly disgusted with himself. How had he managed to make her crisis all about him?

"I'm not playing at all." She stared at him, eyes wounded and searching, and he could no longer hold on to even the pretense of being pissed off. So he sighed, tucking the hurt away as he pulled her into a loose embrace. "I'm sorry. This thing blindsided me. If I promise not to act like an ass anymore, will you tell me what else has been going on?"

He felt the stiffness leak out of her, felt the exact moment when she decided to let the argument go. He stayed like that for a while, his arms around her while their hearts beat in the same rhythm.

When they'd both calmed down a little, he pulled away and said, "Finish telling me about what the cops said."

"That's it, really." She let him pull her over to the sofa, let him cuddle her against him as he stroked her hair. "They want to know about my lovers—present and recent past. I told them that we hadn't even known each other when the calls started and that you were with me when some of the messages were left. So they've ruled you out."

"What about your other lovers?"

She blushed, turned her face away. "There hasn't been anybody but you in over a year. And Carlos wasn't exactly the insane, wreck-a-car-when-the-relationship-goes-south kind of guy, you know?"

"So there's been no one else." His stare was direct and uncompromising. "No one-night stands, no casual hookups—"

"Kevin!"

"I'm not interrogating you, Serena. I couldn't care less. But I've been thinking about this, a lot, and I need to know."

"No! There's been no one. That's why I was so ... you know, when we first got together."

He grinned. "No, I don't know. Do you mean *hot*? *Horny*? *Unbelievably sexy*? But we've been together a couple of weeks now, working on all that pent-up frustration, and you don't seem to have cooled off any."

"Will you stop it?" Her cheeks flamed and she stood, desperate to put a little distance between them. Desperate to get her equilibrium back.

When she'd seen her car, her first thought had been to call Kevin and let him deal with it. She'd known that he would be there for her, would hold her hand and deal with all the messy stuff she didn't want to handle. It was that knee-jerk reaction, more than the car and all that it had implied, that had sent her into a tailspin. Since when did she let someone else, particularly a male someone else, deal with her problems? Since when wasn't she strong enough to deal with them herself?

That was the real reason she hadn't called him. Because she'd wanted to. She'd needed him to be with her. She, who didn't need anyone, had felt the absence of another person keenly for the first time since her twin died. It wasn't a comfortable feeling.

Wrapping her arms around herself, Serena started toward the big bay window at the end of her living room.

His strong arms reached out and pulled her back onto the couch, back onto his lap. His lips skimmed over her forehead, down her nose, across her cheek and then back to her mouth. Their lips met, and though Serena felt the familiar arousal beginning to burn in the pit of her stomach, Kevin kept the kiss light, soothing. Healing.

When he finally pulled away, she was pressed against him, her peaked nipples against his hard chest. They were both breathless, and she was gratified to see that for once, Kevin's hands shook as badly as her own. She cuddled against him, ran her lips up the strong column of his throat. She was weary, emotionally worn-out and desperate for the distraction he could so easily provide.

But instead of giving into the fire that burned so brightly between them, Kevin lifted her off his lap and placed her next to him on the couch. He was careful to maintain some small physical contact with her, but she got the message loud and clear. He didn't want her. She wrapped her arms tightly around her waist, hugging herself though she'd much rather have Kevin's arms holding her. But, though his hand remained on her thigh, he'd never felt so far away.

"Look, Serena, I've been thinking ..." His voice trailed off and as he searched for words.

"Are you dumping me?" she asked incredulously. "Now?"

"What? Are you insane?" Both his face and voice reflected his shock. "Where the hell did you get a crazy idea like that?"

"You didn't want to—" She gestured to the couch. "You're mad about me not calling you, and I know I've been a lot of trouble lately but—"

His mouth swooped down and took hers violently, the tenderness from earlier nowhere to be seen. His lips devoured hers, his tongue thrusting into her mouth, claiming her, branding her with every stroke.

When he finally broke the kiss, her lips were bruised and swollen and her panties were soaked through. "You aren't any trouble. And even if you were, I'd still want to be with you. *Te me rendes fou!* You make me crazy, *cher*. You turn me inside out. When are you going to figure that out?"

Serena stared into his midnight blue eyes, saw anger and possessiveness burning there. His feelings were so intense she wanted to look away, but she forced herself to maintain eye contact. As she looked deeper, she saw past the rage to the caring and concern, saw past the fear to the agony of love.

His hands were still wrapped around her upper arms, his fingers gripping her hard enough to leave bruises, but he seemed oblivious to his actions. She reached up, cupped his face. "Then what were you thinking about? What are you having such a hard time saying?"

His hands dropped away and he looked instantly uncomfortable. "I almost didn't say anything, because I could be wrong. But I've been thinking things over since I got Steve's call." He took a deep breath and finally blurted, "What if it's all connected?"

She looked blank. "What if what's all connected?"

"The SUV in San Diego. The scorpion. Your car. These crank calls. What if it's all the same guy?"

"But who?" She was bewildered, even as her heart rate increased. "We already talked about the fact that you're the first serious relationship I've had in a long time." She paused, backtracked. "Not that we're—"

"Damn right we're serious," he snarled, his expression daring her to contradict him. "But, as you said earlier, I think we can safely rule me out. However, and I'm really sorry to bring this up if I'm wrong, but haven't all these things happened after Damien got out of jail? After you testified at his parole hearing?"

Serena paled alarmingly, her skin turning clammy beneath his hands. She struggled for breath, tried to maintain perspective as nausea threatened to overwhelm her. "That doesn't make sense. Why would he risk his parole on something this stupid? Someone could have easily seen him in front of my house, could have called the police, and he'd end up back in prison for another five years." She shook her head, her tone decisive. "He's too smart. He wouldn't risk it."

"He may be smart, but he's also obsessed. And more than a little crazy, or he wouldn't have been able to ... do what he did."

She thought over what Kevin said, hating the cold logic behind his words. "But the calls started in late June, months before he even got out of jail."

Kevin shrugged. "He wasn't in maximum-security lockdown, right? That means he had access to a phone." His eyes narrowed thoughtfully. "In fact, it should be easy enough for the police to check out the records from the prison, see if there were any calls from the pay phones inside to your home or cell numbers."

"But why? We had almost nothing to do with each other when Sandra was alive. She knew I didn't like him, so after the first couple of months, she kept us apart."

"You were the key witness for the defense, right? Wasn't it your testimony that forced him into cutting a deal?" At her nod, he continued. "Revenge is a hell of a motivator."

"Ten years later?"

"What's that old expression, a dish best served cold?"

Her lungs wouldn't work. She tried to breathe, tried to force air into her starved airway, but nothing was happening. It was as if Kevin's words had broken her, tearing her body apart until nothing worked as it should.

Things started to go black and she felt herself sway. Then Kevin was shoving her head between her legs, calling her name as he pounded repeatedly on her back.

The blackness beckoned, so once again she focused on her breathing, concentrating on drawing noisy breaths. The sounds she made weren't pretty as she tried to force her shock-frozen lungs to accept air, but finally, finally, the darkness began to recede.

When she felt well enough to sit up, she did so, to find Kevin staring at her, his eyes glazed with horror. "*Mon Dieu, bébé.* You sure know how to take the years off a man's life."

She smiled weakly. "I can't—"

"I know, *cher*. I know." She let him cuddle her, let the steady beat of his heart lull her into a sleepy daze, where she didn't have to think about her sister or Damien or the blood that had covered her long after the nurses had sponged her off.

Kevin held her for a long time, murmuring softly to her in French. When he finally spoke in English, it was to say, "We need to call the police. Tell them what we think."

"Not yet."

"Serena—"

"I know, I know. We will. But not right now, Kevin. Not quite yet. Just give me a few more minutes before I open that door again. Just a few more minutes."

He continued to rub her back. "All right, *bébé*. But just a few more."

Chapter Fourteen

"Serena? What are you doing here?"

She turned at the familiar voice, and watched in surprise as Assistant District Attorney Jack Rawlins strode across the battered police station toward her.

He stopped next to her, crouched down. "Is everything all right? Did something happen?" Jack rested his hand over her clasped ones. "Can I help?"

She felt Kevin stiffen behind her at Jack's familiarity, heard the low rumble in his chest before he could stop it. She leaned back against him reassuringly. "I'm fine, Jack. Just dealing with an unfortunate incident that happened yesterday."

Kevin snorted at her "unfortunate incident" comment before saying, "Her car was vandalized."

"You're kidding! Like you need more crap, right? Do they know who did it?"

"We've got a good idea." Once again, it was Kevin who answered.

Jack turned to Kevin, eyebrows raised. "Who exactly are you?"

"Oh, I'm sorry. Kevin, this is Jack Rawlins, the ADA who worked extremely hard to keep Damien in jail. Jack, this is Kevin Riley. He's my ..." Her voice trailed off as she tried to figure out what to say. *Boyfriend* seemed far too insipid for what they shared.

"Lover," Kevin supplied as he extended his hand. "I'm Serena's lover. It's good to meet you, Jack."

"Kevin!" Serena flushed bright red as she twisted in her seat to glare at him. His face was bland as he met her look with a smile.

He shot her an innocent look. "Well, I am, *cher*, aren't I?"

She was too mortified to answer, so she simply glared at him. He winked, then turned back to Jack. "Maybe you can help us," he commented.

"Maybe I can." Jack pulled up an available chair and sat with them as they waited for the detective in charge of Serena's case to return. "Now why don't you two tell me exactly what's going on?"

Kevin nodded, but his chest tightened at the quiet ADA's over-friendly interest in Serena, making his answer abrupt. "Detective Grayson doesn't seem to be taking our suspicions as seriously as I would like. Maybe you can speed him along."

Jack's eyebrows rose questioningly as he pulled out a pen and a yellow legal pad. "We'll just have to see, won't we? Now this is about your car, correct?" His tone grew serious.

Serena related the details from the past few weeks, stopping only when Jack asked for clarification. Halfway through her story, Grayson returned, but was shushed by the ADA as he continued to question Serena.

When she had finished her version of the events, Jack turned to Grayson. "I assume you've checked the prison phone logs?" he asked, his voice and eyes colder than Serena had ever seen them.

"I'm working on it," Grayson returned just as coldly. "How'd you get involved anyway? I'm not ready to call in the DA's office yet."

"I'm a friend of Serena's. And it sounds like she's got a pretty good point."

"I'm not disagreeing. I'm just trying to make sure I've got the facts correct. I'm on my way to LaFleur's house to check out his alibis for the dates and times we've discussed. That okay with you, boss?" The look he gave Jack was sarcastic in the extreme.

"Good. Let me know if you find something." Jack ignored the sarcasm, turning toward Serena and Kevin with his hand extended. "I'll do some looking into this as well. Give me a call if anything else turns up."

He turned back to the detective. "Keep me posted about what's going on, Pete. I'm extremely interested in this case."

"Then maybe you should've done a better job keeping the guy behind bars." Grayson grabbed his jacket off the back of his chair and stalked out of the building without another word.

Jack's gaze was rueful when he looked back at Serena. "Pete and I don't have the best relationship—a case that went bad a couple years ago. But he's damn good at his job. He'll find out what's going on."

"I'm glad to hear that. Thanks for all your help, Jack." Serena extended her hand.

He took it, rubbing his thumb back and forth across the back of her hand. Kevin shifted warningly. If the ADA didn't get his hands off Serena soon, he'd—

"It's nothing. And I expect to hear if anything else happens, understood?" His gaze encompassed both of them, and Kevin found himself staring into Jack's amused eyes. Perhaps he wasn't being as subtle as he'd imagined.

But when Jack leaned over and brushed his lips over Serena's cheek, he couldn't stop the warning growl that started low in his chest. Fuck subtle. He'd rip the guy—

Then Jack was extending his hand and grinning like a fool when Kevin hesitated to take it. When Kevin finally did reach forward and clasp the guy's palm, he found Jack's grip firm to the point of pain. He answered in kind, then felt ridiculous as he saw Serena's gaze resting on their taut handshake.

He dropped Rawlins's hand immediately, but couldn't help watching as the man strode down the hall away from them. What exactly was the ADA's relationship with Serena? And why did it bug him so much to know that there was something more than her sister's case between them?

Hours later, when they were only minutes away from Kevin's house in the bayou, Serena finally asked, "What was going on back at the police station? Between you and Jack?"

Kevin's gaze slid to her face, a slight smile curling his full lips. "What do you mean?"

"You know exactly what I mean!" she said in exasperation. "You told him we were lovers!"

"We are lovers."

"Something I think he could have figured out, even without your advertising the fact."

Kevin shrugged. "I didn't want him to get the wrong idea. He was interested and I wanted him to know you were taken."

Serena steadfastly ignored the warmth spreading through her at Kevin's words, focusing instead on their utter absurdity. "What am I, your bone?"

His smile turned wolfish. "I kind of thought it was the other way around." He grabbed her hand, brought it to the erection currently squeezed behind the zipper of his jeans.

"Kevin!" She tried to look horrified by his pun, but ended up laughing despite herself. "That's terrible."

"That's not what you were saying a few nights ago." He thrust lightly against her palm.

It was her turn to grin as she began stroking him through the denim. Lightly at first, and then with a little more pressure as he groaned in appreciation.

She'd never been in a relationship this free before, had never felt comfortable enough with another human being to do and touch whatever she wanted. With Kevin, everything felt so natural that she often forgot to put a lid on her response to him.

She loved his erection, loved the proof of his desire for her. But she wanted more. Much more than a quick feel in the car. Easing his button open and his zipper down, she was rewarded by Kevin's harshly indrawn breath when her hand finally slipped inside and found him.

"You're not wearing underwear," she accused, her breathing a little faster than normal, despite her resolve to stay in control of the situation.

He winked at her. "Thought that was your own private domain, hmmm?"

His words reminded her, as they were supposed to, of the last time she'd gone without underwear. In San Diego. At the museums. Her nipples peaked and she grew wet, suddenly as aroused and uncomfortable as she'd made Kevin.

"I wasn't complaining," she murmured, her fingers gliding over and around his erection. He really was delightful, a mixture of incredible hardness and velvety softness. She loved the feel of him—in her hand, in her mouth, and most assuredly in her body.

Squeezing her aching thighs together in defense, she murmured, "Hurry," knowing that she sounded as breathless as she felt, but totally helpless to stop it.

"Hurry what?" Kevin asked, his own voice raw with desire.

"Hurry home. I want you." Slipping out of her seat belt, Serena bent down and took him slowly into her mouth. She ran her tongue along his huge, hot, hard length, loving the faintly salty taste of sweat that clung to him.

"*Mon Dieu, bébé!* You'll kill us," he protested, even as he thrust involuntarily against her mouth and hand.

She delivered a long, leisurely lick down the length of his cock and stopped to suck on the head, before turning her face up to his. "Me?" she asked with false innocence. "You're the one driving."

He glanced down at her incredulously. "You're the one making me so hard I can barely see."

"I like that." She grinned as she once again lowered her head. "Let's see what I can do for your other senses while I'm at it."

Her mouth closed fully over him, and he nearly lost it at the wet, sweet pressure of her tongue. Her left hand reached lower, to cup his balls, and he gritted his teeth against the sudden, urgent need to orgasm blasting through him.

He wanted to be inside her when he came. He wanted to prop her hot, little ass down on the kitchen table and drive into her again and again. He wanted to kneel between her legs and lick her for hours. He wanted to fuck her—from the side, behind, standing up, sitting down. Every way he could think of. As long and as hard as possible, until she was so exhausted and so sated that she wouldn't be able to think about leaving him.

"Serena—" Her name was torn from him as she swirled her tongue around his cock, pulling him deep into her throat as she did so. She found the extremely sensitive spot on the underside of his tip and licked it delicately until he was nearly out of his mind.

"Stop!" He took his right hand off the steering wheel, tangled it in her hair. "Serena, *cher*, you need to stop. Now."

"Mmmm," she murmured deep in her throat as she ignored him.

Kevin gritted his teeth and took the turn onto the private road leading to his house at nearly fifty miles an hour. He drove another minute, until he was sure that they were far enough away from the highway not to be seen. Then he jerked the car to a halt, lifting Serena onto his lap before he'd even managed to turn the engine off.

Her smile was teasing and more than a little sensual as she asked, "Why are we stopping?"

Kevin glared at her; then he climbed from the car with her in his arms. "You know why." He let her slide down his body, turning her so that she was facing the car, her hands planted firmly on the hood. He pushed her jeans down to her ankles with one hand while he pushed his own out of the way with the other.

Leaning forward, he ran his lips down her long, elegant neck while his hands reached between her legs to test her readiness. She was hot, drenched with excitement, and he couldn't wait any longer. Bending her over the hood of the car, he surged inside of her with one powerful thrust of his hips.

Serena whimpered deep in her throat. It had been a long few days and the relief of having Kevin inside her was totally overwhelming. She tried to speak, but couldn't form the words around the needy moans clawing their way out of her throat with each slam of Kevin's cock between her thighs.

She reached behind her, raked her nails down his bare ass as she tried to pull him even deeper. Deeper and deeper and deeper, until he was a part of her. "Do it harder," she finally managed to gasp. "Please. Harder."

He heard her strangled gasps and responded with more pressure, even harder thrusts, until he feared he would tear her apart. But being inside her felt so good, and as she met him, thrust for thrust, hungry cries poured from her throat. His left hand moved between her thighs while his right one remained on the small of her back, keeping her bent forward for the best access. He spread her open, stroked her where she pulsed around him. And she responded by pressing back even harder, as desperate for release as he was. Maybe more.

"Come on, *bébé*. Come for me. Let me feel you." He reached for her clit, stroked his thumb over it once, then again and again. She came, screaming his name as he rode her through her climax. Wave after wave of sensation crashed through her, weakening her knees and sending slivers of heat to every part of her body.

Her muscles clenched rhythmically, milking him with every contraction of her strong, young body. He clenched his jaw, fought his approaching orgasm with everything he had. He wasn't done yet, wasn't ready for this one perfect moment to end.

He continued his rhythmic thrusting, so deep inside of her that he swore he could feel her womb. He moved his hand down and with his index finger gently tapped out a pattern on her clit. She moaned his name, her head lolling forward as her questing body arched into his caresses.

"That's it, *bébé*. That's it." He continued the pattern, loving how her hips moved more and more urgently against his hand. "I love feeling you come. I love seeing you, watching how your skin flushes. I love being inside of you when your muscles pulse around me again and again. Hugging me, holding me to you."

He bent his head to the vulnerable line of her neck, licked the thin line of sweat dotting her nape. Followed it until her shirt got in his way. "I love your sweet raspberry nipples and your hard little clit." He brushed his lips over her neck, his tongue sweeping against the sensitive spot on her jaw as he murmured softly to her.

Serena moaned deep in her throat, her body moving feverishly against his, while tears of need streamed down her face. His words were inflaming her, taking her closer and closer to another orgasm, something she had been sure was impossible only moments before.

"I love that you're always ready for me, always wet and willing and open to anything I want to do. I love to fuck you, to thrust inside you and feel you clench around me." He pulled out slowly, then slammed back into her, relishing the scream she couldn't stop. "I love how you take all of me, everything I have to give. I love how you always demand more." His mouth fastened on the juncture between her neck and her shoulder, sucking ravenously.

"I love how you seduce me, with your crazy ideas and your open, honest responses. I love how you let me fuck you wherever and whenever I want. I spend huge chunks of my day just thinking of new ways and new places to fuck you." He pinched her clit between his thumb and middle finger, leaving his index finger free to stroke the sweet bundle of nerves again and again.

"I love your strong, gorgeous body." He squeezed her clit a little harder and was rewarded by a high-pitched scream as she thrust her ass even harder against him. "I love your breasts—how your gorgeous little nipples always taste so sweet." His hands coasted up her stomach to her breasts while he licked a fiery trail down her neck. "I love your legs and how they wrap so perfectly around my waist. I love your pussy"—he gave an extra hard thrust that had her screaming—"and how it hugs me so tightly.

"And I absolutely, positively love your ass." One of his hands drifted down to caress the lush globes before he spread them open and thrust a long finger inside of her. She bucked against him, but he refused to be hurried. Refused to pick up his pace. "I love everything about you, Serena." He slammed into her again and again. "I love the hell out of you."

"Kevin, stop!" she cried, her entire body shuddering as she pleaded for the maelstrom of emotion and sensation to end. "I can't take it. I swear I can't."

He nipped at her neck, her shoulder, the tender skin that covered her spine. "You will take it. And more—so much more. Won't you, *bébé*?" His hips moved harder and faster against her as his control slipped another notch. "Won't you?" He moved his right hand from her back to her stomach, splaying his hand over her abdomen and pulling her even more tightly against him. "Because you love the way I make you feel as much as I love you."

"Yes! Yes! Kevin, please!" She was pleading, sobbing, wilder than he'd ever seen her, and he loved it. Loved her. He thrust again and again, claiming her, branding her as his, so no matter how far she ran, she would always remember that she belonged with him. So she'd never forget the feel of him pounding into her, seducing her with his body and his voice.

He was killing her with his restraint, driving her past the brink of her endurance into someplace she'd never been before. His words echoed in her head, drove her insane. Made her crave him and everything he could give her.

Her vagina spasmed, her body turned inside out by Kevin's dominance. She was shaky, out of control and more desperate than she could ever remember being. All she knew was that she couldn't keep this up—she was going to die if he didn't give in. If he didn't come soon and stop this totally incredible, absolutely amazing torture. Desperate, she closed her legs, trapping Kevin between them, and then clenched her vaginal muscles as tightly as she could.

She was rewarded when Kevin groaned deep in his throat, slamming into her one final time before spilling himself inside of her. His orgasm triggered her own, and she screamed his name, again and again, totally caught up in the hurricane ripping her body apart.

Kevin was lost in the feel of her body, lost in the insane pleasure rocketing through him as Serena's orgasm milked him dry. "*Mon coeur. Mon amour. Je t'aime.*" His love spilled out of him as his body jerked spasmodically against hers.

When the last contractions died away, Kevin collapsed against her, blind to everything but the incredible glory of holding the woman he loved, of being inside her as she recovered slowly from what they'd done together.

Eventually Serena stirred, pushing against him as she reached down to pull up her jeans. Kevin released her, fastening his own pants as he watched her wriggle her fantastic ass into hers.

When she was once again neatly dressed—every button fastened and her shirt tucked sedately into her jeans—she turned to him, a shy smile on her face. He reached a hand to her face, cupped her cheek and brushed his thumb lightly over her mouth.

"I love you, Serena."

"I know." She turned her head so that she could kiss the center of his palm. "Kevin—"

"*Ssh, bébé.* I know it's too soon for you. That's all right." He focused on her, ignored the pain slowly burning a hole in his stomach. He had no right to be upset. He'd known going into this thing how hard it would be to convince her to stay with him. Of course, going in, he hadn't known that he would want to.

But she was studying him carefully and saw the flash of pain in his eyes before he disguised it. "I'm sorry."

His smile was real, yet resigned. "Nothing to be sorry for, Serena. You're magnificent and well worth waiting for."

Serena shook her head. "You're the magnificent one. Kevin, you mean more to me than any man ever has. Can't that be enough for now?"

"Serena, just holding you is enough for now." He tilted her chin up so that she was looking directly into his eyes. "Don't you think you've got enough going on right now? And don't you think I know that? When this thing is over, when Damien LaFleur is back behind bars where he belongs, then we'll talk. All right?"

Kevin cleared his throat. "I wanted to talk to you about that."

She stared at him, mystified. "About what?"

"About Jack Rawlins."

She snorted before she could stop herself. "Are we back to that?"

The look he shot her was sizzling hot. "We never would have left it if you hadn't distracted me."

"Then I'm glad I distracted you."

"So am I." He laid a firm hand on her shoulder as he guided her back into the car. "But seriously, Serena, there's something about that guy I don't like."

"What's not to like? He was more than helpful today, just like he's always been."

Kevin's fists clenched, but Serena was too upset to notice. "What does that mean?"

"It means that he worked really hard to convince the DA not to offer Damien the deal ten years ago, just like he went above and beyond trying to keep him in jail this time."

Kevin's eyes narrowed and she could almost see the wheels spinning in his brain. "So you've known Jack a long time."

"Yes. He's always kept in touch, calling me every few months just to check on me. I've run into him numerous places through the years—"

"What do you mean, you've run into him?" Kevin took his eyes off the road long enough to glance at her. She could tell he wasn't happy, but at the moment she was more than annoyed enough not to care.

"Just that. At the dry-cleaner or the movies. Stuff like that."

"Baton Rouge isn't huge, but it's big enough that repeated meetings seem kind of odd, don't they?"

"We live in the same neighborhood!" she answered, her voice rising in exasperation. "I don't think it's odd that we both eat at the same restaurants!"

Kevin let that pass, but still didn't drop the subject. "Isn't it strange that he's kept in touch with you all these years? I didn't realize DAs did stuff like that."

She shrugged. "Sandra's was the first big case Jack ever worked—he was fresh out of law school. It made an impact on him."

Kevin snorted. "I'm sure it did."

"What is that supposed to mean?"

"It means he's interested in you, Serena."

"No, he's not. We're friends. Friendly acquaintances, really."

He glanced at her again. "He wants to be more than that."

"No, he doesn't."

"Yeah, he does." He held up a hand when she started to protest. "He's never made any moves on you? Never stood too close, never acted just a little too friendly?"

"No." Kevin raised one mocking brow, but Serena shook her head emphatically. "He's never done any of that. And even if he had, it wouldn't have mattered. I was never interested in Jack that way. I couldn't be, not with his connection to Sandra's death."

"Maybe he doesn't know you feel that way."

Her gasp of outrage echoed through the car. "Don't you think you're taking this jealousy thing way too far? You're being ridiculous."

"Am I?"

"Jack's the only one from that whole time period that I trust. That's all there is to it."

Kevin pulled the car to the side of the road with a swift skill she might have admired at another time. "Maybe he doesn't know you don't return his feelings."

Serena studied him, completely shocked by this new side of Kevin. "I never would have taken you for the jealous type."

"Then you're blinder than I thought." He ran a frustrated hand through his hair. "But this has nothing to do with jealousy."

"Then what—" She paused, her stomach twisting sickly as the truth sunk in. "You can't possibly think Jack's behind this!"

"I can't?"

"No! Absolutely not."

"Why not?"

"Because he's not a psychopath, for one thing. And he's always been incredibly kind to me—he would never go out of his way to hurt me like this."

Kevin watched her with hot eyes, but his voice, when he spoke, was ice-cold. "All kinds of people develop obsessions, Serena. Even men like Jack."

"You think I don't know that? You think that I, of all people, don't know the atrocities seemingly normal men can commit?"

"I didn't say that." Kevin's voice held exasperation and some-thing more dangerous. "I know you've been through a lot, *cher*, more than anyone should have to experience. But I think you're wearing blinders when it comes to this guy."

"You met him exactly once, and you think you know him better than I do?"

"I think you don't see him for what he is."

"And you do? Jack was nothing but helpful today—he spent time I'm sure he couldn't afford trying to help us. You're letting some stupid jealousy get in the way of the truth."

"It's not jealousy," he ground out, his teeth firmly clenched.

It was her turn to eye him disbelievingly. "Yeah, right. For a min-ute I thought you were going to grab me by the hair and drag me back to your cave to stake your claim."

His growl was low, warning. "Don't push me, Serena."

Her look was incredulous. "Or what?"

He ignored the question, his hands tightening on her shoulders involuntarily. "I don't want you seeing him again. Not alone."

"I don't take orders from any man, Kevin." She shrugged his hands off, the molten chocolate of her eyes promising retribution. "Not even you. Especially not you."

"He's dangerous, Serena."

"So are you, but you don't see me running in the opposite direc-tion, do you?" She eyed him with contempt. "Although maybe I should."

"That's it. I've had it," he roared, pulling her into his arms and crushing her mouth with his own. It was a kiss meant to punish, to express his frustration. But the second his lips met hers, it softened into something so much more.

At first she fought him, but as his lips moved gently on hers, Serena yielded. He skimmed his tongue over the corners of her mouth, sipping from her, coaxing her to open to him. When she did, his tongue darted inside, exploring every tender recess of her. Trying to connect with her. Trying to gain her trust when he knew she had so very little to give.

With a groan, he ended the kiss, but moved his hands to cup her face. "I'm worried about you, *cher*. I'm scared for you."

She stared at him with wounded eyes. "I know you are. But ultimatums aren't going to get you anywhere with me."

"So what will?" His eyes shot blue thunderbolts at her, though his touch remained gentle.

She shrugged. "I don't know. I don't," she reiterated at his disbelieving stare. "Asking, maybe. Explaining why it's so important to you."

His eyes darkened threateningly. "I'm not real good at asking, *bébé*."

"And I'm not real good at taking orders, *bébé*," she mimicked. "So maybe we should just forget this whole thing!"

Kevin was shocked at the feeling of loss that overwhelmed him. "Do you mean that?"

"I don't know. Maybe." She stared at him with hurt and angry eyes. "We're not exactly bringing out the best in each other."

Kevin tamped down on his own hurt, focused instead on the pain he saw in Serena's eyes. "I'm sorry, *cher*. This whole thing has blindsided me. I just want to keep you safe."

"That's not your job."

"Then whose job is it?" He pulled her into his arms, his heart trembling when she melted against him despite her anger.

"Mine! I can't let myself get used to relying on you. It'll just be that much harder when—"

His mind went blank as fear that had nothing to do with Serena's safety and everything to do with his own swept through him. She was already planning the end of their relationship, when he'd barely gotten passed the beginning.

How the hell had this happened to him? Deb had always accused him of keeping a part of himself away from her—an accusation that he'd never been able to deny. How ironic was it that the one time he gave himself completely to a woman, she didn't want him?

"Kevin?" Serena's voice intruded on his thoughts. "I didn't mean that the way it came out."

"Don't worry about it." He ignored the hurt—this wasn't the time or the place for it. And he pushed his suspicions regarding Jack Rawlins to the back burner, not wanting to upset her any more than he already had. He would mention a discreet word to the police and see what shook out.

Probably nothing, he admitted ruefully. Maybe Serena was right—maybe he was letting jealousy focus his attention somewhere it didn't belong. God knew, he hadn't liked watching Rawlins touch her, had wanted to smash the guy's face in within the first minute of watching him look at Serena.

Tamping down the worry—and the anger that it inspired—he said softly, "When this thing is over, when Damien LaFleur is back behind bars where he belongs, then we'll talk. All right?"

"All right." But the look she gave him was just a little bit sad as he settled her into the car. Because he could relate, he said nothing.

Chapter Fifteen

"Need someone to wash your back?"

Serena stifled an instinctive scream as Kevin slid into the shower behind her, his arms warm and strong as he pulled her back against his front. Damn—this whole thing had her jumping at shadows, and she resented—bitterly—the fact that Damien could do this to her all over again. And with so little effort. It had taken her years to regain some semblance of normalcy, and it galled her that it could be taken away so easily.

Kevin's hand slid up her warm stomach to cup her breast, his long artist's fingers toying with her nipple until it stood straight up. "That's not my back." She struggled to make her voice sound normal, but must not have succeeded because Kevin's hands froze in midstroke.

"You okay, *chere*? You're heart's beating a mile a minute."

"I'm fine." She turned her head to smile at him, enjoying the feel of him hot and hard against her back as the warm water of the shower sluiced over her breasts and stomach. "You just startled me."

His hands slid up her arms to her shoulders, where they began a soothing massage. "*Mon Dieu*, I'm sorry. Sometimes I don't think." His voice was thick with self-disgust.

Suddenly she couldn't stand it for one more second—couldn't stand that he blamed himself over and over again for *her* shortcomings. She was the one who was a basket case. The one who couldn't be a normal lover. The one who was a total and complete failure.

The pain and guilt of it overwhelmed her, and she whirled in his arms, reaching up to pull his mouth forcefully down to hers. Their tongues met, tangled, for long seconds and arousal whipped through her—more powerful for the instants of fear that preceded it.

But she could feel Kevin holding back, his sorrow nearly palpable in the close confines of the shower. Pulling out of his embrace, she cupped his beautiful face in her hands. "It's not you."

He shrugged off her words. "Of course it—"

"No, it's not." She went on tiptoes at the same time she pulled his face down so that she could look directly into his troubled midnight eyes. "*None* of this is your fault. You've been nothing but wonderful to me from the moment we met, and I won't let you take that away from me with your stupid, misplaced guilt." She grinned, and if it didn't go all the way to her eyes, then at least she'd made the attempt. "I've got more than enough neuroses for the both of us."

He studied her as the water continued to slide over them. She wasn't sure what he was searching for, but he must have found it, because he smiled and it lit him up from the inside out. "God forbid I should try to horn in on your neuroses," he teased.

"Exactly." She leaned forward and leisurely licked from his navel to his collarbone. His erection—already long and powerful—jumped against her leg so that she couldn't resist repeating the motion.

He groaned even as his arms came around her. "*Bébé*, let me—"

"Oh, no, not this time." She slipped away, reached for the sandalwood shower gel on the shelf next to the shower head. "You're always taking control, driving me insane."

"And that's a bad thing?" His eyes were nearly black as they watched her rub the gel between her hands.

"Of course not. But this time—" She slid one slippery hand down his chest, pausing to toy with first one nipple, than the other. "This time, I get to make you crazy."

He thrust helplessly against her thigh, his cock so full and hard it nearly bruised her. "I'm already crazy."

"Then you've got a problem." She glanced at him from beneath her eyelashers. "Because I haven't even gotten started yet."

"If that's true—" His breath hissed out as she lapped gently at his chest. "If that's true," he repeated, his voice much hoarser than usual, "then I don't think I'm going to make it out of this shower alive."

Her smile was wicked. "I guess we'll just have to wait and see, won't we?"

Dropping to her knees, she licked the water from the area right under his belly button. He tasted so good—so fresh and clean and wonderful. She loved kissing him, loved running her tongue over his body.

"Lower," he groaned, hands tangling in her hair as she ran her tongue along the light dusting of hair that ran from his navel to the thatch of black pubic hair at the base of his cock. "Lower and harder."

"You need to get some patience," she murmured in between delicate licks. "I want to play a little first."

She covered his abdomen with little nips, her tongue soothing the sting away almost before he could feel it. His hold on her hair was getting tighter and tighter, his muscles tenser than she'd ever felt them. For a brief moment she wondered if she should give in and take him in her mouth like they both wanted. Then she thought of all the pleasure he got from tormenting her and slowed her meandering pace to his cock even more. Let him suffer—he deserved it.

She was killing him, the hot silk of her mouth touching any- and everywhere but the place he needed it most. His body arched toward her of its own accord, his cock begging for her lips, her tongue, her hot and hungry little mouth.

But Serena merely laughed and brushed a cool, soft cheek against the length of him before continuing on her journey down his body. She nibbled at his inner thighs, ran her lips and tongue over his balls, dug her fingers into his ass as she drew him closer and closer to her questing mouth.

His heart was pounding. His cock was throbbing. His lungs were bellowing in and out as he tried desperately to get enough air. His balls had pulled up so tightly that for a moment he thought he would explode, his come shooting all over her before she'd so much as touched the tip of her tongue to his erection.

He opened his mouth—to demand, to protest, to beg that she finish it—but before he could get a word out, she'd leaned forward and slipped his long erection between her breasts. Her elbows pressed tightly against her sides so that the warm, wet pressure of her breasts drove him so close to the brink that ecstasy turned the edges of his world black.

"Fuuuuuuck." He couldn't stop the word any more than he could stop his hands from clenching furiously in her hair as she began to lift and lower her upper body in a rhythm guaranteed to make him even crazier. "*Chere, bébé, mon coeur*—" The words poured out of him without premeditation—she'd taken him so close to insanity that no part of his body was within his control. His brain, his mouth, his unruly cock—she'd taken them all over. In return, she gave him the most incredible pleasure of his life.

Electricity coursed down his spine, lighting him up as the softness of her breasts enveloped him. And when she lowered her head and took the tip of his cock in her mouth, he couldn't hold back the hoarse shout that echoed through the bathroom and beyond.

He arched into the warm wetness of her mouth, helpless to do anything else. Nothing had ever felt this good. Nothing would ever feel this good again. He thrust furiously against her, driving his cock deeper and deeper into her mouth. He struggled for control, fought to keep from thrusting his cock all the way down her throat—but as her throat closed tightly around him for the first time, it was impossible. With a shout, he slipped the reins of his control and let himself go. He strained against her, trying to get closer, dying for her to take every part of him inside her.

Again and again he thrust, his come boiling up hot and uncontrollable. His fists clenched in her hair spasmodically, and for a minute he feared hurting her. But then she moaned deep in her throat, let her tongue tickle the sensitive spot at the base of his head. The world went black and he came apart in her arms.

His orgasm was a violent explosion—it took over his senses, his body, his brain—until the world no longer existed. Until nothing existed but him and her and the incredible fire that burned between them.

The ecstasy consumed him, took him under, enveloped him until he was shuddering over and over again, his hands twisting in her hair, anchoring her wild, wet mouth to him. And still she took him, swallowed his come, continued to suck him until he was longer and harder than before.

"Enough!" His voice was low, guttural—but it was the best he could do as need rode him hard. He tugged on her hair until she reluctantly released him with a last, lazy curl of her tongue. His eyes nearly crossed as he yanked her to her feet, and with one, smooth motion, he turned her until her breasts and stomach and pubic hair were pressed against the glass walls of the shower.

His fingers settled on her outer thighs—wrenched them apart—and then he was thrusting himself balls deep inside of her. Her body was slick and welcoming and so fucking hot he nearly came with his first thrust. And then she screamed, bucking wildly against him as her muscles clenched around his shaft. He gritted his teeth against the urgent need to orgasm—he wanted to hear her scream again and again. Needed to hear her call his time with a desperation that would have bothered him if he wasn't so far gone.

"Take me deeper," he growled right before his teeth closed on the delicate lobe of her ear. "Take me all the way."

She pushed back against him, her ass tilting up s
deed go deeper. Pound harder. Fuck more and more

"Kevin!" Serena whimpered softly, but it felt like he was
her apart. Going at her so hard and deep that she swore she could
feel him all the way to her womb.

A part of her wanted to protest—it was too much, too intense,
too frightening. But the pleasure was insidious, washing over
her in all-consuming waves as he shoved his cock inside her again
and again. She could feel her muscles tightening—protesting his
unrelenting invasion—and the pressure only made the pleasure
better.

And when he slipped a hand down the curve of her ass, his thumb
pressing inside her anus with one unapologetic thrust, she came in
an unbelievable rush. The contractions started deep inside—so deep
that they were almost painful. And then they spread, rippling out a
little more with each second that passed. Spreading through her
womb to her pussy. Taking over her stomach and her breasts, her
nipples throbbing against the cool, clear shower glass.

Until all she could think about was the pleasure. Until all she
could do was feel. Absorb. Scream, as Kevin continued to thrust inside of her, stoking the fire, making her orgasm so intense she feared
for her consciousness.

And then, just when she thought she could hold on to her sanity,
he rocked the very foundations of her soul. His mouth closed over
the spot at the juncture of her neck and shoulder at the same time he
hit her G-spot with a twist of his hips and sent her soaring again.

And again. One long orgasm after another until she was pleading
for relief, begging him to stop and to continue. Pleading with him to
do something—anything—as sobs racked her body. As pleasure
thundered through her. As her heart and her pussy and every nerve
ending in her body wept for relief.

The ecstasy had spun out of control and there was nothing she
could do about it. In those moments Kevin owned her—body and
soul. She would have died for him, would have given him anything
he asked for, given *up* anything he demanded.

The knowledge should have chilled her blood—but the soul-searing delight of belonging to Kevin overshadowed everything else. The powerful pleasure he gave her burned away her misgivings until all that she feared—all that she was—was laid bare for Kevin and his unrelenting, insatiable cock.

She knew the minute he sensed her surrender, felt it in the powerful surge of electricity that arced from him to her and back again. And then his hands were on her hips—bruising her, branding her—as he pushed her forward and slammed her back against his thrusting shaft.

Another orgasm ripped through her. "No more, Kevin. Please, no more." She was whimpering, begging, and she didn't care. All she cared about was ending the insane, never-ending pleasure before she burned up from the inside out.

Clenching the muscles of her pussy tightly around Kevin's cock, she reached back and grabbed his ass. She caught him off guard, and as she slammed him into her, he bellowed in shock and surprise and pleasure. And then he was flooding her, his come jetting into her with each thrust of his hips.

Marking her. Claiming her. Filling her to overflowing.

As the waves of pleasure slowly ebbed, she came back to earth with a thud. And struggled, silently, against the panic suddenly clawing at her throat.

Hours later, she was still fighting the panic as she counted the number of stripes on Kevin's bedroom wallpaper for the fourteenth time.

Even after Kevin's wild and steamy lovemaking by the side of the road earlier and his out-of-control attentions in the shower, she couldn't sleep. Her body was exhausted, completely wrung out by the events of the past weeks and Kevin's insatiable lust. But her mind couldn't settle. Images of Sandra and Damien chased themselves around in her head, while thoughts of Kevin and his unspoken demands trailed directly behind.

What was she going to do? Please, God, what could she do? Part of her really believed that it *was* Damien doing these things—the scorpion in her camera bag, the car, even the accident in San Diego. Not to mention the crank calls. They, in particular, had his sick and demented fingerprints all over them. But she didn't want it to be so, didn't want him in her head again. She couldn't stand even the idea that he'd gotten close enough to her to do those things when she'd been utterly oblivious.

Because she hadn't wanted to think about it, hadn't wanted to know. After Sandra's death, she'd become an expert at burying her head in the sand and ignoring anything she didn't want to see. It was a habit Kevin steadfastly refused to put up with as he pushed her to face reality the way it was, not how she wanted to see it. Which was just one more reason she was studying herself in the mirror above Kevin's bed instead of sleeping.

With a sigh, she rolled out of bed, careful not to disturb Kevin. The light from the nearly full moon shone in through the window, lending support to the night-light he'd installed in the hall the night he'd found out she was afraid of the dark. She looked down at him, smoothed his wild mane of hair back from his face in the same tender gesture he usually used on her.

He really was a beautiful man—even more so on the inside, which surprised her. She'd come there prepared to dislike him, expecting to do her job as quickly as possible and then get out.

Instead, she'd dragged it on. Even though she had enough quality photos to fill at least three books about him, here she was, preparing to take more. For two reasons, really.

One, because she hadn't gotten the perfect shot of Kevin yet. That first night she'd come close when she'd captured the art-god side of him. But she hadn't gotten the human side yet—the one who laughed and cried. The one who yelled at anyone who entered his domain, yet anonymously gave money and food to the poor people of the bayou. The one who had always fought for everything he wanted, yet held her tenderly when she denied him what he wanted most. That was the Kevin that she wanted to capture on film. That was the Kevin she wanted the world to see.

The other reason she was still here was because she couldn't bear to leave him yet. She knew the end was coming, knew that it had to arrive sooner rather than later. Eventually even Kevin would get tired of the baggage and neuroses she wore like a badge of honor.

But not yet. She wasn't ready to say good-bye yet. That, more than anything else, was what had had her lying awake tonight, staring at her own reflection in the mirror. That was the situation making her increasingly uneasy as her time with Kevin slowly turned from days into weeks.

She knew it wasn't fair to him. He loved her and she didn't know how to love. How to be a lover. Not anymore. Too much of her was frozen behind the shell she'd formed after Sandra died—so much of her, in fact, that she wondered if there'd be anything left if she let Kevin melt it as he was so desperate to do.

Pulling the sheet up, she smoothed it over his glorious body and let her fingers linger for just a moment over that beautiful heart of his. She didn't know what to do about him. About them. Like everything else in her life these days, her relationship with Kevin had spun wildly out of her control. This afternoon, as he'd made wild, glorious love to her, the death grip she kept on her emotions had loosened, and for the first time in a decade, she'd feared for her heart.

Afterward, when he'd taken her excuses and her cowardice in stride—when he'd loved her anyway—she'd known that her heart was no longer her own.

She loved him. Wasn't just infatuated with him. Didn't just like him. She really, truly loved him. She loved Kevin Riley and all of the crazy pieces that made him who he was.

Serena tried the words on for size, imagined herself saying them to Kevin. Imagined his tender smile and the way he held her like she was the most fragile thing in the world. As she did, panic skated up her spine to grab her by the throat.

She wasn't ready for this. Kevin had pushed past her barriers, bulldozed over the control that kept her separate from the rest of the world. For the first time in many, many years, she felt vulnerable. Raw. Her emotions on display for the whole world to see. To say it was terrifying was understatement in the extreme.

After Sandra had died, she'd closed herself off from her emotions because the pain of losing her twin had been so intense that she'd contemplated suicide for the first time in her life. Once she'd locked those feelings behind walls, it had become easier to breathe. The guilt and despair were still there, just distanced. She could still take them out and examine them whenever she wanted to, but she'd learned how to wall them back up when she was done. So that she could move on with her life, as her parents, friends and shrink all told her she must.

The side effect, of course, was the emotional chasm she'd opened up between her and anyone who'd ever cared for her. It was why she never spoke with her parents except about the most superficial things. It was why her brother had stopped calling years ago. And it was why she'd never connected emotionally with a man. She'd dated casually, had sex when her body craved it, but had never let her emotions be touched.

Until Kevin. Kevin had scaled the incredibly high walls she'd erected, and now her defenses were threatened. She and her crippled emotions were on their way to being laid bare for him.

She couldn't stand it.

With a sigh, she shrugged into Kevin's black cotton bathrobe. It was miles too big for her, but it smelled faintly of him and made her feel safe. She shook her head at the irony.

How it was possible for one man to embody both total security and absolute threat, she didn't know.

She turned away from the bed they had shared for nearly three weeks. Turned away from him and padded out to the family room to curl up on the couch and watch some abysmal movie on late-night TV.

Sandra had loved late-night movies, had talked Serena into

watching any number of terrible horror movies in the early hours of the morning. The ones with the deranged serial killers and the stupid teenage girls had always been her favorite. If only they'd known ...

It had been nearly eleven years, yet she could still smell the blood—the stench of old pennies mixed with sweat. Her blood. Sandra's. There'd been miles of the stuff. The marble floor had been covered, the walls and art—even the chandelier—sprayed with huge dripping ribbons of red.

The young heroine on TV screamed as she ran through the streets, fleeing the masked madman with a knife. Serena watched with a detached kind of horror as he caught his victim and stabbed her over and over. Was that what it had looked like when Damien had killed Sandra? Had her body been that rigid and tense as she'd fought him, gradually going limp as he'd punctured major organs and her blood had drained from her body?

The screams from the TV were lessening as death claimed the heroine. Serena watched the heroine's face relax, saw her eyes go gradually blank. She continued to watch, torturing herself, as the killer threw back his head and laughed maniacally before plunging the knife into the dead girl a few more times. He ripped at her clothes, bent down to smell the stench of death permeating her. Licked a drop of blood from her face before—

The television clicked off abruptly, and Serena turned to find herself staring into Kevin's enraged face. "What the hell are you doing?"

She shrugged, almost completely numb now. A small part of the wall threatened to crumble, but she shored it up. Watching the movie had reminded her, only too well, what loving someone could do to her. "I couldn't sleep."

"So you decided to come out here and watch a teenage girl get murdered? Have you completely lost your mind?"

She smiled faintly, knowing she should be ashamed. Or at least upset. Concerned. Horrified. Something. Kevin fairly crackled with rage, yet she couldn't work up anything reassuring to say. She finally settled on, "I don't think so. But I couldn't swear to it."

"You couldn't swear to it?" He stalked to the sofa and crouched down beside her so that he could look her in the eye. "Well, then, I'll tell you that I think you've gone completely around the bend! Why watch that filth, Serena? Why torture yourself with it?"

She shrugged off his concerned hand, wandered into the kitchen to get a bottle of water from the fridge. He followed her, his utter silence demanding an answer. "It's no big deal. Sometimes I watch them."

He thrust a hand wildly through his hair, his eyes burning into her back. "Sometimes you—" He stopped, as if just the thought was too much for him. "How twisted is that?" he asked finally.

She turned, a rueful smile on her lips. "Pretty twisted. But then I warned you early on that I wasn't playing with a full deck, Kevin."

He sighed wearily, reached out a hand for her own. But she avoided him neatly, knowing somehow that if he touched her, all of this nice numbness would wear off again. She'd sob out her love for him, her pain, her utter confusion. She'd be back to being Serena the basket case—a role she hated but couldn't stop playing in his presence.

"I'm fine, Kevin. It was the first thing that came on when I turned on the TV."

"And you couldn't change the channel?"

"I chose not to." She brushed past him, headed down the hall toward the bedroom.

He grabbed her arm, spun her around until they were face-to-face. "What's going on in that head of yours, Serena? This isn't like you." His eyes glared furiously at her.

"Nothing, Kevin." She sighed, yanked her arms out of his grasp. "It's late. I just want to sleep."

She crawled into bed and closed her eyes, keeping her back to Kevin as she feigned sleep. Even with her eyes closed and her back turned, she knew that he lay awake, watching her for hours before sleep finally claimed him. Dawn's ribbons of red and orange streaked across the sky before she could say the same.

*   *   *

Serena awoke slowly, gradually becoming aware that she was alone in bed. It was the only time since they'd first made love that Kevin hadn't woken her with a long, leisurely session of lovemaking. She wasn't sure how she felt about his omission. While part of her rejoiced at the distance that would allow her time to think, another part of her wept at the small light that had gone out of their relationship.

She sat up slowly, stretching, as questions whirled through her head. Had she completely blown things with Kevin? Or would he be willing to take what she was capable of offering? It was nothing compared to what he wanted from her and she knew he wouldn't be satisfied forever. But, please, God, let him still want her for a little while longer. Let him not be ready to end things right now, today. No matter how selfish it was, she wanted just a little more time with him. She knew she'd pay for it later, but couldn't bring herself to care. Not when his scent was all around her and the heat from his body still lingered on the sheets.

The smell of freshly brewed coffee wafted slowly into the room. She was dying for a cup, but getting one meant facing Kevin, and she didn't think she was ready for that yet. But she could at least get up and take a shower. Buy herself some time to decide what to do.

Her cell phone rang and she froze in the act of climbing out of bed. Her eyes darted to the nightstand, where she'd dumped her purse the previous night, and for a second she considered taking the cowardly way out and not answering her phone. She didn't think she could take another call from Damien the Deranged.

But in the end she picked it up, because the detectives had put a trace on the phone and because for her the unknown was rapidly becoming worse than the known. UNKNOWN NUMBER flashed across the screen and she took a deep breath to steel herself before hitting the ACCEPT CALL button. "Hello?"

"Serena? This is Steve." At the familiar voice, the tension inside of her dissolved as quickly as it had come. She glanced up to see Kevin in the doorway, a mug of coffee in his hand and a furious scowl on his face as he glared at the phone.

"Oh, hi, Steve," she said, emphasizing his name as she spoke. Kevin relaxed and walked lazily into the room, extending the cup of coffee to her as he got closer. "Lost another phone, huh?"

She took the mug gratefully and sipped, not caring if she burned her tongue. She avoided Kevin's eyes, shocked at how ashamed she felt after last night. She hadn't meant to hurt him, had only been protecting herself. But as she glanced briefly up at his face, she couldn't miss the pained shadows that hadn't been there the day before.

She listened as Steve outlined the plans for the showing he had gotten her, shocked at how many pieces he needed delivered in a relatively short amount of time.

"Steve," she protested, when he had finally wound down, "I'm not sure I can handle that many. At least not with my recommendations for matting and framing. Not with the photos of Kevin almost due and the ad campaign you want me to start next week."

"I've got faith in you, luv. You can do anything. Besides, don't worry about frame and mat recommendations—you know the galleries never like what the artist picks out anyway."

"But—"

"No time to chat! Say hi to Kevin for me, and I'll call you with the rest of the details next week. Meanwhile, make sure you include some shots of Kevin in what you send. And some from your Gulf of Mexico series as well. Those are fabulous. Gotta go!"

Serena stared at the dead phone in her hand with a combination of shock and chagrin. "You're right," she told Kevin, who was still perched next to her on the bed. "He really doesn't understand the whole nurture-the-client-relationship thing."

"I told you. The man's a Nazi." Kevin's grin was at half wattage, but at least the shadows had lifted from his eyes. "I'm making breakfast. If you're interested."

She took his hand, aware that it was one of the few times she'd ever reached for him. Maybe she did know what to do after all. "I am interested. Very interested." She flashed him a smile. "Particularly if there are pancakes involved."

"Waffles, okay?" He raised his eyebrows questioningly.

"Even better." She leaned forward, kissed him smackingly on his lips even as she avoided his eyes. "I'm starving."

Kevin watched her go, bemused and more than a little angry. How could she blow so hot and cold? She'd pushed him away so absolutely last night that he'd been sure she'd try to end things this morning. Not that he'd had any intention of letting her, but he'd prepared for a struggle. He certainly hadn't planned on lighthearted banter over breakfast.

Eyes narrowed, he headed toward the bathroom door, determined to get an answer for her strange behavior last night and even stranger behavior this morning. He had just crossed the threshold when her cell phone rang again, and he picked it up, expecting it to be Steve. "What'd you forget this time?" he asked.

The wave of obscenities that answered his casual question was so filthy that it made him ill just thinking of Serena subjected to it. It was a struggle to keep his voice even as he replied, "Damien, I presume?"

His question was answered with threats and more obscenities, followed by an immediate disconnect. He hit a button to get the last incoming number and dialed it, not in the least surprised when it wasn't answered. Probably a throwaway cell phone.

Fury consumed him. He'd been pissed when he'd heard about the phone calls, shaken after the car accident and royally ticked after he'd heard about her car. But as he'd listened to the filth spewing through the phone lines, he'd grown frightened for Serena. Really frightened. This guy wasn't wasn't just out for some twisted kind of revenge. He was seriously sociopathic, so unhinged that Kevin feared for Serena's life on a whole new level.

"Who was it?" Serena was standing at the door, and he could tell from the look on her face that she knew exactly who had called.

"We need to call Grayson," he answered. "Let him know you got another call. They need to pick this guy up or I—" He trailed off, not wanting to finish the sentence in front of her.

"Or you'll what?" Her eyes narrowed as it was his turn to avoid her gaze. "*You're* not going to do anything. He's crazy, Kevin. Absolutely around-the-bend crazy."

"I got that impression. Which is why I can't just let him keep threatening you, destroying your stuff, *trying to kill you*!"

"Which is why the police are handling it!" She walked to him, pushed against his chest to make sure she had his attention. "Don't do anything stupid, Kevin! This isn't your problem."

"Are we back to that?" He stared at her in disbelief. "Are we seriously back to that again?"

"Yes! No!" He could literally hear her grind her teeth. "I mean, this isn't either of our fights. Now that we've told the police ..." Her voice trailed off as if even she knew how lame her excuses sounded.

"What? So now the Baton Rouge police are your best friends?" He sneered. "That's quite a turnaround."

She turned away, but not before he could see how pale she'd become. "That's not what I meant and you know it."

Shit! Shit, shit, shit! He was handling this all wrong. Handling her all wrong—again. "Serena—"

"Forget it. I don't need another apology."

"Yeah, but maybe I need to apologize."

She turned back to him, and the tears he saw reflected in her eyes made him feel like an even bigger heel. "I don't want anything to happen to you, Kevin."

"Nothing's going to happen.

"You don't know that!" Her voice rose more with each word. "I don't want you going after him."

"I wasn't planning to."

"I don't believe you." She reached a hand out to him but he shrugged it off.

"Well, that's your problem then. I said I'd leave the bastard alone and I meant it."

She came closer, stared into his eyes. Her brown ones were filled with so much confusion and fear that he wanted to relent—to just say fuck it and promise to do whatever she wanted.

"He's not worth it."

"You're worth it." The words were out before he could censor them.

"Oh, sweetie—" Her voice broke, but she continued to stare at him with beseeching eyes. Didn't it just figure that the first time she used an endearment it was when she was asking for something he couldn't give her.

"*Bébé*, don't do this. Don't ask for the only thing I won't give up. I won't compromise on keeping you safe."

"I'm not asking you to."

"Aren't you?" He eyed her challengingly. "Then what do you call this?"

"Trying to keep you alive!"

"My safety isn't what's in jeopardy here." He shoved a hand through his hair, a low growl rumbling in his chest. "Call Grayson, Serena. Tell him what happened."

"I will. But I want to hear you say—"

He swooped down and kissed her, hard. "Don't push me on this." He tossed her the phone and headed down the hall to the kitchen.

She joined him a few minutes later, just as he slid her waffles onto the table. She looked from him to the food blankly. Finally, in a voice barely above a whisper, she said, "Grayson says he's got an alibi."

"For what?"

"For yesterday and for the car accident. For everything." She shook her head and stared at Kevin with dazed eyes. "He just got out of rehab yesterday."

"Rehab?"

"From what Grayson said, Damien got out of prison with quite the substance-abuse problem. His parents rushed him into rehab two days after his release."

"That's no guarantee. Those places don't watch you twenty-four seven."

"I know—and the cops are investigating. But Grayson says that at this point he can't make a case against him."

"Of course he can't." Kevin's voice was viciously sarcastic. "Does he at least know it's bullshit?"

She shrugged helplessly. "I think so. There are calls from the prison phone to my home number. We all know it's him, but any decent lawyer could make a case against circumstantial evidence." She snorted. "Like I know so many other people at Angola."

He sank into the chair next to hers. "I won't let him hurt you, Serena."

Her smile was strained. "Let's not start that again. Besides, is it really even the point? I'm tired of this. I need it to be over."

"Is Grayson going to pick him up and at least talk to him?"

She shrugged. "Not yet. But he is going to have someone follow him for a few days. Since the calls come almost every day, he figures he can catch him in the act. And he's going to fingerprint the phone booth Damien just called from—it wasn't a throwaway phone after all. It's still circumstantial, but the more nails in his coffin at this point ..." Serena's voice trailed off as she fought tears.

Kevin studied her for a minute before commenting, "You need to get your mind off of this crap." He gestured to the full plate. "Hurry up and eat, *bébé*. And then I'll take you on a boat ride, show you the swamps."

"Don't you have to work?"

"One of the benefits of being self-employed. Besides, I will be working."

"Oh, really? Planning on bringing your blowtorch along?"

He shook his head, a familiar wolfish grin spreading across his face. "Just a sketch pad and a few pencils."

Serena's eyebrows rose as he caught her interest. "You're going to do a swamp piece?" she asked.

"I've done lots of swamp pieces. But today I've got something different in mind."

"Like what?" Was that breathless voice really hers?

"Like sketching you, naked and replete from my lovemaking."

Her breath lodged in her chest, but she refused to make things easy for him. "I don't think so. I'll be eaten alive by mosquitoes."

"I've got insect repellant."

"Oh, really?" Her eyebrows rose. "There are certain, sensitive parts of my anatomy that I refuse to put bug spray on."

"That's okay. I'll be more than happy to take care of those spots for you, *cher*. No sacrifice is too much when it comes to your safety." He snatched a slice of bacon off her plate before heading down the hall for his own shower, a wicked grin on his lips.

Chapter Sixteen

Things were working out exactly as he'd planned. She was back in the bayou with that laborer, cut off from everyone and everything that mattered. There were no police stations nearby, and that stupid cop in Baton Rouge was too busy chasing his tail to bother checking in with her every day. That plus the budget crunches of the last couple of years made it impossible for him to have a tail on her. God bless Katrina.

The path to Serena was clear and soon—very soon—he would make his move.

He could barely resist doing a little dance of glee right there in the hardware store, something that would look admittedly strange there among the cattle standing in line to check out. They wouldn't understand his happiness, wouldn't understand anything that existed outside their narrow scopes of existence.

But they might remember, and though he was disguised—amazing what a change in clothing style and hair color could do for a guy—there was no reason to call undo attention to himself.

The line was moving slowly and the chains he carried were heavy and cumbersome. And he was bored, more than ready to get on with things. Patience, he reminded himself as he smothered his natural impatience by thinking about Serena. About how glad she would be to see him once he'd taken care of that bayou rat. How eventually she would be grateful that he'd saved her from a life of such mundane tedium. What he would do to her to teach her to be grateful.

Restlessness quivered in his belly—like a child before Christmas morning, he wanted to rush straight for the prize. But it was a game of skill he was playing and there could be only one victor. One checkmate. He was determined that at the end, his king would not be the one in jeopardy.

And at the end of the game, only he and his queen would be left standing. Serena.

Glancing at his watch—for the tenth time in three minutes—he sighed as the second hand slowly counted down. That bayou rat was already checked; he just didn't know it yet. And if things kept going his way—again he shifted the heavy chains—Kevin Riley wouldn't know what had hit him until it was too late to do anything about it.

Don't worry, Serena, he told her silently. Your king is coming for you, and he's more than prepared to scale the castle walls.

Serena stretched lazily in the shade of the heavy trees. All around her the bayou buzzed with the sounds of wildlife—insects, raccoons, even alligators were out and about. And she was lying there, stark naked, right in the middle of it.

"I can't believe I let you talk me into this," she told Kevin as she moved her eyes so that she could see his face. She was careful not to move her body, because she'd already provoked one glorious temper tantrum when she'd stretched her aching muscles without permission.

"It's no different from those photos you took of me." His reply was absent, his mind miles away as his pencil flew over the sketch pad.

"It's very different. One, we were indoors and away from dangerous predators." She eyed a passing alligator warily. "Two, it took a lot less time than your drawings are turning out to take. And three—" Her voice broke as Kevin looked at her—at her, Serena, not just the subject of his sketching. His eyes were hot and wild and desperately turned on.

She felt her heart rate double, then triple. But he made no move to end the agony of lust she'd been existing in for the last hour. "Just a little longer, *'tite belle,*" he murmured as he came toward her, shifting her slightly so that she was lying on her right hip—her right arm extended straight above her head while her cheek rested on her biceps. Her legs were almost straight—the bottom one bent just slightly. "I'm almost finished."

He skimmed a finger over her nipple, and it hardened instantly, begging for his attention. But he was already turning away, picking up his sketchbook. And as the fever raged in his eyes, she forgot about the pose, about her modesty, about the insects buzzing around them, and lost herself in the powerful heat of his gaze.

It was incredible, watching him work. Thrilling to see the fierce concentration that took him over.

Did he realize what he looked like, she wondered, when he sculpted or sketched or merely contemplated his art? The power, the beauty, the total and complete sexuality that flowed from him to his work and back again? It wrapped her up, took her along for the ride, and she realized she had never felt more beautiful, more desirable, more cherished than she did at this moment.

How had it happened? When had he slipped past her defenses and become the first man—the only man—she wanted to wake up with, to stay with, to take from and give to? She would give him anything he asked for, everything he wanted. It was frightening to realize how much she loved him, terrifying to contemplate what would happen to her—to Serena—if she yielded to him as completely as he wished.

Would she simply cease to exist? And if she didn't, would she even recognize whatever parts of herself were left when the fire between them burnd itself out?

"Serena, *bébé*, come back to me." She shivered as Kevin's voice slipped over her, around her. She refocused her eyes and realized he'd stopped sketching and was standing above her.

She grinned, shrugged off the fears. "I'm right here."

He shook his head and settled next to her, his fingers rubbing soothingly at the sudden tension in her neck. "You were a million miles away."

"Nah." She shook her head. "Just a few hundred thousand."

His grin was quick, but his eyes were quiet. Quieter than she'd ever seen them.

"I'm not like him, Serena. I won't hurt you."

She nodded, leaning into Kevin's strength—because it was there and because she needed him in more ways than she was ready to acknowledge.

He picked her up and settled her on his lap so that she was straddling him—so that they were eye to eye. "Tell me you believe me." His eyes were dark, intense, powerful—all the passion she'd seen him show for his work now focused on her. "Tell me you know that I'll never do anything to cause you pain."

Her heart rose to her throat. "Kevin—" Her voice broke and she had to start again. "I know you won't mean to."

His eyes narrowed while his hips surged powerfully beneath hers, and she realized that he was fully aroused. Huge and long and thick and more than ready to bury himself in her.

She moved against him, but his hands clamped on her hips like a vice—cementing her in place. "That's not what I said." He thrust again, this time so hard that he almost bruised her. She felt an answering heat uncurl deep inside. "Say it."

Serena eyed him disbelievingly. "Do you know how ridiculous you sound, trying to intimidate me into saying I know you won't hurt me?" She struggled to get away, but he held her firmly as he continued to thrust against her, the hard ridge of his jeans riding between her slit.

His eyes turned black, stormy. "That's bullshit and you know it." He lifted and lowered her, and the rough material of his jeans against her wide-open pussy sent rockets of sensation shooting through her.

His callused fingers came up and squeezed her nipples, his thumbs flicking over the hardened tips again and again. She tried to move, to rock against him, but his hands clamped onto her hips. He was still in control and torturing her seemed to be the name of the game.

"Kevin—" Her cry was low and keening as heat streaked from her nipples to her stomach. Down her spine, between her legs, into every part of her. "Come on ..."

He shoved himself inside of her—jeans and all—and she screamed, but couldn't get away. Couldn't get closer. All she could do was take what he gave her, helpless to control his movements or her body's response to him.

"Say it." He bent his head, whispered the words in her ear before his tongue licked the sensitive spot behind her lobe. "Say you're mine and you know I'll never hurt you."

Shivers ripped through her as his breath added another layer of sensation to the feelings already bombarding her. "Or what?" Her voice was shaky, but it was the best she could do.

He lowered his head, nipped at her shoulder and her neck before settling down to suck on the vulnerable curve where the two met. "Or this is all you'll ever get." He slid his hand away from her nipple, down her stomach to her hot and hungry clit. He flicked it once, twice—brought her right to the edge of orgasm with his thumb and his teeth and the powerful heat of his body between her thighs. And refused to send her over.

Again she tried to rock against him and again he held her still. "Kevin, please." She was sobbing—entreating—and she didn't care. Tears streamed down her face and small explosions occurred with every touch of his mouth on her body. With every thrust of his cock between her legs.

And still he wouldn't end it. His mouth slipped over her bare shoulder, down her breasts to her nipples. She screamed at the first flick of his tongue over the hardened buds, pleasure and pain mingling inside of her until she was twisting violently in his arms. Desperate for some freedom of motion. Desperate for the completion only he could give her.

"Serena, *bébé*." His voice was soft and strained against her breasts, his tongue tracing patterns over and around her nipples. "I love you. I love you so much." He lifted her in his powerful arms, held her suspended in midair as he lapped delicately at her clit. Just hard enough to drive her crazy without sending her spinning into space. "If you can't say that you love me, too, at least tell me that you trust me. That you know I'll never do anything to hurt you."

He pulled her clit between his teeth and nibbled softly, and she screamed again. She screamed and screamed and screamed as sensations unlike anything she'd ever felt before coursed through her. Pleasure and pain. Lust and fear. Overwhelming need and incredible vulnerability.

She was on overload—her mind and body craving Kevin and what only he could give her. Only him. Only Kevin. He'd given her so much—she arched against his hips, desperate for a harder pressure, dying for just a little more.

Would it be so bad if she gave him just a little of what he needed from her?

He lowered her back to his lap, his tongue relinquishing her aching clit, and she wanted to howl in disappointment. She'd been so close, teetering on the cliff that would send her spinning into ecstasy. One more lick, one more nibble—one more *anything*—and she would have flown.

"Fuck you, Kevin!" She screamed the words as frustration roared through her and tears poured unheeded down her face. Any other time she would have been embarassed at their lack of restraint, but he'd turned her into a wild thing. Bucking, scratching, biting, tearing, *begging*. *Pleading* with him to end it. Beyond desperate for the pleasure he could so effortlessly give her. If only he *would*.

"Gladly." His voice was hoarse, tense, and for a moment—just a moment—she pulled away from the need raving her with its fiery claws. And saw his clenched jaw, his tense shoulders, his beautiful hands curled into fists so tight his knuckles were white. And for a second—just a second, before he turned his head away—she saw the tears shining in his own eyes.

Her restraint broke, burying her fears under the weight of her desire and Kevin's love. "I need you," she cried as her hips moved agonizingly against his.

"I want you." She lowered her lips to his, her teeth closing over his bottom lip "I trust you—only you." She wrapped her arms around him and pulled him close.

With a hoarse shout, Kevin lifted her away from him and rolled her onto her back in one smooth motion. Reaching down, he unzipped his jeans. And then he was over her, around her, inside of her so deep she was afraid she'd never get him out. Even more afraid that when the time came, she wouldn't want to.

He rode her hard and she came with his second thrust inside of her. He continued to pound into her, his body strong and powerful above her. When he pulled back, draping her legs over his shoulders so that he could thrust deeper, she came again. And again. And again. Until Kevin was all that existed in her world—Kevin and the unbelievable ecstasy he brought to her.

And when he finally came—his seed jetting inside of her in long, powerful pulses—the pleasure was so great that she lost consciousness. Her last thought as the world turned gray at the edges was that she was safe. Kevin would take care of her.

Chapter Seventeen

Darkness was settling over the bayou when Serena pushed the door of Kevin's truck closed with a resounding bang, knowing from bitter experience that it took quite a bit of strength to get it and keep it closed. He'd offered her the Ferrari, but she'd been a shade leery, to say the least. The way her luck had been going lately, she'd end up with a huge dent in the side, and then Kevin would have to kill her. Literally. He wasn't attached to much, but the Ferrari topped the lists of things he couldn't live without.

She smiled as she grabbed the grocery bags sitting on the passenger seat, filled with stuff for dinner and two boxes of Twinkies for Kevin, because his supply was running dismally low. How was she to have known that she'd develop a taste for the little yellow sponge cakes herself?

She was getting downright domestic, she thought as she began putting the groceries away, humming to herself as she went over dinner preparations in her head. In the last few days, she and Kevin had fallen into a routine. He made breakfast, she made dinner and they pretty much scavenged for lunch on their own.

And if she wasn't quite as relaxed about the whole situation as she pretended to be, that was nobody's business but hers. She was learning to trust—albeit slowly, as she waited for the other shoe to drop. But she *was* learning. At least half of her time with Kevin was spent in the moment instead of worrying about things she couldn't control.

Like the fact that she could have sworn she'd seen Michael La-Fleur peering out at her with haunted eyes from the doorway of the drugstore today as she'd driven through town. Stylishly cut brown hair, designer clothes, he'd looked like her worst nightmare. But by the time she'd stopped the truck and glanced back, he was gone.

She shook her head, hating the fact that she was so screwed up she saw the boogeyman around every corner. How long until she lost it completely and had to be put away? How long before Kevin grew sick of her drama?

Pushing the unpleasant thoughts away, she focused instead on a more pleasant subject and one she never grew tired of.

Kevin.

His work was going very well, and though he was extremely secretive about what he was doing, she could tell his latest piece was huge. Not in its size, but in the impact it was going to have on his career. The lines were clean, beautiful, so smooth and flowing that she'd never seen anything like it before. She couldn't wait to see the finished product, with all the pieces assembled in their proper places.

She'd taken lots of pictures of Kevin working, relaxing, trekking through his beloved swamps. She'd also begun a series on Louisiana bayous for her exhibition, and she'd taken some of the most amazing photos of her career. Raccoons sneaking up and eating marshmallows from Kevin's hands. Alligators cruising the swamp looking for dinner. Even an incredible close-up of a cottonmouth snake dangling lazily from a tree.

But her time here was drawing to a close—she knew it and so did Kevin. It was in the way he looked at her, the way he held her and made love to her at night. A new kind of desperation.

But she couldn't stall Steve much longer—the publishing company was beginning to ride him hard. The deadline they had set was in six days, and she had more than enough photos to meet it, if she could just talk herself into going back to Baton Rouge.

But she was so afraid that their relationship would be over when she did. While she was there, doing her job, she could exist in a happy little world somewhere out of time. She pretended that her actions didn't have consequences, that soon she wouldn't have to make a choice.

They had established a fragile peace after her cold, little temper tantrum a few nights ago, and she could tell that Kevin, like her, was reluctant to rock the boat. But he was reckless and impatient by nature, and she knew that he wouldn't wait much longer before drawing his line in the sand.

So she buried her head, letting precious days trickle away as she lived in her little fantasy world. But she couldn't live in a bubble forever. Lately she'd taken to lying awake at night, listening to Kevin breathe as she watched the numbers roll slowly past on the digital clock. She'd begun to hate that clock, detesting its silent smugness as it slowly counted down her remaining time with Kevin.

Serena shut her thoughts down with a grimace. She was starting to sound like a total lunatic, and that *so* wasn't the image she wanted to leave Kevin with. So instead of dwelling on what she couldn't have, she focused on what she could. Namely, a romantic dinner with Kevin. One of their last. She wanted it to be special, and she was making her famous gumbo—a recipe her mother had taught Sandra and her many years before and one that Kevin had loved when she'd made it a couple of weeks earlier.

Serena turned the radio on, danced a little as one of her favorite Clapton songs came on, laughing at herself as she did. Wanting to set the mood, she lit some candles and dimmed the lights a little. Slapping butter and flour in a pan, she began making the dark roux that was the most important part of any good gumbo. When the roux was thick and bubbly, she added some chicken stock and let it simmer as she began chopping celery and onions. A new song came on and she swayed gently while she worked, caught in the romantic lyr-

ics about piña coladas and the rain. Piña coladas sounded particularly good right now. Maybe she'd see if Kevin had some coconut in
his cupboards.

Before she could do much more than reach for the pantry door,
the lights went out, plunging the room into swift and sudden darkness. The candles she'd lit earlier for atmosphere shed enough light
to keep her from freaking out, but not enough to make her anywhere
near comfortable.

Taking a couple of deep breaths as she willed herself to remain
calm, Serena crossed to the kitchen window. The lights should have
gone out in Kevin's studio as well, and he was probably rushing up
to the house to check on her right now. But as she peered into the
darkness, she realized Kevin's lights were still on. He had no idea
that she was alone in the night.

Breathe in. Breathe out. She repeated the words to herself as she
searched the shadowy kitchen for her shoes. She was a big girl. She
could handle walking over to the studio by herself. It was simply a
matter of keeping calm and—

"Hello, Serena."

A startled scream escaped her, and she whirled around, a death
grip on the chef's knife she still clutched in her hand. Her heart beat
wildly out of control as she made out the outline of a dark figure in
the doorway, only feet away.

But who? It wasn't Kevin, of that she was sure—the silhouette
illuminated by the candles was too small, the voice too soft.

Serena's breath caught in her throat. "Damien?"

"I've been waiting for you to get home."

No, she realized as panic made her hands shake, not Damien.
The voice wasn't right. A small part of her panic-stricken brain
picked up on that even as she told herself she was crazy. How long
had it been since she'd heard him speak?

But she'd heard him in her nightmares for ten long years. And
this voice—it wasn't his. It had the same rhythm, the same accent—
but it was lower, smoother, with a familiarity that tickled at the corners of her mind. But her heart was pounding out of control, her fear

making it impossible to grasp the slender fingers of memory poking at her subconscious.

Squinting into the darkness, she realized that the size wasn't right either. Damien was shorter, leaner.

So who—? She grabbed the knife even more tightly, lifting it up to chest level. Whoever it was wouldn't find her an easy target—not this time.

And then he moved deeper into the room—closer to the candles and to her—and relief turned her knees to water. "Jack." She lowered the knife. "What are you doing here?"

"I'm here for you."

"Did something happen? Damien—"

"Forget about him, Serena. I'd never let that scumbag close enough to touch you."

"Then what—" He came closer, and as she got her first good look at him, she paused in the act of putting the knife down. Dressed impeccably in designer clothes, his hair died brown and cut into an expensive new style, he was as handsome as ever. His angel's face looked almost pious—if she didn't look too closely at his eyes. And ignored the pistol dangling carelessly from his fingers.

Shock rocketed through her, made her stumble.

Not Jack. Please, God, not Jack!

But as he advanced menacingly, she knew there was no other explanation. Her stomach revolted, and she fought to control the nausea rapidly turning her inside out.

How could this be happening?

How could it be Jack?

Betrayal wound through her and tears pricked the back of her eyes. She beat them back, mercilessly.

"What are you doing here?" She knew—dear God, she knew—but she couldn't stop herself from asking. From praying it was all a huge misunderstanding.

But the gun gleamed menacingly in the candlelight. And Jack's smile—when it came—made a mockery of her hasty imprecations.

"I wanted to surprise you." He reached forward, ran one cold finger down her cheek. "Did you think you could fool me? Living out here in the bayou with that dirty, disgusting laborer? Really, Serena, it's beneath you."

"Jack, don't." Her voice was rusty and harsh-sounding next to his melodious tones, but she couldn't stop the plea from breaking free.

She'd trusted him. The words ran through her head again and again. For ten years, he'd been the *only* one she'd trusted. Yet Kevin had been right all along.

What little heart she had left shattered in her chest.

"How can I not?" His perfect bow lips curled into a snarl. "I've spent ten years waiting for you to notice me, ten years waiting for you to get over your sister. I stayed close, knowing I would be the one you turned to when you were finally able to move on."

A chill skated down her spine as naked madness moved in eyes she no longer recognized. "I even went to the prison regularly, started those ridiculous calls expecting you to turn to me for help. Instead, you've been consorting with the most unsavory of characters."

"It doesn't have to be like this." She tried to reach out to him, to stop this before it was too late. But the insane rage radiating from him told her how useless her efforts really were.

There was no getting out of this.

Terror crawled through her at the realization.

"Oh, yes, yes, it does. I want you to suffer as I have. I want to see you stripped of everything, totally humiliated, as I've been, watching as you let that animal touch you. And then"—his laugh was high-pitched, out of control—"then I'll make you mine forever. One way or the other."

He was insane. Completely, absolutely, around-the-bend insane. How could she possibly have missed it for so long? If she could have had any doubts based on his behavior of the last few weeks, his cold delivery of her torture and possible death sentence would have alleviated them. Whether he had always been so, or if something in the last ten years had pushed him over the edge, she didn't know.

Nor, she realized, did she particularly care. But the thought of

Kevin walking into the house, totally unprepared, and getting shot by this psycho, chilled her more than any threats Jack could possibly make. She had to do something and quickly.

"Jack." She kept her voice soft and friendly, though she wanted nothing more than to claw him bloody. "I had no idea you felt that way. I wish you'd told me. We might have been able to—"

"Shut up!" The first chink in his impeccable armor appeared with the vicious scream. "Stop lying!"

"I'm not—" She broke off as she heard the gun cock, watched him step back and raise it to chest level as he pointed it at her for the first time.

"Slut!" His agonized scream ripped through the house, tore up Serena's spine before she could brace herself against it. "I loved you. I always loved you. And you pay me back like this?"

His voice broke and he sank, shuddering, into a kitchen chair, the gun falling to the table with a clatter as he activated the safety. He buried his head in his hands for a moment, and Serena tightened her grip on the chef's knife as she slowly sidled toward the back door.

Jack's head came up at her second step, the gun coming up one second later. "Where are you going?" he asked, a singsong quality to his voice that creeped her out more than everything else combined. "You can't leave the party so soon."

"Nowhere. I just wanted to get something out of the fridge. I'm making gumbo and I don't want it to get ruined." Was she seriously talking about dinner with a crazed, gun-wielding murderer?

"I like gumbo." His voice was still high-pitched and childlike.

"I know you do," she replied soothingly, her mind desperately searching for a way to warn Kevin. "That's why I'm making it."

"You knew I was coming?" A hint of his long-lost charm lit the sudden smile that flashed across his face.

"I hoped you would." She pitched her voice low and seductive, fought the intense urge to vomit with everything she had. "I've missed you."

"I've missed you, too, Serena." His eyes were crafty as he studied her. "Come here."

And get close enough to let him touch her again? Not without a fight. "But I've got to make dinner. Remember? The gumbo?" Oh, God, Kevin, please stay in the studio. Stay safe.

"It can wait, can't it? I've been wanting to hold you for such a long time."

"Later. I promise." She nearly choked on the lie.

"Put the knife down and come to me."

Serena's head jerked at the command in his tone, her startled eyes meeting his suddenly clear ones. "Jack—" She tried a placating tone, but his gun was pointed once again at her. This time he had it aimed at her head.

"Now."

"But how will I—"

She stopped dead as he cocked the gun. "I'm not an idiot, Serena. Nor am I a child. Now please do as I ask, or, I fear, the results will be disastrous."

It seemed it was time to lay her cards on the table. "From what you said earlier, I figure it'll be disastrous no matter what. So why should I make it easy for you?" If soothing didn't work, maybe tough would.

"Because you can die easily or with more pain than you could ever imagine exists. At the moment, the choice is yours. But I'm running out of patience and soon the choice will be mine." His smile was cruel. "Somehow, I doubt you'll like my choice."

Her fingers went numb and the knife clattered to the floor before she could stop it. He wore the same smile on his face that Damien had worn eleven years ago, when she'd answered the door and called her sister to her death. When he'd plunged his knife into her and locked her in the closet. When he'd returned to finish the job.

What could she possibly have done to attract the attention of *two* psychopaths in her lifetime?

And now that she had Jack's attention, how was she going to get out of this alive? More important, how was she going to keep Kevin alive as well?

She walked across the kitchen toward Jack—small, dragging

steps designed to buy her time to think. But memories were crowding into her brain, clamoring for attention, demanding that she run as fast and as far as possible. Messing with her ability to think rationally.

He wore the same cologne Damien had worn so many long years before, and the scent made her stomach churn sickly. Calvin Klein's Obsession. More appropriate than the designer would ever know. That stench of it had stayed with her even longer than the smell of her sister's blood. Walking by the counter at the mall always made her queasy, and she'd turned down dates from every man who'd ever asked her out while wearing it. How had she overlooked Jack's predilection for it?

Her heart beat faster and her breathing turned harsh. Panic crawled through her veins, overpowering her attempts to keep calm. She was going to die. She knew it, could even accept it if it meant that this was finally over and that Jack would spend a big part of his miserable life rotting in jail.

But she couldn't stand the idea of Jack killing Kevin, too. Beautiful, talented Kevin whose only fault in this was to fall in love with her. To make her love him back. She couldn't let that happen. Jack might kill her, but she had to take him with her. Better she should die painfully than spend eternity knowing that she could have saved Kevin but hadn't been brave enough to try.

She was a few feet away from Jack when she stopped walking, the beginnings of a plan suddenly forming in her overwrought brain. "Didn't you hear me?" he demanded. "I said, get over here."

"Make me." Her voice wasn't as strong as she would have liked, but it didn't shake either.

Jack fired an almost soundless shot at the floor near her feet, and she used it as an excuse to jump backward, pretending to cower in fear against the kitchen cabinets. Not that it was all pretense. She *did* have a madman with a gun stalking her, after all. And the fact that the shots made no sound—due to the silencer attached—only made the whole thing more eerie.

"The next one rips through your flesh instead of the floor," he sneered. "Now move it."

"I can't. Please—" She made her voice tremulous, lowered her lashes as she pretended to look away from him.

He stalked toward her, swearing. "Get up!" He plunged a fist into her hair and pulled, lifting her up as pain ripped through her scalp. He drew back the hand that held the gun, prepared to punch her. But she whirled at the last second, ignoring the sharp pain in her head at the action. Her hands closed over the handles of the huge gumbo pot on the stove, and she turned as she lifted it, dumping the hot broth down his front.

The stove was electric and had turned off with the lights, so the soup wasn't nearly as hot as she would have liked. But it did the job. Jack screamed, his hands releasing both her hair and the gun as he tried desperately to rip the hot shirt from his scalded flesh. She didn't take time to examine the damage, but ran, heart pounding, straight through the utter darkness of the living room to the front door—the one closest to Kevin's studio. She was fumbling with the lock when she felt an arm around the waist, and Jack flung her facedown on the wood floor.

Serena hit the ground hard, but was rolling over to face him even as he leaned over her, screaming obscenities. She kicked her right leg up and out with everything she had and her loafer-clad foot connected with the angry skin of his stomach.

He fell backward and she scrambled to her feet, biting back the instinctive screams welling in her throat. Jack was making enough noise to wake the dead—if she added to it, Kevin was sure to hear and come running—a scene she wanted to avoid at all costs.

She turned to run, hoping to hide somewhere in the pitch-blackness of the house, but his hands closed around her left calf.

Then he was on her, shoving her to the ground, turning her face up as he straddled her prone body. His hands tangled in her hair and he smacked her head, hard, against the floor, again and again. Things turned fuzzy after the second hit, but Serena refused to give up without a fight.

She bucked against him with her hips, desperately trying to unseat him. Or at least make him lose his balance enough to give her a shot at escape. But his legs were strong, catching her hips in a vice that seemed unbreakable.

Keeping one hand in her hair, he pulled her head tight against the floor and lowered his face to hers. "How does it feel, knowing you're going to die, bitch? How does it feel, knowing you'll never see pretty boy again? That the last dick you'll ever feel inside you will be mine?"

He tilted his pelvis so that his erection pressed against her stomach and she gagged. "What's the matter, baby?" he jeered, fumbling with his wet and slippery zipper. The jeans had obviously protected that part of his anatomy in a way the thin dress shirt had been unable to protect much of the rest. "You like what the laborer does to you. Maybe you'll like it with me as well."

She whimpered despite herself, bucking wildly against him as desperation overwhelmed her for the first time. She couldn't let him rape her, couldn't stand to die with some psychopath inside of her, as Sandra had.

She wiggled her hands between them, forced herself to ignore the way he pushed and tore at her khakis—and the tender skin below them—as she waited for the perfect moment. Her button and zipper gave way, and he lifted onto his knees in an attempt to push her pants out of his way.

It was the move she'd been waiting for, the chance to get her arms between them and rake his burned skin with her short, sharp fingernails. Curling her fingers into talon, she dug in, drawing blood with every swipe of her hand.

He bellowed in rage and agony as he crashed his fist into her jaw. Pain exploded through her face and she tasted blood as the world went dark around the edges.

Kevin hung up the phone after Grayson's call, uneasiness eating at him. The police had been tailing LaFleur for the last couple of days since he had gotten out of rehab—not expecting anything to pan out, but trying to shake him up nonetheless. And now he had escaped his police tail, shedding them nearly four hours before in a mall dressing room. Grayson figured that it wasn't deliberate, that the cops had simply gotten distracted and missed him.

But Kevin wasn't so sure. If it had been sheer dumb luck that had enabled LaFleur to lose them, why hadn't they found him by now? And if it had been deliberate, what exactly was he up to? He glanced uneasily out the big bay window at the side of his studio, saw his truck once again parked in front of the house. Serena was back from the store, yet hadn't come by to see him. Which wasn't totally unheard-of behavior, he had to admit, particularly if she had just returned. But it made him nervous enough to want to check.

With narrowed eyes, he headed toward the house. If she was fine, he would warn her about what Grayson had said, and they could figure out what she wanted to do about it. The detective had also promised to look into Jack Rawlins, but he thought Kevin was way off track. For Serena's sake, Kevin hoped the detective was right. She didn't need another disappointment in her life.

And if she wasn't okay, well, then he would figure out a way to deal with whatever was wrong himself.

But the closer he got to the house, the more uneasy he became. Something felt different, wrong. Even the bayou animals were quiet, as if sensing danger. Then it hit him—the lights were out. There was no way Serena had turned them out voluntarily. He broke into a run and heard the scream of an animal in pain as he hit the porch full force. Every instinct he had told him to push through the open door, to rush in and save the woman he loved.

But he had just enough sense left to stop and look through the window, to try to find out what he was up against. The room was black and he couldn't see anything. But he heard Serena moan, the sound quickly followed by a high-pitched masculine giggle.

Damien.

With a bellow of rage, Kevin crashed through the open door and launched himself in the direction of the sound. His hands connected with warm flesh, and then he was dragging the half-naked bastard off Serena like a man possessed. He grabbed him by the hair and held him in place as he plowed his fist into his stomach again and again.

LaFleur sagged against him, retching, and Kevin shoved him to the ground. Then Kevin banged the intruder's head against the hard wood—once, twice, a third time.

But Serena hadn't made a sound, hadn't moved since he roared into the room, and fear was wild and torturously alive inside of him. Abandoning LaFleur, he turned to her motionless body, desperate to know if she was breathing. He couldn't see well enough to tell if she was bleeding, but when he put his hand on her, he felt the rise and fall of her chest. Relief, acute to the point of pain, flooded him.

Crouching down beside her, he smoothed her hair from her face, murmuring, "*Bébé?* Serena? *Chere*, are you okay?" His hand came away sticky and his blood ran cold.

Serena's body jerked, her eyes opening even as she pushed feebly against him. "Jack," she said, her hands clutching at him as she wiped her bloody nose against her shoulder.

"What about him?" He stared at her, confused.

"You were right. It was Jack all along." She began to cry, powerful shudders wracking her slender form.

"What?" He glanced behind him at the lifeless body lying facedown on the floor. "That's Rawlins?"

"I trusted him," she sobbed. "How could I have trusted him?"

"It's okay, *bébé*. He won't hurt you." He looked again at Jack's shadowy form, wanting to be sure that the sniveling, retching mess was still no threat. "You're okay now."

"He's got a gun, Kevin." Her hands groped desperately for his. "He dropped it in the kitchen when we fought. I think it's still there."

Kevin felt a surge of admiration for this strong, sexy woman who refused to give up, no matter how badly life battered her. He brushed his lips over the top of her head before jumping to his feet. "I'll get it and be right back."

He bent over Jack, wanting to make sure he was out of commission. But Jack moved abruptly, his arm coming up in a stabbing motion that had Kevin stumbling before he could catch himself. That stumble saved his life, twisting him just enough so that the knife sliced his upper arm instead of plunging through his heart as the attorney had intended.

Cursing he drew back and eyed Jack with disgust. He wanted to yell for Serena to run, but he was afraid she was too badly injured to go very far. If that was the case, he didn't want to draw Jack's attention away from him and onto her.

Jack stumbled to his feet, and Kevin and he circled each other warily, each looking for an opportunity to strike. Kevin's arm hurt like hell, and he wanted to get Serena to a hospital. But the situation they were in now was his fault—if he'd killed the guy earlier, when he'd had the chance, Serena would be safe. It wasn't a mistake he would make a second time.

Jack feinted left and lunged right, his knife cutting quickly through the air. Kevin threw himself to the left, narrowly avoiding the blade, searching for an opening to make his move.

Ignoring the pain richocheting through her, Serena pulled herself laboriously to her feet—her entire being focused on Kevin and the danger he was in. Hysteria welled in her throat, but she fought it down. There had to be something she could use to help Kevin end this thing once and for all. But the darkness was absorbing and she didn't know which of the big men was which.

Feeling her way to the built-in cabinets against the left wall of the room, she crouched and pulled out the flashlight Kevin had shown her after the blackout weeks before. Afraid of blinding Kevin, she pointed the flashlight at the ground before turning it on.

She turned the light toward the men in time to see Jack lunge at Kevin with the knife again. Kevin blocked him and used Jack's own momentum against him, flinging the attorney to the ground and kicking him in the ribs as the knife clattered across the floor.

Jack wrapped himself around Kevin's leg, pulling Kevin down next to him. The two men rolled across the floor, punching and kicking, struggling for supremacy. At one point Kevin was on top, but

Jack twisted and pinned him beneath him. His hands wrapped around Kevin's throat and squeezed, even as Kevin plowed his fists repeatedly into Jack's stomach.

Refusing to give in to her terror, Serena shone the flashlight around the room, desperate to find something she could use to help Kevin. Jack was fighting with a strength and desperation born from insanity—he took whatever hit Kevin threw at him and kept coming, despite the damage Kevin was inflicting.

Her eyes fell on the fireplace set Kevin kept on his hearth. Slowly—too slowly—she dragged herself toward it, desperate to get it before Jack got a clean shot at Kevin. Her hand closed around the sharp iron poker, and she nearly wept with relief.

Across the room, Jack screamed and lost his grip on Kevin's throat long enough for Kevin to drag in a few ragged breaths. At the last minute, Jack regained his balance and his grip tightened once again.

Desperate, terrified of hitting Kevin by mistake, Serena waited until she had a clear shot at Jack's back. Then, with a muttered prayer, she pulled back her arm and thrust the poker into Jack's upper back with every ounce of her waning strength.

Jack's fingers dropped from Kevin's throat, his high-pitched screams once again filling the room. Kevin pushed Jack backward, following him as he hit the ground on his left side. Like a man possessed, Kevin plunged his fists into Jack again and again—hitting his stomach, his face, anywhere he could reach.

Jack rolled over, screaming, as the poker pushed deeper into his body, his blood dripping steadily from the wound.

Kevin pressed his advantage, his massive fists making contact again and again. In the grip of a killing rage, he wanted nothing more than to destroy this man, ensuring that he would never threaten Serena again. His fist plunged into Jack's face again, and this time he felt the satisfying crunch of bone as his hand connected solidly with Jack's nose.

Kevin pulled back his hand again, fully prepared to beat the now-unconscious man to death. But Serena rested her hand on his arm, her touch calming him as nothing else could have.

"Kevin, stop," she murmured quietly. "He's not worth it. He's just not worth it."

Kevin turned his head, looked into the warm chocolate of Serena's eyes illuminated by the flashlight, and the rage receded. Not completely, but enough to let him think a little more clearly. He climbed off Jack and gathered Serena in his arms.

"Are you okay?" he asked, his hands running desperately over her as he searched for any wounds.

"I'm fine." Her voice was gentle. "You're the one who was stabbed."

"I've done worse to myself in the studio." He shrugged. "It's nothing. But we need to call the police."

"I already did. Once I realized you had things under control. They're on their way."

"Once you realized I had things under control?" he repeated incredulously. "Is this before or after you plunged an iron poker into the man?"

"After." It was her turn to shrug. "You looked like you needed help."

Sirens sounded in the distance and Kevin wrapped a hand around the back of her head, pulling her in for a gentle kiss. "I thought women were supposed to scream in situations like this. That's what they do in books and movies."

She raised an eyebrow, managing to look imperious despite the bruises, blood and ripped clothing. "Screw that."

He laughed, ignoring the pain in his bruised throat. "I love you."

She swung the flashlight around, surveying the mess in his kitchen and living room. "I don't know why."

Kevin relinquished his hold on Serena reluctantly, then took the flashlight from her and bent down next to Jack. He shone the light directly in the bastard's face while at the same time delivering a few well-placed nudges that assured him the man really was unconscious and no longer a threat.

He shook his head in amazement. He didn't know many women who would have had the guts to do what Serena had done. Was it any wonder he was crazy about her?

Pulling her up and out of the house, he settled both of them on the porch steps with the flashlight as they waited for the police to arrive, yet again. "There is one thing that's been bugging me," he said, loving the way she fit into the curve of his arm. Thanking God that he had a chance to hold her again. "Why was he wet? It isn't raining."

She met his eyes. "I dumped the pot of gumbo I was making on him."

"Was it hot?"

She grinned, a poor, lopsided smile that made his heart ache. "Close to boiling."

"Hot damn. You really are my kind of woman, Serena Macafee."

She glanced behind them, as if expecting Jack to come barreling through the door at any second. "Exactly how twisted does that make you?"

"Just twisted enough to keep up with you."

Her answering snort was music to his ears.

Chapter Eighteen

Hours later, after having his arm stitched up and giving a statement to the police, Kevin found himself hesitating outside the door of Serena's hospital room. While she had escaped serious injury—which was more than he could say for Jack, who was currently stabilized in the small hospital's intensive-care unit—she had a mild concussion and enough bumps and bruises that the doctors had decided to keep her overnight for observation. The decision was not sitting well with *her*.

"Serena, *bébé*, let the poor people do their jobs." Kevin held out the flowers he'd bought her at the hospital gift shop. "If you're a good girl, they'll let you go home tomorrow."

Her lower lip poked out in the first pout he'd ever seen from her. "I don't want to go home tomorrow. I want to leave now. I hate hospitals."

The nurses shot him an exasperated look, clearly pushed to the limit by this strange and demanding Serena. "You've got a concussion, *mon amour*. They just want to watch you for twenty-four hours."

She snorted. "I don't care what they want. I'm going home. Now."

He shook his head, though his heart warmed at hearing her refer to his house as home. "Not today you aren't."

"Kevin!" Her voice was a wail. "I can't stay here. You don't understand. I can't."

"Have you given her a sedative?" he asked the nurse closest to him, shocked at how wound up Serena still was.

"Two. And a pain pill." The nurse shrugged at his incredulous look. "She's so uptight that they're not working."

"I don't understand. She's usually so calm. This is totally unlike her."

"Hey, I'm still here! You don't need to talk about me like I'm not around."

Both nurses gave Kevin looks of sympathy before heading rapidly for the door. "Call if you need us," one said on her way out. "Good luck."

Good luck? Just how badly behaved had Serena been? He turned back to the bed, warily, the lilies still clutched in his hands. "Serena, *chere*, what is going on?"

"I told you what's going on! I'm not staying here." She pulled at the IV in her arm, nearly succeeding in ripping it out before he could stop her.

"Whoa, whoa." He dropped the flowers on the bed as he reached for her hands. "What are you doing?"

"I can't stay here. Nobody will listen to me. I can't stay here." Tears swam in her eyes, thickening her voice.

He settled onto the bed next to her. "It's just for one night, *bébé*. Then I'll take you home."

"No! Kevin, please. The last time I was in the hospital was after Sandra …" Her voice trailed off. "I lay in bed for weeks, staring at the ceiling and reliving my sister's murder. I can't do that again. I can't lie here and remember. Please. Please, don't make me stay."

"*Mon Dieu, bébé!* I'm sorry—I didn't think." He gathered her into his arms, stroked her hair away from her battered face. She held herself stiffly against him, unwilling to sink into the comfort he offered her. "I'll get you out. But you have to behave. Give me a few minutes, okay?"

She nodded against his chest. "Okay."

He strode down the hall to the nurses' station. "Where's her doctor?" he asked the blond nurse who'd been in Serena's room a few minutes before.

"He's doing rounds. He'll be done in a little while." Her eyebrows rose inquiringly. "Is there a problem, sir?"

"I need to take her home."

She sighed impatiently. "I know she's upset, but the doctor wants her here. She's pretty badly bruised and she needs to be observed."

"I understand that. But she's not going to calm down. Being this agitated can't be good for her."

The nurse threw her hands in the air. "There's her doctor. Take it up with him." She pointed to a small balding man in a blue shirt and golfing tie.

"What's his name?"

"Dr. Alexander."

"Thanks." Kevin approached the doctor warily. "Dr. Alexander?"

The man turned. "Yes?"

"My name's Kevin Riley. I'm with Serena Macafee. Do you have a few minutes?"

The doctor took in Kevin's blood-spattered clothes and various bandages and sighed. "Of course you are."

"Can I take her home?"

"No, Mr. Riley, you cannot. While her concussion is relatively mild, I still think she needs to be observed. She's taken a pretty bad beating."

"I know. And I've tried to calm her down, tried to convince her to stay." He acknowledged the doctor's skeptical look. "I have. But look, she's had it rough." He explained the situation, watched the doctor's expression change from impatience to horror and finally to acceptance.

After studying Kevin for a minute, he sighed loudly. "Let me talk to the nurse and check Serena one more time. Then we'll talk."

The doctor returned a few minutes later, shaking his head. "You're right. She isn't going to settle down here." He looked Kevin in the eye, his gaze direct and absolute. "If I let you take her home, you have to promise to watch her closely. And I want to see her in my office tomorrow morning."

Dr. Alexander pulled a card out of his pocket and handed it to Kevin. "Call and make an appointment. Tell my receptionist I want to see her first thing in the morning. And if she doesn't look good, I'm putting her back in the hospital. Even if I have to knock her out to do it. Do I make myself clear?"

Kevin nodded. "Absolutely. Thanks, man. I really appreciate this."

"Take care of her."

"I will."

The doctor merely shook his head. "The nurse is working on the discharge papers. Your friend should be ready to go in about twenty minutes.

Hours later, Kevin sat in a chair by the side of his bed, a small light burning on the nightstand and his sketch pad in his lap. Serena was sleeping, finally, though she tossed and turned restlessly. He reached out a hand to soothe her, loving the feel of her petal-soft skin beneath his.

She'd insisted on a shower when she'd gotten home, and he hadn't had the heart to deny her. Though the hospital had cleaned her up pretty well, he understood her need to wash away the day's events. So he'd taken one with her, holding her limp body up and washing her hair before settling her in bed with a bowl of canned chicken noodle soup.

She'd eaten a little, but by then she'd relaxed enough for the medication to finally take effect, and she'd fallen asleep over her tray. He'd been sitting by the bed ever since, watching her, thinking about how close he'd come to losing her.

He needed to call Grayson. The police who'd answered Serena's 911 call had assured him that they'd get in touch with the detective, but he still felt the need to touch base. To find out what was going to happen to Jack Rawlins now—if he had even lived after Serena's fireplace-poker stunt. Surely he couldn't buy his way out the way LaFleur had—he didn't have the money or the status to pull it off. And if he tried, well, Kevin had a lot of money of his own to throw around.

Kevin stroked his pencil lightly over a piece of blank paper, drawing more for comfort than any artistic purpose. He sketched the fine lines of Serena's face and the long, slender column of her neck. Then he began to fill in the details—the high cheekbones, the long eyelashes—but the paper kept blurring in front of him.

He blinked the tears back, astounded that he was crying for the first time in his adult life. As much as Deb had hurt and angered him when she'd dumped him publicly in order to gain notoriety and make a name for herself, he'd never shed one tear for her—had never even come close. But Serena had nearly died today, with him less than fifty yards away. And he hadn't even known she was in danger until it was almost too late.

Standing up he crossed to the window and looked outside into the darkness of the bayou. He loved this woman; he'd known this for weeks. But he hadn't made a move, hadn't cemented things between them. Structure had never been that important to him before—he lived his life his way and to hell with what others had to say.

But he wanted Serena, and not just for a little while. He wanted her for a lifetime, tied to him legally, emotionally, in every way a man could bind a woman to him. He wanted to watch her grow ripe with his child, to see what she'd look like at forty. And fifty and sixty and seventy.

But what did she want? She'd never said the words, had never told him that she loved him. But he felt it—in the way she touched his hand, in the way she kissed him, even in the way she always came home with an addition to his stash of Twinkies.

She had to love him—now that he'd found her, he couldn't handle the thought of life without her. When Deb had left, it had hurt, but if Serena left him, he didn't think he'd ever recover. She was it for him. This was the woman he was destined to spend the rest of his life with. As long as she cooperated.

Serena moved restlessly, moaning as she shifted in her sleep to find a more comfortable position. Rawlins had really done a number on her—there was barely an inch of her poor body that wasn't black-and-blue.

Anger rose in him again, and he wished, not for the first time, that he had killed Jack Rawlins and gotten him out of her life for good. This new bloodthirsty side of himself surprised him. While he'd never run from a fight, he'd never looked for one either. He lived out here alone because he liked it, because any extended contact with people—harmless or violent—was too much for him. He craved his isolation.

Of course, that was before Serena. Now he could picture himself living happily with her, seeing her face everyday, hearing the laughter of their children as they played in the backyard. Not that he was ready to do anything as drastic as moving to the city, but having a few people around wouldn't be so bad.

Serena moaned again, crying out as she rolled onto a badly bruised shoulder. He was furious that Jack had gotten his hands on her, but he was also incredibly proud of the woman he loved. Never in a million years would he have put her as the type to pour boiling gumbo on a man and then stab him in the back with a fireplace poker.

But he shouldn't be surprised. He'd known all along that there was a lot more to that calm, cool exterior than she showed the world. Today he'd simply found out that there was even more there than he'd ever have guessed.

"Kevin?" Her voice was husky with sleep and he turned to find her sitting up in bed, staring at him.

"Are you all right?" he asked, crossing to her and sinking to his knees at the head of the bed.

She smiled. "I'm fine. But I miss you. Aren't you coming to bed soon?"

"I promised the doctor I'd watch you."

"You can watch me from bed." Her smile was frankly sensuous. "Anyway, I'm fine."

"I know. But I'm going to make sure of it." He brushed his hand over her hair in a gesture so achingly familiar it nearly broke her heart. "Are you thirsty?"

She shook her head. "No." She patted the spot next to her. "Come to bed, Kevin. I want you to hold me."

"I'm coming, *bébé*." Facing her fear of the dark was definitely not something she needed to do tonight, so he turned on the bathroom light before flipping off the bedside lamp and easing himself gingerly onto the bed beside her. Ignoring his concerns, she reached out and dragged him closer, laughing when he protested.

"Stop treating me like glass. I'm a little sore. So what? I still want to feel you against me." She wrapped herself around him, pillowing her head on his chest and throwing her left leg over his.

Serena breathed deeply, letting Kevin's familiar smell wash over her. She could finally sleep now, with his warm and solid body against hers. She could finally feel safe. She didn't know where Jack was now, or where he was going to end up. In the morning she knew she'd want to know why he'd done the things he'd done. But for tonight she didn't want to think about him—refusing to give him any more importance in her life than she already had.

Snuggling closer to Kevin, she listened as his heart beat rhythmically beneath her ear. "You're not going to sleep, are you?"

"Nope."

"Why not?" She pulled away, looked at him in the dim light. "I'm fine."

His smile was gentle. "I know. But it doesn't hurt to be sure."

"Kevin—"

"Stop arguing and go to sleep." He gently pressed her head back to his chest. "It's the best thing for your headache."

"But—"

"Enough, Serena! Get some rest or that doctor will send you back to the hospital tomorrow."

She sighed huffily, but didn't say another word. He found himself grinning at the ceiling as she drifted off to sleep.

Serena fought to keep from snarling as she watched Kevin leave his studio and head to the house. He'd taken her to the doctor yesterday, who had pronounced her definitely on the mend. But had that stopped him from coddling her? Not even close. He hadn't left her side once yesterday, and this was the fifth time today he'd made the trek from his studio to the house—how he was getting any work done, she didn't know. God knew, he was certainly interfering with her work.

With a grimace, she closed the screen of digital images she was categorizing. All she needed was Kevin leaning over her shoulder, complaining about each and every picture. Especially with her deadline looming two days closer.

She had to leave tomorrow. Much as she'd tried to ignore her responsibilities and pretend that she didn't, she knew that her time with Kevin was drawing to an end. She closed her eyes, rubbing her temples in an effort to alleviate the pounding headache that had suddenly broken through the pain pills.

What was she going to say to him? How would she tell him that it was over? He thought he loved her, told her so nearly every day. But she couldn't love him back, *wouldn't* love him back. She'd lost everyone she ever cared about, and she wasn't strong enough to make it through losing him, too.

Look at Jack. Besides Kevin, he was the only person she'd truly trusted in the eleven years since Sandra's death, and he'd ended up being a certified, documented sociopath. Detective Grayson had called late last night, had told them of the heavy-duty medication in Jack's apartment. Of the sick shrine he'd built to her—complete with copies of her sister's homicide photos and the voice distorter he'd used during the crank calls. Of the room in the back of his house equipped with chains and every torture device imaginable.

Kevin had nearly lost it then—shouting and cursing in French, throwing the phone across the room. She'd known, instinctively, that he was imagining her in Jack's little shop of horrors—something that she had tried very hard not to do. She found it so hard to believe that she'd trusted Jack, had gone to him for help, had defended him to Kevin. What on earth had she been thinking? How had she been so blind to what was really going on in the ADA's head? Her radar had never so much as beeped.

So how could she trust her judgment again? Her heart told her Kevin would never do anything to hurt her, and she believed it. But she knew herself—knew how much more fragile this latest betrayal had made her. She was a total basket case—only one small nervous breakdown away from the same mental institution that was currently housing Jack. And Grayson's casual mention last night of how Damien was fitting into society like a model citizen only made her grip on sanity more tenuous.

Yet the thought of leaving Kevin now ripped her apart. How much worse would it be if she stayed and something happened later on? She'd never recover. Kevin would be smart enough to figure it out, kind enough to stay with her when leaving was the best option.

Which was just one more reason that it was time to move on. Maybe she had refused to acknowledge her love for Kevin—but she cared about him and wanted what was best for him. She wasn't good for herself, let alone anyone else. Her life was a slippery, nightmarish slope, and asking anyone else to share it was absurd. Kevin—for all his surly masculinity—craved his solitary life. What would her absurd, horrifying existence end up doing to Kevin if she stayed?

If he really believed that he loved her, a clean break was better. She'd thought long and hard over the past twenty-four hours about whether or not she wanted to continue the relationship. But it wasn't a matter of want. Or even need. She couldn't continue with this thing, couldn't let Kevin start building his life around hers. Her life was such a mess—as evinced by the events of the past forty-eight hours—how could she ask him to take on all of her baggage?

Besides, it would have to end eventually. She'd rather finish it now, when there were good feelings between them, than let it drag on and end with broken promises, missed meetings and burning bitterness. No, clean and quick was definitely better. And if her heart hurt just looking at him, that was one more reason to end it.

Kevin had reached the porch, though the tears in her eyes blurred her view of him. Serena blinked, rapidly, desperate to hide the signs of her emotional weakness. She was smiling when Kevin reached the kitchen, and if the smile didn't touch her eyes, it would be hard for him to notice around the bruises.

"Hey there, gorgeous!" she said, wrapping her arms around his waist, absorbing his wonderful scent for one of the last times.

"Hey, yourself." He looked around the kitchen, eyes narrowed. "You've been working," he accused.

"Only a little." She turned her back on him, closed her computer. "Besides, it's not like I've got a choice. The deadline for the book is looming, Kevin."

"Call Steve. Tell him to explain the situation to them. They'll understand."

"I don't miss deadlines."

"I know, *cher*. But this is different. You're *malad*. Sick," he elaborated at her blank look.

"I'm not sick. I was punched. And pardon me if I don't want to broadcast that fact to the world."

Kevin sighed wearily. "Serena, *bébé*. You don't have to tell him the whole story. Though I don't understand why you're ashamed of it. You're the victim here."

"I'm done talking about it, Kevin." She put a hand up when he started to protest. "No, I mean it. I'm finished."

His looked at her sternly, though he didn't say another word. Serena eyed him just as suspiciously, not trusting his easy capitulation. It was so un-Kevin-like. What exactly was he up to?

"So when do you need to head back to Baton Rouge?" he asked, his voice a rough velvet rasp that curled her toes.

"Tomorrow. I have pictures that need to be developed and sorted through, though I have a pretty good idea which ones I want to use in the book."

His eyebrows rose in surprise. "Already?" he asked.

"Pretty much."

"Then come with me. And bring your camera. I have something I want you to see."

"What is it?" she asked, reaching for her camera bag.

"You'll see. And while I know that it's your vision that's going into the book, I really want this to be a part of it."

Her furrowed brow smoothed out. "You've finished your sculpture! Oh, Kevin, that's wonderful! I can't wait to see it!" She stepped out the door in front of him, practically dancing in her eagerness to see his newest creation. She'd watched him work on each of the various parts of it in the last couple of weeks, but she'd been dying to see the whole thing put together.

This sculpture seemed special to her, and not just because he'd commented more than once on it being the best thing he'd ever done—his talent was so great that nearly everything he did was head and shoulders above the competition. Maybe it was the intimacy of her connection to the piece—watching it form from nothing into pieces that were beautiful on their own. She could only imagine how stunning it was when completely assembled.

"Hurry up. Let's go," she said, rushing across the grass that separated the two buildings.

Kevin grinned at her enthusiasm. "What if you hate it?"

She rolled her eyes. "I won't! I've been wanting to see it finished forever!"

"I've only been working on it for a couple of weeks. It's come together much faster than a lot of my work."

"Blah, blah, blah. It's seemed like a lot longer, let me tell you. Can you tell me what it is now? You wouldn't before."

"I said that you'd either see it—"

"Or I wouldn't. I know, I know. But I really want to be able to see it."

He pushed open to door to his studio. "You will. I've got faith in you."

Serena walked in, her face raised expectantly to the ceiling. But this piece was nowhere near as large as his other sculptures, rather it was quite petite and delicate in stature. Her eyes widened as she looked at the graceful lines, the metal curved and flowing like water from the top of the sculpture.

She tilted her head, her eyes growing wider and wider. It couldn't be, but it certainly looked— No. It couldn't be. She walked around the sculpture slowly, searching for something beside the obvious.

She glanced at Kevin, who was watching her closely. "Do you like it?"

"Of course I do." Her smile was a little forced as the old, familiar panic began to claw at her stomach.

"Are you sure?" he asked. "You don't look too certain."

"It's not that." She wrapped her arms around herself, studied the abstract sculpture, which looked more and more like a woman the longer she stood and stared at it. Her eyes fell on the smooth chunk of metal clutched between the woman's hands, and her heart skipped a beat. It was a camera.

"Kevin!" Her voice came out high and panicked, but she could do nothing to change it. "It's me. Isn't it? You've sculpted me?"

His smile was blinding. "Yes. It's not what I intended, but every time I came down here, all I could see was you."

It was beautiful, stunning really. The work of a genius who had truly outdone himself. The colors were brilliant—he'd heated the metal to such a state that it bled colors, a shimmering rainbow that added much to the personality of the piece. She tried to be objective, tried to look at the artistic value alone. But everywhere she looked, Kevin's incredible emotions stared back.

The metal was so smooth, the lines so fluid, that the woman actually looked like she was moving. No matter what angle Serena studied her from, the sculpture seemed to be staring back. Its lines were so graceful, so defined, that her face and the back of her head were interchangable, the curve of her breasts and buttocks the same. No detail was too small for him to notice, no part of her not represented.

From the crazy winged butterfly in the sculpture's hair—identical to the one on her hip—to the fists tightly clenched around the fanciful camera, this sculpture was her. It was a labor of love, Kevin's testimony to his love for her. She'd have to be blind not to see it. And though she was stubborn and repressed and often rigid, she was definitely not blind.

Fear crawled through her. She couldn't handle this, couldn't handle the visible evidence of Kevin's feelings for her. He wouldn't have done this if he wasn't serious, wouldn't have put himself on display for the world to see if he didn't mean it. Maybe that was what scared her the most. Kevin wasn't like so many of the artists she knew—falling in and out of love with each new model they used. He never let anyone get close, never opened himself up enough for others to see what really made him tick.

But he had with this piece. Everything he felt was obvious, laid open for even the least observant person to see. Oh, God, what was she going to do? *What was she going to do?*

"Serena, *cher*? What do you think? Do you like it?"

"It's—" Her voice broke. "It's the most beautiful thing I've ever seen."

"Like you." His arms came around her from behind, and it was all she could do to stop herself from weeping. "I love you, Serena. It astounds me how much feeling I have inside of me for you."

"Kevin—"

"No, you always stop me. Let me get this out." He took her hand, laced his large, callused fingers with her own. "I hadn't planned on doing this yet, hadn't planned on doing it here. But somehow it seems perfect."

She started to interrupt again, but he covered her mouth lightly with his other hand. "I know you, *bébé*. Whatever you think, whatever you'd hoped to hold back, know that I see it. I see the real you."

He pulled her to him, turned her around so that her back was to his chest and her eyes were focused, once again, on his sculpture of her. "That's the real you, Serena. Every bit of it."

"No." She shook her head, tried to push his hands away but his hold remained firm. "Kevin, you don't know the real me. All the dark, disgusting parts. You can't—"

He turned her toward him again, cupped her face in his beloved hands, while his beautiful blue eyes stared into hers. "I know you're afraid. I know you're raw inside. Who wouldn't be after everything you've seen, everything you've had to live through? But you can do this. I know you can."

"I'm a mess," she protested, fear nearly strangling her with its frigid claws. "More now, I think, than when Sandra first died. I can't do this. *You* can't do this."

"Can't do what, Serena? Can't want you? Can't need you? Can't love you more than I've ever loved another human being? Too late, *cher*. I already do. And I want to marry you. I want to build a life with you."

Panic raced through her, a living, breathing entity shredding her insides until it was nearly impossible to breathe. Her head spun and the world went gray for the second time in as many days.

She bent over, braced her hands on her knees, as she sucked in great gulps of air. Tried to find the words. Tried to find the courage to say what needed to be said. Kevin crouched beside her, reached to touch her but she backed away. If he touched her now, she'd be lost. And she couldn't make this mistake, couldn't let him throw his life away on someone who'd never be whole.

He reached for her again, but she knocked his hand away. She straightened slowly, not wanting to risk another bout of dizziness. Watched as Kevin did the same. His eyes were wary but his gaze held steady as he stared at her, taking in every emotion she didn't have the strength to hide.

"Don't do this, Kevin."

"I have to." His hands gripped her arms right above the elbow and lifted her onto her tiptoes. "Because you won't."

He kept his eyes opened and focused on hers as he slowly leaned down to kiss her. She'd expected it to be punishing, had prepared herself to taste his anger and hurt. But his lips caressed hers gently, his mouth tender as he slowly slipped his tongue between her lips.

She should fight him, should turn him away—after all, she couldn't give him what he wanted. But if this was it, if this was the last time she would ever kiss him, she wanted everything she could get.

Her arms crept around his neck as she eagerly pressed her body to his. His big arms wrapped around her, slid down to cup her ass and pull her against his erection. She spread her legs before she could stop herself, relished the sudden dampness of her panties as she rubbed herself against him. He thrust himself gently against her, increasing her need to fever pitch as his mouth continued to devour hers.

His tongue slid teasingly between her lips, tangled with hers before retreating, again and again, She moaned in frustration, pressing herself more firmly against his body as her hands yanked his soft, well-worn T-shirt from the waistband of his jeans. She wanted to touch him, needed to feel his body against her own. One more time.

Tears sprang to her eyes, rolled down her cheeks unheeded as she gave Kevin everything she had to give. It wasn't enough, but it was all she had. With a sigh, she bit gently on his lower lip, relishing his answering groan. Loving how he backed her against the wall and thrust himself between her legs again and again.

His jeans were rough on her bare thighs but she barely felt them. Everything she had was focused on Kevin and this one perfect moment. Her hands worked their way up his back—his flesh was warm and toned, his muscles rippling with each movement he made. He smelled like Kevin—the scent of trees and rain and heat so familiar that her tears almost became full-fledged sobbing.

But she controlled herself, knowing that Kevin would stop if he sensed her pain and inner turmoil. And she wanted this, needed this one last time with him almost more than she needed to breathe. So she swallowed the sobs threatening to choke her and fought against the tears that continued to fall. She would love Kevin long enough and well enough to last her a lifetime. Because she had no other option.

She pulled slightly away from him, angled her body so that he was now the one braced against the wall. "Serena, it's too soon. You're still in pain—"

"*Ssshh,*" she cut him off, pulling his shirt over his head before he could stop her. "I love your body," she murmured, trailing her lips teasingly over his heavily muscled chest. "So strong, so beautiful." Her tongue darted out, teased his nipple once, twice, three times before moving on. "So responsive."

He groaned, fisting his hands in her hair. Serena smiled to herself and set about driving him wild—moving her mouth over every inch of his upper body. Kissing his neck, licking his chest, skimming over his nipples and his incredibly flat stomach. Her tongue circled his belly button, shimmied inside, and she laughed as he jumped.

She was wet, her body restless and aching for the pleasure it knew he could give. But she wanted this to be for him, needed desperately to give him just a little taste of what he'd given her. She traced her tongue over his belly button and down his happy trail, loving the raggedness of his breathing as she tasted the musky warmth of his skin.

She reached to pop his button and release his zipper, but Kevin's hands covered hers as he sank down beside her. His eyes were hot, aroused, and extremely serious as they gazed into her own. "Don't do this if you don't mean it, Serena. " His hands tightened, squeezing her fingers nearly to the point of paint. "I couldn't take it if this didn't mean as much to you as it means to me."

She tried to look away, but he lifted a hand to her chin, tilted her face until her eyes met his again. "I'm serious. I love you and I want to spend the rest of my life with you." His midnight eyes searched hers desperately, looking for a truth she couldn't hold back any longer. "Serena?"

"I love you, Kevin. I didn't want to. Told myself it was infatuation, lust, obsession." Her smile was sad. "It's all of those things and more. I do love you, Kevin. I love you so much it hurts."

His breath whooshed out before he could stop it and relief poured through him. Serena was meant for him, just as he was meant for her. And now she was his. Finally. He cupped her face in his hands, lowered his lips to hers before she could say another word. In that moment, nothing else mattered for him, nothing else existed. He knew she was afraid, knew she was vulnerable, and if it took the rest of his life, he would soothe those fears. He would make her trust in her love for him and in his for her.

His lips skimmed over her hair, down her cheek, across her eyes, and over her mouth. He tasted the saltiness of leftover tears, hating that he had made her cry. But it was okay now. Everything was okay because she was really, truly his.

"I need you, Serena. *Mon coeur, mon amour, cher*, I need you so much."

He ripped at the brown polo shirt she wore, desperate to feel her skin against his. He hated these shirts and the long-sleeve oxford ones she wore so often. Drably colored, buttoned up to her neck, hiding as much of her skin as she possibly could. As he ripped the shirt from her body and flung it halfway across the studio, he promised himself that he would buy her clothes that showed off her beauty—clothes that helped her see who she really was when all those tightly held emotions were let out.

He was hot and hurting, desperate for her. He pushed her bra down, fastening his mouth on her breast and sucking as hard as he could. She screamed, arched against him, and rational thought ceased. Desire and desperation took over until all he could see or smell or feel was her. She filled every one of his senses, every corner of his mind and he knew that he'd die if he couldn't be inside her soon.

He reached under her skirt, ripped her panties away with one yank. She gasped even as she pushed against his hand. His lips raced over her stomach, sinking lower and lower until, finally, he could take her in his mouth. She screamed, her hands fisting in his hair as he thrust his tongue inside of her, licking, stroking, savoring the tangy sweetness that was the essence of Serena.

He pulled her clit into his mouth and rolled it gently between his teeth. She screamed again, louder and longer, as her first climax roared through her. But he wasn't done yet, nowhere near it. He thrust his hands under her hips, lifted her so that she was sitting on him, her beautiful clit positioned directly above his mouth.

He'd been dying to try this, dying to have Serena above him while he kissed and licked his fill of her, his face buried beneath her thighs and her beautiful ass moving up and down on his chin. Ignoring her gasp of surprise, he swirled his tongue around her clit, loving the soft sound of her. But when he grabbed her hips to hold her in place, she squirmed away from him laughing.

Before he could protest, she'd turned around, balancing herself on her knees and elbows. She kept her gorgeous clit centered above his mouth, a move he was decidedly grateful for, but positioned herself so that she could go down on him as well. A move he was even more impressed with. Her lips closed around his aching cock and he groaned, thrusting helplessly against her mouth.

It took all of his self-control to keep from coming, and even then it was a close thing. He slid his tongue over her clit and between the plump, pink lips of her sex, relishing the taste and smell of her as she pulled him deeper and deeper into her mouth. Her tongue swirled over his cock as her lips moved slowly back and forth over him and he nearly whimpered.

He'd never done this before, never realized how incredibly arousing it was to go down on a woman while she went down on him. His every sense was on high alert, every nerve ending involved in the incredible, unending pleasure of Serena's erotic lovemaking.

He increased the pressure of his tongue, sweeping it faster and harder against her clit, loving the feel of her lips doing the same. Her hips moved more and more quickly against him and he found himself thrusting against her with the same rhythm. Moans and strangled screams filled the air and he was hard-pressed to decide if they came from him or from her.

He thrust two fingers inside of her, relishing how tight and hot she was around him. He hooked his fingers, searching for her G-spot, was rewarded when she jerked against him, her mouth taking all of him. His climax boiled up, and he tried desperately to hold it off until Serena was ready to come with him. But he was unprepared for her to reach under his balls and find the spot she had helped him discover only a couple of weeks before. She pressed her fingers firmly against it at the same time she swirled her tongue around his cock and he exploded, pouring himself into her mouth as he sucked desperately at her clit, his fingers flying over her G-spot again and again.

She shattered less than a second later, and he savored her contractions as he pulsed inside of her. It was the longest, most intense orgasm of his life, and as her hips jerked repeatedly against his mouth, he prayed it was the same for her. When her final tremors died away, he slowly pulled his fingers out, loving her low moan of protest. But he wanted, needed to hold her. Wanted to stare into her eyes as he told her how exciting, and moving, he'd found their lovemaking.

He smiled at himself, shocked at how much he'd changed since meeting Serena. The Ironman was gone, and in his place was a man so in love with his woman that she could melt him with a soft look or light touch. He should hate this new Kevin, should be shocked and astounded by how much of himself he'd given to another person. But he didn't. In fact, he loved the freedom he had to be himself with her, loved the way he could tell her anything.

He turned her to face him, burying his head in her throat and soaking up her scent. Serena. His woman. "Serena, *bébé*, I—"

Her lips closed over his before he could tell her how much he loved her, how much she meant to him. Her tongue stroked his lightly, slipping in and out of his mouth with quick, sure strokes that aroused him all over again.

She pulled back and smiled into his eyes, "I know." Her hand wandered down his belly to his cock, which, amazingly, sprung to life at the first light touch of her hand. "You don't actually think I'm finished with you, do you?" she asked, her fingers sliding up and down in a rhythm that had him arching off the floor.

He raised an eyebrow, his blue eyes gleaming wickedly as he reached a finger up to trace her lips. "Not even a little bit."

Her lips curved and she reached for a condom. "Did I mention your stamina is just one of the many things I love about you?"

He threaded his fingers through her hair, pulling her down so that their lips met. Right before he showed her a few of the many, many things that he loved about her.

Chapter Nineteen

Serena examined the last batch of negatives of Kevin listlessly. It had been four days since she'd left him. Four days since she'd crept out of his studio while he slept, thrown her things into her suitcase and run away with his truck. She hadn't planned on ending things like that—sneaking out without a word to him. But when he had fallen asleep after the most intense lovemaking of her life, she'd been left awake, staring at his statue of her. Left awake reliving every word he'd said to her. Left awake wondering how her life had spun so incredibly far out of her control.

And then she'd panicked. Running while he was asleep had seemed her only alternative—if she tried to leave when he was awake, she knew she'd never make it out the door. Not that he would keep her against her will, but when she was with him she didn't have any willpower at all. All of her rational thoughts and feeling disappeared under the force of his desires.

Never in her life had she acted the way she acted with Kevin. Sure, she'd had lovers. And while she'd enjoyed having sex with them, she'd never craved it. They'd never been in her blood, had never inspired the lust and longing that Kevin could without even touching her. Her control evaporated and she was helpless, totally mesmerized by his magnetism and desires. It was that loss of control, that loss of self, that she feared most of all. That reminded her so much of Sandra right before she'd died.

Sandra had given everything she was to Damien, had held nothing back. And he had killed her for it. If she'd been more suspicious of him, less susceptible to her own need for him, she might still be alive. But she'd surrendered herself willingly to the passion between them, ignoring Serena when she'd tried to warn her that it bordered on obsession. Now she was dead.

Sandra was dead, and Serena seemed destined to repeat her mistakes. Not that she thought for one second that Kevin would kill her—he was too gentle, too loving to even contemplate such a thing. But her feelings for him were overwhelming, bordering on obsession of the most base kind. When she was away from him, he was all she could think about. When they were together, all she could think about was getting him inside of her as fast as possible.

It wasn't normal. Admittedly, she'd never been in a serious relationship before—after Sandra she'd kept everything casual. But she'd never felt anything close to this with any of the men she'd seen before Kevin. Sex with them was pleasant, enjoyable, but certainly not mind-numbing. It was nothing like the soul-searing, body-tingling, explosive experience she had whenever Kevin put his hands anywhere near her.

And he loved her. She knew it, deep down, which is why four days after she'd left him she still couldn't sleep. Couldn't eat. Couldn't work up any enthusiasm for anything, even her work. The photos were due in six days, and while she now had the negatives developed, she was no closer to organizing them than she'd been when she was out in the bayou.

The phone rang, but she made no move to answer it. It was probably Steve calling to harass her about her photos for the gallery showing, and she just couldn't deal with him right now. Wishful thinking had her listening eagerly for the answering machine to pick up, hoping and praying that it was Kevin. But he hadn't called in three days.

By the time she'd gotten home, a little over three hours after she'd left him sleeping, there had been three messages from him on her home answering machine and another four on her cell phone. Demanding to know where she was, if she was all right, why she'd left the way she had.

The calls had continued all evening and most of the night, and she'd ignored every one of them, too raw and hurt to try to explain what she'd done and why she'd done it. She'd suffered hugely as she'd listened to his hoarse, desperate voice on her answering machine. Begging her to talk to him, to let him know that she was all right. Not picking up the phone and blurting out all of the confusion and pain and need inside of her had been one of the hardest things she'd ever done.

But she'd refused to cave, and sometime early the next morning the calls had stopped. The only time the phone had rung since was when Steve wanted to bug her or when the police called to fill her in on what was happening with Jack.

She shivered just thinking about Jack, remembering how crazed he'd looked standing in Kevin's kitchen, looking and acting just like the man who had killed her sister.

She'd come from that, had all that ugliness inside of her. She had scars on the outside from the knife Damien had plunged into her over and over again, but they were nothing compared to the scars she carried on the inside. Rage, bitterness, agony seethed right below the surface—the rigid control she kept on herself the only thing keeping them from destroying every part of her life. Kevin threatened that control, and she was terrified that if she let go, the darkness of the past would destroy them both.

Staring blindly at the negatives, Serena replayed her thoughts, knowing that she was on the brink of a major revelation. And when the truth hit her, it was so simple she could barely process it. She wasn't afraid of Kevin or their obsessive passion for each other. She wasn't even afraid of losing the real Serena inside the maelstrom of emotion he called from deep inside her. No, she was afraid of losing control and having all of her past, all of the darkness inside of her, boil up and onto Kevin. He shook her to the very foundations of her being, made her happier and sadder than she'd ever been in her life.

Tears slid silently down her face, and she wiped them away as she continued down the path her thoughts had turned onto. He took care of her, held her when she cried, loved her when she couldn't love herself. Protected her when she didn't know how to protect herself. Could she do any less? Kevin loved her, but loving her wasn't good for him. She was dangerous, an emotional black hole. And she was so afraid that she would absorb Kevin into her, destroying him for all time. Already, in the short time they'd known each other, he'd put his life on hold to take care of her—he'd held her when she cried, loved her when she'd begged, saved her life when she couldn't save herself. If she loved him, how could she subject him to a life like that?

She couldn't. The answer was as simple as that. Which is why she'd run away as fast as possible. Why she'd dodged his calls. Why she'd holed up in her apartment with the blinds closed as she nursed her misery. Because it was best for him.

She reached for a tissue and blew her nose as a sense of resolve filled her. She could do this. She could cut all the ties between Kevin and herself. Not for her, but for him. So that he could live a healthy, happy life without her.

With a heavy heart, but a renewed sense of purpose, she settled down with the negatives. Not because she was dying for any glimpse of Kevin she could get, but because she had a job to do. And if she could give him nothing else, she could give him the best damn book he'd ever seen.

Kevin slammed his blowtorch onto the workbench, heedless of the damage he was inflicting on one of his most important pieces of equipment. He'd never been more miserable in his life. He couldn't sleep, couldn't work. Couldn't close his eyes without picturing her face, couldn't walk around his house and studio without thinking of every single place they'd made love and every single place he had yet to take her.

Damn Serena for doing this to him. For making him love her and need her and then running away without a word. He'd spent the first twelve hours after she'd left calling her every five minutes, desperate to hear her voice. When that had failed, he'd driven to Baton Rouge to make sure she'd gotten home safely. When he'd pulled up at her condo and seen his truck parked in the driveway, he'd never been more relieved. Or more furious. He'd wanted to storm the house, to demand that she see him, speak to him, tell him why she'd left. How could he fight for her when he didn't know what he was fighting against?

He'd been halfway to her door before he'd stopped himself, halfway to knocking the door down before the truth hit him. He couldn't make Serena love him, couldn't make her want to be with him. He'd done everything in his power to show her that she could trust him, done all he could think of to show her how much she meant to him. Now it was up to her to decide what to do. If she needed time to make that decision, then the least he could do was to give her that time.

But it had been seven days since she'd left, seven days since he'd spoken to her, held her, loved her. And she hadn't come back. Two days ago a delivery service had shown up with his truck, along with a note from Serena thanking him for its use. Polite, to the point, and completely impersonal. He'd read it over and over, while the need to shake her grew stronger with every second that passed. He hadn't deserved that stupid, impersonal note, hadn't done anything to her but love her and try to take care of her.

He smiled bitterly, turning the smooth piece of whittling wood over and over in his hands. Hadn't done anything but rush her, but try to make her fit into the mold he had created for her. He shook his head, shocked and angered at his own stupidity. He loved Serena, with all of her baggage and all of her quirks. He loved how when she smiled, really smiled—it came from within and lit up her whole face.

He loved that she'd faced down her biggest nightmare, as cool and collected as if she was going to a garden party. Loved that she'd been smart and quick enough to stab a fireplace poker through Jack without batting an eye. Loved how she defended him. Loved her strength and her softness. Her passion and her control. Her stupid button-up shirts and the amazing lingerie they hid.

Why then had he tried to change her? Why had he tried to rush her, to force her to make a decision that she wasn't ready to make? He knew she had to think things through, had to measure the good points and the bad points. Yet he was so used to getting his own way, so used to running over any obstacle in his path, that he'd used the techniques of a lifetime on the woman he loved.

He was an idiot. An absolute, total fucking idiot.

His gaze fell on the sculpture he'd made of Serena. Two nights ago, drunk and half mad with pain, he'd tried to destroy it. Had planned on smashing it to bits. In the end, of course, he couldn't do it. Too much of her, too much of him, too much of them was in that sculpture, and if that was all he'd ever have of her, then he would cherish it. Once he got over the crushing pain of her desertion. Of his own stupidity in trying to push her into something she wasn't ready for.

What was he going to do if she didn't come back? How would he learn to live without her?

He glanced out the window, his heart jumping as he saw a car making its way down the driveway. Had she come back to him? His heart beat faster, and his eyes narrowed as he strained to clearly see the car. But his heart sank when he got his first clear look—it was a bright red convertible with the top down, a car so different from his cool, controlled Serena that it existed in a whole different realm.

Damn the tourists and their stupid desire to see the bayou. If they couldn't follow a map, not to mention the signs marking the main road, why the hell did they come? He was sick of chasing them away. Maybe he'd get a big, mean dog. Two dogs. And post huge BEWARE OF KILLER DOGS signs all along the road. Surely that would discourage the idiots.

But the car bypassed the main house, continued down the rough driveway to his studio. He walked onto the porch to get a better look, and his mouth dropped open when he saw Serena park the car and slowly unwind her long, curvy body from the driver's seat.

She stretched, arching her back and extending her arms above her head. Her lush breasts pushed against the low-cut neckline of her hot pink blouse, threatening to pour over the top at any second. Her short blond hair was windblown, and sparkling earrings dangled from her ears. His eyes narrowed, even as his cock hardened predictably at all that smooth, glorious skin on display. Who was this blond bombshell, and where was the woman he loved? He studied her through slitted eyes, searching for some sign of the Serena who'd left here one week ago. He found it in her wary eyes and uncertain smile as she turned to face him.

"Hey," she said.

He raised one sardonic brow. "Hey." Just because he'd admitted to himself that he was partially to blame for her disappearing act didn't mean he had to make it easy for her. Plus his tongue was tied in so many knots he didn't think he could get another syllable out of his mouth anyway.

She reached in the car to get her briefcase, and he nearly groaned at the way the long, slim skirt molded her fabulous ass. He turned and headed back inside before she noticed him looking. Before he embarrassed himself by coming at the mere sight of her.

Though he hadn't issued an invitation, she followed him, her thin stiletto heels tapping sensuously against the wood of the steps. He bit back another groan. Was she trying to kill him?

"Kevin?" Her voice was uncertain as she tried to capture his attention. Like he wasn't aware of her with every cell of his being.

"Yeah?" He turned to look at her, steeling himself as he did.

She swallowed, clasping her hands tightly in front of her before taking a deep breath. "Do you still want to marry me?"

His heart stopped, stalling in his chest as he looked at her beloved, bewildered face. "What did you say?"

She cleared her throat. "Do you still want to marry me?" The words were evenly spaced, and he noticed that annoyance was beginning to replace nervousness. Good. At least he could recognize that much of her.

He tried to hang on to his self-righteous anger and remember the fear and hurt that had raged through him for the past week. But with her standing there, looking so vulnerable and beautiful, so different and yet so familiar, he couldn't think of anything but having her in his arms. "Yes."

A huge sigh escaped her, even as the first real smile of the day bloomed across her face and she headed toward him. "Thank God. Then I accept."

Both brows rose before he could stop himself. "Why?"

She stopped dead. "Why what?"

"Why do you accept? And why should I believe you? The last time I saw you, you told me you loved me and then left so fast you forgot your panties."

"I do love you, Kevin."

He shrugged. There was no need to make this easy on her, after all. "You loved me last week, but you still ran away as fast as humanly possible."

Fury began to simmer in her eyes, and part of him wanted to back down, to take what she was offering. But he was fighting for the rest of their lives, and she had to know it. Their future was too important to leave things unsaid.

"I was frightened. I wanted to do what was best for you."

"Best for me?" he asked incredulously. "Making incredible love to me and then sneaking out while I was asleep was best for me? Not answering my calls and driving me half out of my mind with worry was best for me? Making me love you and then leaving—how exactly was that best for me, Serena?"

"Kevin, I'm so sorry. I—"

"I don't want an apology. I want to know what happened. I want to know why you left, and I want to know why you came back! You can't just come in here and tell me that suddenly you'll deign to marry me and expect me to just say okay. Or can you? Is that how you thought this would go?"

She shrugged. "A girl can hope." Her smile was more sad than sardonic.

"Well, hope springs eternal." He slammed out of the studio, his pain so great that the massive room couldn't contain it. He went down the steps, dragged huge gulps of air into his burning lungs.

Serena followed him and there were tears in her voice when she said, "I'm sorry, Kevin. I'm so sorry."

"I don't want your apology!" He grabbed her arms, had to fight the urge to shake her.

"Then what do you want? Tell me what you want and I'll do it."

"I want you, Serena. All of you. Not just the parts you're not afraid to let me see. I want to know when you're scared. I want to know when you're happy, when you're sad, when you're hurt or angry or all of the above. You can't run away every time things get out of your control."

"That's not fair."

"I'm done with being fair. You asked what I wanted. I want you in my bed every night and in my arms every morning. I want you to love me and marry me and have children with me. But most of all I want you to trust me. The way I trust you. With everything that I have and everything that I am. If you can't do that, then this will never work."

"I want to, but—"

His hands dropped away and he turned his back on her. "There can't be any buts, Serena. I can't compromise, not on this." He thrust one hand into his hair while the other rubbed his aching chest. "I can't believe I'm saying this. Really, I can't.

"I love you so much that I want to forget about everything, carry you in the house and make love to you until neither of us can walk. But I can't do that, because this is too important to let it go and just hope it comes in time. I know I'm pushing you. I know that it's too soon and too hard for you. I know that I should compromise. Hell, before you got here, I told myself I was an idiot because I hadn't compromised.

"But it turns out I can't. I can't marry you and always wonder if you're going to leave me when things get too hard. I can't build a life with you and then worry every morning when I wake up if today will be the day it all comes crumbling down. I love you, but I can't do that."

He turned back then, saw the tears running unchecked down her cheeks. *"Bébé, mon coeur*, don't cry. Please don't cry. It's okay. Really, *cher*, I understand."

She shook her head. "No, you don't. You don't understand anything, you big, stupid idiot. I didn't leave because I didn't trust you. I left because I didn't trust myself not to hurt you, not to screw this up."

"Serena—"

She held up her hand. "No, you had your chance to talk. Now it's my turn. I love you. I love everything about you. You're the strongest, kindest, most irritating and most gentle man that I know, and I almost threw it all away because I didn't think that I deserved you, didn't think that I could really make you happy. Not with all my fears and my baggage and my incredibly boring blandness. I look at you and see every color of the spectrum, and I'm nothing but shades of gray."

He started to protest, to tell her how much he loved her subtleties and her strength, how there was nothing bland about her. But she talked over him, determined to say what she'd come to say.

"But then I went through the pictures that I took while I was here, all of the pictures—from the first day to the last. And I figured something out." She wiped carelessly at the tears that continued to fall. "I make you happy. Despite the fact that I'm a basket case half the time, despite the fact that I seem to come with every sociopath in Louisiana attached, I really make you happy."

He pulled her into his arms, buried his face in her neck and breathed in her spicy, familiar scent. "You make me deliriously happy."

She pressed herself against him and rained kisses over his beautiful hair. "I know I do. It was in every look you ever gave me. Even when you were angry or exasperated or just plain exhausted." She cupped his face in her hands, pulled his mouth to hers for a slow, sweet kiss that rapidly got out of hand. When they finally pulled apart, she was breathless but the tears were gone and her eyes sparkled with happiness. "Almost from the first I knew that you were good for me. I just didn't know that you were crazy enough to think that I was good for you."

"I don't just think, *mon amour*. I know." He tenderly stroked her hair back from her face. "You're the best thing that's ever happened to me, and I can't give you up."

"You have no idea how happy it makes me to hear that." She grinned as her hands reached down and cupped his ass, pulling his erection firmly against her.

He looked over her head. "I do have one question, though."

She rubbed herself suggestively against him and he almost forgot everything but Serena and the amazing way she made him feel. "What's that?" she asked.

He glanced over her shoulder. "What's with the car?"

She smiled. "I wanted a little color in my life."

His eyebrows rose inquisitively. "I thought you liked gray?"

She shook her head. "You like gray. I'm finding that I like all the wild, wonderful colors that life can throw at me."